Bruce

Murder at Home

Detective Inspector Skelgill Investigates

LUCiUS

THERE'S NO PLACE LIKE HOME

DRIFTING ABSENTLY in *The Doghouse* on Bassenthwaite Lake, Skelgill has a feeling that he is being watched. From his wheelchair in the adjoining grounds of Duck Hall Nursing Home an elderly man looks on. They exchange a wave; it becomes a regular occurrence. And when later Skelgill engages with his bankside supporter he learns of his tragic circumstances. The helpless man has surely fallen prey to unscrupulous next of kin. As Father Time looms, there ensues a race against the clock, and the realisation that this may not be their first victim.

BRUCE BECKHAM brings a lifelong love of the outdoors to the contemporary crime novel. He is an award-winning author and copywriter. A resident of Great Britain, he has travelled and worked in over 60 countries. He is published in both fiction and non-fiction, and is a member of the UK Society of Authors.

His series 'Inspector Skelgill Investigates' features the recalcitrant Cumbrian detective Daniel Skelgill, and his loyal lieutenants, long-suffering Londoner DS Leyton and local high-flyer DS Emma Jones.

Set amidst the ancient landscapes of England's Lake District, this expanding series of standalone murder mysteries has won acclaim across five continents, with over 1 million copies downloaded, from Australia to Japan and India, and from Brazil to Canada and the United States of America.

"Great characters. Great atmospheric locale. Great plots. What's not to like?"

Amazon reviewer, 5 stars

TEXT COPYRIGHT 2024 BRUCE BECKHAM

All rights reserved. Bruce Beckham asserts his right always to be identified as the author of this work. No part may be copied or transmitted without written permission from the publisher.

This is a work of fiction. Names, characters, places and incidents either are the product of the author's imagination or are used fictitiously. Any resemblance to actual persons, living or dead, events and locales is entirely coincidental.

Kindle edition first published by Lucius 2024
Paperback edition first published by Lucius 2023
Hardcover edition first published by Lucius 2023

For more details and rights enquiries contact:
Lucius-ebooks@live.com

Cover design by Moira Kay Nicol
United States editor Janet Colter

UNCLE BILL
1929 – 2022

EDITOR'S NOTE

Murder at Home is a stand-alone mystery, the twenty-second in the series 'Detective Inspector Skelgill Investigates'. It is set in the English Lake District, in particular the area surrounding Bassenthwaite Lake, along with scenes in the Cumbrian settlements of Carlisle, Kendal, Penrith and the coastal port of Whitehaven.

Absolutely no AI (Artificial Intelligence) is used in the writing of the DI Skelgill novels.

THE DI SKELGILL SERIES

Murder in Adland
Murder in School
Murder on the Edge
Murder on the Lake
Murder by Magic
Murder in the Mind
Murder at the Wake
Murder in the Woods
Murder at the Flood
Murder at Dead Crags
Murder Mystery Weekend
Murder on the Run
Murder at Shake Holes
Murder at the Meet
Murder on the Moor
Murder Unseen
Murder in our Midst
Murder Unsolved
Murder in the Fells
Murder at the Bridge
Murder on the Farm
Murder at Home
Murder in the Round

Glossary

SOME of the Cumbrian dialect words, abbreviations, British slang and local usage appearing in *Murder at Home* are as follows:

A&E – Accident & Emergency
Alreet/areet – alright (often a greeting)
Any road – anyway
Arl fella – father/old man/husband
Arl lass – mother/old lady/wife
Auld Reekie – Edinburgh ('Old Smoky')
Beck – mountain stream/brook
Blether – gossip/chatter
Blighty – Britain
Bookie – bookmaker
Brew – tea/make tea
Brown bread – dead (Cockney)
Brummie – person from Birmingham
Butchers – a look (butcher's hook, Cockney)
Caw canny – play it carefully (Scots)
Chap – tap/knock
Conny-onny butty – sandwich, spread with condensed milk (Liverpool)
Come 'ed – come here/come on (Liverpool)
Cop – catch/get
Cur dog – fell sheepdog
Deek – look/peep
Donnat – good-for-nothing
DWP – Department for Work & Pensions
Everton F.C. – soccer team; local city rivals of Liverpool F.C.
Fanny about – do nothing (naval slang from 'Sweet Fanny Adams')
FIU – Financial Investigation Unit (police department)
Gee – horse ('gee-gee')
Geordie – person from Newcastle
Ginnel – narrow alley between buildings

Happen – maybe
Hause – col, pass, low point
Howay – come on
Jill pike – female pike (male = jack)
Ken – know
Knock-off – stolen property
Lamp – hit
Lecky – electricity/'the electric' (Liverpool)
Mardy – in a bad mood (East Midlands)
Marra – mate (friend)
Mash – tea/make tea
Merseyside – the metropolitan county that includes the city of Liverpool
Mincers – eyes ('mince pies', Cockney)
Mizzle – precipitation that is somewhere between mist and drizzle
Nowt – nothing
Offing – the more distant part of the sea in view
Owt – anything
Pop clogs – pawn shoes (= pass away)
Reasonable suspicion – probable cause (legal term)
Reet – right
Scotch – of Scotland (often misused instead of Scots, for a person)
Scouse – a stew of leftovers; Liverpool accent
Scouser – person of Liverpool
Shedload – large amount
Shooting brake – station wagon
Soft lad – from mild insult to term of endearment (Liverpool)
Stotting – raining heavily
Summat – something
Swim – a pocket of water frequented by fish
T' – the (often silent)
Tarn – small mountain lake in a corrie or coomb
Tebay – Skelgill's favourite motorway café
Theesen – yourself
Us – often used for me/my/our

Wipers – Ypres
Yowe – ewe

QUOTATION

"Loveliest of trees, the cherry now
Is hung with bloom along the bough,
And stands about the woodland ride
Wearing white for Eastertide.

Now, of my threescore years and ten,
Twenty will not come again,
And take from seventy springs a score,
It only leaves me fifty more.

And since to look at things in bloom
Fifty springs are little room,
About the woodlands I will go
To see the cherry hung with snow."

From *A Shropshire Lad*, by A.E. Housman, 1896

1. AUTUMN LEAVES

Bassenthwaite Lake – 6.25 a.m. Saturday 23 September

The Gregorian calendar is an imperfect human invention, for the outdoorsman a discomfiting stricture imposed upon Mother Nature's biological clock. So inadequate, in fact, that a day must be added every four years, and the odd second here and there, to make a correction. No academic, Skelgill nevertheless has a practical investment in such matters, to the extent that they interfere with his habits, and intersect with his natural curiosity. Why, for instance, does it continue to remain dark later each morning until the New Year if the twenty-first of December is the shortest day? By Boxing Day the first singing great tits reliably tell him that the solstice has passed.

Further imperfection, this very day, takes the shape of the autumn equinox; it is unequivocally a tangible astronomical event, especially if one dwells on the equator. But in a place that shares a latitude with Alaska, the fractional inching of the sun a tad closer to the southern horizon passes unmarked by birdlife and unremarked upon by Skelgill. If it is meant to herald the onset of autumn, it does not.

A family of swallows chitter on the wing as they hawk for hatching olives and sedges; not yet for them the agitated gathering upon telegraph wires, awaiting their flight to Africa to be called. A chiffchaff chaps out its onomatopoeic rendition of *Chopsticks* from bankside alders; its swansong, sure, but why depart for Iberia when there is yet ample to eat beside Bassenthwaite Lake? And no trees show signs of turning; summer green remains the dominant theme of the landscape.

But occasional leaves do sit proud in the meniscus.

If Skelgill squints he can imagine them as a scattering of fishing boats, laying up, on a slack tide out in the Solway.

And there are other subtle harbingers of seasonal change. At the first hint of dawn a fifty-strong skein of Icelandic pink-footed geese came flighting down from the north, their eager chatter *("Are we there yet? Are we there yet?")* redolent of a school playground just in earshot, another autumn sound, as the kids go back and holiday hordes retreat from Lakeland, unobtrusively replaced by a riper generation that treads more softly about the fells.

And there has been a nip in the air.

Initially overheated from rowing a good half mile; thence preoccupied with putting out a couple of lines; now inactive for the last half hour, he becomes self-aware.

Like most anglers, not catching fish forms an important part of his existence.

Decompression might be the watchword.

Also on offer, in his particular case, is a mode of deliberation that lies somewhere between analytical thinking and gut feel; quite where it is rooted between brain and viscera he is not sure. It would be tempting to say the heart, but that is too busy with running the show, when round-the-clock resilience is called for.

Accordingly, he emerges from his present brown study suspecting an innate resistance to acknowledge the onset of autumn. True, it might reasonably be ingrained by successive boyhood summers – fishing, foraging, farm work – reluctantly given over to an inexorably rising tide of impending back-to-school melancholy, ultimately irresistible, and the satchel-burdened traipse into daily captivity and darkening evenings, those surreptitious sneak thieves of fun and freedom.

But there is a deeper insecurity than that to which he gradually became inured as a juvenile; it is more a birthmark than a scar – and something that no amount of telling himself that it is merely a cyclical phenomenon, that spring will come around soon enough, has been able to assuage.

For there is no denying one less year.

Fewer. He hears DS Jones's voice. One fewer year.

He shivers.

Though the air is still and the water shows no trace of a ripple, his boat has drifted imperceptibly – it might be a current;

Bassenthwaite Lake is, after all, a mere widening of the River Derwent as it drains down through the post-glacial dales to its journey's end; the cold fell-water stream that creeps along the lake bed must surely send its tentacles to explore the subaquatic contours.

He shivers again.

But it is not the cool morning air; instead another indefinable sensation stirs him.

He is being watched.

That's what it is.

He has drifted to within a hundred yards of the eastern shore, a small secluded bay fringed by an arc of ancient Scots pines, their upper boughs the telltale burnished brass that looks like a trick of the light, as if the sunrise has reached them prematurely. It is a favourite haunt of his for beaching – Scotch Wyke, he calls it, though it is officially innominate – the private parkland of a long-empty mansion house and shooting estate, Duck Hall, that decays out of sight beyond a dense rhododendron understorey. A narrow overgrown ride leads down through the shrubbery to a raised turf bank; under the shelter of the evergreen canopy it is a perfect base for a bivouac and a spot of night fishing.

There sits a man.

Skelgill blinks, as if his eyes deceive him.

It is a man – yes – but even at this distance plainly a very elderly man, small and frail, sunken in demeanour – and left all alone in a wheelchair.

Left is Skelgill's first reaction – for how could the person have got there? There is no bankside footpath – nothing resembling public access for a mile in either direction. He looks too infirm to have wheeled himself. Moreover, the position is somewhat precarious.

Then Skelgill gets a bite.

For a good two minutes he becomes preoccupied – it is a modest pike, under ten pounds (though a decent weight for a jack, and worth a dozen in the pub) – but feisty all the same, and demanding of his undivided attention until he has it by the tail. When he lets go it seems in no hurry, as if it is a matter of pride –

but as he is about to nudge it, it gives a kick and is gone. He rubs his hands together in the clear water and casts about for a rag. Water alone is never sufficient when it comes to slime and scales, and it is a moment before Skelgill looks up, and across to the shore.

The man is gone.

2. KER-CHING

Lowther Street, Carlisle – 10.15 a.m. Friday 29 September

Morten Jenner licks his lips. The moment of anticipation, the click of the returned plastic card and the rumble of the automated teller as it counts the crisp banknotes as a precursor to their climactic ejection is almost as adrenaline-inducing as their ultimate function. Habituation to the stimulus, that's what it is, like Pavlov's dogs.

And here they come, four hundred pounds.

He separates half of the money and folds the notes and fastens them into the left breast pocket of his shirt; the remainder he slips into the concealed inside pocket that zips down the hem of his leather bomber jacket.

A sly smile turns up the corners of his wide, full-lipped mouth. Beneath a prominent ridged brow to which lank strands of oily hair cling, beady brown eyes, so dark as to be almost black, glisten in triumph. There is the extra satisfaction of making his first collection within sight of the Department for Work & Pensions, the scene of his just-concluded quarterly assessment.

Indeed, doubly so, that he had confounded his new case worker – and the man's boss, come to that! By the end of the interview he had them trussed up like a spider with a couple of juicy bluebottles in its web, mesmerised by his spinnerets, pinioned by his silk, injected with just enough poison to subdue and disorient them.

It had been useful practice, recounting his story; there are always subtle changes, and it was about due for an edit. The new assistant – what was he, late thirties – some no-mark in a dead-end occupation, like most of the others. Gullible. Bored. Lights on, no one home. Where do they get them from? This one sounded like a Cockney. Is the pay so bad that they have to scrape the barrel of the waiting room and recruit from the steady stream of hopeless jobless lowlife that pollutes the place all day long?

No waiting for him. Priority disabled access and a blue badge to boot – not that he would risk parking outside. He smirks once more as he reverses and turns and rumbles towards The Crescent, obliging pedestrians to move out of his path. He reprises the conversation for his own pleasure.

"Your mother – she is not attending?"

"My mother is far too infirm to leave the house. Besides, my own condition means it would be inadvisable for me to attempt to bring her."

He knows they're too busy to check. They're short staffed and badly managed like all these government departments. Not that they could be bothered; it's an easier life for them to go through the motions.

The man had clearly not even read the file.

"And your ailment, sir – there has been no improvement?"

He had relished the question.

Spreading his palms sagaciously, he had indicated his predicament, the glaringly obvious fact – that he sat before them in a wheelchair. He had made them wait several seconds, revelling in their disquiet. He had plied them with an expression of resignation tinged with courage. And he had proceeded to blind them with science.

"Myalgic encephalomyelitis – what you may know as chronic fatigue syndrome – or simply ME or CFS, has a recovery rate of less than five percent. And while I might appear hale and hearty to you this moment, undergoing an ordeal such as this will set me back for weeks. The medical profession call it post-exertional malaise – the worsening of symptoms after even minimal physical, mental or emotional effort – all three of which are inflicted upon me by the necessity of appearing here today. Tomorrow I shall undoubtedly suffer from muscle fatigability, sleep disturbance, and even cognitive dysfunction."

Hah! He knows more about this conveniently undetectable ailment than his own GP. He has been able to run rings around him – the ancient Dr Baldwin, the stupid buffer is old school – probably doesn't even believe the thing exists – hadn't he made the joke when Morten first suggested it, that ME stood for Malingerer's Excuse? Morten secretly likes that. But old Baldwin's another who wants an easy time – he just keeps renewing the sick note and prescriptions, no questions asked.

The new Benefits Assistant's boss had seemed mortified by his slaying of her subordinate's question.

"Of course, sir – we're terribly sorry to put you to such trouble – we really appreciate the effort you have made. Next time, perhaps we should arrange to come to you."

He clicks his tongue in self-reproach. He'd left a little open goal and they'd taken a shot at it. He'd had to call their bluff and agree it would be a good idea. Deal with that if and when the time arrives. At the merest ring of the bell he and Rina are well practised when it comes to playing possum. And the high-walled garden and secure gates mean they can't be caught unawares.

The assistant had quickly fallen into line.

"And, naturally, we'll do everything we can today to make sure you are receiving the full package of benefits to which you and your mother are entitled."

Hah! They had thrown the book at him – the government's *cheque* book! He'd scored an extra hundred a week. Extra pension credit for Rina, attendance allowance, cost-of-living allowance, winter fuel payment, support for mortgage interest on the loan Rina doesn't know she has just taken out on the property; incapacity benefit and housing benefit for him … the list goes on. Long live the welfare state!

He turns jauntily into Warwick Road and slews across to the next cash machine. He selects a different card from his wallet and – hesitating for just a moment as he recalls the correct PIN – withdraws another four hundred pounds. He adds the notes to the safe stash inside his jacket. It is a warm day and he reminds himself that, after the third collection, he should lock the garment in the boot of his car; better than on the back of a chair where it could be tampered with.

He moves on and crosses Warwick Road at the pedestrian lights, taking his time, not minding that he holds up the traffic that would go through on flashing amber if their way were clear. He senses that he is the subject of sympathetic eyes, and he milks the moment, basking in the invisible but warming rays of pathos.

One more ATM and he swings into Alfred Street and rattles over the cobbles as he reaches the relative grandeur of Portland Square. The central gardens, lush green lawn, are bathed in dappled sunshine that angles through the majestic limes, still green save for the odd yellowing leaf. In a patch of sunlight he spies a young woman seated on a bench, reading a novel; an infant must snooze in a fancy perambulator at her side. He pauses for a moment. His features tighten as he stares through the wrought-iron railings.

Perhaps it is coincidence, but the woman looks up, directly at him. She must be fifty feet away. She is attractive, a brunette in her thirties, tastefully attired – expensively so. Perhaps she lives in one of the mansions. A wealthy husband and no need for her to work. She regards him blankly for a couple of seconds and then returns her attention to her book.

Morten emits an involuntary snarl and goes on his way. He scrutinises the buildings that surround the square, sandstone terraces with their great bay windows and colonnaded portals, three main storeys with attic rooms and basements – five floors in all. This is where he should be living, a neighbourhood fit for his status. He must rake in more per hour than a millionaire in the short time it takes him to come into town and complete his little round.

Hah! And they said it's a shame he's fifteen years too young to claim his own state pension!

This is his job and his pension rolled into one. And it has been hard worked for. A thousand pounds or more every Monday – the culmination of a career that has had its ups and downs. Some big investments of time – months, over a year in one instance (the Rich Bitch) – that never paid off. But now he has settled down to a kind of working retirement. It's the least that's due to him after all these years of living hand to mouth.

He casts a last glance back as he turns out of Portland Square. Perhaps he could move here when Rina is gone. But could he leave Troughdale House behind?

On the flip side it would certainly make his job easier. And his interests. It would simplify everything. Though they'd try to take away his mobility allowance if he were no longer living in the sticks and there was no Rina to drive about, to get her hair done, to get to the doctor, damn shopping trips.

And it would be nice if Rina could find just one more good one. One last one while she's still got it in her and they've still got the granny flat. It would be the cherry on top of the icing on the cake.

He could come into the city twice a week instead of once.

He isn't sure if the latest one – busybody Harriet – is going to be suitable. She knows what a fair rent is round here.

But that's for another day.

As he takes the sharp left, an acute angle, into Aglionby Street the morning sun dazzles him, though his grimace might equally be one of disapproval. An obstacle course of grey wheelie bins is strewn along the pavement; the trees are irregularly spaced and amateurishly pruned; and the more modest red-brick terraces a rung or two down the property ladder. Is this more likely what he could afford?

He reaches his car. It is in a bay reserved for the two-hour Disc Zone; but he has displayed his disabled badge – he can stay as long as he likes. He has wheeled himself quite quickly and he is a little out of breath, and getting warm. He doesn't want to turn up sweating.

He makes a big play of rising with difficulty from the chair and folding it into the boot. Anyone watching would think he was in pain, the care he takes in his slow movements. He folds his jacket on top of it and closes the lid. Then with one hand on the vehicle he edges round to the driver's side and lowers himself in, gripping with knotty fingers the metal above his head.

Now he waits. His eyes traverse a route from one mirror to the next – nearside, rear-view, offside. Then to the fore. He scrutinises parked cars, but in none can he discern the shape of a watcher.

A movement in the passenger-side mirror catches his eye – a woman is barrelling along the pavement from behind. She is both shabbily and garishly dressed and carries two bulging plastic supermarket bags. He sits still as she approaches, and pretends to be looking at his mobile phone as she passes. She is overweight, and unsteady, and shows no sign that she is aware of him.

What lengths would they go to? They say that in the really good agencies, you'd never in a thousand years spot the private investigator, the ones they employ for surveillance only. But the woman suddenly halts and laboriously climbs the five or six steps up to the door of a house. She puts down one bag and finds a key in the pocket of her misshapen pink cardigan. She enters; she just lives there.

Satisfied that the street is now empty, Morten returns his attention to his phone. He finds a conversation and taps out the words "Am parked" and transmits the text.

He stares at the handset for maybe thirty seconds, but he can see that he's over ten minutes early and he places the phone on the dashboard. He rubs his hands together with a vim not exhibited hitherto this morning. He checks the offside mirror for approaching traffic and pushes open the driver's door.

He springs to his feet – now a car has rounded from a side street and comes at him from the front and he is obliged to jog out of its path. He makes the opposite kerb and continues apace, a brisk walk into the road the car came from. Halfway along, at the next turn, there is a corner shop. The regular woman is seated low behind the counter. She looks up from her phone and seems to know what he wants, for she is reaching for the vodka when he has only uttered the words "a quarter bottle". And she sidles to the National Lottery stand as he is asking for fifty pounds' worth of scratchcards. While she is counting them out he takes a tube of Polos from the rack on the counter.

He strides rapidly back to his car and reaches in for his handset. There is a message displayed over the locked screen.

"Come now."

The scratchcards can wait until after. R&R. He slips them into the door pocket. He pops a blue pill from a blister pack and washes it down with a large gulp of vodka. He opens the mints and tosses two into his mouth and the packet onto the seat. Then he locks the car and checks his reflection in the driver's window.

He brushes at his hair, and then smiles, manically.

3. ROLL CALL

Police Headquarters – 11.45 a.m. Friday 29 September

'It's a while since we've had bacon rolls. You seem to have been favouring the old Cumberland sausages lately, Guv.'

'Hark at the kettle. And they're tea cakes, Leyton, not rolls. How long are you going to have to live up here before you start calling them by their proper name?'

'Cor blimey, I dunno, Guv. I thought roll was what you'd call the lingua franca. But – I mean – it ain't a cake, is it? It's bread.'

Skelgill scowls, but cannot delay further biting into the said sandwich, thoughtfully organised by DS Jones for their review, ahead of Skelgill's attendance with other senior officers at the Chief's last-Friday-of-the-month meeting.

DS Jones has a more conciliatory take on the argument.

'It seems to me that wherever we go they have a local name for them. It was morning rolls in Edinburgh.' She flashes a look of corroboration at DS Leyton. 'In Manchester they call them barm cakes.' Now she glances to Skelgill; a point in his favour. 'When we were in the East Midlands they were just plain cobs. At uni I shared a flat with a Geordie who called them buns and a Brummie who insisted it was a batch.'

Now Skelgill chips in.

'The arl lass calls them oven-bottom cakes – that's how she bakes them – so they're black underneath.'

DS Jones turns again to DS Leyton.

'What about in London?'

Perhaps unexpectedly, DS Leyton looks puzzled.

'Baps?'

However, he seems to colour, and row back from the suggestion, as though worried he might have offended his female colleague, given the euphemistic double-meaning. He ruffles his dark hair and shakes his head.

'*Nah* – come to think of it – that was a geezer I used to work with from Shrewsbury – a DS, when I was a rookie – he liked his bacon sarnies. London – I reckon it's mainly just rolls. Course – there's rhyming slang – *brown bread* – but you know what that means.'

Skelgill waves his half-eaten bap-barm-batch-bun-cake-cob-roll like a conductor wishing to restore order in the pit.

'On which cheery note, what have we got?'

His colleagues understand they should move on.

He adds a further point of direction.

'Start with Operation Community Chest – I'm tight on time.'

DS Leyton now chuckles.

'What's so funny, Leyton?'

'How did we end up with that title? It reminds me of Monopoly. The press'll have a field day – they'll be calling it Operation Chance – or Operation No-Chance.'

Skelgill shrugs.

'I'm no fan of it, Leyton. The Chief wanted something that sounded inclusive. She knocked back my suggestion of Operation Dole Cheat as tone deaf.'

DS Leyton grins a little sheepishly; he assumes Skelgill is being sardonic with his liberal jargon, but he takes the underlying point.

'Right enough, Guv. After my three mornings in the benefits office last week, I can see we're treading on eggshells. It's a political hot potato. A proper dog's breakfast.'

His colleagues simultaneously settle just slightly back in their seats; DS Leyton glances from Skelgill to DS Jones to see they are each suppressing a grin of sorts.

'How come you get all the glamorous undercover assignments, Emma? I feel like I should just carry a short straw round with me – save the false hopes.'

DS Jones pulls a face of apology. DS Leyton grins self-effacingly; he continues, with a sigh of resignation.

'They'd never make a detective thriller out of this one. And I don't mind admitting it's been a bit of a minefield. It's just as well there's a supervisor sitting in with me. I mean – it puts you in the front line – you get to see the whites of their eyes – them that's claiming benefits. All these folk who can't make ends meet – and all manner of ailments you never knew existed. It makes a policeman's lot seem a cheerful one, I can tell you.' He shakes his head ruefully. 'As for organised crime – or at least – systematic fraud – I can't say I've seen enough yet to begin to form a view. I've got a meeting on Wednesday with the branch manager – that might shine a bit of light on it. Maybe I'll start seeing the wood for the trees.'

He blinks like a creature that has emerged late from hibernation to find his fellows already enjoying the spring sunshine. Though it is autumn cloud that darkens Skelgill's office this morning – and perhaps his colleague's action prompts Skelgill to rise and step across beside DS Jones to raise completely the venetian blind.

He stands and stares for a few seconds, though his gaze locks on to the no-man's land of the middle distance. DS Leyton's description has struck some kind of chord, though it is just a vague, ineffable echo that is barely discernible.

His colleagues wait patiently.

He snaps out of the trance and seems surprised that it has occurred.

He resumes his seat.

'Jones?'

She nods.

She has a report – substantial – it must run to twenty or more sheets, but she wavers and opts not to hand out copies. Instead she manipulates the screen of her electronic tablet. She finds a coloured graphic and props up the device on Skelgill's desk where they can all see.

'I started with national statistics – this is from the UK Government website. The largest and most common type of benefit fraud is the under-recording of self-employed income. And when people are paid in cash, it's almost undetectable.'

'Double bubble.' DS Leyton appropriately uses prison slang for being paid twice the normal rate.

'That's right. Someone who wouldn't qualify for income support if they declared their true earnings.'

Now she indicates again to the pie chart.

'The second biggest area is household composition fraud – such as where people claim for non-dependents who no longer qualify, like children who have left home or who have finished full-time education.'

Her colleagues nod, and continue to listen.

'Third is classed as capital fraud. It's where people fail to declare their savings – which would exclude them from qualifying for benefits more generally.'

DS Leyton now chips in.

'Yeah – I reckon we had one of those on Wednesday – geezer who'd sold his window-cleaning business a couple of years ago – says he had to pack it in because of a bang on the head from a fall – reckoned he'd spent all the dough he got from the sale. He remembered all the details of the injury – but then started to claim memory problems when we asked him for copies of his bank statements.'

Now the attention is on DS Leyton, as they wait for his story to unfold.

'Thing is – I felt a bit sorry for him. I mean – he was sixty-one – worked his fingers to the bone, an' all that. He's paid up his full stamp – but he's got six years' to wait until he gets his state pension. So he's supposed to survive off've his life savings – while folk who've never bothered their backsides swan in and cop a shedload of benefits.'

There is a pause as they each consider the quandary.

It is DS Jones who breaks the silence.

'I think that hits the nail on the head. And it exposes part of the flaw in what we're trying to do with Operation Community Chest.'

Skelgill gives an involuntary expulsion of air – but the repressed meaning is made clear by his words.

'You volunteering to tell that to the Chief?'

She smiles a little coyly – for she knows he is being equally a little facetious; but she counters without answering directly.

'Well – there are two strategic aspects that struck me.'

Skelgill folds his arms, but nods that she should elaborate.

'The first is that all three broad categories of fraud that I've described are made up of hundreds – thousands – of small cases. The loss is twenty pounds a week here, thirty pounds a week there. For a worthwhile result it would take enormous resources – in fact I doubt if it would be cost-effective.'

'Can't argue with that.' It is DS Leyton. 'That's the long-standing problem, ain't it? It's cheaper to swallow the loss.'

DS Jones nods in response. Then she turns her gaze on Skelgill.

'The second aspect – it's more about the positioning of Operation Community Chest.' She indicates to the pie chart on the screen of her tablet. 'These benefits – this is Westminster money – it comes directly out of the national purse, from the Treasury in London. I know it's perverse, but there's an argument that the more fraud a region can get away with, the better that region's doing. A kind of guerrilla warfare version of Levelling Up. I'm not saying it's officially countenanced, or even that it's a widely held public opinion – but I read a research report that showed among more deprived strands of the community it's regarded as a legitimate redistribution of wealth.'

Skelgill is listening intently. His normally two-tone irises seem particularly grey in the flat light, although it would be hard to say if it were a reflection of his degree of enthusiasm for her case. He can think of plenty of hard-working farmers who have never taken a day off in their lives, let alone claimed a state benefit. Men and women who can barely keep their small farms afloat, but who would never dream of turning to alms.

But he seems to understand that she has something of merit.

'So, what are you saying – we're barking up the wrong tree?'

DS Jones regards him earnestly.

'Well – in a way – yes. I think we should focus on fraud in which the victim is not the anonymous state but a real person – a local person that anyone round here could identify with. If we openly target fraudsters who are parasitising their own community, I think our initiative will garner a lot more public support.'

DS Leyton inhales to speak. There seems to be an inherent flaw in her logic – but she quickly moves to pre-empt it, and swipes at the screen of her tablet to reveal another pie chart.

'This is something that has not been looked at for a while. But

I found a report by a reputable firm of accountants – excuse the oxymoron – one of the Big Four, as they call them. They estimated that over £300 million a year is being lost in what's called 'deceased person fraud' – that's people who continue to claim the pension of their partner or relative, by failing to report their death.'

DS Leyton starts.

'Yeah – me and the Missus, we just watched a programme about that – it was a drama based on a real case. Couple shot the wife's parents and buried them under the patio. Lived the flippin' life of Riley. Only got caught when an official from Buckingham Palace got in touch to arrange for a letter of congratulations from the monarch for reaching a hundred. They'd kept it going so long, they'd scammed something like a quarter of a million quid.'

DS Jones nods.

'That's exactly my point. Each individual case is likely to be of high value. Provided the fraudsters have assets – such as the family home – then there's capital for the legal team to take aim at. So, we score not only on local support, but also cost-effectiveness.'

Her argument seems to have justice on its side – the artificial justice of the law in which they are inculcated, and the natural justice of moral reprehension when rogue members of a community cheat the system.

Skelgill is listening, seemingly in agreement. But he checks his watch, and peremptorily rises.

He addresses DS Jones. 'The meeting's in three-quarters of an hour. Can you knock me up a couple of charts?' He indicates to the electronic tablet. 'Like those – pictures where possible.'

She nods amenably.

'Sure.' She glances at DS Leyton, to enlist his backing. 'We'll put our heads together.'

Skelgill forces a thankful grin and takes his jacket from its blunted fish-hook peg and departs. He needs some bait for the early morning and it may be his only window of opportunity. And maybe another bacon roll. There is no telling how long the Chief's meeting might run; the entire rest of the day is not unknown.

But he feels a small spring in his step – with a small caveat of trepidation. DS Jones has correctly identified a strategy that ought to win the Chief's approbation. But there is little worse than presenting a suggestion and having a gleeful DI Smart cackling in the corner when it is shot down in flames – doubly so if he is the one doing the shooting.

4. RINA'S ROSES

Troughdale House, Whitehaven – 12.40 p.m. Friday 29 September

Rina Jenner enjoys dead-heading. Sacrifice the dying to feed the living. It's especially true for roses. When they came to Troughdale House there were no roses and the big west-facing walled garden was crying out for them. People say they're a lot of work, but they've always been a rose-growing family; even when their Da had the French polisher's shop on West Derby Road there were roses in pots in the tiny slabbed yard at the back, between the privy and the coalhouse. That was a long time ago, seventy years, probably.

It was their Da that had been keen on roses. When he died, and to be near the rest of them Mam and Billy moved to Middlemarch, they never had roses in their garden. Brother Billy grew vegetables to please Mam; she liked the thrift. It was she, Rina, and sister Joy that inherited the love of roses. And even Joy was haphazard about it. Her garden was always a bit of a jumble – boys belting a ball about, the dog digging up the borders; and Bryden was too busy with his job.

But Joy did have a blue rose in her garden in Middlemarch. An actual blue rose. Not one of these artificial things, dyed or genetically tampered with. Back in those days it was a real rarity. She'd got it from the little local market garden. It was a throwback from when the place was still a village; she'd persuaded the old nurseryman who'd bred it to part with his prize specimen. He only had one to sell every few years; it was a secret he'd taken to his grave. She was good like that, Joy – she wouldn't take no for an answer; it's another thing they both inherited, they were streetfighters – but that more likely from their Mam.

Joy had planted the blue rose in pride of place near her and

Bryden's front gate, so she could point it out to passers-by.

It was a shame for Joy when her blue rose had died.

Rina feels the muscles of her face relax into a contented smile.

The blooms under her nose drift back into focus. She waggles her secateurs absently, and her small dark eyes dart about in search of victims for the snip.

But it seems she has vanquished them for the time being. She takes a step away, and slowly swivels on her heel, scanning for tasks to be done. Autumn tidying for Morten.

Prune the climbers where she can't reach them. It's a job that needs a ladder. Cart in the sacks of horse manure from outside the gates. Mulch the beds. Not that they need mulch, the rain they get here. Nor fertiliser.

If anything, they've grown too well this summer – at least, the beds of grandiflora either side of the pergola that Morten built, and the ramblers that have engulfed it. Thomas's Bed and Richard's Bed, planted in memoriam. Some people do it with their pets; they actually bury them in their gardens – or perhaps they get their ashes nowadays. That would be another kind of fertiliser. Though roses don't like the soil to get too alkaline.

Her mind wanders again, and she stares across at the sandstone wall with the rustic arch at the centre of the two flourishing rose beds. She'd thought about putting in those little vases with holes in their lids, for spare blooms that she'd pruned, but Morten had turned up his nose at the idea. He hadn't liked Thomas or Richard. Perhaps he'd be better with a woman.

The hint of a smile tweaks at the corners of her mouth – she thinks of what he'd said when she'd told him about Harriet perhaps coming to stay. "That's all you need – Tom, Dick and now Harriet!" He could be funny, Morten, when he was in a good mood.

Harriet's due tomorrow morning; her regular Saturday appointment. She's been a reliable client; she's never once cancelled, or even been late. And she gets here by herself, on her mobility scooter. Morten had objected at first – called her a busybody. But Rina had persuaded him that Harriet would come on a trial basis – rent the granny flat while she tried to sell her house. The place needs a lot of work, her having been a widow for so long – and it might not sell easily. She'd told him about Harriet's heart condition, and about how she's on benefits – and then Morten had said he could help to spruce it up a bit, to get a quick sale – that the longer a property sits on the market, the harder it is to shift it.

She scans the garden. Where could they put another bed? Unless they dig out a new patch in the lawn, there's only really the long window in front of her treatment room, but that faces east. It gets the morning sun, but roses don't thrive without at least half a day of sunlight. That said, there's a section in her catalogue that advertises roses for north-facing gardens. Perhaps she should try a couple, as an experiment.

There's some of her clients that would like that. Those who find it claustrophobic and prefer the curtain open. They're not all shy of being seen in their underwear – and it's not like Morten's some kind of Peeping Tom. Most of them have met him at one time or other, when he's shown them into the waiting area when she's finishing off with her previous client. They've all commented on how polite and charming he is. How she's fortunate to have a son who's so attentive when he's got his career as a financial adviser to think of, when most of them don't see their children or grandchildren from one month to the next. One advantage of Harriet is she says she's got no relatives – Morten doesn't approve of visitors arriving unannounced.

She rotates her head a little. Isn't that his car, now? He's usually in high spirits when he comes home from Carlisle; and he always seems to have a hearty appetite. Perhaps it's still warm enough for them to eat at the wrought-iron table on the patio. She's got his favourite shepherd's pie ready, and tinned peaches with evaporated milk for after, which always reminds her of growing up in the back-to-back in Tuebrook. There was still rationing then, and peaches and 'cream' were a Sunday treat, with a small joint of beef, if they were lucky, and scouse if they weren't. Much of the rest of the week, midday dinner was a conny-onny butty, or more often jam. On Saturday nights, their Da would bring in fish suppers if Everton had won, and brown ale for him and Mam if one of his gees came in.

The electric gates make the little telltale metallic clang that precedes their opening, and Rina watches as the two halves rather jerkily separate, and Morten's silver Mercedes begins to nose its way through the gap. He likes his big car; especially this new executive saloon with its personalised number plate. And she feels like Lady Muck, being chauffeured round in the back seat.

She waves the secateurs, but she can't tell through the tinted glass whether he waves back. And he waits in the car, as usual, until the gates have banged shut behind him. Just in case there's someone watching across the road. He's warned her about giving them away, but where she's standing she can't be seen. And it might be a suburban street, but being detached and up on the high side of the little valley, Troughdale, means no one overlooks them.

Perhaps he hasn't noticed her; she's wearing green with yellow patterning, and she must blend against the foliage and the flowers. He seems a little distracted – he gets out of his car and strides back to the gate to the post box. She watches his reaction as he reads the senders' addresses on the back of the envelopes. Some of them are the cheap government manila type. He doesn't give much away, even to her.

But now he looks up, directly across at her, and his face breaks into a broad smile. He makes a beeline over the gravel of the drive, onto the lawn. He looks down, and makes a sweep of the arm, as though he's fanning the grass with the letters.

'I'll give this a cut tonight, before it gets dark – might be the last one of the year.'

Rina nods thankfully. Morten thinks of everything. He only mows the grass after working hours; he says you never know who might be listening from outside in the street – that it's one of their tricks, checking up on what jobs you do around your house. Assessing your mobility. He says there's some idiots that get caught playing golf or carrying great bags of shopping. He says there's a purge at the moment, and they should be extra careful.

She plies him with a motherly smile.

'There's a bit of pruning needs doing.'

Morten has a briefcase in his other hand, a worn brown leather one; it was Richard's, and it had seemed a shame to throw it out. Now he raises it, triumphantly, like the Chancellor of the Exchequer on his way to deliver the budget.

'Got us another fifty quid a week.'

She beams upon him proudly.

'I knew you'd get us more. Your dinner's ready – your favourite – any time you want it. I thought you might like it on the patio.'

He acts out a rather uncomfortable contortion of his shoulders.

'I'll have a shower. It's close, today. It was clammy in that meeting. I had to battle hard.'

'You just suit yourself, Morty. I can wait.'

Rina looks at the envelopes, now held at his side. Morten does not volunteer to share them.

But she already knows who they're from.

He'll probably open them in his study and lock them in his desk. He normally has a nap after his trips into town. She'll look at them later.

She watches him go inside, and then she turns back to the rose bed. There are still some blooms that have got a few days in them, but you have to be ruthless.

She smiles to herself.

You can take the girl out of Liverpool.

5. WILLIAM

Duck Hall Estate – 6.45 a.m. Saturday 30 September

It had troubled Skelgill, the disappearance of the lone man in the wheelchair.

Last Saturday he had rowed in, close to the shore, to reassure himself that the fellow had not somehow toppled in. That raised section of bank is steep, and the water easily deep enough to submerge a seated person.

From time to time during the week the image had revisited him. Not the spectre of a drowned man – but the just slightly spectral watcher, still and silent and strangely knowing. And there was the dual mystery of his presence, and his departure.

Today, having tried a different stretch since before dawn, down towards the swampy southern reaches, Skelgill has paddled back up the eastern bank, pulling vigorously, faster as the prospect of breakfast nears – though now rounding into Scotch Wyke instinctively he relents, and hauls only with his right hand; the boat slews to port, the pines swing into view over the stern.

The man is there.

Skelgill suffers mixed emotions.

His breakfast spot is occupied. But the man is safe.

And there is a third dimension that arrests his attention: a young woman stands at his side.

Moreover, even at a distance, she provides some explanation: she wears a royal blue nurse's uniform. And he can just discern an ID badge on a lanyard.

And now the man raises a mittened hand – it seems to Skelgill less of a wave and more of an imploring gesture. He squints for a moment at the incongruous scene. The man is muffled; as well as the mittens he has a blanket over his knees and he wears a lopsided eared hat. The woman – evidently his chaperone – in contrast seems under-dressed in her short-sleeved tunic, her arms and legs bare. Briefly she leans down, it seems to listen to something the man says.

Now she waves, too, more vigorously.

Skelgill finds himself turning the boat and pulling towards the shore.

He grounds the craft and scrambles around to find that the nurse has come forward, as if she feels she ought to help. He jumps from the prow, just putting one boot in the water and the other making dry land.

Before he can speak, she addresses him.

'He thinks you're his son, or grandson or something. You're not called R.O., by any chance?'

'R.O.?'

Skelgill begins to shake his head and inhales to question her further, but she quickly elaborates. Her accent sounds local, but not strong.

'He suffers from dementia – it's quite advanced.'

Skelgill gestures erratically about their locus – and he must produce a suitably puzzled expression – such that she launches into an explanation.

'He's been transferred here from Belmont Manor at Carlisle. The care provider went bust. The council have had to step in. They've requisitioned Duck Hall until suitable placements can be found. There are eighteen residents and twelve staff. I've been seconded from Lancaster.'

'I thought the place were a wreck?'

She shakes her head.

'The interior has been refurbished – the National Trust is going to make it a visitor attraction.'

'Reet, then.'

There ensues a moment of silence. Skelgill's somewhat impetuous arrival has them both tongue-tied now, as if quite wondering what they are each doing there.

Then the woman stretches out the lanyard, displaying her photograph, and offers her right hand.

'Ashanti.'

To Skelgill's ear it might almost be a greeting, were it not for the lettering on the badge. It states *Nurse Ashanti* and he is unsure if it is her given name. In her photograph there is an eruption of dark hair which today is immaculately braided, a score of shoulder-length strands with loose curls beneath. He realises that in making the comparison he might seem to doubt her credentials. Hurriedly he rubs a still-wet palm against a buttock, but grimaces at the result, and instead offers a fist which she readily bumps with an amused grin.

'Er, it's – Dan.'

'Pleased to meet you.' She leans a little closer. 'You're *not* his relative, by any chance?'

Skelgill does not need to look past her at the man. He might have an extensive family, especially on the side of the maternal Graham clan, but they are all accounted for.

'Afraid not.'

'That's a pity. We saw you – last week.'

'Aye – I saw you – well – the chap. Then he were gone.'

'He'd dropped a glove – it was just up in the bushes. I fetched it and then took him back – I thought he was getting cold.'

The same morning chill does not seem to bother Nurse Ashanti. Though Skelgill can see goosebumps that are surely more prominent than the natural pores on her smooth skin.

'You come out early.'

'Oh, yes – well – insomnia – or at least, irregular sleep patterns – it's a common symptom of dementia. And – since we saw you – he's asked to come down to the lake each morning.'

'Ah.'

'Will you speak to him? Before I take him up.'

'Aye. What's he called?'

'We think it's William.'

Skelgill does a slight double take – but then he walks purposefully towards the man, his wheelchair safely set some eight feet back from the water's edge. He has sat patiently, like a person accustomed to the waiting room, looking ahead, blandly out across the lake and not inquisitively at them, as one might expect. Nor do his rheumy eyes track Skelgill's approach.

Skelgill drops to one knee, in front, but slightly to one side. The man continues to gaze past him, his expression placid but otherwise unengaged.

'Alreet then, William?'

The man does not respond.

Skelgill glances at the nurse. She gives an encouraging smile.

'You saw us fishing – last week, eh? It were a jack pike. Took a piece of old rotten herring.' Skelgill scowls extravagantly. 'I've blanked this morning. That's fishing, eh, William?'

But Skelgill's words get no reaction. He is not is his element, and flounders. He tries another tack, rather struggling for what to say.

'I believe you like Bass Lake. It's the only lake in the Lake District, you know? It's a kind of joke – a play on words. The rest are all meres and waters. And behind us – the mountain – it's Skiddaw – fourth highest in England – it'd qualify as a Munro if it were in Scotland.'

Still there is no response.

Skelgill looks appealingly at Nurse Ashanti.

Now she plies him with a grateful expression, that it was a good try.

He rises a little stiffly; he is reminded he ought to flex his spine after rowing. He steps across to the woman, when unexpectedly the man speaks.

'Come 'ed, R.O.'

Several things are incongruous to Skelgill. The frail old man has a rich voice; there is no hint of tremor or creakiness; the accent might just be Merseyside. But he continues to stare unblinking over the water. He does not look for compliance, or even an answer; he might almost be talking in his sleep.

Skelgill regards the nurse with a look of bewilderment.

Though she speaks quietly, they are not out of earshot; evidently it does not worry her.

'Sometimes he's more lucid. He's said several times this week – about the lake – and about you – well, R.O.'

Skelgill frowns.

'Have you asked his relatives?'

Suddenly the woman – who can only be in her late twenties – looks much younger than her age; she regards him with the mournful deep brown eyes of a forsaken child.

'We don't have any contacts for him.'

Skelgill is nonplussed.

'What – none at all?'

She shakes her head, the braids rippling.

Skelgill's detective training now picks up on a point that might have passed another person by.

'What did you mean – when you said you *think* William?'

The girl understands the gist of his query. She purses her full lips for a moment before she responds.

'It's just me. I mean – William – it's what we have on the system. But I feel he would react to his name – he doesn't.'

They both turn to regard the man; still he gazes sedately across Bassenthwaite Lake.

Though he is tempted to put the point to the test, Skelgill feels it would be demeaning to call out the man's name. Nurse Ashanti abruptly looks at her electronic wristwatch. Then she puts a hand on Skelgill's arm.

'Ah – I'm being paged. I had better take him back up.'

Skelgill seems momentarily lost in thought. Then he snaps out of it. He makes as if to move towards the man in the wheelchair.

'Aye. Can I lend a hand?'

'Oh, no – there's no need, thanks. He's not very heavy – and the exercise is good for me. Besides – you must have a fish to catch?'

She grins; it seems she has registered his performance to date.

Skelgill scowls.

'Aye, well – there is that.'

She walks across to her charge and turns his chair; she seems to move it with ease; the ground is dry and the turf cropped short by rabbits and waterfowl.

'Perhaps we'll see you again?'

'Aye, why not.'

As she pushes the man away, Skelgill hears his voice, again clear and vigorous.

'Where's me shirt, for church?'

Nurse Ashanti turns her head over her shoulder, and flashes a broad white smile.

Skelgill gives a wave, acknowledging the challenge she faces. He watches for a few moments, until she passes out of sight, soon hidden by the dark green rhododendrons that crowd the ride.

Then he turns and stands for several moments, like the man, unblinking, gazing out over the calm waters of Bassenthwaite Lake.

6. RINA'S REDUCTIONS

Troughdale House – 10.15 a.m. Saturday 30 September

Rina Jenner hums happily to herself as she goes about with the feather duster. *A Hard Day's Night*. She still knows all the Beatles' songs off by heart. She remembers their Da used to sing along to that one when he was working late; they'd listen, the three of them shivering in their beds in the tiny room above the shop, and he'd come up and tuck them in, smelling of shellac and bringing extra army blankets, knock-off from the docks that he'd bought in the pub.

He was a hard worker, their Da. A true grafter. *Eight Days a Week*. She knows that one, too. How could you not, growing up in the same city as the Fab Four. And she's always been a grafter, too. Something else she's inherited from their Da. Whatever anyone might say about her, she's always worked. She's always liked the money – she pauses her humming to smirk – that from their Mam. Definitely their Mam.

Put them together and what have you got?

From that little back-to-back. Humble beginnings. And now look at her. A place with its own name, Troughdale House. Not a silly romantic name like people give to their retirement bungalows by the sea, like *Shangri-La* or *Dunroamin*. A place that's had its own name since it was built. A place of substance in sandstone. Detached. Its big walled garden – made for roses. An annexe – a granny flat that can bring extra income.

And Harriet seems to be taking a long time in there with Morten, which must be a good sign.

Morten has his own study. A sea view from the attic – that he says he's going to put a proper stair up to, to replace the loft ladder that he doesn't know she can climb. He's a good boy Morten, but he's not a grafter in the same way as her. But he does have an engine of his own sort. What he calls himself is an Ideas Man.

Ever since he left school – and even before that – he was having his ideas. This scheme, that scheme – a little carpet cleaning business that got him in the local paper, an enterprising schoolboy making extra pocket money. But they'd not all worked out, his schemes. He had a chink. A soft spot. He's clever, Morten – but once or twice a woman has been his downfall. Men are just not as naturally smart as women.

That Sadie Brown. He helped her with her legal problems, her divorce, and she got a couple of million and didn't give him a penny. Kicked him out when he tried to put up a fight.

And the time when the New York investment went wrong and Rina had had to sell up in Cornwall to bail him out. That was a woman – an online scammer, they call them. He fell for her – thought it was love – and it was love of money. A foolproof investment. Morten was fooled all right.

And it wasn't the only time she'd had to sell up to bail him out.

There was Leicester, and Leamington, as well as Land's End.

This is the last place, near the Lakes.

It works better from home. There's no overheads or nosey landlord. No money-grabbing scrooge.

Just as well she'd listened to their Da. Get yourself a skill. Something that people always want, like being a French polisher. Except he would have been wrong about that. It might have seemed furniture restoration would never end. Then IKEA came along and now people treat furniture as disposable. French polishers have gone the way of chimney sweeps and video shops and Yellow Pages.

But not so her line. All these years, and it's still going strong. Cash coming in, and that cash can explain away a lot of things, if push comes to shove. And people will always put on weight. They're putting on more than ever. And then they want to take it off.

It's her little goldmine. *"Rina's Reductions – Lose Pounds For Less!"* Morten had the little appointment cards made with a shapely mature woman on them. Half the price of a high street slimming salon and no VAT – all perfectly legal. She and Morten still laugh about it – people think it's pounds weight they're losing!

A never-ending stream of portly elderly ladies who want their adipose tissue reduced. They keep putting it back on. She keeps taking it off. Taking off the pounds avoirdupois, raking in the pounds sterling.

Harriet especially puts the weight back on.

Harriet's been a model client. Twice a week, at least, for a full hour. Then Morten says he's seen her in Asda with a trolley full of cakes and biscuits and chocolate.

She wonders what Morten will negotiate with her – whether he'll throw in a free session every week with the rent. She'd agreed he could offer that. It's better that he does the deal, then Harriet doesn't have to feel awkward with Rina. And it gets Morten off on the right footing with her – with her finances. Like he's the landlord figure. They can start off with her renting – and if Harriet decides to buy the granny flat, then he can help with that, too. She might want a mortgage to free up some cash. He can arrange it for her. And he can help her with her benefits. He can even do the shopping, for all of them – why wouldn't he, he has to get theirs?

Harriet will probably put on a lot more weight, once she moves in.

They'll surely be finishing soon, and she'll just leave it for Harriet to tell her what has been agreed.

Harriet will probably have questions for her.

Harriet knew about Billy being here, even though he never met her clients. He liked to keep himself to himself, is what she always told them. That he was socially inept, and shy. There was something in that. He never married, and he was reclusive, and he was happy to live with their Mam. But then so is Morten, and he's not socially inept at all.

But she'll need to be ready to speak to Harriet about Billy. After all, that's why the flat's available.

Rina frowns, pausing as she arranges the towel on the treatment table. She tries to think what difficult questions Harriet might ask. Like what did Billy die of, how long was he ill, what were his habits

– and has the granny flat been deep-cleaned? And she might ask about the funeral. Some people notice these things, they always read the classified ads in the Gazette. But Billy was never from around here. It would be natural that his funeral would have been in Middlemarch – or Liverpool, even.

Besides, she's got her stock answer. She doesn't share her domestic troubles with her clients. Her job is to settle them down and listen to *their* problems. It's what every good beautician does. That's what she'd be called if she were setting up nowadays. Back when she started it was called electrotherapist. Her machine is years out of date. It looks more like an old-fashioned telephone switchboard, with its plugs and wires. But, like her, it's not age-dependent. And it still does the trick. Morten thinks it's probably illegal now. Health and safety. But she's never electrocuted anybody yet. And her clients come from a generation that doesn't worry about that sort of thing.

It's a generation that prefers cash.

And that suits her, too. She's never liked these debit cards and credit cards. Especially not credit cards. Especially not credit.

She gives an involuntary shudder – and then pats the fluffy white towel that's she's put in place for Harriet to rest her head. She pats it urgently, as if she's reacting to some unpleasant memory.

It took her a long time to recover from Morten's last difficulty.

Until just over a year ago, really.

But they'd had little choice. Like Morten said, they were lucky to get the mortgage in the first place. And lucky they found a part of the country where property was so cheap. Things were even more depressed then. They'd just closed the steelworks at Workington. On top of all the years of redundancies round here. And, yes, they were lucky to buy somewhere big enough to run her business from.

But it was a relief when they finally managed to pay off the loan. It's a last resort, an interest-only mortgage. It was all she could afford to take out at the time. And the years rolled by, and the two hundred thousand seemed to rise and rear up, a great big wall of water lurking out there in the Irish Sea – a tsunami that one day would crash over them and wash everything away.

But between her and Morten they'd fixed it. Paid it off, the capital sum. And the title's in her name, debt free. No bailiffs can come knocking. No mortgage instalments to pay. Just cash coming in, tax free, for them to spend how they like.

And now it's all word of mouth, and she's more careful about which clients she takes on. It's under the radar – a need-to-know basis, they call it. The Inland Revenue don't need to know.

And Morten didn't waste much time with his new Mercedes; he said he got an interest-free deal on that.

Morten's ups and downs. And she's been the reliable grafter, filling in the gaps, shoring up the defences. Morten needs her. Morten might have the flair – but what else has he really got?

He thinks he's handsome – but truth be told he's getting on a bit now. He's got quite a pot-belly, and he tries to make the best of his hair, but she hasn't got the heart to tell him it looks ridiculous. He'll be fifty-three at his next birthday. That's too late to settle down and start a family.

She wouldn't want him dividing his attention between her and another woman.

Morten's her insurance policy. But she's his pension plan, isn't she? Without her, they couldn't have built up their income to what it is today.

No more moving about, giving creditors and their henchmen the slip. Now they can live in peace. No need for Morten's schemes. Between them they've finessed a better one: for cover, her little business with its bloated ladies; and the bloated state system, a great cash-cow so morbidly obese that it can't tell that it's being milked. Her job, and Morten's job.

So it's a mutual dependency. For Morten, if she went, a lot of their benefits could unravel.

Though she's not sure if he owns up to all the cash he takes out. True, he has to pay for car servicing and fuel, the groceries and so on. But then she makes her own money, and gets her pension credit. She's never paid her stamp. She's never declared a penny. They've always believed her when she's said she's not able to work because of her nerves.

Yes, they need one another. She'll be seventy-six at her next birthday. She's fit and mobile at the moment. But who knows what's in store for her. Just look at Joy. She went into hospital for a check-up and was dead within three days.

Yes, Morten might be their front man – out in the world, thinking up his ideas – but he's also companionship. Someone to look after her. Billy stayed with Mam until the very end. And he didn't do it for the money. He even carried on in Mam's house, living frugally – the same thrift that Mam liked – and only gambled a bit from his pension each week, when he could have mortgaged the place or sold off some of the garden to developers.

She frowns.

Of course, Morten tried that, didn't he? But it fell through when the local planners rejected his application. Billy never found out.

And the Last Will and Testament that Billy made out – so he said – was going to be split between her and Joy. He was trustee of Mam's house – and she'd said it was to be his two sisters' equally after he'd gone. They never found that – Billy's will – but it doesn't matter now.

Rina looks up, cocks her head to one side, listening.

That sounds like they're coming through – Morten's voice, honeyed and smooth-talking; and she can hear him laughing at things Harriet must be saying.

It's not just her that's got the gift of the gab.

Morten inherited it from her – but where did she get it from?

Not really from their Mam or their Da.

Those back streets of Liverpool?

That's what Joy would have said. She knew – saw her growing up, getting her way when others couldn't. And Joy had some of that – just not what Morten would call "business acumen".

And Joy knew it.

What was it Joy used to say to her? *Little Sis, butter wouldn't melt in your mouth.*

Rina grins, and begins to hum once again.

I Me Mine.

7. RESCUE

Blencathra – 4.15 p.m. Saturday 30 September

Skelgill sits astride the arete. It isn't the ideal stance from which to belay a man, but he estimates he has enough weight on his side – the tarn side – to arrest the arl fella if his mates should slip up. And they're almost there; another few feet and they'll be on a decent ledge, where they've got the titanium stretcher laid out ready. Now that the poor chap's off the edge, his role is just a token back-up. But he keeps the rope taut, nonetheless – it gives them a bit of purchase – helps your balance when you can't look at your own feet, where you're planting them. But, as far as he knows, no one's ever died falling down the north flank of Sharp Edge.

The same can't be said for the south flank. The death toll is well into double figures – and three figures for serious incidents – more than any actual rock-climb he can think of. But there's the rub. Sharp Edge isn't a rock-climb. It's something that, on a calm, dry summer's day an agile person with a good head for heights can skip across with hardly a blink of the eye. The guide books have it as a mere grade 1 scramble. So hillwalkers think they can do it with impunity.

Except it's a grade 1 scramble with grade 3 exposure.

He gets a shout from below and feels them untie the working end. He releases the free end from the sheriff and carabiner on his harness. Automatically, methodically, he draws in the rope, winding elbow to heel of hand, and forms a bight and ties it off in a mountaineer's coil.

His eyes are narrowed, his features set in a severe grimace. A grade 3 grimace. It might appear a reaction to the elements. A stiff breeze is coming up vertically, ripping at his cagoule; his hair is plastered down, part-perspiration, part-mizzle that isn't quite rain, or even drizzle, but which seems to transfer itself to the human body in a way that mist alone cannot do.

And he stares down into the abyss – it could be an abyss. The visibility is so poor and the premature darkness such that, beneath and beyond the ten feet of almost sheer, slick black rock under his stance there could be anything. Ironic – that he knows it to be one of the most spectacular close views in the Lakes. On a clear spring morning, with the rising sun creeping into the coomb, Scales Tarn glitters like a sapphire in a burnished setting. He recalls the sounds; of meadow pipits parachuting in stereo, and the cuckoo chiding its own elusive echo, and the resonant cackle of red grouse high up in the heather ... and, below, the babble of Scales Beck at its outfall.

He shifts position. What was it Wainwright said? At its most razor-sharp point the traverse can only be tackled *à cheval*, at risk of some damage to tender parts. But sprightliness was not a trait that would be associated with the great cartographer; cantankerous obduracy, more like. And, cryptically, he also described Sharp Edge as a sight to make a person forget all their worries, up to and including a raging toothache. Was that a brickbat or a bouquet?

Skelgill gets another shout; at best he can discern vague shapes moving in the dark fog.

But they've done their job. He's strapped in. There's enough of them to carry the patient – besides, he's done his bit, too. They ribbed him (earlier, out of earshot) about him surely being a trained negotiator and best suited for talking down the crag-fast old chap. And he wasn't even on call. Just by chance was he making a small repair to *The Doghouse* when they came barrelling along the A66 and rang his mobile on the off chance that he was about. He was – and even kitted out for the stretch of the legs he had intended for Sale Fell to the Bishop of Barf and back.

They are not hanging about. And quite right. The arl fella seems okay – he's in one piece – no breaks – but he was quaking with cold, and they'll need to get him treated for that. Eighty, apparently – and the son no spring chicken at fifty-four. Though he looks fine to walk out under his own steam. He'd been more sheltered, and he'd done the right thing, getting himself on the safe side, albeit it was just a doubled confidence rope they were tied together with.

'Howay, Skelly, lad – we shan't be coming back for thee – Jack here wants a pint!'

Skelgill barks a confirmatory response to team-leader Woody's entreaty.

Though on the careful descent – seventeen hundred feet to the waiting ambulance at Scales – he finds himself hanging back, a little aloof from the banter, and the encouragement the team doles out to the man on the stretcher and his son – who to his credit keeps offering to take a handle, and is in decent shape.

At the foot of the fell the conditions are – as ever – more benign. They have dropped through the cloud base and the wind is revealed to be convectional rather than cyclonic – and the sense of emergency, the battle against the clock in growing darkness and worsening weather and fading victim seems mitigated.

The elderly patient has been loaded aboard. He has recovered his wits and went into the ambulance under protest, even causing a laugh with a rendition of *"I don't want to go on the cart"* that had the Monty Python aficionados among the rescuers chuckling.

Skelgill is still a little detached. The mountain rescue team are steaming up the windows of Woody's Defender, cracking jokes of their own and waiting for him to join them. He sees that the elderly man's son is speaking with the paramedic at the driver's window of the ambulance; he spies Skelgill and gives the woman a thumbs-up and breaks away.

He moves towards Skelgill, raising his hand to indicate he wishes to speak, his expression somewhat contrite.

'I'd like to thank you. I realise you guys will probably just split.' The man's accent is Scots, fairly mild it seems to Skelgill. 'If you could tell me your website address or something – I'd like to make a donation. Do you think five hundred would cover it?'

Skelgill regards the man shrewdly. This is a reaction that is all too rare. Most folk seem to think the mountain rescue is some public service funded by the government, the taxpayer. It is not. The volunteers give their time freely and rely on donations to buy the gear they need.

'That would be appreciated.' He tries not to raise an eyebrow at the generous sum. Instead he inclines his head in the direction of the ambulance. 'What are they saying?'

'They think mild hypothermia. They want to admit him to the cottage hospital at Cockermouth – just to get him checked over.'

Skelgill nods. There is a white Range Rover parked nearby and it matches the fob the man holds. 'You going to follow on?'

'Well – yes. To be honest – they probably won't let me in with him at first – knowing the protocol. I'd like to buy you guys all a pint.'

Skelgill gives a bit of a grimace. The team prefer their own company. Though he feels a certain deference to the man's age, a good half-generation above him.

'Tell you what. You could give us a lift. If you're heading for Cockermouth – my motor's on the way.' He jerks a thumb over his shoulder. 'I was picked up. This lot would prefer to drive straight to Keswick.'

'Sure. I'd be glad to do anything to help.'

Skelgill clears his plan with his teammates, promising to catch them up.

It takes just fifteen minutes in the smooth and silent 4x4. They make some small talk; Skelgill learns the man is Kenneth Muir, an anaesthetist from Edinburgh, and his father a retired surgeon of some repute. He contrives not to reveal his own occupation – he is not sure why – and further, finds himself not wanting to reveal the exact location of his shooting brake. He eschews the near-hidden slip off the A66 and directs the man to turn at the crossroads where The Partridge is signposted. As they swing into the double-oxbow the ancient long and low building is revealed – and Kenneth Muir exclaims in recognition.

'*Och*. I ken this place. But I've not been for years. It's an old coaching inn, right? Tremendous character. I pray they've not modernised it.'

Skelgill is silent for a moment.

'Careful what you wish for.'

'To be frank – I quite wish for a pint. Are you sure you can't be tempted?'

Skelgill shapes as if to hem and haw.

'I do need a quick word with Charlie – the landlord.'

'It's a deal. You find your man and I'll get the beer.'

Skelgill locates Kenneth Muir a few minutes later in the old bar. He raises his glass approvingly as Skelgill settles opposite him. Skelgill prefers to sit facing the room, but the position is taken.

'Apologies – I started. I realise I needed a drink. Shame it can only be one for the road. This is a decent pint.'

Skelgill reciprocates, saluting with his beer held aloft.

'Aye. Can't complain.' He would not be averse to a couple himself, not least that the rapid climb was dehydrating work. 'Happen you've got Deuchars in Edinburgh?'

The man sips and scowls, as if the local Cumbrian bitter is suddenly beyond tart. He puts down his glass, and shakes his head dejectedly.

'The big boys bought it. Closed it down. Auld Reekie's last traditional brewery.' He snaps his fingers. 'A hundred and fifty years of history, gone like that. They brew the brand under licence elsewhere.'

His expression tells Skelgill all he needs to know about the imposter. Skelgill regards his own local pint with unforeseen trepidation, and he hears an echo of his words of a few minutes earlier, about being careful what to wish for.

But the sharing of peril for a second time in the day has in its way broken the ice between them, and Skelgill now regards the older man squarely.

'So, Kenneth, what made you think it was a good idea, in cloud and rain, to take an eighty-year-old chap up Blencathra via Sharp Edge?'

For an instant the man looks alarmed – but then he registers there is just enough mischief in Skelgill's tone that his defence will receive a reasonable hearing. However, he raises both palms to his shoulders in a gesture of mea culpa.

'You've heard it before – but I got caught out by a change in the weather. I knew cloud was due to come in, that pressure was falling – but not until we were scheduled to be well past the summit.' He hesitates, and makes a somewhat rueful intake of breath. 'Dad was a lot slower going up – I should have anticipated that.'

Skelgill watches over the lip of his glass as the man continues.

'I'm a fairly experienced mountaineer. When I was younger I climbed in Africa, Nepal, the Alps – I've done most of the Munros – the tricky ones like the Black Cuillin and the In Pinn, the Aonach Eagach and so on. As you saw, I had him on a confidence rope – and there's a bothy bag in my rucksack – although I'm not sure quite how I would have got him inside that.'

'Aye – he were proper crag-fast. Happens to the best of mountain yowes. Except you can send the cur dog to fetch them.'

The man nods. He raises his eyebrows as he takes a pull on his pint.

'I guess so. I was reluctant to call you guys out.'

Skelgill shakes his head vehemently.

'Nay. You did right. Besides – that lot, they've been getting too fat and happy – now winter's on the way – it was just the ticket. Reminder of what's to come. We've spent the last six months fetching lost holidaymakers who thought it would be a clever idea to have their picnic on Scafell Pike because they've heard it's England's highest mountain – wearing flip-flops and trainers and nowt but a t-shirt, and thinking the satnav app on their phone will work in the fells.'

Kenneth Muir scowls in sympathy.

'It must be frustrating.'

But perhaps to the man's surprise, Skelgill gives a resigned shrug.

'What would be the point – if folk didn't come out? Decent folk who care and want to explore a bit – push the envelope, as they say.'

It seems a broad philosophical question – but sufficiently rhetorical that the man feels able to answer by reference to his own circumstances.

'My Dad's never exactly been into the outdoors – but he introduced me to all sorts of things that he didn't really do himself. Golf, skiing – fishing, even. Opened my eyes to the potential. He used to bring me down to the Lakes – he's half-English, so he says he always feels at home here. We'd do some of the tops, the better-known fells. We always said we'd do Sharp Edge – somehow we never made it.'

He pauses to drink, his features pensive.

'Then Mum died – and he told me he'd got it on his bucket list. I discovered he's devouring the Wainwrights – climbing vicariously. Now, the last of our kids has gone off to uni – I've got a bit more spare time. I thought it was something I could do for him.'

Skelgill has listened and is looking at the man; but perhaps rather disconcertingly now seems to be staring excessively. But he snaps out of the momentary diversion, as if there is some realisation. Indeed, he drains his pint, ahead of Kenneth Muir who still has a quarter left. He begins to rise.

'Look – that was a good thing you did. Come back in spring – and I'll go up with the pair of you. Phone here – Charlie knows how to find us.'

Before the man can answer or try to rise to shake hands, Skelgill has left him.

Outside, the mizzle has persisted in its relentless descent as the barometer has continued to fall. Even at lake level dusk is pressing upon the dale, and along the wooded lane to Peel Wyke Skelgill moves catlike in deep shadow. At the little harbour, surrounded by the ancient oaks that give the Derwent its Brythonic name, the paler rectangle beneath the bridged trunk road draws him to the edge of a becalmed Bass Lake. Of Skiddaw, there is nothing to be seen, but – rather curiously, it seems to Skelgill – the distant dark smudge of pines that fringe Scotch Wyke is a feature that catches his eye, when it has not before. Perhaps the two Scots just encountered have obliquely raised his awareness. And not just in common provenance, but also the dutiful son and the intrepid father – Skelgill smiles to himself, recalling the senior man's protest at being shipped ignominiously to hospital.

He stands and stares for some while, before he turns and marches to the back of his car, long and shabby and dun-coloured, almost invisible in the gloom. The interior light seems excessively bright when he raises the tailgate. He scowls as he rummages about, foraging first in a box of supplies – and he gives a small growl of triumph when he produces an unopened packet of chocolate digestive biscuits.

He rounds to the passenger side and climbs in. Now he delves into the glove compartment – and emits another, more moderate, grunt of satisfaction. In the palm of his right hand he has a small but not insubstantial pocket guide. *The Observer's Book of Freshwater Fishes*. On the well-thumbed jacket are pictured a perch and a pope (aka ruffe) – those twin terrors with spiny dorsal fins designed to catch out the uninitiated. Inside, the edition, *Reprinted 1964*. And, much later by date, the dedication, in manuscript: *"Daniel, tight lines, JRH"*.

A much-prized boyhood gift from the good Prof's own library.

He stares long and hard.

8. PHANTOMS

Duck Hall – 6.35 p.m. Saturday 30 September

Skelgill has waited a good three or four minutes before he hears footsteps beyond the heavy panelled front door of Duck Hall. But as he listens, his ear close to the wood, if anything the soft patter of feet seems to cross what must be a tiled hallway and fade away. He has found no bell; he knocks again, vigorously, hoping to catch the person before they pass entirely from earshot. The approach has brought him along a winding wooded drive, the trees mainly ornamental conifers that crowd the back of the Georgian mansion house and conspire with the overcast sky to produce a premature nightfall. Drops of rain are beginning to land; it seems to be coming on quickly, though he is sheltered in the unlit porch.

Then more footsteps, heavier shod, these more urgent.

The door is opened by a slim young woman in a nurse's outfit, her fair hair drawn tightly back by a band and her features equally strained.

'Oh – I thought you were Agnes.'

'I'm sorry?'

'I've lost her.'

The girl vacillates – she rocks back on her heels – it is plain she is preoccupied with a missing charge.

Skelgill quickly jams a metaphorical foot in the door.

'Nurse Ashanti?'

'What? Oh – she's just finished her shift – she'll be coming out any minute. I didn't know she'd booked an Uber.'

The nurse looks anxiously over her shoulder – she seems reluctant to admit Skelgill.

He intervenes for a second time.

'A moment ago – I heard footsteps – like someone trotting

barefoot.' He gives a wave of the hand, indicating the capacious entrance hall behind her. 'Left to right.'

She makes a face of realisation, but also perhaps relief.

'The kitchen. She'll be there again.' She takes a step back and gestures to a wooden settle beneath a large oil painting, a dramatic stormy landscape of mountain and moor. 'You'd better come in and close the door.'

She hurries away. She turns right into a side passage. Skelgill hears her voice calling, "Agnes, no more cheese, dear – you'll be having nightmares again."

He does not sit, but stands to attention before the artwork. He recognises Souther Fell with the distinctive saddle of Blencathra behind, but not the straggling army of tiny figures that must stretch for half a mile across its brindled flanks. He stares with some wonder at the scene of smoke and mist; it is like something from the Napoleonic Wars – but he knows of no such conflict that took place hereabouts. He ducks to squint at the legend, a tiny hand-engraved brass title plate. It states, *The Phantom Regiment, 1745*. He frowns; a question for next time he sees Jim Hartley.

New footsteps interrupt his musings; not phantom, like the first might have been, but brisk and echoing in the resonant vestibule. He turns.

Momentarily he is further disoriented – expecting the uniform – instead the young woman is clad all in black, close-fitting jeans and sweater that reveal a figure that was merely hinted at by the nurse's tunic. Her appearance makes him doubt it can be she. She has her head down, intent on the screen of her mobile phone.

'No signal?'

Surprised, she stops in her tracks. She looks up; she too is plainly bemused. Then she beams her Colgate smile.

'I didn't recognise you.'

She approaches to within a few feet.

Skelgill takes her lapse as a small tribute, without exactly calculating that in mountaineering garb he looks less like a scarecrow than when unkempt and unbrushed and fishing in the early hours.

A little self-consciously, however, he now raises a polythene supermarket carrier bag that has dangled at his side since his arrival.

'I brought some stuff – for your chap, William. Some chocolate digestives – and a book I thought he might like – that someone could read for him. It's got plenty of pictures. Fish. *Fishes.*' He adds hurriedly the peculiar correction.

But she quickly responds to his broad proposition.

'Oh, that's so kind of you.' She takes a step closer, so much so that he feels the opposing poles of their unfamiliarity must surely propel him back half a yard. 'I left him settled in the TV room. Would you like to take them through? They've had dinner – I'm sure he'd love a chocolate biscuit with a cup of tea – and the book. You can't imagine what a treat that will be.'

Skelgill begins to think he is to undertake this errand himself. But she reaches to touch his upper arm, a guiding motion.

'This way.'

She steers him around into a corridor to the left, opposite that taken by Agnes and her pursuer. The place has the ambience of a country house hotel, high-ceilinged with what might be public rooms to either side, though in one smaller he glimpses an office set-up, a computer on a desk and an angle-poise lamp that is casting a cone of light, though no one is present. But where the hotel might smell of roast dinners or old pipe smoke or damp dogs, there is an altogether less endearing piquancy, not entirely masked by that which he recognises as disinfectant, from his many boyhood visits to the local cottage hospital, for the insertion of stitches, or the extraction of fish-hooks.

The room they enter is carpeted and dimly lit, and a widescreen television provides additional flickering lighting, its volume low, when the converse might have been expected. Skelgill realises that figures sit immobile, absorbed deep in individual armchairs; more phantoms, emaciated and pale; God's waiting room. Despite the forgiving pile underfoot, he finds himself treading reverently.

Beside a great bay window against which outer darkness presses – though Skelgill knows it must afford a view down towards the lake – Nurse Ashanti rounds a winged chair and stoops attentively – but in her face he sees disappointment. She rises, and Skelgill joins her.

William is sound asleep.

Skelgill is conscious that his inadvertent grimace betrays a reaction that he would not want the man to register, were he able.

Again the girl presses a palm against Skelgill's upper arm, and she stretches up to whisper.

'He can be a little disturbed when he's woken unnaturally. I think he dreams – and it makes him doubly confused – distressed. We normally move him through to his room when he wakes. Then give him his medication.'

It is plain she is torn about what to do.

Skelgill responds in correspondingly hushed tones.

'It's alreet, lass. I mean – you can give it him tomorrow.' He holds out the bag. 'I'm not needing to take the credit for it.'

'Oh, no – but he would love it to be you. He keeps speaking of you – well, R.O. – he's convinced you're one and the same person, whoever R.O. might be.' She looks imploringly at Skelgill, her large eyes dark pools in the gloom. 'Couldn't you pop back? He doesn't get any visitors.'

Skelgill regards the small, wiry figure in silent repose, his sunken chest barely heaving.

'Aye – I figured that – from what you've said.'

Skelgill gnaws at the corner of a thumbnail. He nods, and then gives a little jerk of his head – the suggestion that they should move away, so that they may speak more freely.

Outside the room, a little along the corridor and opposite the vacant office, he halts.

'His clothes – they all look far too big for him. And isn't that a woman's top he's got on?'

Nurse Ashanti seems suddenly deflated.

'He doesn't have any budget. He's just on the most basic care package. It's all the council can fund. We get him what we can – bring in our own spare toiletries. But I'm afraid some of the clothes – when he needs a change – we have a little store – donated, from residents who have passed away.'

Skelgill glowers, thunderously.

'This can't be reet.'

The girl shakes her head sadly.

'I know – it's just that, well – there's very little on his record.'

Perhaps subconsciously, she glances into the office. Skelgill needs no further invitation. He takes a step across the threshold and leans in, checking that the room is empty.

'Can you show us?'

Nurse Ashanti is suddenly a little guarded.

'I should go through Miss Bostick – she popped out to a meeting with Social Services at Bothel – about a place for one of our residents at a care home there.'

Skelgill regards her evenly.

'Can you work the computer?'

She hesitates.

'I only have restricted access to the system. Just to update a patient's notes.'

He manufactures a boyish grin. However, he rejects the phrase that is on the tip of his tongue, *while the cat's away.*

'There's no harm just looking. Someone needs to help this arl fella.'

His two-pronged entreaty seems to do the trick. She enters and takes a seat at the workstation. The desktop computer is not the latest model, and is in no hurry to power up. Skelgill watches from just behind, stooped with a hand on the back of the girl's chair; she wears a cloying, honeyed perfume that is not altogether unpleasant. They stare intently at the screen, willing it into life.

'And what is going on? And who are you?'

The pair so addressed look up as one.

Silhouetted in the doorway, a short, sturdy figure stands, arms akimbo. The woman wears a two-piece suit that is too small for her – or, rather, she is too large for it; a visual effect that for Skelgill reveals something of an uncompromising nature. He guesses she is mid-fifties; she has short, dark hair, indistinct doughy features, and an expression of indignation that appears comfortable with itself.

Nurse Ashanti has pushed back the wheeled chair and has both risen and taken a step backwards; to Skelgill's eye she seems unduly troubled for what can only be a minor indiscretion. Her reaction galvanises his own response. He remains at his post.

'Miss Bostick?'

The woman appears all the more vexed at being questioned in her own domain. Stiffly, she moves her hands to her hips.

'And what is it to you?'

Skelgill now steps casually towards her. His left hand drifts to his back pocket.

'Then you'll have heard of Operation Community Chest.'

She opens her mouth to speak, but no words emerge.

Skelgill now presents his warrant card.

'DI Skelgill, Cumbria CID. I'm investigating the background of one of your residents.'

There is a noise – a gasp, an intake of air – it is Nurse Ashanti, who stares at Skelgill wide-eyed. He shoots her a sideways glance, his expression stern, but in its own way conspiratorial.

'Madam, your colleague was kindly trying to help, in your absence – as I'm a bit pushed for time. But now you're here –' He gestures with an open palm, inviting her to her own desk. 'I'm sure the nurse would agree you'll be more proficient.'

A little battle seems to take place behind the angry eyes, but Skelgill's compliment seems to do the trick, and just tips the balance from authoritarian hubris to grudging compliance, with no loss of face. With a glare at Nurse Ashanti, she bustles into position. However, she deems it fit for there to be a small sting in her tail.

'An appointment would be preferable.'

'Aye, that's what I'm always telling burglars.'

When the woman might bristle, it seems his rank outweighs his impertinence, and she merely gives a small twist of her narrow lips.

However, she makes them wait, composing herself rather like a concert pianist, whose piano stool and music have been minutely adjusted so as to cause untold inconvenience.

'Who is it that you want to know about?'

Skelgill now looks again at Nurse Ashanti.

'I gather you just know him as William. I take it there's only one.'

'William Nobody.'

The placeholder name has Skelgill biting his cheek. After a minute or two, and some self-important clicking of the tongue (and the mouse), little bursts of typing, and irregular breaths, the woman seems ready to share her findings. He notes, however, that she introduces a little caveat, one perhaps revealing of underlying insecurity, just in case there might be repercussions for her.

'What is your particular interest in William?'

Skelgill finds himself in two minds about how he wants to answer the question. He senses that Nurse Ashanti is regarding him with concern; after all, from her perspective the honest answer would seem to be entirely altruistic. Again, he lets his gaze linger on her for a moment longer than needed. A white lie comes quite easily.

'He fits the profile we need for an initial sample inquiry. I expect you have been briefed through the usual channels on what Operation Community Chest is all about – from a point of view of criminality.'

That he puts the ball in the manager's court, and that she would certainly not want to admit to any weakness or failing in knowledge in front of a subordinate, brings a response of just a curt nod.

Now she pronounces. She leans a little closer to the screen.

'We have limited records. He was admitted first to Callington Clough residential home. He was diagnosed with partial dementia and other conditions judged to need nursing care. He was transferred after three weeks to Belmont Manor nursing home. It was private sector but it took a quota of state-funded patients. That establishment of course has gone into liquidation, which is why he is here – why we are all here. We are direct employees of Cumberland Council, drawn from the local authority care system. This is a holding situation – a temporary arrangement.'

For the first time she looks at Skelgill with some equanimity; that they are now on professional terms.

'What about this business of his name – and there being no contacts, no relatives?'

The woman's expression seems to soften, and indeed her voice takes on a note of hitherto unheard compassion. There is perhaps also a reasonable defence of her small realm.

'Naturally, for most patients, we hold contact details of next of kin. In case of emergency – or we may need approval for something, such as an inoculation. But beyond that – our role concerns only the wellbeing of our residents. Care packages, finance, occupational therapy, family background – that is the remit of Adult Care – part of the council.' She turns back to the computer and manipulates the mouse. With a final flourish a click causes a green light to blink in a dark corner of the office, and a printer purrs into motion. 'I'm giving you the details of his social worker. I'm afraid I can tell you no more at present.'

She rises and retrieves the document. Skelgill gives a bow of his head as she hands it over.

'I shan't detain you two ladies any longer.' He steps back and now addresses Nurse Ashanti directly, and at the same time holds out an arm to indicate that she should leave ahead of him. 'Sorry, Nurse – I hijacked you on your way home. Perhaps you'll see me out – make sure I don't mess up the security on the front door.'

Nurse Ashanti is quick to read his intention. It is to save her from the possibility of a dressing down. She wastes no time in leaving. Skelgill follows, giving a deferential wave of thanks with the sheet of paper.

Outside, beneath the porch, they both halt. Rain, though invisible in the darkness, is coming down in stair-rods. Skelgill, however, has something to else to say.

'Happen it's not just William we've got in common.'

'Oh?'

'Does the word battle-axe mean owt to you?'

She chuckles, throatily.

'Your boss, too, you mean?'

'Sometimes you just have to roll with the punches.'

'Oh, I think her bark is worse than her bite. She's territorial – and naturally she's worried about accidents, or someone wandering off. This place is not purpose built for nursing care. And – you, know – there's the lake.'

'Without which, I wouldn't be here.'

Skelgill perhaps surprises himself with his words – and he adds a qualification.

'That's all straight up – what I said about Operation Community Chest.'

The girl regards him thoughtfully, though in the gloom he can discern little of her expression. Her words, however, are more revealing.

'But you came anyway – you care about right and wrong. It never occurred to me that you might be a police officer.'

It goes unspoken that it was perhaps just as well, but also that this fact is a convenient coincidence. Skelgill skips such steps in the debate.

'There must be someone – some way of getting to the bottom of this. No right-minded person would want him in this situation.'

'No right-minded person would put him in it, would they?'

And now a longer pause for deliberation. The patter of the rain on foliage and the gravel of the driveway seems to increase in tempo and volume. Skelgill detects the change.

'You've booked a taxi, aye?'

'Oh, no – there's a bus that passes the gates. It's a request stop. There's one every half-hour until eight.'

Skelgill scowls into the darkness beyond what little light diffuses from the property. The muffled hoot of a tawny owl seems timed to create a sense of apprehension.

'Where are you heading?'

'They've got me temporary lodgings – a B&B in Keswick.'

'I'm driving that way. No point in you getting soaked. This is in for the night.'

'But – what about your burglars?'

Her tone is just a little tongue in cheek. Skelgill replies in kind.

'Believe it or not, burglars are human. They don't like when it's stotting down.' He pauses, still squinting into the night. 'Besides – it's fraudsters I'm after, right now.'

The girl stands motionless; she seems to be watching him intently.

In his mind's eye, vague and indistinct and almost lost amidst the inner darkness, Skelgill is visited by the spectre of a frail old man, clinging waterlogged to a precipice as torrential rain beats down.

She gives a little cough; Skelgill snaps out of his trance.

'Howay, lass – wait while I open the door – then you make a

dash for it.'

9. SOCIAL SERVICES

Carlisle – 10.40 a.m. Monday 2 October

'It states that he was admitted to A&E at Westmorland Infirmary. That was – let me see – last September – the fifth. So, just over a year ago.' The young woman adjusts her spectacles and manipulates the information available on her computer screen. 'It appears that there was nothing life-threatening and he was transferred to Callington Clough care home in Kendal. However, he was subsequently diagnosed with dementia and also to be suffering from a chronic alimentary condition and was deemed to require nursing care. There was a case conference on the twentieth of September and a care package was filed for approval. On the twenty-ninth of September last year he was transferred to Belmont Manor, until –'

Skelgill steps into the little hiatus.

'Aye, we know this bit. The staff at Duck Hall filled us in. Belmont Manor's gone bust. Meanwhile he's got no money and no visitors.'

The woman's hand drifts to her thorax and she closes her fingers around the lanyard that attaches to her ID. She continues to stare at the screen, evidently disconcerted that the police inspector has not pulled his punches.

'Well – he is fully funded by the council – by the local taxpayer.'

Skelgill frowns but opts not to press the point. Nurse Ashanti, on their drive through the rain, had reiterated her lament that William Nobody – as her superior Miss Bostick has labelled him – is not getting the quality of life that is expected; that the very basic package provides little more than subsistence.

He looks to DS Jones to take up the baton; she can be relied upon to be less confrontational.

She leans forward, better to catch a reminder of the young

woman's name badge.

'Karen, what would be your normal procedure for arriving at a care package?'

The girl – for she must be younger than DS Jones by a good couple of years – looks up hopefully.

'Oh, well – obviously we don't make people hand over a credit card before receiving care. They are dealt with according to medical assessment. The first big distinction is between residential and nursing care. Once we know what ongoing level is appropriate, we identify possible placements and their costs. Naturally, nursing care requires extra resources and more highly qualified staff.'

DS Jones nods.

'And how are the costs met?'

'Typically a person is already receiving benefits – state pension or pension credit – and they may be a property owner. The state benefits are diverted as a contribution, and arrangements may need to be made to sell the house – unless there is a surviving spouse, in which case there is a financial reconciliation with the executors of the estate when that person passes away.'

DS Jones has listened carefully – and she reads between the lines of what she has heard thus far.

'Does a person's income and wealth affect the quality of care they receive?'

Despite DS Jones's neutral intonation, the young woman seems uneasy.

'Most care homes are private businesses. The council has limited resources with which to purchase care on behalf of the local population.'

DS Jones lays a palm on the desk, as if to reassure the girl of their mutual interest.

'I understand – that is a bigger issue than for between these four walls. But what can you tell us about William, in particular? The financial picture.'

Now the girl nods, willingly – but as she manipulates the information on the screen before her, her expression seems to drain of hope. Her free hand drifts again to her ID; beneath her name, Karen Abbott, is her title, Newly Qualified Social Worker.

'I wasn't here then – and my predecessor who dealt with William's case has left.' She bites her lower lip, as if she would wish to say more – but in the silent body language is the implication that she has been cast out of her depth and that staff resources are not, and have not been, what they should be. She gives a sigh. 'The sections for next of kin, the income and assets statement – they are all just blank. No home address – not even a national insurance number. And no GP or medical records.'

She looks up forlornly.

'This can't be –' DS Jones can sense Skelgill's frustration – and she shares the sentiment – but she adjusts her question, for the girl cannot be blamed for what is emerging as a systemic failure. 'This can't be the first time that someone comes into council care and initially you don't know who they are. A single elderly person who lacks capacity. How would they be dealt with? Do you have a procedure for identification?'

But it is plain from the girl's reaction that she has not experienced the situation before.

'I suppose, you see – with limited resources – we have to deal with what's in front of us. That's the patient and their immediate needs. Crossing the t's and dotting the i's has to take a back seat.' However, she seems to gain a little confidence, and now regards DS Jones more squarely. 'But I think it is really unusual. I mean – even at least you would know where they came from – that it would be recorded at the hospital, as that's the first point of contact.'

DS Jones takes up the discrepancy.

'You said William was admitted to Westmorland Infirmary – that's Kendal. Do you have anything more about that?'

The girl checks her screen, but after a moment shakes her head. She answers without looking up.

'Just the date. Then, in the case notes, a record of the hospital contacting us – when they were looking to discharge him into the care of the local authority.'

DS Jones regards her evenly.

'In my experience, Karen, it's normal – unless it's a dire

emergency – that on arrival at A&E there's a triage process, and a person is identified and their medical record called up – this happens at the front desk – in case they have an underlying condition.'

The girl nods but looks helpless.

DS Jones contrives a sympathetic smile. She changes tack.

'Do you have any indication that the police were involved?'

This seems to assuage Skelgill's agitation, for he slides back in his seat and runs the fingers of one hand through his somewhat unkempt hair.

The girl peruses her records.

'It says a report was made to the police on the twenty-first of September – in case of there being a missing persons inquiry.' She clicks a couple more times. 'Yes – an email was sent by my predecessor. We got a reply that the notification was received. But … there's nothing else in the thread. It looks like the officer's name to whom it was forwarded was "A. Smart" – judging by their email address.'

Skelgill and DS Jones each know they avoid exchanging glances. Skelgill crosses his arms and lets out a small expiration of disparagement.

DS Jones remains outwardly unperturbed.

'Okay – so, we can look into some of these aspects. Let me ask, Karen – you are his assigned social worker, is that correct?'

'Yes. Well – I'm based here. I'm not sure if they'll keep me with him, now that he's been moved. It's quite a way down to Bassenthwaite – and I'm still learning to drive. Also – he will be moved again – that's ongoing – that we're trying to find permanent places for the residents who were at Belmont Manor.'

'But until recently you were – what – visiting him? How does it work?'

'If you're the case manager you would try to visit a patient every month – to make sure their needs are being met and coordinate any specialist appointments, medical assessments, occupational therapy – and you're another point of contact for relatives as well as the care home.

'But William has no known relatives.'

The girl's eyes are downcast.

'No. I'm afraid not.'

'Has Adult Care made any efforts to trace friends or relatives?'

Despite that DS Jones places the onus upon the department for which she works, Karen Abbott shifts uneasily in her seat, and her interrogation of the computer seems haphazard.

'I don't know what they did – that's not been recorded.' She glances up nervously. 'Obviously – when I took over William's case – I met him. I tried speaking with him. But – I realised he often wasn't able to answer coherently. To give a surname, for instance. Or where he had come from. I mean – he said Liverpool – but obviously we knew he had been brought in locally. And at his age he was hardly likely to be a tourist.'

'What age is he – do you know?'

'He's been assessed as being about ninety.'

The girl's response causes a pause for reflection; the silence seems to prompt her to elaborate.

'I mean – I tried asking about various things – such as did he have a bank account. He actually said yes. But when I started naming banks, he just said yes to them all. When I asked where the bank was, he replied Liverpool – but it seemed he always said Liverpool if you asked him anything about a location. I would have tried more – but since I started I've also had to cover for one of my colleagues who's off with long COVID. And we've got two staff on maternity leave at the moment.'

DS Jones nods. She can sense Skelgill's impatience is rekindled at their lack of progress; but it seems they must accept that this particular avenue of inquiry is in fact a cul-de-sac.

She closes her notebook by way of suggesting that she has reached their final question. But she has one supplementary.

'You must have a finance department who have a vested interest in getting to the bottom of his case?'

But now the girl looks baffled, as if it has not occurred to her that such a motivation may figure.

'There is a finance team, yes.'

'Are they likely to have investigated? If he's been in care for over a year, that must be quite a bill that has been run up.'

'I don't know how they operate – what they might have done.'

'Are they in this building?'

'I think they mostly work from home – it can all be managed online. Or they might have moved to Kendal – what with the changes – the split into two councils.'

Skelgill at this juncture makes another indeterminate noise of discontent – but his colleague knows it is the unpopular absurdity of recent boundary changes. She ignores the potential diversion.

'Karen, could you find the point of contact for William's case.' DS Jones issues the question as a polite but firm instruction. She hands over a card. 'My email address is on here.'

Skelgill remains taciturn as they leave the building and his stride is below its regular challenging pace. The pavements are slick after a recent shower, though now the sun glints between broken cumulus clouds that sail in from the Atlantic; despite the urban environs, the air is keen after the windowless office. Skelgill's gaze tracks the aerobatics of a lesser black-backed gull that harries a feral pigeon for a sandwich crust, but the determined pigeon has the speed to outrun its cumbersome assailant.

Reaching the end of Warwick Road, however, he has them skipping through traffic into The Crescent, and DS Jones realises they are not returning directly to his car. Across the busy thoroughfare is Carlisle railway station.

'What are you thinking, Guv?'

'Kendal.'

'The hospital?'

'Aye.'

'Rather than just phoning?'

He plies her with a look like, "Aye, that'll work."

'True.'

There is a pause, then DS Jones ventures a query.

'Guv –'

He recognises the tone.

'I sense a complaint coming on.'

'No – no – not a complaint. Just – obviously – this lead – William. It's kind of – informal?'

Skelgill shrugs.

'There was nowt informal about that meeting.'

'No. But – I mean – well, you know – reasonable suspicion?'

'Don't you smell a rat?'

'Oh – well – yes – there's definitely something not right here – if it's not administrative failure.'

Skelgill scoffs.

But DS Jones persists.

'I just wondered – the nurse you mentioned, who's looking after William – how much this is personal.'

If his colleague is angling at there being a more subtle ulterior motive, any nuance in her question seems to fly over Skelgill's head.

'Aye, it's personal alreet – I've seen the arl fella.'

He seems sufficiently unabashed that DS Jones reverts to the technical caveat.

'Public services aren't very joined up. It appears to be a compartmentalised system. People just do the job in front of them. And they're plainly under-resourced.'

Skelgill is not entirely convinced.

'What's with her job title? *Newly Qualified* Social Worker. It's like those P-plates folk use after they've passed their test. You can either drive safely – or you shouldn't be on the road.'

DS Jones is more inclined to the young woman's predicament. Her own days as a probationer lie not so far back in her rear-view mirror.

'When did you stop feeling imposter syndrome, Guv?'

Skelgill grins wryly.

'Wait, while I ask my invisible friend.' DS Jones chuckles – but he has a further cynical rejoinder. 'At the end of the day, the council will pick up the tab. The buck stops at no-one's desk. No need to bother your backside.'

Now she prefaces her response with an *ahem*.

'It seems like they're not the only ones to have failed on that score.'

'Another surprise.'

DS Jones allows a pause before she continues.

'Do you want me to look into it?'

'Smart?'

'Aha.'

Skelgill's features become constricted.

'I'll come back to you on that one.'

'He'll only be defensive if you speak to him, Guv.'

Skelgill does not answer.

DS Jones checks the time on her mobile phone.

'Are you thinking we'll get a sandwich on the train?'

Her timing is apt, for Skelgill abruptly swings into the open doorway of a fish and chip shop. He halts and turns and jerks a thumb over his shoulder. He grins broadly.

'It's ages since I've had a patty. I can never decide between cheese and curry.'

DS Jones shakes her head resignedly; she stands her ground.

'I'll save myself for some Kendal mint cake.' She waggles her mobile phone. 'I'll check my mail while I wait.'

When Skelgill emerges two or three minutes later he brandishes triumphantly a greasy brown paper bag.

'Special limited edition. Cheese-and-curry combo.'

'I suppose it avoids having two – thinking of the waistline.'

Skelgill's brow furrows.

'Nay, lass – I've got two – in case you change your mind, obviously.'

DS Jones plies him with a somewhat cross-eyed look, but she dutifully falls in beside him as they begin to retrace their steps, the purpose of his little diversion now revealed. It seems they will drive to Kendal, after all.

They turn back into Warwick Road. Skelgill is evidently restraining his hunger until they reach his car, parked a short distance away in Aglionby Street. The pavements are busy with pedestrians, and when a man in a wheelchair abruptly reverses around from a cash machine without looking over his shoulder they are obliged to wait for him to complete his manoeuvre and begin to move ahead.

Almost immediately is a right turn into Alfred Street – their intended route – while the man in the wheelchair seems bent upon crossing. From behind them an Asda truck swings suddenly into the junction, necessarily cutting the tight corner, and Skelgill instinctively darts to grab the back of the wheelchair. If its occupant is hard of hearing, he is about to be crushed.

'Oi! What the –? Get your filthy hands off me, you effing idiot!'

The invalid's violent reaction is hardly to be expected from one plucked from the jaws of misfortune. Equally, the average person in receipt of such a tirade would surely recoil in horror at whatever wrong they have evidently committed.

Deviating from the demographic mean in both character and life experience, Skelgill first resists the very tiny but profound urge to propel the ingrate under the rear wheels of the articulated trailer, and, realising that his unwilling charge is now in fact trying to turn right along the pavement, instead gives him a healthy shove on his way.

'Suit theesen, marra.'

Further, he shapes to hurl his weighted paper bag as a parting shot – but that is never going to happen – and instead he rotates like a baseball player who has pulled his pitch, and finds himself facing DS Jones. She regards him with a mix of alarm and amusement – and a small frown of sympathy that his cameo of guardian angel has been rejected with such petulance.

The man in the wheelchair does not look back. Indeed, he accelerates to put twenty feet or more between them. He would appear to be in his mid-fifties, reasonably able-bodied despite being wheelchair-bound. Now they see just hunched shoulders in a black leather pilot jacket and a retreating bald pate, smeared with a straggle of oily black hair. They had only caught his profile; a prominent brow, a hook nose, an angry eye small and beady, and malleable lips twisted in their vitriol.

'Some folk never can get out of the right side of the bed.'

As they follow, casually, he rattles over cobbles ahead of them into Portland Square and swings into the open gateway of the iron-railinged public garden. They pass without ado. DS Jones glimpses through bordering shrubs the leafy oasis with its central expanse of glistening rain-drenched lawn. Skelgill is busy checking that his patties have survived the various forces to which they were briefly subjected.

The brown shooting brake stands just around the next left-hand corner, Alfred Street's junction with Aglionby Street; it is a handy destination for visitors-in-the-know coming to the city centre from the M6 motorway in the east, an old residential area with liberal parking restrictions.

Ensconced, Skelgill wastes no time tucking in.

'How's the cheese-and-curry?'

He makes a grunt of approval. And he speaks in due course.

'Sure you can't be tempted?'

DS Jones laughs; she recognises the note of reluctance in his voice.

But she becomes distracted; they have the windows down, and an approaching rumble from the nearside pavement draws her eye to the wing mirror. It is the ill-tempered man in the wheelchair. Again he is making considerable haste. Instinctively they remain motionless as he passes, apparently oblivious to their presence.

They watch further as he moves away, Skelgill munching in silence. Given that they are all three seated, the man soon disappears from view beyond the straggle of parked cars that line the kerb.

Skelgill's attention shifts. He has finished his first patty and is debating whether to start on the second; these things take more eating than he remembers.

'Look.'

Skelgill glances at his colleague and then along the empty street, following her line of sight; but he is too late.

'What?'

'That chap – he just crossed the road – a good way down. He was out of the wheelchair – pushing it.'

Skelgill gazes, pondering for a moment, but is not unduly moved. Such dual abilities are not entirely miraculous.

'A chair can double as a walking frame.'

'He seemed to move completely normally.'

Skelgill carefully folds the bag holding his pardoned patty and slips it into the door pocket. He reaches for his seatbelt.

'Howay, Miss Marple – save your sleuthing for Westmorland Infirmary – we'll need it.'

He pulls away briskly, pinning her back in her seat while she is still trying to buckle up. In order to turn right they have to wait for an oncoming executive silver Mercedes; it veers to its left ahead of them without indication. Then, as Skelgill follows, it slews across to the opposite kerb, again with no signal, and jams to a halt on double-yellow lines outside a corner store.

An idle police patrol (if there were such a thing) would not let the misdemeanours pass, without at the very least dispensing a reprimand – indeed there is ample for a charge of careless driving and causing an obstruction. But uncouth witlessness is such everyday fare on England's roads that the two detectives do not even pass comment; though their silent disapproval is palpable.

DS Jones is first to speak; there is a loose association in her question.

'Sure you don't mind driving to Kendal? It must be quicker by train. And less hassle.'

Skelgill grimaces briefly.

'It's six and half a dozen. By the time you've fannied about at the other end.' He taps the steering wheel. 'We'll be there in under an hour. Plus we shan't have to come back for this.'

DS Jones nods contemplatively.

'And I suppose there's always Tebay.'

10. RED MIST

Carlisle – 11.45 a.m. Monday 2 October

'Seventy pound 52p – seventy for cash. *Ha-ha-hah!*'

Morten does not smile.

He hands over three twenties and a ten, and turns brusquely, clutching the polythene bag that contains his regular purchases. He bangs out of the door. The woman behind the counter seems unperturbed; she continues to grin, now transferring her delight to the crisp banknotes.

Reaching the pavement, Morten's rage intensifies. He erupts for the second time in ten minutes.

'Oi! Can't you see I've got a Blue Badge? You bloody fool!'

He glares at the traffic warden, a uniformed female, short and stout. But she looks like she would brook no nonsense; her moped, its idling engine popping erratically, is parked belligerently in front of his car, so close as to prevent him moving off without crushing it. He would happily do that.

'It disnae give ye the right tae cause an obstruction.' The accent is West Coast Scots, the voice gravelly. 'Your age – ye should ken the Highway Code. Thirty-two feet frae a junction's where ye should park. Ah could have the polis tow this away. That'd be points on yer licence. Think yersel lucky it's just a ticket.' As she utters this last word her hand-held printer spits out the said item and she slaps it unceremoniously onto the windscreen of the Mercedes. She adjusts the visor of her crash helmet, an action that makes it look like she is thumbing her nose. In a jiffy she is on the scooter and wheeling away in search of her next victim. She is plainly inured to any abuse that an offending motorist might hurl at her.

To Morten's surprise the moped circles and the stocky helmeted figure leans perilously.

In good Glaswegian style, she doubles down on the final say.

'And ye dinnae look disabled tae me, pal.'

Morten could scream – *"Not all disabilities are visible!"* – the mantra he has seen posted on the doors of disabled lavatories – but she is gone before the idea comes to him.

In a fit of pique he rips the ticket from the car and crumples it and hurls it ineffectually in the direction of the warden as she disappears around the next corner.

He curses viciously and climbs into the driver's seat, slamming the door.

He swallows a mouthful of vodka and tears open a chocolate bar and gorges until it is gone.

He takes several deep breaths.

He reproaches himself.

Mustn't attract attention, Mort.

Getting a parking ticket attracts attention. And disputing it would attract even more. He'll have to pay it. Better to pay within the amnesty period before it doubles in price.

He climbs out and fetches it.

But he is not quite there yet – and he tosses it rebelliously into the passenger footwell.

Another swig of vodka.

He reflects on his condition; he is still agitated.

Several reasons.

He attracted attention to himself with the young couple. *Youngish.* The girl, maybe.

He'd watched her through the bushes.

What's a looker like her doing with an untidy bloke like that? What could she possibly see in him?

Mind you, he was powerful – a lot stronger than he looked.

It was a hell of a shove he gave him. It ricked his neck. And when he arrested his progress – it was an iron grip – like that time as a teenager the farmer had caught him about to try out the quad bike that had been left by a locked field gate with its key in the ignition.

It needn't have happened – the grab and the push.

True – he wasn't concentrating after he'd left the cash machine.

His temper had flared. That was reasonable enough – why wasn't the payment through, dammit? Have they changed the due day or something? That's another thing he'll have to live with until it sorts itself out. He can't be phoning up or messing about online. Rattling their cage. Remember the watchword: do nothing that might arouse suspicion.

That ill-matched couple – they could have been DWP snoopers.

But why fork out on a couple when one person's enough?

Besides – the chap wouldn't have treated him so roughly. They'd be briefed not to engage. To keep their distance. If he'd gone under a lorry, so be it – one fewer suspected benefits cheat. Not that he would have gone under the lorry – he'd seen it at the same instant he'd been grabbed.

And they weren't snooping in the brown car. The bloke was eating. And they were indicating to turn right – before they could have known he was going to turn left in front of them. And they drove past.

He scans about – his neck hurts and he curses again.

But they're nowhere to be seen. And there's no missing that old rattletrap. The aerial was a bent wire coat hanger.

He considers whether he should change his routine. Even change location? But where else is he going to find ATMs of three different banks handily close together? Whitehaven's not an option. Workington's too close to home. Penrith? He doesn't know his way around Penrith.

Besides, there's the other thing.

But right now it's also another niggle.

He checks his phone.

She still hasn't confirmed.

Dammit.

It's a minute to their regular meeting time. His last message does not say delivered.

Now he thinks about it, she's let him down once before. No explanation and no mention of it the next time.

Why is that? It can't be that she gets a better offer. He preens himself imperiously and surveys the interior splendour of his Mercedes.

Maybe her phone's out of charge. Or out of minutes or data or whatever.

He could go and knock.

No – he doesn't want that – to stand there on the steps in full view. When she knows he's coming she watches from some spyhole and the entryphone buzzes as he approaches. Push open the door – disappear from sight without breaking stride.

Dammit.

He could look online now. Find someone on tour, like he used to – that would be anonymous. Except you never know where they might stay. You never get the address until the last minute. It could turn out to be one of those flats right next to the benefits office. He could hardly march up to the door.

And it's short notice.

He glances at the clock on the dashboard. It's past twelve and he said he'd be back for two. That great behemoth Harriet's coming to discuss terms.

He reflects, momentarily distracted by the thought.

She seems pretty keen. He still has reservations. But she's well-padded in more ways than one – she's already let slip that she's got investments. PEPs and ISAs, and no heirs to speak of. But there's the immediate hurdle – she wants to pay the rent for her trial period by direct debit. That means giving her his bank details. He needs to find a way of talking her into paying in cash. Why shouldn't she? She's always paid Rina in cash – Rina only accepts cash.

He could say he doesn't have a bank account – but, no – not when Rina's bragging that he's an Independent Financial Adviser. That's not credible – and Harriet's not stupid, that much he can tell. That's her main drawback, as far as he can see.

He needs to sell her the benefits of cash. He needs to talk her into letting him collect it for her. That way, he gets her PIN. If he fetches it, she doesn't need risk the traffic on that mobility scooter. She says she likes going out – that it does her good. But what about when it's raining? And what about when the scooter develops a fault? That can happen – that can easily happen, a loose connection. And then she needs her weekly prescription. Morten

81

to the rescue. He'll get her prescription, get their provisions, get the cash she needs. Buy cakes, a little daily treat. Morten at your service. Service with a smile.

She'll need to change her address. She'll need to write to her bank. He doubts she'll have online banking – most people her age don't trust the internet. And he'll offer to post the letters – insist. Once he's got the details, he'll set up remote banking – Rina can pretend to be Harriet on the phone, for the security questions. After that, they can sign in with impunity.

He'll need to brief Rina. She's got Harriet wrapped round her little finger. Rina's always had the gift of the gab, a born and bred Scouser, unlike him. She can conjure up a smile – insincere as you like, and you'd never know. Nothing's too much trouble – she's good at pretending to be interested in people. She finds out all about them. About their families. About their finances.

He's inherited it in his own way, but he's more of a suave charmer.

And people always want to listen when it comes to making money, it's just like being a surgeon or a solicitor.

He sits motionless.

His thoughts, momentarily stalled, become diverted – a young woman in a short skirt passes his car; his eyes track her progress until she turns into the corner shop.

His anger has subsided but there is still the frustration to be assuaged; one layer is peeled away, another lies beneath.

Who did that traffic warden think she was? Who was she to talk about his age? The old bag.

His ears are burning and he can still feel the thump of his pulse at his temple.

He swallows one of his tablets with a mouthful of vodka.

Damn her.

He takes up his phone and opens the browser.

11. ROAD TEST

Westmorland Infirmary, Kendal – 12.50 p.m. Monday 2 October

Good to his word, Skelgill has them at their destination within the hour, having argued the time-saving case for the taxpayer of 90mph, and – "any road – the cylinder head on a straight-six needs a good de-coking every so often".

DS Jones raises an already well-exercised eyebrow when he slews into a parking row reserved for disabled drivers.

He must sense her mild disapproval. As he leads the way he flashes a grin over his shoulder – then he falters in his stride and shoots a hand to the small of his back. Now he moves in a positively ungainly fashion.

'Guv – it says administration block to the left.'

Ahead of them a large rectangular awning juts out over hatched tarmac, a sheltered drop-off designated for ambulances. A row of empty wheelchairs that offer a choice of red or blue plastic-covered cushioned seats wait for custom rather like supermarket trolleys, save for one in which a post-operative occupant puffs profusely under a no-smoking sign. Above a large rotating door arrangement are the words Accident & Emergency. Indeed one ambulance waits with its engine running and rear door open – inside DS Jones glimpses someone being tended by a green-clad paramedic.

She notices a discarded cigarette packet, and instinctively stoops to pick it up and diverts to drop it into a litter bin.

When she looks round, for a second she does not see Skelgill – then she realises he is seated in one of the wheelchairs. He has opted for red.

She approaches, frowning patiently, thinking this is still his little act of flippant bravado. But when Skelgill remains resolutely in place, she puts her hands on her hips and regards him questioningly.

'He didn't come by ambulance.'

His statement is a question, a challenge and – for DS Jones – a sudden realisation – that Skelgill is up to something shady – and it begins to take shape at the hazy event-horizon of her consciousness. She nods reflectively.

'Give us a shove, lass.'

The chair has no means of self-propulsion. She steers him through the ponderously rotating doors.

They emerge into a sizeable foyer smelling of cleaning fluid and toasted sandwiches that gives the impression of a shopping mall, a central tiled concourse with side avenues where people move purposefully, like extras crossing a film set, their carefully choreographed routes designed to avoid collisions. These are mostly hospital staff in various colour-coded outfits; members of the public are less decisive, outpatients or visitors who vacillate in trying to decipher signs loaded with medical jargon and abbreviations. They pass a board affixed to a pillar that lists a score of departments, the likes of IPCU and REDU.

Directly ahead of them behind Perspex screens three receptionists like bank tellers are all occupied; a small queue waits.

'Over there. Then check us in.'

Skelgill points tangentially to a wide opening, signposted Waiting Area, that evidently expands into a more capacious atrium. Motionless figures are seated around the perimeter and back-to-back in perpendicular rows.

DS Jones has caught up with his unspoken plan.

'What shall I tell them?'

He makes a casting motion.

'Monster pike – back spasm.'

She wheels him in and finds a space and returns to the desk, departing his line of sight, shaking her head.

His arrival has attracted little attention – perhaps just a few pairs of eyes raised to check that his case is not so serious as to bump their own malady down the priority ranking. Indeed, along such lines, he peruses his fellow citizens – and the paradox further dawns upon him. There is one teenager in a Sedbergh School rugby kit, accompanied by what might be his resigned-looking games master. The boy's right cuff is pinned to his left shoulder, the shirt pressed into use as a makeshift sling; his face is smeared with mud and tears, but now he is braving it. Skelgill flashes him a grin of encouragement, as if to say I've been there and you'll survive. And then the contrast – at a quick count there are forty people and – the boy aside – not one to his eye is a case of either *accident* or *emergency*. There are neither the pained nor the haemorrhaging, merely the glum-faced and downcast. They look more like dispirited travellers in an airport departure lounge whose flight is interminably delayed.

'It could be four to six hours.'

DS Jones's voice interrupts his analysis.

Skelgill springs to his feet. Again, there are anxious looks in case he is queue-jumping.

'That makes me suddenly feel a lot better.'

He flexes his spine.

Then he grabs the wheelchair and swings it around.

'Howay, lass.'

He starts rapidly towards the exit.

'Hadn't I better tell them?'

'Aye, do that.'

While DS Jones is at the desk he returns the conveyance to its place in the line and scans about. There is a CCTV camera over reception. Another monitors the ambulance bay. But the impression is not comprehensive.

DS Jones joins him. By mutual telepathy they follow signs for the administration block.

'What did they ask?'

'Name and date of birth. That's enough to call up your medical record. Then they confirm the home address.'

Skelgill gives a slight tip of his head, but does not comment.

'Did you know you're still registered at Buttermere?'

'I'm not exactly a regular at the Doc's.' He has no idea who is his GP. But he has a question. 'What about you?'

'They didn't ask. I guess they just assumed I would wait with you. I suppose, unless you're accompanying a minor, they don't need to know.'

'So, you could have dumped us in the waiting room and done a runner.'

DS Jones regards him with a small degree of alarm, though she understands this was the aim of their experiment.

'Yes – I suppose I could have just said, that's William through there – I've left my engine running – I'll move the car before I block an ambulance – and never returned.'

Skelgill shrugs.

'You needn't have said owt. Just straight into the waiting room – and off you go.'

'Except they got his name – William.' She looks again at Skelgill, more questioningly. 'Could he have told them that much?'

Skelgill does not meet her gaze, but he narrows his eyes.

'The nurse, Ashanti – at Duck Hall – she reckons it's not his name.'

DS Jones watches him for a moment; but he continues to stare ahead as they move quickly.

'I saw you looking for cameras.'

'I'm not holding out any hopes on that score.'

And his pessimism is soon borne out.

Seated presently in the Acting Hospital Director's office – DS Jones having explained that they would like to interrogate the movements of a patient admitted one year and 26 days previously – and the man, a diminutive, rather nervous type in his late fifties, having explained that he is merely "holding the fort" until a permanent appointment is made for the position, had wrung his small hands and appeared constipated.

'What I can tell you, officers, is that I have been charged with a review of a proposed budget for the forthcoming year. My background, you see, is in finance. I know that CCTV records are deleted after twelve months.' He perhaps detects disappointment, and seems to shrink further into his over-large chair. 'It is the cost of cloud storage, you see? The hospital has over 100 cameras, producing approximately 100,000 gigabytes of data per month. That's an annual cost of roughly £40,000. The proposal is to reduce storage time to six months. An analysis showed that over

95% of requests for footage occurred within a week of an incident – the vast majority concerning the drunken abuse of admissions staff.'

DS Jones nods sympathetically, but does not give up.

'Is there any possibility that the deleted data could be recovered?'

'I would have to inquire.' He looks unhappy, and speaks tentatively. 'Is this a matter of life and death – a serious crime?'

DS Jones might be tempted to say there is in fact no evidence of any crime whatsoever, beyond Skelgill's whims. She avoids eye contact with her superior.

'It could be a serious matter. We are part of the multi-agency team assigned to Operation Community Chest – I expect you will be aware of that.'

Now the Acting Director looks puzzled.

'I thought that was concerning fraud?' He gives an open-handed gesture; it seems of futility. 'We have no monetary transactions.'

He appears a little relieved in this regard. Certainly it is not easy for a member of the public to steal from a service that is free at the point of delivery.

DS Jones has a reporter's notebook, and quickly writes a few lines. She tears off the top page and hands it over with her calling card.

'These are the details we have obtained. William – aged ninety – a possible Liverpool connection. And the date of admission to this hospital. The patient is effectively unidentified, and may be a victim of financial exploitation. Indirectly, that would be a fraud against the county council. We're working on the premise that he was brought here by private means. But if he had been collected by ambulance, and it has been overlooked, that address would represent a significant breakthrough in our inquiry.'

The man nods, rather timidly.

'Yes – I see. There will certainly be records of all ambulance movements. As you may know, response time is a matter of great civic controversy, given the geographical nature of this region.'

This lament stimulates a flicker of interest from Skelgill, himself a first-responder of sorts. He is well versed in the so-called 'efficiency programmes' that may see a heart-attack victim driven past one hospital that formerly housed a cardiac unit to a 'centre' of excellence – *centre* being a misnomer – forty miles away in Lancaster, eating into the 'golden hour' during which survival is more likely.

But if he has learned anything in life it is to pick one's battles judiciously, and not allow one's resolve to be drained by exposure to the relentless blood-letting that is political discourse.

The Acting Director senses some emanation of displeasure from Skelgill. He places the page of notepaper carefully in the centre of his desk, and staples DS Jones's card neatly to one corner.

'I shall see to it as a matter of urgency.' He gives a nervous cough. 'There are, of course, certain data protection protocols to be observed.'

DS Jones regards him evenly.

'In general terms, what's your procedure for identifying an unknown patient? Say, a hit-and-run when the victim is carrying no ID?'

The man is momentarily baffled by the question.

'Well – you see – that would normally be a police matter – wouldn't it? It would be unusual for an ambulance, alone, to attend the scene of an accident.'

DS Jones glances at Skelgill.

She tries again.

'Well – an elderly person, then – someone who has just collapsed in the street. Let's say a vagrant. Surely you want to know who they are – to understand their medical record?'

The Acting Director is plainly uncomfortable with this line of questioning.

'Look – I'm no clinician – but, well – I think a person's vital signs are quickly monitored and any irregularities treated accordingly. Our role is to stabilise a patient and prepare them for discharge – as soon as reasonable, to prevent bed-blocking. If they are not identified in the ordinary course of events, and judged as lacking capacity, statutory responsibility for them passes to Social Services.'

Skelgill lets out an involuntary gasp of frustration. While the man has been perfectly amenable, and cooperative within his limited means, it feels like asking the proverbial yokel – chewing a straw and loitering at a lonely crossroads – how to reach someplace thereabouts.

DS Jones can tell that Skelgill has had enough, and she brings the interview to a close, to the relief of all.

They pace back more slowly towards Skelgill's car, despite that a light drizzle has now begun to fall.

'He seemed a fish out of water, Guv.'

Skelgill flashes her a curious look. It might simply be that she uses words that resonate with him, but he is undoubtedly a little conflicted. And it is not the unsatisfactory nature of this latest interview – other than that it is reflective of his attachment to this case, which his colleague has more than once intimated is in excess of what might be justified by its facts. The corollary being that he is letting his heart rule his head, and these two organs of wisdom face off in a silent duel, while he is a less-than-unbiased second.

But for Skelgill there have been the opening encounters, almost spectral and surreal, with the old man and his nurse that have left a deep if ineffable impression upon him.

When he does not answer, she tries again.

'Penny for your thoughts.'

Skelgill starts.

'I'll take you to meet him.'

'Oh – right.'

'First – I need to see a man about a dog.'

This all-purpose expression for a diversion might range in meaning from a brief visit to the gents' to an afternoon's fishing expedition. Skelgill seems to understand that qualification is needed.

'Actual dog. The arl lass – she's been minding Cleopatra. Likes the company, I reckon.'

'That's nice.'

'Aye – except she spoils her rotten, on the quiet. Dog won't touch her kibble for a week.'

DS Jones, having observed some of Skelgill's erratically liberal behaviour after a couple of pints with packets of crisps, inhales a touch sanctimoniously. But she has switched back on her mobile phone and now she is distracted as messages crowd her inbox. She has matters she would like to initiate, and feedback to her inquiries may have arrived.

'Will it take us long from here?'

Skelgill looks a little askance.

'From here? *Buttermere?* You can't get there from here, lass.'

12. HARRIET OVERHEARS

Troughdale House, Whitehaven – 2.20 p.m. Monday 2 October

'I can't think what's keeping Morten, he's usually so punctual. I hope he's not had a problem with his new car. If he's much longer, perhaps we could start your session. It could be your first free one, Harriet – an introductory bonus. And then you could chat to him after.'

Harriet brushes a biscuit crumb from the dieting magazine on her lap that she has been perusing in Rina's absence. She is seated in what will become her armchair, unless she brings some of her own furniture. She isn't sure how she feels about using second-hand items, that were the province of someone now passed away. A bed, especially – it would be like you were wearing their old clothes.

'Och, I don't know about getting a free session before we've agreed anything. Besides, it can't be cheap for you – the price of electricity these days – it must be one of your biggest costs. I want to pay my fair share of the bills. I'm not hard up – I've told you that, Rina. I'll be doing it for company – for the two of us.'

Rina turns away, ostensibly to adjust the yellow roses in the Clarice Cliff vase that came from Mam's. (She never thought of the place as Billy's). But she glimpses herself in the gilded mirror, also from Mam's. For a fleeting moment she is shocked by what she sees. A portrait of unbridled avarice, a predator.

She quickly lowers her eyes, but continues arbitrarily to adjust the stems.

Back in the day, living in West Derby Road, every other house was on the rob – fiddling the lecky. But their Da would never do it. "I didn't fight Hitler at Wipers to come home and steal off my own nation." Well – times are different, now. It's everyone for themselves – that's what Morten says.

And he has a way of circumventing the meter. Just like that time in Cornwall, when he disconnected the odometer on her Fiat Panda to stop it clocking up the miles. The trouble was, she never knew what speed she was going. She got flashed three times by cameras and eventually had to give up her driving licence.

'That's very good of you, Harriet. I try to be fair with my clients. You know I've never increased my prices – even now that they're saying electricity's gone up by triple.'

Harriet frowns at something in the magazine – perhaps the naked salad that fills most of the centrefold – and speaks only absently.

'Does this part have its own meter? And there's council tax – did you split that out for your brother – or did he get a separate bill?'

Rina looks for a moment a little disconcerted. She leans down and pushes the biscuit plate closer to Harriet, and takes up the teapot, but it is empty.

'Morten handles all the finances – I've told him to make sure you get a preferential deal, like.'

Harriet seems more engrossed by the article than interested in what Rina has to say. She does not respond, other than sigh a little as she shifts position.

Rina goes to the window and presses her cheek to the glass, trying to peer at an angle. The window gives on to the end of the driveway as it runs along the side of the house. She can just see Harriet's mobility scooter, but not beyond, nothing of the front section.

'He said he'd be back by two. He knew you were coming half an hour early to discuss things.' She pulls away and rubs her hands together. 'Let's get you started on your session – and then I'll go and ring him up.'

Harriet reluctantly folds away the magazine, and with some difficulty levers herself from the undoubted comfort of the armchair. Rina extends a guiding hand.

'Look – I'll show you – you can get through to my treatment room this way – so that'll be a nice shortcut from your flat. And you can keep the door locked on this side, for privacy, if you want.'

Harriet moves ahead, half tentatively, half inquisitively.

Rina follows, close on her heels.

'There we are, you see? You just get undressed and make yourself comfortable while I get the slimming machine warmed up. I think we should go for all sixteen pads today, don't you, dear? Since it's after the weekend.'

It takes Rina a good few minutes to get the electrotherapy pads in place, and some not inconsiderable gasping on Harriet's part as she raises unwilling limbs and torso from the treatment table to enable Rina to pass the securing bands from one side to the other.

Rina switches on the power – and waits a moment, her lips pursed – always wondering if one day the machine or her supine client will go up in smoke – and always secretly pleased when neither does.

'How's that? All feel okay?'

Harriet responds with a grunt in the affirmative. She is rather conscious of the implied confidences she shares with Rina – not least that Rina gets to see her twice a week in her underclothes, when outfits can be much more forgiving.

'I'll leave you in peace. Are you happy with the curtain open? I'm thinking of planting some roses just out there. The window's ajar – my last client had wanted it closed, with the heating on – but I thought you'd find it a bit too warm. You're more robust – and what with your Scotch blood.'

Harriet confirms she is happy with the arrangements, despite the backhanded compliments. Rina will often stay and gossip with a client – sometimes for the entire forty-five-minute session (the hour including time to set up beforehand and shower afterwards). Today, however, it is plain she is distracted.

'I'll just go and check that Morten's not been trying to ring me. He might have forgotten his little remote that opens the electric gates. It's not like him – but the battery could have died.'

Harriet consents. She rather likes the idea of tranquillity.

Rina leaves.

Harriet's eyes dart about.

From the open window filters the mournful autumn song of a robin.

She lets out a deep sigh. One thing is for sure, there's no traffic noise here, unlike her present place, where the road seems to get busier and more perilous by the day.

There is just the gentle hum of the archaic slimming machine and the rhythmical ticking of the wall clock, a casement type of about thirty inches in length in plain oak that looks like it would benefit from the attention of a French polisher. Rina has told her it is nearly a hundred years old; that it was a wedding present given to her parents – and that the dent in the brass bob of the pendulum was caused by her mother throwing a cup at her father when he was winding it one day, when she found he'd lost the family allowance on a horse. She said her mother had a tigerish temperament.

But now from the clock emanates only a hypnotic aura; its resonant *tick-tock* soft and deep and satisfying, and redolent of an old vicarage or library or schoolroom during an examination – or her office in the Victorian council building where she worked as Chief Accountant before she retired early due to her heart condition.

She listens. The ticking intrigues her – for all its restful properties, she wonders that Rina has it in here instead of the piped New Age music they play at most salons.

There is an old-style neon digital display on the slimming machine, a timer, and Harriet waits for it to click down to 42:00 and then begins to count. It is quite a high frequency, certainly not a second between each movement, but perhaps not half a second, either.

Still she is surprised to reach 50 after just 30 seconds – which means the clock must tick and tock 100 times a minute … that's 6,000 times an hour … and 144,000 times a day … and – come on Harriet … how many times a year … hmm …

Harriet opens her eyes.

The digital timer shows only twenty minutes left.

She feels alarmed.

Has her name been called?

There is a slight draft from the window. She shivers. She must have got chilled during her unintended nap.

Then something else from the window – something more disturbing.

A voice. An angry voice.

Though she can't completely discern the words – it comes again in a hateful expletive-laden tirade. There are obscene, horrible names. Slang for female animals peppered among human body parts.

It is Morten's voice.

And now it is answered – with interest – by Rina's shrieking retort.

It is a full-blown, no-holds-barred quarrel.

Teenage tantrum plays the incensed parent.

As Harriet strains to decipher the content, she hears a car door slam and the squeal of an engine in reverse gear and the crunch of tyres spinning in gravel.

And now only Rina's voice – a charge hurled after her departing son.

'Don't blame me, Morty – you never accept responsibility for anything you've done wrong!'

And then a more specific, if paradoxical defence.

'And I've neither filled in a bloody form nor *not* filled in a bloody form!'

A car roars away.

There is silence.

Then the faint sound of footsteps on the loose stones, coming towards the house.

A door closes.

Harriet exhales – she has been holding her breath – and now she feels her heart straining to restore the oxygen level in her bloodstream.

'Are you getting on alright, dear?'

Rina is all sweetness and light.

'You're looking very good, Harriet – that must be your new diet

– and the magic of the machine, of course.'

Rina chuckles, and – as she moves around her client's not inconsiderable form, adjusting the pads and tightening the bands – hums a little ditty, *Hello, Goodbye*.

Harriet is about to make an inquiry when Rina saves her the trouble.

'Morten had a puncture after all. He had to change a wheel all by himself. He's such a clever lad. And then he rushed back – but when I told him you'd started, to save time – he offered to pop down to Asda to buy some fruit scones for afternoon tea. He thought you'd like that. He's so considerate.'

Harriet murmurs her agreement to the proposition.

'You're lucky to have him.'

'That's right, Harriet – I am. And so will you be, too. Morten will be able to help you in lots of ways. I think it's going to be a very good arrangement for us all. I think it's going to be a good year for the roses – don't you?'

13. WINDING ROADS

Buttermere – 4.30 p.m. Monday 2 October

'I didn't say you were with us, lass.'

Skelgill pre-empts a protest from DS Jones by letting Cleopatra into the back of his car. The Bullboxer immediately swarms through into the front, enveloping DS Jones in a tornado of elated wriggling.

Skelgill rounds to the driver's door and watches, waiting for the storm to subside.

'She weren't that pleased to see me.'

DS Jones grimaces, not entirely appreciating the attention.

'She recognises a sister sufferer.'

Skelgill growls disapprovingly – but he embellishes his excuse for not introducing his partner on this occasion.

'She's got Verena in there. They'd be all over you like a rash. They can blether for England.'

He is bearing a bulging duffel bag and a translucent Tupperware container. He rattles the latter.

'Upside – Verena's Welsh cakes. Melt in your mouth.'

It is said the average dog recognises 89 words and 'cake' would seem figure in the present canine company's lexicon. Skelgill opens the box and tosses a sweetmeat onto the rear seat. Cleopatra follows, much to the relief of DS Jones. She is not so much huge, as dense.

Skelgill frowns, and moves away.

'Second thoughts, I'd better put these out of reach.'

He takes the Welsh cakes and the duffel bag to the rear and secretes them among the collection of crates and tackle and outdoor gear.

When he returns, DS Jones acknowledges his somewhat unconvincing apology.

'It's okay – I literally just finished a call. Can you believe the Acting Hospital Director got straight back to me?'

Skelgill shrugs.

'Accountants – they're nowt if they're not efficient.'

DS Jones eyes him with a twinkle of amusement. In characteristic style, he has avoided asking for the news.

'As we suspected. Firstly, there's no record of William being brought in by ambulance. All movements on that day were of persons identified. Secondly, they don't have the historical CCTV. Moreover, they discovered that the reception area security cameras had not in fact been working for about six weeks during that period. He said, thanks, we got him a discount.'

Skelgill makes a scoffing sound.

'Hundred percent strike rate, I'll take that, for now.'

DS Jones frowns.

'Fifty – at best – surely?'

Skelgill turns to check the dog; she has settled on a reassuringly aromatic army blanket.

'Even if the cameras had been working – I can tell you – pound to a penny, we wouldn't have been able to identify the person who brought him. He's been abandoned, lass.'

'Disguise?'

'Aye. Or lob a bung to a taxi driver – summat like that.'

He starts the ignition.

They are both quiet as they move away, leaving the hamlet – officially a village, by dint of its church and hostelries, if not by its population of just over a hundred. As they do so Skelgill eyes the Buttermere sign in his wing mirror and thinks of his schoolboy record for hitting it with a stone from distance. He realises he has forgotten the yardage, if not the satisfying clang. He finds himself pondering the economy of the name, shared by the settlement and its eponymous lake. The other way around, of course.

As the road rises they come alongside Crummock Water. It is on the passenger side, and to DS Jones's eye a foreboding, cold-looking body in the fading autumn light, flanked on its far side by the long, dark barrow of Mellbreak.

Skelgill drives swiftly and efficiently, knowing the road, travelled ten thousand times. But she notices his concentration is intense, when he might ordinarily be tempted to scan the lake for only he knows what.

On the descent to Hause Point the way narrows as rocky outcrops erupt ominously on their right, while a neatly dressed dry stone wall rises nearside – not an ancient sheep enclosure, but a barrier raised more recently for traffic safety, for there is a steep drop down into the lake – and barely room for two cars to pass – and to boot a blind corner fast approaching.

Skelgill, as invariably is the case, has his side window down by a few inches. He says it is better to detect traffic, and birds, and country sounds.

But now his colleague sees him check urgently in his rear-view mirror – for Cleopatra has risen to sample the airstream, straining her snout at his shoulder.

Rather than take the bend on trust, like he has many of those ten thousand times he instinctively slows to little more than walking pace – and – sure enough – in the centre of the narrow lane, four Swaledale sheep lie ruminating on the tarmac, a parliament of yowes.

Skelgill yields to an exasperated expletive.

He switches on his hazard lights and reverses twenty yards or so, obliging any aft-coming vehicle to slow. He jumps out and, producing a hank of baler twine which he loops through the dog's collar, he sets off on foot, Cleopatra straining at the leash.

It is a minute before the pair return, Skelgill jogging, Cleopatra trotting, ears pricked.

'What did you do?'

'Chased them up the fell – Rannerdale Knotts. It's less steep round the corner – it's called Buttermere Hause.'

'You didn't let her off the leash?'

Skelgill shoots his colleague a sharp glance.

'You must be joking. Old Jack Nicholson – his eyesight's not what it used to be.'

He seems to bear no malice against the landowner –

acquaintance or not – that it is the farmer's first right to protect his livelihood and discover later what or whom he has peppered with shot.

But Skelgill adds a rider, as if to reassure DS Jones.

'I've never yet seen her show the slightest inclination to chase a sheep – but they think she's going to chase them. The sight of her works a treat – puts a rocket under them, faster than any amount of my yawping.'

DS Jones grins.

'I'm surprised there aren't more casualties – just here, I mean – this bend is a death trap – there's no escape off the sides.'

Skelgill frowns reflectively.

'It's after lambing's the main problem. These big lumps of yowes – they're a lot easier to spot and they can probably take the odd dunt in the hindquarters. But – like everywhere – you get idiots not fit to drive.'

DS Jones is about to remark, how many incompetent motorists have they seen today – they might have issued a book of tickets. But, then, there was the 90mph motorway dash.

No vehicles have come during the hiatus; they move on.

There are many more sheep to avoid, notably populating the edible fringe of the open bracken-clad slopes that spill like frothing lava from the great bulk of Grasmoor. They skirt the grounds of Crummock Hall without passing comment; then plunge into winding wooded narrows, a single-track stretch thankfully guarded by a cattle grid that shadows Liza Beck before it snakes beneath the road to meet the nearby River Cocker. There is the turn onto a marginally wider B-road that takes them due north through Low Lorton. Skelgill glances as they pass the village shop, but does not speak.

Presently Skelgill turns east, eschewing the main roads for a back route, *All Saints Lane*, he calls it, for it passes the tiny isolated churches of St Cuthbert, Embleton and St Margaret, Wythop.

DS Jones is less familiar with this way – though she might suspect his reverence has something to do with an alternative strand of communion, when at a junction she realises they have arrived within a stone's throw of The Partridge.

Skelgill must detect her suspicion.

'Ten minutes.'

He means their ETA, and hauls at the wheel like a horseman turning a thirsty steed away from a watering hole.

'Do you think we ought to phone ahead?'

Skelgill hesitates to answer.

'The nurse – who looks after him – she said come any time during reasonable waking hours – but after high tea around five was always good.'

DS Jones nods amenably.

When they park in front of Duck Hall Skelgill stalks to the rear. Noisy rummaging ensues, and DS Jones sees he has the duffel and a supermarket carrier bag.

It looks like Cleopatra is being left behind – but she has other ideas. Albeit inelegantly, she scales the seatback and scrambles out before Skelgill can get the tailgate down. In short order she is at DS Jones's side.

Skelgill shakes his head. He frees a hand and digs into his trouser pocket.

'Catch.'

He tosses the hank of baler twine.

'Just be ready to brace yourself if she takes a liking to someone.'

'Do you think they'll mind?'

'I reckon there's folk paid to bring in therapeutic animals.' He shrugs. 'So long as they've cleared all their plates away.'

101

14. FISHES

Duck Hall – 5.20 p.m. Monday 2 October

'Dan – I knew you'd come back. He'll be so pleased. And he's awake – they've just finished their tea – I mean, you know, dinner?'

While they have waited in the lobby Skelgill has once again been drawn to inspect *The Phantom Regiment* – there is something macabre and fascinating about the silent host and its imagined march into oblivion. DS Jones meanwhile, has settled to peruse her mobile phone in a shady alcove where visitors' chairs have been arranged.

That the nurse is in uniform heightens the incongruity of her informal greeting; more so that she steps close and reaches to place the palm of her hand against Skelgill's heart.

He reacts self-consciously; the hall is gloomy, though there is surely a flush of crimson on his cheekbones. He seems to stagger backwards, as if she has pushed him. He raises the bags.

'I've got the stuff – some clothes, an' all.'

DS Jones watches quietly. There is no sign that Skelgill will introduce her.

She rises; now the nurse notices her. They each take a couple of steps towards one another.

'I'm Detective Sergeant Jones.'

There are now exchanged appraising looks; an unspoken dialogue in a language entirely alien to Skelgill.

But he does sense something – and rather clumsily he thrusts the duffel bag at the nurse, now holding open the mouth so she can see its contents.

'We stopped at me Ma's place – she sorted these out, vests and whatnot – they've been gathering dust in the arl fella's wardrobe. I reckon they reek a bit of mothballs.'

The nurse flashes her broad smile.

'Oh, that's so thoughtful – *of her.*'

The rider causes Skelgill to hesitate.

'Aye – I'll tell her thanks.'

Now he shakes the carrier bag.

'And I've got the biscuits – and the book.'

There is a curious hiatus. It is in order that they would proceed to see William – but it is as if the nurse is expecting that DS Jones would resume her seat and wait.

Instead she takes charge.

'We have begun formally to investigate William's case. It is clear there are irregularities. It is essential we identify him.'

The nurse inhales to speak – but she becomes distracted. Urgent footsteps approach from the corridor to the left of the hallway and evidently their cadence is familiar.

The detectives follow her gaze to see Miss Bostick emerge. She halts at the junction. She eschews formalities.

'I have more information. Come into my office.'

Command issued, she swivels on her heel with military precision.

The trio left standing are reduced to a condition of neutrality, approaching alliance.

Skelgill remembers Cleopatra.

He issues a low whistle, a two-tone summons that brings her from the alcove. DS Jones swoops to pick up the trailing leash. The nurse seems intrigued, but does not remark. Instead, she leads the way.

They find Miss Bostick seated at her computer.

They stand in line; it is like the headmistress's study.

She looks up questioningly; first at the dog, then at the duffel bag held by Nurse Ashanti.

The latter takes half a pace forward.

'Dan – Inspector Skelgill – he has brought some clothes for William.' She raises the bag and then places it on a cabinet, where what appear to be other such donations are waiting to be distributed.

Miss Bostick permits herself a perfunctory smile.

She taps her keyboard.

'I have retrieved his records – all of his notes pertaining to his time in care. They do not cover Social Work observations and decisions, or their procedures – but it is a log of information relevant to his ongoing treatment. I'm afraid that it does not make entirely pleasant reading.'

They wait.

'It seems he was admitted to hospital with an episode of delirium – a state of disorientation. Dementia is the biggest single risk-factor – we see it regularly. Delirium is a condition poorly understood but known to trigger a worsening of dementia symptoms – it can be a step-change – but without his medical history there is no knowing his capacity beforehand.'

She looks up – it seems she is about to share a significant point.

'It states that his wife died. There are no details – but that might be the explanation for the onset of delirium. This is in the notes supplied by the hospital. It is not clear whether he told them about his wife, or if it came from some third party.'

DS Jones wastes no time in requesting clarification.

'Are there any details of the wife?'

But the manager merely shakes her head. She looks up briefly at Skelgill.

'As I mentioned – he was discharged from hospital in Kendal to nearby Callington Clough care home – but his combination of dementia and a bowel problem led to him being moved out of the district into nursing care at Belmont Manor in Carlisle.'

The three listen patiently. There is the implied corollary that the transfer put paid to any likelihood of uncovering William's domestic connections.

Hitherto the manager has been matter-of-fact in her delivery – but suddenly she seems to suppress an expression of dismay. As she reads the notes and prepares to relate their content her voice catches and she swallows a couple of times.

'It states that he was initially unsettled. And agitated. There are notes of concern made following a DoLS assessment – that's Deprivation of Liberty Safeguards, required by the Mental Capacity Act, 2005. There are two direct quotes. He repeatedly asked, *"Why am I here?"* And stated, *"Get me out of here!"* He made several attempts to escape. The culmination was that after six weeks he was found in his room with a polythene bag over his head.' Again, her voice falters, though she remains stern-faced. 'Extra precautions were taken thereafter. Gradually he seemed to acquiesce to his circumstances.'

Miss Bostick rocks back in her chair and regards her audience. She is momentarily alarmed by Skelgill's wrathful countenance – but correctly does not regard it as a sentiment aimed at the messenger.

'That is all, I'm afraid. William's is an unfortunate case – but far from exceptional in these straitened times.' She pauses, though she raises a hand to suggest she has something to add. Her gaze comes to rest on the Bullboxer. Again there is the softening of the expression, that Skelgill had noted on his previous visit. 'Perhaps you can learn something before it is too late.'

Skelgill inhales to speak – but before he can she points to a wall clock, and addresses Nurse Ashanti.

'I mean to say – it's getting on for six.'

Her expression is pained, however. Plainly, she had meant not late in the day, but late in the life.

They troop a little dejectedly out into the corridor after Nurse Ashanti. While the three humans walk softly on rubber-soled shoes, the dog's claws tap out a languid *ticker-tacker* on the tiles.

Inside the residents' lounge they find William in what might be his regular seat, turned towards the big bay windows and, beyond, the sweep of parkland and the pines that shield Scotch Wyke. Dusk descends with drizzle from a leaden sky.

Nurse Ashanti moves ahead and stoops before her charge.

'William? William – you've got visitors.'

Skelgill notes that the man does not react to his name – but perhaps there is a touch of movement at the word *visitors*.

He sidles into William's sightline.

The rheumy eyes flicker.

'Alright, R.O.?'

Skelgill glances at DS Jones – it is a look of self-rebuke – he has not explained this, being somewhat in denial, sensing her scepticism of his motives. He shakes his head – that she is not to trouble herself.

Nurse Ashanti now brings a pair of lightweight visitor chairs; Skelgill relieves her of them.

Then DS Jones rounds into sight with Cleopatra.

William looks up at DS Jones – there is no hint of recognition – but then he sees the dog and, as if the dying embers of the sun have penetrated the mist that smothers the distant fells, his countenance lights up.

'Kelly! Come 'ed, soft lad!'

A wizened hand reaches out, shakily to touch the hound's muzzle.

Cleopatra, to Skelgill's relief, hitherto seems to have left her alter ego the Canine Cannonball at Buttermere, and – unaffected by the incorrect name and gender – allows herself to be petted. She shuffles around to sit upright at one side of the armchair.

Skelgill is inured to the attenuated form and depleted condition of the elderly man, but the little cameo nonetheless has him choking on any words he might wish to utter at this juncture. And he looks at DS Jones to see the consternation in her hazel eyes, and with her fingertips she brushes away a tear that teeters upon each prominent cheekbone.

'Get settled – and I'll bring the three of you some tea.' Nurse Ashanti knows to intervene, in businesslike fashion. 'William – you've got a special treat – chocolate biscuits.'

There is an urn set up on a sideboard and she quickly supplies three mugs while Skelgill sequesters an occasional table intended for such a purpose.

William sits motionless, save for the fingers that stroke the top of Cleopatra's head, his eyes cast down – but when Skelgill produces the chocolate digestives the crackle of the wrapper attracts his gaze. He takes an offered biscuit and without hesitation dunks it into his tea. His audience watches with bated breath – but he instinctively seems to know the optimum timing and successfully transfers it to his mouth.

He reaches for a second as soon as it is offered, and repeats the feat.

Attention having shifted from dog to biscuits, the former drops prone, snout resting upon front paws, her mournful gaze seeking out Skelgill. She seems to read his wink of commendation, and sighs, and closes her eyes.

DS Jones has taken over the supply of biscuits.

Nurse Ashanti steps back.

'Why don't you have a little chat?' She indicates to the pager in her belt. 'There's a colleague that could do with a hand upstairs.'

Skelgill seems apprehensive.

'Go ahead.' She beams encouragingly, and presses a hand against his upper arm and begins to back away. 'I'll just be a few minutes. He won't bite.'

He realises he should try. After all, he is 'R.O.'

Still, for a moment he is tongue-tied.

He glances at DS Jones. She mouths the word, *'Football?'*

He takes the cue. He leans closer.

'Liverpool had a good win on Saturday. Did you hear that – they beat Man U?'

The man does not move; his gaze seems fixed on his mug. But he speaks.

'Yes – yes, Liverpool.'

Skelgill glances again at DS Jones, and she gives a nod of encouragement.

'Just remind me – do you support Everton or Liverpool?'

There is still no movement.

'Yes – yes, Liverpool.'

Skelgill frowns – he realises the leading nature of his questions, and that these could be no answers at all.

'Which part of Liverpool did you live?'

'Yes – yes, Liverpool.'

Skelgill gives a pained grimace.

'Your wife – was she from Liverpool?'

'Yes – yes, Liverpool.'

Skelgill bites at the corner of a thumbnail.

DS Jones offers another biscuit which the man takes and dunks and eats without looking up.

Skelgill tries again.

'What was her name? Your wife?'

There is no answer. The man chews methodically.

'Your wife – she died. When did she die?'

Still there is no reaction.

And then he speaks unprompted.

'Where's me shirt, for church?'

The man chuckles, as if he knows this is some private riddle.

The detectives exchange puzzled looks.

Skelgill now delves into the carrier bag and produces the book. He slides it across the small table, so that it falls into the line of sight of the man's downcast eyes.

The man starts forward, and reaches to touch the cover, with its two illustrated fishes. He leans close over the book.

'Perch. The Green Pit, R.O.'

'The Green Pit.'

The man does not answer. But he has correctly identified one of the species.

Skelgill reaches and turns several pages; he is looking for common types. He stops at one such.

'Roach. The Black Pit, R.O.'

'The Black Pit.'

Again, no response.

Skelgill finds a picture of a tench.

'Tench. Mill Pond, R.O.'

Skelgill glances up at DS Jones. She is taking notes. He nods – it is to signify that the identifications continue to be correct.

He ponders for a moment, and locates a rainbow trout. There is now a little method in his approach – it is a choice for a reason.

But the man seems to peer blankly at the fish, with its blaze of purple scales along its lateral line.

'Do we catch this one?'

There is no reply.

Skelgill frowns, and begins to turn pages trying to think what would serve him best – when the man reaches to stop him. The illustration is of a common carp.

'Carp. Foster's Pond, R.O.'

Skelgill glances more urgently at DS Jones; she gives a reassuring nod – she has it down.

'Just remind me – where was … Foster's Pond?'

But there is no response; the man stares at the conspicuously scaled fish.

Skelgill continues to leaf speculatively – he pauses at minnow – merely to get a better grip of the book from his somewhat awkward stance – but there is a reaction.

'Minnow. Sorebrook, R.O. *Hah!* Sorebrook. Your first fish!'

Skelgill can feel his pulse racing; he keeps the page open, and taps the picture.

'A tiddler, eh? Sorebrook, of course. Where's that again?'

But the man does not move. His breathing seems to come more heavily. A few moments pass.

DS Jones slips off her chair onto one knee, better to see his face. She looks up at Skelgill. She tilts her head and signs with her hands at her cheek. Again she mouths a word. *'Asleep.'*

Skelgill frowns pensively – but now he feels a warm touch on his shoulder. Nurse Ashanti has returned quietly over the carpeted floor.

'You can come back – in the morning, if you like.'

Skelgill recalls what she told him about disturbing William from slumber.

He rises, as does DS Jones – he takes their chairs aside.

Cleopatra struggles to her feet, looking surely disappointed.

Skelgill is prompted to look at the half-eaten packet of biscuits. The nurse follows his gaze.

'Remember your book – it was good of you to bring it.'

Skelgill rocks a little on his heels.

Now DS Jones is watching him closely. She has glimpsed the faded inscription from his mentor, the old professor.

'Keep it for him.'

The nurse smiles.

'Oh, he'll like that – I'll read it to him later, if he has trouble sleeping.'

They are beginning to move away.

Skelgill realises the opportunity.

'If he happens to mention any more places – anyone – anything –'

'Yes, of course – I'll make a careful note. Come – I'll see you to the door.' She touches his hand. 'Thanks for all you're doing – and for Saturday night.'

15. SCOUSE

Room 101, Police HQ – 9.15 a.m. Tuesday 3 October

R.O.
*Wife (d)
Kelly – former pet dog?
Accent – Liverpool/Merseyside
"Where's me shirt, for church?"*

*Green Pit – perch
Black Pit – roach
Mill Pond – tench
Foster's Pond – carp
Sorebrook - minnow*

'Allo, allo, allo?'

DS Leyton, emerging from the kitchenette and using one foot to negotiate the sprung door while his hands are occupied with a tray of teas, spies the notes that DS Jones has neatly transcribed upon the whiteboard in his absence.

He stands and stares for a moment, while she snaps the cap on the dry-wipe pen and returns to her seat beside Skelgill.

'What's with the shirt bit?'

He unloads the mugs and joins his colleagues, now three in a row, facing the screen.

Skelgill takes a gulp of tea without first testing the temperature. He smacks his lips in approval; evidently DS Leyton has remembered the sugar.

'I've heard him say it twice, Leyton. Once on Saturday, again yesterday.'

DS Leyton ponders.

'You thinking he was connected to a church?'

Skelgill grimaces.

'Search me, Leyton.' He raises his mug to indicate the whiteboard. 'That's about all we got. It's not easy – he doesn't say much and it's not all coherent. He called Cleopatra Kelly – and he thinks I'm someone called R.O.'

There is a silence, before DS Jones turns to Skelgill.

'I noticed you didn't call him William.'

Skelgill shrugs.

'It weren't working. You saw that. He didn't bat an eyelid when the nurse said it. If it's not his name, he might think you're talking to someone else.'

She nods – and then addresses DS Leyton.

'However – he correctly identified a series of fishes – associated with each of the places.'

DS Leyton runs the fingers of a hand through his dark hair.

'That's a sight more than I could do. I go into the chippy – can't tell a cod from a haddock to save my life.'

Skelgill looks at his subordinate askance.

'When they're battered?'

'That's right, Guv – they even taste the same, to me.'

Skelgill continues to regard DS Leyton with disbelief – but there is just the small possibility that it is not a wind-up, which leaves him in a quandary as to the most apt retort; consequently, he holds his peace.

An amused DS Jones pushes on.

'There was one fish he didn't seem to recognise.'

Her tone is questioning, and it puts Skelgill back on track.

'Aye – a rainbow trout. Not a native British species. The others – perch, roach, tench, carp, minnow – they're all coarse fish. Ponds, canals – that sort of thing. Float fishing or maybe ledgering, with bait. Rainbow trout you'd need to go to a reservoir where they're stocked – for fly fishing.'

DS Leyton looks puzzled as to the logic underlying this line of inquiry; DS Jones helps him out.

'It sounded as though he used to take this R.O. character fishing. The nature and method might just help narrow down where they fished – and in turn, who he is.'

DS Leyton squints intently at the whiteboard.

'Foster's Pond – surely we can find that?'

DS Jones draws his attention to her laptop.

'It's coming up as a lake and nature reserve in Massachusetts.'

'*Whoa.* Don't suppose the Chief'll sign off that trip.'

DS Jones grins ruefully.

'But if we can just get a peg in the ground, we might work outwards from there.'

DS Leyton does not move for a moment, until he begins in slow motion to perform a little cameo familiar to his colleagues. Gradually he raises a finger as if half testing the wind and half wanting (but with trepidation) to introduce an idea which is not quite fully formed.

Then it comes.

'Remember the Harterhow case? I visited Liverpool CID. I got on well – after a few teething problems – with one of the officers. He was big on fishing. We could ask him.' DS Leyton pulls out his phone. 'I reckon I've still got his number. DC Rankin, he's called.'

It takes DS Leyton a minute to find the contact and get a response, and another to hold his own in a small battle of jovial banter along the lines of his being a soft southerner, and when is he thinking of following a proper football team? Though reminded of DS Leyton's East End, Millwall-supporting credentials the precocious DC yields up a draw, admitting that in reality there is probably not a cigarette paper between a true Cockney and a true Scouser.

Putting his handset onto speaker, DS Leyton further introduces his colleagues and explains their mission to identify 'William', whom they believe to be of Merseyside provenance.

He hands over to Skelgill.

'Leyton reckons you're into fishing?'

'I do my bit, sir.'

Skelgill baulks at the recognition of his rank – but he presses on.

'What kind of thing?'

'Just occasional match angling, these days, sir. But as a kid I roamed everywhere – there was no stopping me – I'd fish in a puddle if it had rained enough.'

113

Skelgill is encouraged.

'Seems this chap used to take a younger bloke – possibly a relative as a child – coarse fishing. He identified the likes of perch and roach and tench – and named the places they caught them. Chances are, these were local to where they lived.' He glances across at the whiteboard. 'We've got Green Pit, Black Pit, Mill Pond – and most distinctive – Foster's Pond?'

There is a short silence, and an expiration of air.

'Crikey. You've got me there. Foster's Pond? It sounds vaguely familiar, like – but I can't think of anywhere round here. The others – they're ten a penny, aren't they?'

DS Jones chips in.

'We've done an internet search – Foster's Pond is coming up as Massachusetts.'

The DC breaks into a brief but surprisingly tuneful rendition of *And the lights all went out in Massachusetts.*

Then he quickly poses a question.

'He couldn't be American, like?'

DS Jones retains the floor.

'His accent is definitely Merseyside. We've also got the name Sorebrook – with reference to catching minnows.'

The constable makes a clicking sound with his tongue.

'I've not heard of it. We've got a central district called Tuebrook, adjoins Everton – urban terraces, back-to-backs. West Derby Road runs right through it. There used to be a stream, the Tew Brook – it's completely culverted. The only fish you'd catch there now would be if you robbed a fishmonger's van.'

A short hiatus ensues – Skelgill is staring at the whiteboard, his expression troubled as their options narrow – and it is somewhat self-consciously that he relates the next point.

'He's come out with this phrase a couple of times. *Where's me shirt, for church?*'

The man instantly laughs.

'Keep practising the accent, sir!'

But there has been the suggestion of recognition. Skelgill persists.

'Does it mean owt?'

'*Where's me shirt?* It was a Ken Dodd song. You know – the comedian – Ken Dodd and the Diddymen? Must have been back in the Sixties. Our arl fella used to sing it when I was a nipper – getting ready for his work. *I feel a twerp, me – Wyatt Earp – with me shirt shot off've me!* The little stanza gets the same musical treatment as before. 'I don't know about the church bit, like. But it sounds like he's a bona fide Scouser, alright.'

Skelgill flashes his colleagues a wide-eyed look.

'When I approach him, he appears to recognise me. He says, *come 'ed, R.O.*' This time he merely emphasises the words and does not attempt the brogue.

'Owen?'

'Come again?'

A frisson passes between the three detectives.

Between Skelgill's question and their silence they convey to DC Rankin that he is inadvertently onto something.

'What I'm saying – he thinks you're called Owen.'

The Liverpudlian has joined dots invisible to outsiders.

'How do you work that out?'

'From personal experience, sir.' He clears his throat. 'You must have noticed – in Liverpool you don't get to go by your own name. If you're Frank, you're Frankie. If you're Steve, you're Stevie. Tommy, Edie, Jeannie – so on. Everyone gets an "ee" sound on the end of their name.'

'So far so good.' It is plain this can only be half of the explanation.

The DC obliges,

'I'm Iain, right? But I don't get Iain-ee – it doesn't scan, obviously. So I just get plain "Ee". Me arl gran says it all the time – "Come 'ed, our Ee, here's yer jam butty and yer cuppa tea." Owen – same principle – it's just "O". and if he's saying "*Our* O" – more likely he thinks you're one of the family.'

Silence.

Not R.O. but Our O. Our Owen.

DS Leyton pipes up.

'What about Oscar?'

'That'd be Ozzie.'

And DS Jones.

'Oswald?'

The DC laughs.

'Another Ozzie. Otto – that'd be Otty. Oliver – Ollie. I can't think what else "O" would be – unless it's some obscure foreign name, but that seems unlikely. I reckon you're talking Owen.'

*

'So, we're looking for a geezer named Owen?'

Thanks conferred and parting banter negotiated, the trio are left to mull over the findings. Even in the negative there is something – the suggestion that 'William' and 'R.O.' (our Owen) did not fish in Liverpool. Skelgill has drifted to the windows. The elevated perspective to which he is unaccustomed has an inherent draw, and since he last surveyed this scene there has been a subtle shift into autumn, despite that the foliage has not really turned; but it is on the cusp. There is the sense that the great cloak of greenery that shrouds the countryside has served its seasonal purpose; all growth has stopped, gone into reverse in herbaceous verges, and from now on the sheep that dot the landscape will munch from an ever-diminishing reserve. Soon the trees that line the River Eamont will shed their leaves, for them to sail downstream to sea and oblivion; skeletons will stand sentinel over the waterway.

He stares across the flood plain. It is the confluence of the rivers Eamont and Lowther. Substantial here – worthy of the descriptor, but not so far away in the fells each begins as a modest trickle. Indeed, follow them upstream and soon they acquire the title of beck.

'River Soar.'

It is no answer to DS Leyton's question – but no surprise to his colleagues.

Skelgill resumes his seat and casts a hand at the whiteboard beyond the long table.

'The River Soar. It runs through Leicester. S-O-A-R. Runs into the Trent. The Trent runs into the Humber. The Humber runs into the North Sea. The Soar's not much of a river – you'd hardly know it was there. It's alright for bleak, though.'

DS Leyton is puzzled – and the angling afterthought passes him by entirely.

'Leicester – that's miles from Liverpool, Guv.'

DS Jones begins tapping at her keyboard.

'Oh – yes. I remember this – from history class. The River Soar. Legend had it that Henry's men dumped Richard III's body there after Bosworth – until they found him buried underneath the letter R in that car park.'

But Skelgill sticks to geography.

'Chances are, it starts off as Soar Brook. Put it on the screen, lass. A map.'

Herewith is the original reason for Skelgill's choice of meeting room – the projection facility that they may collectively view.

While the technology takes a few moments to power up, DS Jones steps around to wipe the board clean of her notes. By the time she is seated the display shows Google Maps.

Skelgill objects.

'We want Ordnance Survey – it's got the names of features. Search "River Soar, Leicester" and we'll work back upstream.'

She finds the website, but now she cuts a corner – she enters the words, "Soar Brook".

'*Lumme!* Would you look at that!'

DS Leyton cannot contain his excitement. The search engine has produced a close-up map of countryside centred upon a green rectangle labelled "Soar Brook Spinney". Horizontally through the patch of woodland runs a fine blue line, a watercourse, albeit innominate.

'That must be Soar Brook, Guv.'

Skelgill's eyes are burning with the green flame of copper.

'Pull out a bit.'

DS Jones does as bidden.

Intently, Skelgill reads the landscape; his colleagues wait patiently for his translation.

It is farmland with small patches of woodland, intersected by lanes and bridleways. Just to the north, Middlemarch, a village close to the Leicestershire-Warwickshire border, marked by the conventional dash-dotted line.

DS Leyton is first to yield.

'What are those blue splotches, Guv?'

'Ponds.'

Skelgill narrows his eyes.

'Zoom in on the triangular one – to the west of the wood.'

He has followed the course of the brook to its source in what must be a moderately sized body of water, quite likely dammed, going by its shape, and the contours.

DS Jones enlarges the image to reveal a layer of labels.

The Lake?'

'That ain't much of a name.' DS Leyton sounds his disappointment.

But Skelgill remains focused.

'When was the survey?'

DS Jones regards him questioningly.

'Hover the mouse over the key.'

She does so – and a dialogue box informs them that it is continuously updated. But Skelgill is dissatisfied.

'That's satellite information. It's not the same as the orthography.'

He inhales and holds the breath.

'Search for "Old OS map of Middlemarch" – see what comes up.'

Again DS Jones obliges.

'National Library of Scotland?'

'Aye – they're good on maps. 1887. Click on that one – third from the top.'

The contrast is both stark and yet familiar – monochromatic, yes, and the Baskerville font archaic to the modern eye, but the segment of landscape is instantly recognisable as largely unchanged, with its spinneys and field boundaries, albeit there are – there were – many more smaller enclosures than the present day.

The map is conveniently zoomable. She homes in on their target.

'Cor blimey!'

DS Leyton's latest burst of exuberance is for good reason.

More recently the ubiquitous 'lake', the triangular body is labelled – was called – *Foster's Pond*.

DS Jones breaks the ensuing silence.

'Soar Brook – and Foster's Pond. What are the odds of there being two others, never mind in such proximity?'

The question is rhetorical, though DS Leyton produces a facial contortion that implies he would open a book on the matter, if pressed.

'Long.' It is Skelgill's simplified answer. He rises and walks round to the screen. 'See these little ponds – they'd all have local names. It's the same round here. As kids we knew every one – same for farmers, watering their stock, getting material, giving directions – how could they function? Green Pit, Black Pit – that'd be the colour of the water. Mill Pond – a mill of some sort. But the names would rarely appear on actual maps.'

DS Jones has a question.

'Are you suggesting we find an elderly local who would know the names of these ponds?'

Now it is Skelgill's turn to cut a corner.

'I'm suggesting we find an elderly local who knows the proper full names of William and Owen.'

DS Leyton pipes up.

'You thinking door-knocking, Guv?'

Skelgill makes what might be an angling action with his two hands close together.

'I'm thinking there's decent carp in that Foster's Pond.'

16. HARRIET HUNTS

Troughdale House, Whitehaven – 10.00 a.m. Wednesday 4 October

'There you go, Harriet, dear – make yourself comfortable. I've just got to nip out with Morten for a doctor's appointment. We shan't be any longer than your session – I'll be back to unplug you before the timer ends. You just relax – feel at home, like. After all, it is your home now, isn't it dear?'

Eyes already closed, Harriet mumbles her assent; the garrulous Rina going suits her; not least that she has been somewhat overwhelming, fussing and clucking like an old mother hen (though they are the same age), almost every minute it seems since her rather sudden move in, following Morten's impromptu suggestion on Monday (was it only two days ago?) that she pack a suitcase and have a trial fortnight – on the grounds that someone else was showing interest in the granny flat and they absolutely wanted her to get first dibs, her having been such a loyal client of Rina's, and since she and Rina got on so swimmingly.

"And possession is nine-tenths of the law, Harriet."

Morten had even driven her straight round to her house, and while she had packed he had checked about, dealing with what he called "security and maintenance" – turning down the thermostat to a minimum and turning off the water at the mains (in case of frost, which seemed unlikely to Harriet this early in the autumn), making sure the windows were all closed, and the back door locked, and the curtains arranged and a few side lights left on, so that it didn't look like the house was unoccupied. He had even inspected the radiators in every room, to make sure none of them was leaking.

She makes a little face of annoyance. But quickly she covers it up with a half snore. She was ill-prepared to leave her home in a hurry, and she could tell that Morten was getting impatient, even though he kept insisting she should take her time. And she'd piled a few things on the kitchen table – including the charger for her mobility scooter. When she was finished (not really happily so) he'd ushered her into his big car to wait while he went back for the case and the other items, such as a couple of bags of food from the fridge that otherwise would have gone to waste. When they got back to Rina's, she realised he'd left the charger. "Not to worry, Harriet," he'd said, grinning, as though nothing was too much trouble, "I'll pop by and collect it later. You've probably got enough charge for any small trip – and, besides, you've got me to run most of your errands from now on."

Harriet had demurred. But she had felt reluctant to hand over her keys to Morten – except now he has made her feel obliged, and there is no way round it. Morten's going to call into her house after he's dropped off Rina, instead of sitting in the waiting room at the surgery. As it happens, it has mainly rained during the two days since she moved in, and there has been neither need nor has she felt the inclination to go out.

She can hear Morten bustling about somewhere; it sounds like he's doing something with a ladder. He always seems to be on the go, which is slightly strange, because Rina has told her many times how he suffers from bouts of ME, and she hasn't seen any sign of it.

'There you go, dear. The heating's on, but I'll leave the little window open a touch, for your fresh air, like.'

Harriet responds with a further half-snore, half-acknowledgement.

Rina tiptoes away and quietly shuts the door.

This is the first time that both Rina and Morten will be out of the house. The first time that she will be left alone.

She can hear the rain now, above the hum of the slimming machine, a patter on the foliage of the rose bushes out in the garden. Then she hears the slam of the external door. There is a chatter – a terse interchange – more Rina's voice than Morten's, though she cannot make out the words. Then the car doors close. There is the throaty roar of the big engine. The clang of the gates.

Silence. Only the melancholy refrain of the robin.

She opens her eyes and lifts her head.

Between her on the bed and the slimming machine on the wall unit (with its countdown neon display telling her there are forty-three minutes left) stretch sixteen rather worn black wires that connect from little plug-in sockets to the pads strapped to her torso and limbs.

Harriet wonders if Rina is taking no chances, and going out while she is tied down, so to speak. Immobilised. There's a slyness about Rina that she can't hide, despite all her flannel and flattery; it's deep in her eyes; congenital, you might say.

But she's not actually immobilised. It's not that she's strapped to the bed – if there were a fire she could jump up and barge out of the French window – wires attached – machine attached, dragging behind – whatever it took.

She ponders her dilemma.

For what she wants to do, what is the best tactic? What will she most easily be able to replicate?

The quick thing would simply be to pull out the plugs from their sockets. A twenty-second job – and the same to plug them back in. It takes Rina a good five minutes – sometimes ten – to get all the pads in place and fastened down with the straps. And then, would she be able to fit them back so that Rina didn't notice?

But would she be able to remember the order of the plugs?

She's got a good memory. Better than good – exceptional. Photographic, they all used to say in the office – they'd often come to her to ask this and that, where things were kept – even the long numbers of combinations and passwords; she knew them all off by heart, and never needed to try hard. "Harriet Houdini", they used to call her – she was always getting them out of tight situations.

She stares hard at the arrangement of pads, wires and plugs – she takes a mind photograph. It strikes her that if she had her mobile phone she could take an actual photograph – but she'll have to trust the old grey cells.

With a groan and a not inconsiderable effort, she rolls off the bed, getting her feet down on the carpet, and turns to the machine – she feels a bit like a cow must when it is being milked, connected up to all those tubes and suckers. One by one, she pulls out the electrical plugs with her right hand and gathers the wires together in her left.

It will be clumsy, waddling about with all the pads and straps on, and one hand occupied with the wires. Then she spies a pink towelling dressing gown on the back of the door to the corridor. It proves to be far too small – but not only is it better than being in just her underwear, also she is able to trap the wires together at her side with the belt, and feed their loose ends into the capacious pocket. Perfect. Two hands free.

In the passage opposite the door to her flat (she notices she is already thinking of it as hers) Rina has a little butler's pantry where she stores towels and beauty treatment products that she sells to her clients. There is an old-fashioned bureau, quite a decent antique, and Harriet lowers the lid and then quickly rifles through the two drawers beneath – but there is nothing much in the way of paperwork, mainly just a random assortment of small domestic items, from scissors and thread to metal polish and cleaning cloths. There's no trace of anything resembling a sales ledger or an accounts book. And no laptop or desktop computer.

Rina has stressed several times that Morten – being a financial adviser – deals with all the household admin, as well as that related to his job. But Harriet on one occasion or another has seen all of the downstairs rooms – if Morten has an office it must be upstairs. She moves to the foot of the flight. She frowns – but at least, this being such a big house, the staircase is broad and shallow, not the steep cramped stair of her own place, that has seen her move to sleeping downstairs for the last few years. The ground-floor location of the granny flat is another aspect of its appeal. She lumbers up, puffing nonetheless, and even the small exertion has her heart going twenty-to-the-dozen – but that might be nerves. They may have gone – but the first few minutes are always risky, when someone might have forgotten something. Her husband Jim was always back before he ever properly went away; she knew to stay her hunger a good five minutes.

She pads about on the carpeted landing, opening doors and peering inside. The unmade beds and discarded clothes and relevant accessories tell her which are Rina's and Morten's bedrooms respectively. Both still have a slept-in smell and need to be aired. There is a bathroom and three other bedrooms – one perhaps in which lip service is paid to its function as a guest room; the other two are crammed full of furniture, like store rooms in the back of an antiques warehouse, with a job-lot from a house clearance that has not yet been processed for sale. Some of it looks quite good – rich mahogany and paler teak, a dining table and set of four chairs, wardrobes and dressers. It is puzzling. But she doesn't have time to hang about. The main thing is there's no sign of a study.

She returns to Morten's room and ventures inside, trying not to inhale the odour that is somewhere between a dirty linen basket and a stale ashtray – then she realises it – behind the door, originally out of her sight, an aluminium loft ladder rises steeply through an open trapdoor, the lid hanging down. It is hard to tell what is up there – she can see a switch within reach at the top – and there is a faint hue of ambient light as if there is a skylight. But she doubts the ladder will hold her weight – never mind whether she could climb it, nor perhaps fit through the narrow hole that the scrawny Morten might have designed for the very purpose. She doubts if Rina even could squeeze through. She might be small but she is stout.

Harriet returns to the landing to recover her breath. There is another avenue that may bear fruit, and one that she now intends to explore. It requires a bit of luck – but not that much luck. She descends the staircase, noticing now there is an excess of furniture crowding the upper areas in a way that is less obvious downstairs. She progresses to the kitchen where there is a side door. The key is in the mortise and it is unlocked. It gives onto the driveway. She pokes out her head slowly to check all is clear.

The rain seems to have become heavier. The gown has a hood. She wouldn't have an excuse for wet hair. She pulls it up but now there is the realisation that she is barefooted. A pair of wellingtons stand near the door. She stares at their position, taking a mental shot. She steps into them; Morten must have big feet, though they are too tight around her calves and she cannot get them properly on. She steps out and waddles awkwardly over the crunching gravel.

Despite the rain the atmosphere is uplifting; after the stuffiness of the house – the bedrooms, especially – the air is fresh, infused with a mixed bouquet of bruised rose petals and damp vegetation, and rich, peaty earth.

She reaches the pair of gates. They must be a good seven foot high, their tops flush with the copings of the stone wall that encircles the property. She realises there is no pedestrian gate – just the two halves driven by an electric motor that requires a little remote to operate. This is something that neither Rina nor Morten has mentioned – and she has as yet had no cause to explore the grounds. Despite the pleasant environs, this place shares some of the qualities of the exercise yard of a prison compound.

She puts the small troubling thought aside. On the back of one half-gate is a mailbox that feeds through from the flap on the outside. At home, her own post comes before ten – and she lives not that far away – and, sure enough, when she lifts the flap she sees the morning delivery has been made.

She is conscious of the rain – but then again mail often arrives sodden – either the postie's bag leaks or it's just careless handing, openly carrying a bundle for the block. So dampness would not necessarily be a red flag. Nevertheless, she leans over, and quickly leafs through the little stack of envelopes. They are mostly white, commercial letters – and quite a bit of junk mail, one for hair restorer, and one suggestive of male bedroom problems without precisely giving away its contents, but its cover image of a flaccid glum-faced cartoon balloon not leaving much to the imagination. She notices it is addressed to Mr Morten Jenner – it gives her pause for thought.

And there are others. But it is a plain DL manila government envelope near the bottom of the pile that stops her in her tracks. Her luck is in. *Bingo*, she might be tempted to utter.

She stares for a moment. Her heart is in her mouth. She had not expected to strike quite so soon.

She realises she needs to act quickly.

She returns the remainder of the mail to the box and stumps back to the kitchen.

She would rather keep on the wellingtons – since she intends to replace the letter – but she realises she will make wet prints and possibly muddy marks on the kitchen floor. She pauses at the threshold, and with an effort, and the loss of a few valuable seconds, removes and replaces them in their spot. Just in case. And she leaves the kitchen door ajar – another little precaution.

There is an electric kettle on a worktop beside the cooker and it still contains tepid water. She turns it on and as soon as it reaches boiling point she holds down the switch and begins to steam the back of the envelope. She almost scalds her fingers – it is tricky one-handed.

She gives it half a minute, sliding the seal to and fro across the jet of vapour. Then she tries to peel back the flap, but maybe they use a better glue these days, and it is not yet yielding. She is conscious she must not overdo it and damage the fabric of the paper. It can be tricky to reseal an envelope without leaving it looking creased and obviously tampered with – albeit that the rain and a careless postie would offer some explanation on this occasion. She could deliberately dampen the other letters so it would blend in.

The rumble of the kettle subsides – and just as she is thinking of getting a knife to loosen the edge she hears a tinny click. It emanates from the gap in the open door. She freezes. She holds her breath. She listens, ears pricked.

And then there is a much greater metallic booming – the gates are opening. They must have come back. How long has she been? Nowhere near the half-hour or so that Rina led her to believe she had to herself.

Harriet pushes the kettle into position against the wall below the overhead cabinet and tiptoes – for no good reason – to the kitchen door and presses it shut, just as she hears the crunch of Morten's tyres on the gravel.

Even as she flees the kitchen she hears the engine die and the muffled thump of car doors – they are not going to hang about in the rain. At most Morten will make a minor detour to collect the mail.

Harriet lurches into the corridor, momentarily disoriented, a human bagatelle ball bumping and smearing along the walls. She crashes into Rina's treatment room and shuts the door, just as she hears the kitchen door open.

She sees the slimming machine with its display telling her there are thirteen minutes left – and she sees the array of sixteen empty plug sockets.

And suddenly – heart pumping, head throbbing, hands shaking – her mind goes blank.

'Harriet – we're home, dear!'

Rina has wasted no time. She is coming straight through.

Rina does not knock – it's her house.

'Morten!'

Rina screams out before she has even properly taken in the scene.

Harriet is lying prone in a tangle of wires.

'Harriet – Harriet! Harriet – wake up!'

Playing possum, sprawled in her underwear with unbecoming authenticity, beneath the panic Harriet detects a curious note of despair in Rina's voice.

Her exhortation does not so much ring of "wake up from sleep" but rather more like "please be alive" – but perhaps it is Harriet's imagination, for she is consumed with her own perilous predicament.

She begins to move and gasp.

The pads and straps are largely in place, if distorted, pulled by the trailing wires which must have offered resistance as they themselves were jerked from the machine, which has toppled over, dragged, but luckily has not crashed to the floor like Rina's more cushioned client. The ancient device might not have survived the impact.

Harriet rolls onto her back, but now she is like a beetle that cannot right itself.

'Och, I'm awake. I fell asleep and must have toppled off the bed.'

'Harriet – thank heavens!' Rina does not offer assistance, but sticks her head out into the passage and screams once more for her son.

'Morten'll help you up. Are you okay? Have you broken anything?'

When Morten still does not immediately come, Rina is obliged to pitch in and haul at her much larger client and lodger. Between them they manage, and by the time Morten does arrive, spotted with raindrops, to insinuate himself between the door and the jamb, a panting Harriet is supporting herself on her elbows at the end of the bed and Rina is peeling away the belts and pads, evidently now more concerned for damage to the wires and plugs than to Harriet.

Harriet offers some further explanation.

'I woke – of course – but I thought I should just lie for a moment – my heart, you know. Then I think I might have passed out for a few minutes until you came.'

'Are you sure you're okay, dear? Do you want a nice cup of tea? Or Morten could fetch you something stronger – like a brandy or a spot of gin?'

Harriet looks at Morten, who seems in a rather distasteful way to be leering at her.

Smeared across his crooked features, a ghoulish grin suggests he finds some unnatural pleasure in the situation.

She lowers her eyes – and her gaze falls on the pink towelling dressing gown on the back of the door – just inches from him, at his side but out of his line of sight.

Protruding from the albeit deep side pocket of the gown is about one inch of a manila envelope.

Rina is still preoccupied with the pads and wires.

Harriet swallows and shudders a little melodramatically, and sways as though she has suffered a wave of nausea. But as Rina steps back clutching the last of the electrical paraphernalia, Harriet indicates to her clothes draped over the chair beside the French window.

'Perhaps – if I could just get a wee minute by myself – to get dressed in privacy. And I'll come through – and have a cup of tea?'

Rina seems content with the suggestion. She heaps the belts and pads and wires over the machine and turns to address Morten.

'Morten – don't stare, you're upsetting Harriet.'

Harriet's heart is in her mouth. The envelope might almost be crying out like the golden-egg-laying hen clutched by burglar Jack, of beanstalk fame.

But Rina's eyes appear to be fixed on Morten – and she gives him an ushering wave with the back of her hand. He retreats to make room for his departing mother.

Rina turns in the doorway.

'Morten's bought you a lovely chocolate cake from the local baker's. It was for afternoon tea – but I think we should make it elevenses. You fetch it, Morten – it's still in the boot of the car.'

She addresses Harriet as she steps into the passage.

'You take your time, dear. I'll put the kettle on.'

She closes the door.

Harriet lets out a protracted sigh of relief.

But there is no time to waste – Rina might return without knocking at any second. Harriet retrieves the envelope and slips it into her ample underwear. It will have to 'arrive' in tomorrow's post – or perhaps even after that, if she does not get the opportunity to return it to the box on the gate.

Then she stares at the door.

Her features crease into a picture of concern. She moves a hand over her heart as though to still a palpitation.

Rina is putting the kettle on.

17. TEMPTATION AT TEA BREAK

Carlisle – 11.25 a.m. Wednesday 4 October

'It must be so exciting – being a detective.'

The woman at DS Leyton's side leans closer – and he wonders again why she hasn't sat opposite him, when the bench seat in the café's alcove is a little tight for two – and he feels the heat of her presence as he wrestles uneasily with conflicting impulses. On the one hand there is the temptation to play up to the admiration; on the other to play down the hyperbole. While the former is not in his nature, he senses to counter, "Exciting? Look at me now," would be to denigrate the work of his companion – glad though he is of a tea break as respite from the doldrums of their desks.

Right now the contrast with his regular employment is particularly acute. While he is back at his assignment at the Department for Work & Pensions, blundering through one depressing interview after another, his CID colleagues have an overnight jaunt to the Midlands. Skelgill has succeeded in convincing the powers that be that there is a case to investigate.

He shifts uneasily in his seat and settles for a diplomatic response.

'Deidre, I reckon it's like most jobs – it has its moments – but in between there's a lot of wearing out of shoe leather to little or no good effect. Knocking on doors that never get answered – or if they do it's an XL Bully staring you down.'

He casts a hand about the café – as though to illustrate the humdrum world, devoid though it is of devil dogs. Deidre Wetherspoon, the benefits assistant with whom he has been paired – presently his out-of-office chaperone – looks unconvinced.

She gives a shake of the head, tossing her peroxide mane like an untamed filly, as though she rejects his attempt to step down from the pedestal on which she has put him. She twists a ring on her right hand viciously – as if some unwelcome thought has just assailed her – and turns to regard him with wide blue eyes.

He is obliged to return the eye contact. In the time that he waited on the street for her to catch him up she had seemed different somehow – and now that he thinks about it he does not recall from their last joint claimant interview the lipstick, the blusher and – especially – the cleavage revealed by the blouse that is carelessly fastened – but then he was neither sitting opposite her nor so close; moreover he now detects her rather cloying but not entirely unpleasant perfume.

She persists.

'But what about – organised crime – bank robberies – gangsters – *murders?*'

There is the impression that she is eager to reach the word *murder*.

'I mean – do you get to see dead bodies? And – you know – the autopsies – where the pathologist is cutting them up?'

DS Leyton glances anxiously in the direction of the serving counter; there is the suggestion in his features that the conversation might be incompatible with his appetite. However, after a moment's hesitation he musters a response to his workmate's somewhat ghoulish fascination with his regular occupation.

'To be honest, Deidre – seeing a dead body – I wouldn't know one corpse from the next. There's all manner of expert forensic scientists to deal with that. They interpret the evidence, and provide us with clues about the probable cause of death. I'm happy with that. Sure – you want to inspect the crime scene – but that's more to get the lie of the land than to see the victim. I'm not one for the gory detail.' He gives a sigh of resignation. 'The Missus expects me to turn up at six and clear me plate and entertain the nippers.'

Deidre Wetherspoon persists with her line of argument.

'But kids – they love gory detail, don't they? You must have some fantastic bedtime stories.'

DS Leyton grins amenably.

'I don't really let on about the day job. The only crooks they hear about are the Baddun brothers in *The Hundred and One Dalmatians* and the Snarget gang in *Stig of the Dump*.' But he gives a resigned harrumph. It is the small realisation that even in children's literature there is little escape from malefactors and ne'er-do-wells.

'You're very conscientious – fighting crime all day and being a dutiful Dad at night. I hope your wife appreciates your efforts.'

She places a lingering hand on his wrist.

He wavers in his answer. To bask in the ill-informed flattery has its appeal, but there is the factual rejoinder – a little voice that reminds him of his honest opinion that a day managing the Leyton brood is a far more onerous task than a day on the beat. Before he can express the argument his companion is applying more pressure to his forearm.

'The warrior returns home to domestic bliss. I hope she greets you at the door in a negligee and with a gin-and-tonic. I know I would.'

She gives a husky laugh.

DS Leyton is somewhat unnerved, and now resorts to a counterpoint.

'More likely I get handed a screamer in a dirty nappy, and instructions for what clubs I'm driving to, and shopping needed in between.'

But the attempt at plain realism plays further into Deidre Wetherspoon's hands.

'A hard-working man wants a break – an outlet for his needs – a distraction from the pressures. Perhaps I should invite you for a drink after work, next time.'

She chuckles suggestively – but respite for DS Leyton arrives in the form of their order – two mugs of tea and the waitress's recommendation of banana dessert cake – billed as the local speciality of the rather obscure and secluded café, tucked away as it is along a narrow alley close to the market cross.

Deidre Wetherspoon takes charge of affairs, smothering DS Leyton's helping of cake with a generous share of custard from a small jug – so much, that he is prompted to protest.

'*Whoa* – save some for yourself. If these trousers get any tighter I'll be for the high jump.'

Her hands occupied, she responds with a gentle nudge of her thigh against his.

'Don't be silly – you're a fine figure of a man.'

DS Leyton takes refuge in his mug of tea; but in good café tradition it is piping hot and he is forced into a small pantomime of huffing and puffing.

If the distraction were intended, it seems to work, for Deidre Wetherspoon – with a spoon – takes a mouthful of her own cake and savours it sensually. When she finishes, and speaks, to DS Leyton's relief she changes the subject.

'How are you getting on with your investigation? It's all a bit cloak-and-dagger at the moment as far as we can see.'

He interprets her reference to mean herself and other staff members at the Department for Work & Pensions.

'Cor blimey – I'm still just finding my feet. You talk about difficult jobs. I reckon you've got one, Deidre. I said to my guvnor, I don't know when I'll see the wood for the trees.'

She leans a little closer.

'But you must have something in mind – or is it all so top secret that you can't share it with a dumb blonde, in case I spill the beans?'

She has him on the horns of a dilemma. She is surely fishing for compliments, but it would be unchivalrous to let her remark pass uncontested.

'Deidre, it's obvious to me that you're far from dumb – even if you are blonde – and attractive.'

'*Ooh* – you are a one.'

She shoots a hand onto his thigh and presses for a moment before removing it.

Give an inch and they take a mile. DS Leyton is panicked into revealing perhaps more than he ought.

'Well – you'll know about this multi-agency initiative, Operation Community Chest. It's a bit controversial – whether it's even going to work. We're trying to find a local interest angle – one that involves large sums. Criminality that will outrage the public.'

'And what are you thinking of?'

DS Leyton shrugs, as if he is not entirely sold on his own strategy.

'One idea we've had is fraudsters who are still claiming state pension for their relatives who've passed away. There was an example not so long ago on the TV – an eye-watering amount of money – and that involved a murder, an' all.'

He plies her with a knowing look, as if to stress that it covers both bases in which she might have an interest. But her reaction surprises him, for it is somewhat lukewarm. She folds her hands on the table and glances away momentarily.

Then she turns back and again reaches to press a hand on his arm. She leans closer, and regards him intently.

'You know – I don't think that's your best bet. I've heard of that kind of case – but they're few and far between. That's not what you want.'

When DS Leyton might be expecting an alternative suggestion, nothing is forthcoming. Instead Deidre Wetherspoon returns to the unhurried delectation of her cake; and she cannot reasonably be expected to eat and speak.

DS Leyton, wondering what should be his next move, absently checks his watch – and he realises the time.

'*Crikey*. Hadn't we better be getting back? That's our next appointment in ten minutes.'

The woman nods and moistens her lips. She reaches to take hold of his sleeve, and gently pulls him so that he turns a little towards her. She leans forward, her heavy lashes fluttering.

'Listen – give me some time today – I'll speak to someone who knows about all this. I think there's a better option – if it's large sums of money and local interest that you want. Maybe even actual suspects. Something that you could really make a name for yourself with. And I'll tell you about it, later.'

She pats his knee several times, and rises and squeezes past, brushing against him when she could go in the other direction. She does not speak, but inclines her head to indicate her destination is a small door marked for the toilets.

DS Leyton takes the opportunity to settle their modest bill. At the glass-fronted counter he considers that he might impress Skelgill with a takeaway order of the last of the banana dessert cake. But it would have to survive until at least tomorrow afternoon – and he is reminded of his waistline.

Applying distance in place of will power he exits the café and waits at the end of the alley. Now he notices that the grand thoroughfare is called English Street, which strikes him as curious. Perhaps, with Scotland a mere ten miles hence, it is to remind visitors that they have strayed onto foreign soil.

'Here you go – duck under.'

There is a hand at the small of his back. In contemplative mood he has not noticed the rain – and before he can object Deidre Wetherspoon links arms and draws him beneath an inadequate collapsible umbrella.

He yields to the force and the replenished aura of her heady fragrance.

18. DIVINING

Watling Street – lunchtime, Wednesday 4 October

'Cob or batch – what's your guess?'

Skelgill raises the bacon roll two-handed before his eyes. He turns it from side to side – and it would seem he is making an assessment in order to answer. But it is simply that he seeks the most propitious angle of attack, and he takes a great bite.

Thus occupied, he shrugs.

DS Jones supplies the missing information.

'He called them cobs.'

Skelgill gives a nod of approval and reaches for his mug of tea.

'He said this is Leicestershire.' DS Jones glances out of the window beside their table. Beyond a dilapidated sign that states, "Stan Hicks' Truckstop" heavy traffic rumbles past. 'The other side of the road – that's Warwickshire.'

Skelgill finishes his first bite but immediately moves in for another. However, he follows her gaze. The vista is of farmland, fairly flat, the immediate roadside hedgerow a pastiche of autumn colours – olives, browns, yellows – the impression of leaves curling – a speckling of red clusters of hips and haws. A bird of prey wheels, its eagle eye distracted by some find, the manoeuvre revealing a forked tail.

'Kite.'

'Guv?'

'That bird – it's a red kite. They've started to appear in the Lakes.'

'Oh. Is that good?'

Skelgill grins wryly.

'Far as I know, they don't eat lambs.'

DS Jones raises her eyebrows. Skelgill has close friends with conflicting allegiances when it comes to matters of tooth and claw.

She reverts to the subject of geography.

'It's the Watling Street – the old Roman Road – the border between East and West Midlands.'

'No wonder you took so long – chatting up the locals.'

DS Jones smiles sweetly.

'He said we'd be best to leave the car here. It's a clearway and there are no pull-ins. There used to be a public footpath – but he thinks it has fallen out of use.'

Skelgill relents – there was method in her engaging the café owner in conversation.

'Did he ask why we're interested?'

She shakes her head.

'I said we're from the British Amphibian Trust. Doing a pond survey. It seemed to do the trick.'

Now Skelgill laughs – he does not quite believe her.

'Then he don't know owt about newts.'

'How come?'

'They only live in water in the spring. Newts are terrestrial.'

'Oh.'

'Same as frogs and toads. And they're mainly nocturnal. That's why folk never see them.'

DS Jones seems intrigued by the prospect.

'Do you ever catch them? I mean, angling – by accident?'

Skelgill regards her quite intently – as though she makes a good point, and one that he has not considered. He shakes his head slowly.

'I never have. I mean – as bairns we used to fish for them. Spawning time – you fix a net on a beanpole and wait for them to come up for air. Or chuck in a weighted string with a worm tied on – best way to catch crests – great crested.' Skelgill frowns pensively. 'I suppose they could take a bait intended for a perch. But newts are mostly in small ponds – where you wouldn't fish with a rod. And they don't cohabit well. Get newts in your garden pond – they'll eat all the fry.'

DS Jones looks sideways at Skelgill, as if to suggest there are some problems she never expects to suffer. However, she is prompted by the general theme.

'By the way – the owner – when I mentioned Foster's Pond – he knew the name.'

Skelgill nods, encouraged.

'Eat up, lass – and we'll put us boots on.'

It takes them just a few minutes, rather stumbling along the overgrown and littered verge, buffeted by eddies from trucks and speeding cars, and nearly tripping into unseen land-drains, to reach a spot that Skelgill has earmarked, where a wood begins on the opposite side, Warwickshire.

'Here – run.'

He grabs his colleague by the wrist and unceremoniously hauls her across the trunk road, and pulls her into the relative sanctuary of a small arbour.

'Look.'

They are facing away from the highway, and he indicates to their right. Just beyond a broken-down fence runs a clear stream, a yard wide and a couple of feet deep to its clay bed, overhung by brambles and nettles and an untidy matrix of fallen branches.

'Soar Brook?'

Skelgill grins. 'Dr Livingstone, I presume?'

She reciprocates. 'Well – I know it's not the Nile.'

'Reckon it'll do us – see.'

Skelgill has borne in one hand an Ordnance Survey map, stripped of its cover and refolded so that the area displayed is that of farmland bisected by the diagonal of the Roman road. He points with a long index finger.

'We're here – where it passes through the culvert. Soar Brook Spinney's downstream – two-thirds of a mile – and "The Lake" – Foster's Pond – ahead.'

Their way is barred by more dilapidated fencing and sprawling brambles, and a minor tributary that joins Soar Brook from their left. Skelgill picks a route, judiciously avoiding the stingers – they might be fading, but they can still pack a punch, even at this season. He vaults the fence and ditch in one and turns to his associate, but she clears the dual obstacle with aplomb before he can even lend a hand. The spinney angles to a corner, and they quickly push out into a modest expanse of overgrown marsh, with the brook on their right bordered by a high hedgerow of mixed shrubs – holly, hazel, hawthorn, and many others, indicative of its age. The marsh gives on to a stubble field, and the woodland swings round from their left to complete an arc that limits their horizon. Directly ahead, at about four hundred yards distant, joining the woods to the hedgerow and forming an amphitheatre of sorts, a line of erect poplars runs along a level embankment.

'There's the dam.'

DS Jones eyes the landform reflectively.

'You think they used to come this way?'

Skelgill narrows his eyes.

'Makes sense. If you look at the map, it's the obvious access. Any other direction and you're talking miles from the nearest road. And the footpath is marked.'

DS Jones inhales as though to develop the theory – but Skelgill moves off; his body language suggestive that further bridges can be crossed in their own good time. He leads the way through the damp sedges and rushes at the edge of the marsh; it has rained earlier and overnight, and the brook runs swift and silent at their side. Birdsong is absent, excepting a woodpigeon that coos its throaty five-note refrain from some concealed perch. Ahead, a family party of bullfinches feeds on the rusty dangling seeds of dried dock, flashing white rumps and emitting soft contact calls as the flock moves in short flighty bounds, driven by the walkers.

Skelgill becomes aware that they are not alone – there are geese in the field, well camouflaged, a flock of some fifty feral greylags that have risen from resting and now stalk away, beginning to chatter uneasily. According to the map, the path is an old right of way, and now it should cross the field at a tangent, which would better suit their purpose. But he has no wish to debate the matter with an irate landowner. Rather than spook the geese and advertise their presence, he sticks to the field edge.

They make it to the corner where the brook pours from a pipe on the dam. It is fenced in, the weathered frame topped with barbed wire. They take a sharp left and walk parallel to the earthwork, the ground rising gently, to the point where it meets the spinney. From here, at the corner of the lake, they can glimpse a view of its surface.

'It's quite big, isn't it?'

Skelgill scowls. All is relative. True, it is no mere pond, but it is small compared to Bass Lake – but Bass Lake is a puddle compared to Loch Ness – and Loch Ness, monster or not, less than a puddle compared to the likes of Lake Superior.

As he takes a photograph on his phone he settles for a conditional agreement.

'Aye – it probably is, for round here.'

'Why do you say that?'

'If you look at the map – we're smack bang in the middle of England. There's no rivers of note – because what there are, start here as trickles. There's no hills to speak of, no valleys – so there's no lakes, nor even sites where they could make a decent reservoir – even if there were enough flow.' He inclines his head towards Foster's Pond. 'This is about as big as it gets.'

They fall silent. After a few moments Skelgill turns and gazes back the way they have come. The landscape is unfamiliar to him, mostly in that it is benign. In the Lakes – in the fells – he is rarely on the flat; he needs his wits about him constantly. Lose concentration for more than a couple of seconds and he could fall a thousand feet, tumble into a tarn or a rushing beck or a mineshaft – even heather and bracken conceal jagged rocks and ankle-twisting cavities. Here it feels like he could sleepwalk for an hour and wake up safely back in bed.

'And what about the fishing? William said there were carp.'

DS Jones's question rouses him from his brown study.

He turns and squints analytically at the lake. On the far bank the grass is mown and it is grazed by a small collection of waterfowl, coot, mallard and a pair of Canada geese.

'They were commonly farmed, back in the day – this place would have been ideal. So there'd still be a remnant population.' He looks along the line of the dam. There is good access to the water and a nice flat surface. 'Wouldn't mind giving it a go – though for carp it's more like camping than fishing. Specimen hunters set themselves up to stay for days on end.'

DS Jones casts about and shudders.

Skelgill plies her with a grin.

'You thinking of the loo?'

She makes a face accordingly.

'Well – there is that, I suppose.'

Skelgill is about to comment – but checks himself, and instead turns on his heel.

'Howay, lass – let's find these ponds.' He rattles the map. 'Through this wood, I reckon.'

Skelgill shows DS Jones on the map – it is called Ash-Pole Spinney and would likely have been planted for the so-named purpose. Unlike an ancient wood it lacks shrub layer and their progress is comparatively easy. The air is still and smells of mulch and fungal spores, and woodland sounds resonate – the harsh porcine screeching of jays and the fine ticking of robins. Beneath an ivy-shrouded tree Skelgill pauses to inspect a scattering of owl pellets, a small-mammal cemetery of sorts, tiny yellowed incisors and bleached bones projecting from the parcels of desiccated grey fur. He cranes his neck, but there is nothing to been seen of the tawny owl that is the scourge of wood mice hereabouts.

It takes them just ten minutes to pick a route through the length of the copse. They meet a perpendicular ride where the plantation joins the next spinney – but here Skelgill refers to the map and takes a turn to the right, along the trackway. Almost immediately they come upon a steep-sided pond, some fifty feet by twenty, tucked into the edge of the wood and heavily shaded by the canopy.

'Ah – you said it would be black.'

Skelgill nods. He stares at the dark water, seemingly bereft of plant life. Occasional drips mimic poor rises, but he is not fooled.

'Looks like they would have dug it for clay. Hard to believe there's roach in there.'

But he moves on, pausing only to take a quick photograph – and in the field at the end of the short ride there is another pond, part-ringed by trees. Lily pads and duckweed cover the surface.

'It's green.'

Skelgill chuckles; again, he captures the scene on camera.

'It's not rocket science, is it, lass?'

'That just leaves the Mill Pond.'

Skelgill taps the edge of the map against his temple.

He leads them through the adjoining spinney – it has an older feel, with great oaks where the odd grey squirrel shells acorns as they pass beneath. At a clearing with gnarled elders Skelgill points out a badgers' sett; there is extensive fresh debris, berms of fine pale soil showing the creatures have chosen a sandy rise for easy tunnelling and good drainage.

They reach the far edge of the wood and Skelgill unfurls an arm.

DS Jones follows his line of indication.

Across the field, in the centre, stands a dilapidated pylon with a single broken propellor blade dangling at the top. A ring of hawthorns marks the perimeter of the pond.

'A windmill.'

'Aye – a windpump – the pond's probably fed by a spring. They would have used it to pump water to the farm – mainly for drinking troughs. But you could see why they called it the Mill Pond.'

DS Jones nods pensively.

'So that's it – all five of the places that William mentioned. They're all here. In what – a single square mile?'

'Nay – nowt like that – hardly fifty acres.'

Skelgill turns and begins to retrace their steps.

DS Jones hesitates, still gazing at the rusted frame of the windmill.

'It feels like we're close.'

Moving slowly, Skelgill is staring at the map. Under a mile to their north is Middlemarch. In the centre of the old village he decodes the symbols he learned to recognise as a schoolboy. A circle topped by a cross: a church with a spire. Directly opposite, by the look of it, PH: a public house.

'Let's pay a visit to the graveyard.'

19. THE CROSS KEYS INN

Middlemarch village – 6 p.m. Wednesday 4 October

Skelgill sits with arms folded.

He has picked a corner table and an oak settle with his back to a window. At the far end of the public bar DS Jones leans at the recessed serving counter where it is plain she is in receipt of overtures from the young bartender. The half-dozen or so males seated at tables affect interest in the conversation, although more likely the newcomer's appearance is their real object.

She had entered alone, because Skelgill had dwelt in the hallway to peruse the pub noticeboard. There was news of the football team, the darts team, a meeting of the local natural history society, winners of the hundred club – but no fishing club and no obvious germ that might yet bear fruit.

He considers the modest rectangular bar to be cosy without being frivolously so. There are twin hearths in which smoulder coals, showing it was once two smaller rooms; the dividing beam is exposed, less cracked and warped than others. There is a sense of age without great antiquity – and it is basic without being austere. There is a welcome absence of TV sets tuned to sport, and no loudspeakers to offend the ears. These whitewashed walls have long endured one-way traffic, and could tell a thousand tales and not be done.

DS Jones turns gripping a bag of crisps between the knuckles of each hand and bearing a dark pint and a half of the same. As it becomes apparent that she is heading for Skelgill's table there seems to resolve an outstanding issue among the male clientele; eyes are averted under the stern stranger's proprietorial stare, and conversation returns to what must have been its level before the incomers' arrival. One of two venerable gents competing assiduously at a cribbage board catches Skelgill's eye and winks knowingly.

'He recommended the local mild – he says it's their most popular session ale.'

Skelgill regards his colleague quizzically, as if to convey that he reads entirely her affected ignorance of what has been going on; that he has no truck with her diffidence, but is not resentful.

If obliquely, she acknowledges his inference.

'He was such a keen salesman that I decided to humour him.'

Skelgill turns his attention to the drinks as she settles opposite him.

'Are you thinking of having a session, then?'

DS Jones chuckles.

'Well – it's only 3.2 percent ABV – if that means anything to you?'

Skelgill gives a growl in his throat; now she is certainly being facetious.

'Woody swears by dividing it into twenty, and that's your hangover-proof number of pints.'

'That's after you've done a rescue, I take it?'

'It's a dehydrating business.'

She grins and indicates to her own half-pint glass.

'I still can't quite imagine drinking twelve-and-a-half of these.'

Now Skelgill shrugs nonchalantly.

'It gets easier as the night goes on.'

'I rather suspect the calculation becomes flexible as the night goes on.'

Skelgill reaches for one of the packets of potato crisps. With a fisherman's dexterity he carefully pulls open the wrapper at three of its seams and lays it down as a platter. He indicates with a palm that she should go first.

'I thought we might find a chippy. As I recall they do decent steak-and-kidney pies in this neck of the woods.'

DS Jones raises her glass in a sign of accord. She sips the coal-black beer curiously, but she seems to approve of the taste and takes another mouthful before sitting back and licking the froth from her upper lip.

'Anything strike a chord?'

She refers to his examination of the noticeboard.

Skelgill has his nose in his pint; he gives a restricted shake of the head.

'No more than the church.'

DS Jones's gaze shifts past him. Dusk presses on the latticed window; beyond, just across the street, the pale retaining wall of the churchyard rises to about six feet; the impressive stone church with its spire is built on raised ground; in turn it steeples into the shadowy gloom, part shrouded by a pair of great spreading cedars, heavy with age and import, in the way of twin undertakers standing sentry, imbued with sombreness by virtue of long association.

In the fading light they had wandered about the hallowed ground. They had arrived without Skelgill revealing a specific objective or DS Jones questioning what it might be. He probably would have been unable to answer. Dusk and decorum demanded a solemnity in their proceedings; beneath ancient gnarled yews flaking gravestones tilted precipitously, like rows of uneven teeth; there were collapsed sarcophagi and more modest plots gone to seed with just a planter filled with dried droop-headed marigolds. They found no family plots, as such, but in places clusters of presumably local surnames, Aylesbrook, Campton, Gretton, Pilgrim.

Lights had begun to glow behind stained-glass windows. They had stopped at the porch, lit by a naked under-strength bulb. There hung a notice, "Welcome to the holy catholic church of St Catherine". They might have entered, but then had come faint sounds of the choir practising for the harvest festival: strains of the organ, and the refrain, with gusto, *All good gifts around us*, an earworm that Skelgill has been periodically humming since.

DS Jones turns her gaze back to him, conscious now of his silence.

'You seem distracted.'

He shakes his head – but more in dissatisfaction than disagreement. He takes another drink and grimaces.

'A life's too large to end up as a line on a lump of slate.'

She observes him, her expression sympathetic to his profound if crude analysis.

'You're thinking of William?'

Skelgill grins.

'Where's me shirt, for church?' This time he makes a better fist of the accent, getting *shert* and *cherch* and even imbuing the phrase with a hint of the famous Scouse lenition.

DS Jones chuckles.

'I suppose there could be a worse epitaph. Imagine if it were voice-activated as you passed a grave.'

'That's probably been invented.' Skelgill sups his beer reflectively. 'It would make it less of a wild-goose chase.'

DS Jones speaks more practically now.

'But you wouldn't have held out too many hopes – not if he comes originally from Liverpool?'

Skelgill makes a face that precedes his counterpoint.

'I was thinking more of the wife. It could be a reason why he was here – if she were a local. She might have family – even be buried here. "Here lies Enid, the wife of William" – that sort of thing. Except we're not even on sure ground with William.'

'Presumably, that would have been a new memorial.'

Skelgill nods.

'Aye – and he'd have been in no state to organise it. Happen he doesn't even know she's gone – the nurse reckons he's never mentioned her – one way or t' other.'

DS Jones nods musingly.

''Tis but thy name that is my enemy.'

Skelgill half-closes one eye.

'What's that, a quote from Miss Marple?'

DS Jones is not sure whether to take him seriously. She skirts a direct answer.

'We can probably rely on the dog's name – Kelly.'

Skelgill approves.

'Folk often know dogs' names before they do their owners' – if ever.'

'Someone might put two and two together. We've got Kelly the dog, a Liverpool accent, fishing, a man and a boy –'

But Skelgill raises a palm to slow her in her tracks.

'We don't know it's a man and a boy. It could be two kids, brothers.'

DS Jones looks like she has not considered this point, the possible variation in the composition of the twosome. Her expression becomes more analytical.

'What do you read into the fact that he seems to have identified you – as a representation of R.O. – or Owen, if that's the name?'

Skelgill ponders for a moment, but folds his arms. What does he feel? What exactly is the unspoken affinity that he has experienced in the company of the old man? Has it anything to do with the man, at all?

He gives an unprompted twitch of the head.

'It seems like he's recognising me now – now he's seen me close up a couple of times. But according to Ashanti he were calling me R.O. when I were nowt but a silhouette out on Bass Lake. I reckon he were triggered by the fishing – not by me.'

DS Jones regards Skelgill contemplatively.

'The description – the first fish in Soar Brook – he was excited – and proud.'

Skelgill inhales to speak, but his words seem to catch in his throat and he takes a drink instead; when he looks up he sees a glisten mirrored in the eyes of his companion.

But he turns and picks up the map from the settle at his side.

'Let's look at what we do know.'

He rotates the map so they can both read it. It is still folded to show the locality, a square of about four miles, with Foster's Pond at its centre. He slides it between them. But when he might be expected to expound upon a theory, his gaze loses its focus.

DS Jones seems to know to wait.

It might be argued that they could have performed the afternoon's research from a desk, zooming in on digitised maps and searching for terms that included the names of the waters. But in Skelgill's book there can be no substitute for the physical recce. They have walked in the footsteps of William and R.O. – there can be no doubt about the location being correct. And Skelgill's own experience, starting with boyhood – predominantly his boyhood, where horizons were limited by time and tiring feet – tells him much about the significance of that location. He had fished in every trickle and beck, every puddle and tarn within an hour's trek of his home.

He places a finger on the point of the culvert, where the Watling Street crosses Soar Brook, and, almost unseeingly, traces a line that runs due north towards the village. It begins as a dotted footpath, but becomes what is evidently a trackway and – as it reaches the village centre, possibly a metalled section with the beginnings of habitation.

'I reckon they lived here.'

DS Jones leans closer, narrowing her eyes to see better under the pale light of the inn.

'It's called Bull Furlong Lane.'

Skelgill's lids are lowered.

'They would have walked. The lad would have sussed out these places – it's what any lad would do. Then maybe the arl fella – he knew how to fish – so they went along together – he passed on his knowledge. He liked taking the kid.'

DS Jones looks up; she sees that, despite his objection, in his mind's eye it is the man and boy that pervades.

20. BULL FURLONG LANE

Middlemarch – morning, Thursday 5 October

'What was your friend Woody's equation, again? Twenty divided by the ABV?'

'Don't remind me, Jones.'

'I rather suspect there was a reason why they only sold that barley wine in half pints.'

Skelgill scowls at his full English breakfast; the regulation greasy spoon variety, with a double helping of fried bread and a lake of beans, courtesy of Stan Hicks' Truckstop.

'It would've been rude not to try the full range of local offering.'

'Just as well I'm on your insurance.'

He regards her a little sheepishly.

'We can go on foot from here. It's under a mile to the village centre. Just above half to the first houses. I'll be fine to drive home.'

'I only crashed the gears once.'

'There's a knack when you're slowing down. You have to double-declutch to get the flywheel up to the right revs.'

DS Jones is looking at the map.

'That sounds like a collective noun for the clergy. Do you think we should speak to the vicar?'

Skelgill's gaze shifts to where her finger touches the symbol for a church with a spire.

'We could do worse. Let's see how we fare.'

DS Jones frowns a little over the pattern of lines, fine black angular field boundaries intersected by paler brown curving contours.

'But what if we have to cast the net wider? I looked online

before we left – there's a newish housing estate to the north of the village.' She shifts her point of indication. 'Here – what used to be Middlemarch Common.'

Skelgill appears to disapprove – if only a reaction to the loss of a habitat; though he answers by way of logistics.

'Chances are, if it's new – they wouldn't have lived there.'

'I suppose so.'

A thoughtful silence ensues. Skelgill begins to tuck in. Hangover or not, his appetite seems unaffected.

By the time they reach the culvert, the fats and salts are working their magic and his mood is jauntier. This time, instead of crossing the busy Watling Street he investigates the unkempt hedgerow on their side.

'There's a stile.'

Sure enough, there is not only a stile, but also an ancient cast-iron public footpath sign. Just discernible is *Middlemarch ¾*.

In the field beyond, they leave Soar Brook behind; it winds away to the east, while they follow a perpendicular line into an area of farmland that time seems to have forgotten. They cross small enclosures bordered by high hedges of hawthorn interspersed by towering English elms; it is a rarity in these days of factory farming and big-boom sprayers, for which the bloated hectare might have been invented.

The day has dawned clear and cold, and the low autumn sun is beginning to seek out the fine mist that lingers in shady corners. Grazing rabbits scatter before them as they emerge into a well-cropped hay meadow, and from beyond a hedge a cock pheasant shocks the silence with its gunshot call. Narrowing his eyes, Skelgill can discern the silhouettes of ragged village children, bending to hoik potatoes in the wake of a toiling tractor.

After about ten minutes their path meets a five-barred gate where an oncoming unmetalled bridleway takes an abrupt turn to their right. The map tells them it leads to Rowe's Farm – the village ahead.

'This must be Bull Furlong Lane.'

Skelgill murmurs an agreement; though he seems preoccupied with some experience, if not deep in thought.

DS Jones reveals her mind to be working at a less abstract level.

'What actually is a furlong? I mean – I know it's a measure they use in horse racing – eight to a mile, right? But where did it come from?'

Skelgill takes a moment to respond; he regards her with mild bewilderment.

'It's a plough-length – a furrow length. The long side of an acre. It's what the oxen could manage without resting. Then they'd turn them. That's why an acre's a rectangle – a furrow long, by a chain wide.'

'So it's a kind of literal description?'

'Aye, I reckon so – Old English, summat like that.'

'A bull furlong – is an oxen furrow length.'

Skelgill gives the kind of shrug that might include a small puffing out of his chest, having impressed his companion with his agrarian knowledge. But DS Jones is not quite satisfied.

'On the map – the lane is surely much longer than a furlong?'

But he gives a shake of his head.

'Aye, down to the farm, maybe – but not where the folk lived. That's just a short stretch from the village street.'

'Okay.'

The prospect of reaching houses causes them to quicken their pace, by unspoken accord. Underfoot the substrate is hard clay embedded with smooth pebbles and occasional fragments of flint. While the lane is free of ruts there are large puddles that keep them to the centre line, at times in single file. There is little to see to either side, for the bordering hawthorns still have plenty of foliage. The old village, pre-dating the Domesday Book, is set on higher ground, and the gradient rises gently.

Some instinct stops Skelgill and he veers to one side, where low bushes border the lane.

'What is it?'

DS Jones joins him.

'A pond.'

She stands on tiptoes. It is a small pool, maybe ten feet across, crowded by thick vegetation and the spikes of a few fraying bullrushes. There is a faint trickle of water, suggesting it is fed by a modest spring.

'We don't have a name for this one.'

Skelgill pontificates.

'It's too small to fish – I doubt there'd be owt in it – amphibians aside.' He scowls reflectively. 'Alreet for the bairns. This would have been a drinking pond for livestock.'

Skelgill is always content to stare at what is to the layman a sterile sheet of water. To the angler it is a blank canvas, ripe for the imagination; it is just a matter of conjuring some vignette from the complex narrative that swirls beneath.

Waiting, DS Jones finds it is her underlying doubts that surface: Skelgill's faith in their mission; his uncharacteristically blinkered drive. She finds herself re-testing a small point of logic.

'Guv, if they were an essential part of traditional agriculture – and a source of raw materials – there must be ponds all around this village.'

Skelgill, roused from his musings, looks unsurprised – and he seems to grasp the query that is at the root of her observation.

'Aye – there were – there still are. The Ashby canal's not much above a mile to the north. It's decent for bream and chub. I'd fish there in a trice.' He raps the map vigorously with the back of his hand. 'But you'd start with your own stamping ground – not someone else's patch.'

DS Jones nods pensively.

'Howay, lass – we're nearly there. Want the left or the right?'

She grins as they move away. She senses superstition at play.

'You take the left.'

The residential properties are irregular in appearance and well spaced, mainly set back from the lane – here still unmetalled and deeper pot-holed through more frequent use – with mature front gardens, mainly ornamental, and glimpses of longer rear plots which, in the traditional village, would be tended as allotments for vegetable growing. The dwellings themselves are of Edwardian appearance, and predominantly in red brick.

That said, the first house on the right, to which DS Jones splits off, is a new kit-built bungalow that looks like it might even be a holiday home or an Airbnb – it has a combination-lock key safe affixed next to the front door. It seems unoccupied; there is no car in the driveway and venetian blinds in the windows are uniformly tilted to inhibit prying eyes. She is not surprised when there is no immediate answer to her ringing of the bell.

Though she knows it to be futile, she does not want to accept refusal at the first hurdle, and persists, pressing again each time the distant chime has died away.

Then she realises there is another tune reaching her ears – a human whistle – but not from within. And it is familiar, the opening two bars of the theme music of the TV soap opera, *Ennerdale*.

Skelgill.

They have their various codes, secret signs and sounds that are essential to detectives working in tandem, such as when they do not want to give the game away to a suspect under questioning.

This one is simply, *something of interest.*

She hurries down the driveway to see Skelgill striding away from her, up the hill. He appears to be heading towards an elderly man, another fifty yards beyond, who has the tailgate of his car open. He is loading what looks like fishing tackle.

While she would ordinarily be sceptical of Skelgill's motives – any opportunity to talk about fishing – hitherto it has been the crux of their search, and she hastens to catch up.

She sees Skelgill show his warrant card and turn towards her; he indicates that she is with him. The man, short and stocky and glowering with beady eyes through a tangle of grizzled facial hair, softens. She estimates he is in his seventies.

Skelgill meanwhile does not beat about the bush. They each have, on their phones, a photograph sent by Nurse Ashanti.

'Sir, we're looking for anyone who might recognise this man. We think he may have lived in the neighbourhood.'

The would-be angler casts a questioning glance at DS Jones, as though he will trust her reassurance: that this is not some ruse that leads to double glazing. She nods encouragingly.

He further screws up his features.

'Lumme! That's old Billy, ain't it? What's he gone and done – popped his clogs?'

The striking distractions aside – the man's London accent and his colourful turn of phrase, that call to mind their left-behind colleague and stand out of place in the rural Midlands – the detectives must simultaneously experience the same overwhelming frisson.

Billy?

Billy ... is *William*.

Skelgill takes a moment to respond.

'You knew him, sir?'

Instead of answering, the man turns stiffly towards his house and bellows.

'Evie!'

To the detectives' surprise a woman of a comparable age, though neatly coiffured and maybe in better fettle pops up from behind the extensive shrubbery bordering the lane. She has on green gardening gloves and holds up a bunch of dried lavender in one hand and red-handled secateurs in the other.

'Come here, will you, girl. These bobbies are looking for old Billy.'

The woman moves rather awkwardly; emerging into view, the source of her impediment is revealed to be a pair of strap-on foam kneeling pads. She waddles boldly up to them. She too is stout, and stands hardly five feet.

Though they have not performed introductions, she seems amiable enough – she smiles, especially at DS Jones.

'Have a butcher's, girl. That's old Billy, ain't it?' The man jerks his thumb at his wife, for the benefit of the police officers. 'Her mincers are better than mine.'

Skelgill presents the handset.

The woman looks with widening eyes. She turns her face up to Skelgill.

'*Ooh* – he's not looking well. Is he alright, me duck?'

She speaks in the local vernacular.

Skelgill has questions queueing up in his mind, jostling for prominence. DS Jones seems to realise he has not processed the enquiry, and she intercedes.

'He's in a care home, madam – in our area – Cumbria. He's

suffering from dementia and we're trying to understand how it came about. It's nothing criminal, as far as he's concerned.'

'*Hah!* Just as well – probably had a fortune stuffed under his mattress!'

'Barry!'

The man's wife admonishes him with a swish of the lavender, scattering scores of tiny dried florets.

The detectives' antennae are twitching, nonetheless – and Skelgill has gathered his wits.

'You're sure you recognise him, madam?'

'That's Billy, alright. The poor soul.'

'Do you know his full name?'

'*Booth.*'

The man has interjected again. His wife shakes her head unwaveringly.

'No, Barry – it weren't Booth – it were Boothroyd.'

The man acquiesces – he makes a facial expression exclusively aimed at Skelgill: that unfortunately women always know better.

Skelgill glances at DS Jones; this is not a surname they encountered in the churchyard. She continues.

'And how did you know him?'

The woman points down the hill with her secateurs.

'He lived at the end bungalow on the other side. Except it's gone – there's that new 'un, now.'

She refers to the modern property that is apparently unoccupied. Its low garden wall is just visible, though not the building itself, which is set back by about thirty feet.

'When did he move away?'

'*Five years ago.*'

'Barry! It weren't nowhere near that long. It's you that's getting dementia! Three, more like.'

The husband, despite his fierce and belligerent appearance, seems accustomed to being put in his place, and bears no grudge. He shrugs resignedly, and holds his peace.

But the woman now seems keen to offer some explanation for any failings on her spouse's part.

'We didn't know him very well at all. He were a bit of a recluse.

It's a dead end down there – you've got no cause to go that way. He used to come past every morning and back with his shopping and his racing paper. Then you'd see him going up to the bookie's before the first race. He'd sometimes say how-do – but you could tell he didn't want to make conversation. He wouldn't look you in the eye – he was shy, or something.'

Skelgill now addresses her directly.

'We understand his wife recently died.'

'*Hah!* He kept that one quiet – he's a dark horse! Talking of horses!'

Notwithstanding his inferior rank, the man is ever ready with insubordination. He receives the customary short shrift.

'Barry – *shush.*' The woman, Evie, looks earnestly at Skelgill and then DS Jones. 'He didn't have a wife. He wasn't married. He used to look after his old mother. But she must have died above twenty-five years ago.'

The detectives exchange glances, when they might wish to rein in their reactions. The sudden non-sequitur threatens to derail their extraordinary progress. It is a reminder that they should not get ahead of themselves. All information should be treated with caution.

DS Jones's mind works quickly; she applies a parallel test.

'Do you recall that he had a dog – named Kelly?'

This time Barry glumly shakes his head – perhaps chagrined that no quip presents itself.

But Evie again comes good. She points the secateurs chidingly at her partner, as though he has pronounced anyway.

'No, Barry – *he* didn't – but the family across the road did.' She turns to the detectives. 'That were his sister – it were their dog – Kelly. I remember them shouting it often enough, because it used to chase the dustmen – until they ran it over with their lorry.'

Skelgill grimaces, but continues with his question.

'What kind of dog were it?'

'One of them sheepdogs – black and white. A big 'un it were. I heard they got it from Rowe's Farm.'

Skelgill is perhaps more diverted by the canine aspect than he ought to be, and DS Jones steps into the breach.

'Madam, you say there was a sister?'

Evie nods but then immediately shakes her head to cancel the positive impression.

'They didn't stay long after we'd moved in. Only about a year. They moved south – because of the husband's job. Went to London.'

'Saw sense! *Hah!*'

Evie shoots a reproachful glance at Barry.

'Pearly Kings Road, I'm sure it were.'

Barry now guffaws. '*Hah!* There ain't no such thing, girl. Purley Way, Croydon, more like.'

DS Jones moves to bring them back on track.

'Were there children – of the sister?'

Barry shrugs.

Evie remembers.

'A lad – a teenager with a motorbike – that were a right nuisance.'

'Do you know their names – the family surname – or the boy's name?'

After a pause both interviewees shake their heads.

'Which house did they live at?'

The secateurs are again brought to bear.

'Their'n were the end terrace. The old farmworkers' cottages.'

'The far end?'

'No the end nearest to us.'

'And when did they move?'

'1966.'

'Barry – don't be ridiculous.' Evie glowers at Barry and then addresses the detectives, a little apologetically. 'He says 1966 to everything.'

'It were a good year, girl.'

Skelgill inhales as if to comment, but Evie continues quickly.

'No. It were in the Seventies. We've been here forty-eight years this Christmas – and it were just before our first Christmas that they moved.'

DS Jones nods amenably. She has been taking notes in rapid bursts of shorthand, but here she lingers somewhat.

'Okay – we can work that out. They must have lived there for a good while beforehand?'

Evie hesitates – she might almost be waiting for Barry's inevitable riposte, in order to set her moving with a counterpoint – but it does not come, and she has no ready answer.

'I s'pose so.'

There is a small hiatus. Skelgill now brings them to the crux of the matter.

'Do you know where Mr Boothroyd moved to? Or why he moved?'

'Hah – the bookie shut up shop!'

Barry is back on form.

Evie jabs him with the point of the secateurs – Barry is well padded, and seems to feel no ill effect – indeed they both look rather blankly at one another, as though disappointed that stalemate ensues. They reach a reluctant accord. Evie answers on their joint behalf.

'It must have been because of his age. Perhaps he went to the sister.'

Skelgill has his eyes narrowed; he nods reflectively.

DS Jones interposes a question.

'Do you think she was younger?'

The chronological triangulation gives Evie some pause for thought.

'I should have said so – but she were older than us. They'd got a teenager – we were in our twenties. She'd be a good age now – but then so is Billy, int he?'

DS Jones nods, but does not dwell on the aspect.

'Can you remember anything about him moving?'

This generates a nodding of heads. Barry is first to the draw.

'I said it – I said he'd gone.'

'No – it were me that said it, Barry. I said I hadn't seen Billy pass for a while. It were during that Beast from the East – and remember you went down to check. And you came back and said there weren't no answer and there were a For Sale board up.'

Barry seems to accept this more menial role in the episode.

DS Jones continues.

'Do you remember the name of the agent?'

'*Hah!*' It seems Barry does – or at least he has something. 'It were private – homemade sign – and just a mobile phone number. I remember that. Remember I told you that, Evie. I said, old Billy, he's too miserly to put it with an agent. Stupid thing to do though, ain't it? You could get ripped off – specially a daft old cove like that.'

'*Ooh!*'

For once the exclamation emanates from Evie. It seems she suffers a sudden remembrance.

'What it were – I were putting the bin out one morning. A big car came past, too fast, like. It skidded to a stop outside Billy's. And a man got out and slammed the door and I saw him pull up the sign and chuck it into the front garden – like he were in a fit of temper. A right mardy thing to do.'

'Did you recognise him?'

But Evie shakes her head.

'He might have been in his fifties – he had on winter clothes – a hat and gloves. It's a long way off.'

'Could it have been the son – who previously lived opposite?'

But Evie looks severely doubtful.

'Like I say – I couldn't see much – and I doubt I'd have recognised someone after all these years. The lad always had a crash helmet with a skull painted on it. I wouldn't hardly have known him, then.'

Skelgill interjects.

'Do you recall the make of the car? The year of the plate?'

Barry cannot suppress a snort.

'She don't know a Zephyr from a Zodiac.'

Despite the long-outdated reference, Evie responds with a suitably baleful glance.

'Why would I look for that kind of thing? I only noticed it 'cause it were going too fast.'

'See, Evie – if that'd been me –'

But DS Jones intervenes to quell further dispute.

'Was there anything else – about that incident?'

There is a pause, before Evie does have a small rider.

'Only that I noticed the sign were back up – a few days later, it were. Then it still took a good time to sell – except the next thing, there were builders' trucks and they'd knocked it down – built the new 'un – and there's no one's lived in that, yet.'

'You wouldn't know who owns it?'

'It'll be some tax scam – Russian money laundering – mark my words, girl.'

Barry's retort is suitably hyperbolic.

'Don't be stupid, Barry – the Russians are not going to come here, are they?' She turns to the officers, shaking her head resignedly. 'He watches all these silly detective programmes.'

Evie seems to realise that she may have inadvertently disparaged the well-intentioned visitors. She brushes Skelgill on the arm with her bunch of lavender.

'Do you want a brew and a nice cheese scone, me duck?'

DS Jones has sensed that Skelgill is nearing the point when he would ordinarily terminate the conversation; they have much to discuss and plans to make. But now she sees he has on his bears-and-woods expression.

21. REFLECTION

Tebay Services, M6 motorway – 6.45 p.m. Thursday 5 October

'Where are we?'

'Thought you might need a pit stop.'

DS Jones blinks and rubs her eyes. It is more or less dark and nightfall is exaggerated by the floodlights of the parking area. Driving rain spatters the windscreen on the slant; now that Skelgill has turned off the ignition the view is blurred as shadowy figures dash for the sanctuary of the illuminated motorway service station.

'Sorry – I didn't mean to fall asleep.'

Skelgill tuts as if it is no matter.

'You didn't miss owt. It was stop-start past Manchester, then roadworks at Preston. It's only since Lancaster we've had anything like a shift on – except this rain's got worse and slowed folk down.'

DS Jones stretches and yawns. They were earlier held up by congestion through Birmingham that dragged into Staffordshire, and further becalmed on the Cheshire plain, where she had been lulled into unconsciousness by a combination of fatigue, the motion of the car, and – with the onset of rain – the hypnotic, metronomic swish of the wipers.

She finds herself still in the thrall of lassitude, heavy limbed with the pseudo-paralysis that comes with an untimely arousal – and she senses there has been a dream that has troubled her, without leaving a clear record of its narrative.

It was a dream perhaps borne out of what had been a series of small setbacks encountered before they left the village. After tea and homemade Leicester cheese scones (a snack that had vindicated Skelgill's maxim of never eschewing a gift horse, for it had proved also to be their lunch) they had explored leads that had emerged from the extended interview with their eccentric hosts, Barry and Evie, surname McClay.

First, there had been a relating of contextual history. Barry, a Londoner, had trained as a mechanic in the army and met local girl Evelyn at the "Humber" in Coventry, where he was a fitter on the production line and she assistant manager in the canteen; as Barry put it, "in the days when you were proud to drive a motor built in Blighty". The newlyweds had chosen to live in the Leicestershire village a few miles from Evie's family home, half an hour's commute from their place of work, across the border in Warwickshire.

They were able to reiterate that, yes, Billy's main interest appeared to be horse racing, and add that, no, they had never seen him go fishing – something Barry insisted he would definitely have noticed, being a keen angler himself. Barry – an incomer, and a townie in Skelgill's book – was unaware of the local ponds reached on foot by Billy and his protégé – and typically drives to his favoured haunt, near the old wharf on the Ashby-de-la-Zouch canal.

The McClays did not recognise the name Owen – or the phrase, *"Our O"*.

They did concede that, yes, perhaps Billy did have a Liverpool accent, and Boothroyd was not a local surname – northern, more like. But they knew of no other relatives, neither in the vicinity, nor in Merseyside or Cumbria.

Taking their leave, the detectives had first knocked on nearby doors – notably the terrace of four farmworkers' cottages where Billy's sister and nephew had lived. But they had come away with nothing more than the postal address. No one was at home – in fact only one cottage had produced an answer – and, like other enquiries roundabout, yielded only a vague awareness of an elderly chap in the dilapidated bungalow, both now gone.

Skelgill had taken more photographs, and they had walked up into the village centre.

But, as they had been warned by Barry McClay, at the most likely place – the bookmaker's premises – a To Let sign hung precariously. The village store had changed hands since Billy

Boothroyd had left the area, and – unsurprisingly, given his solitary nature – he was unknown at the Cross Keys, where a manager of recent appointment held the fort. Had they been present, Skelgill would have interrogated the cribbage players. Finally, as to DS Jones's earlier suggestion of consulting the local reverend, a visit to the vicarage had revealed him to be away at a meeting with the Bishop of Leicester.

DS Jones suppresses another yawn. She leans to check the time on the console. Delays have cheated them of a couple of hours, when they might have initiated inquiries and requests for information.

That said, another fifteen minutes and they could be at headquarters.

(That said, this is Tebay, which might be named especially for Skelgill.)

And now she notes something about his manner. He is excited.

He does not keep her waiting for long.

He displays his phone. The contact is headed "Ashanti".

Left-aligned is the portrait of the elderly man, looking wan and bewildered.

Beneath, right-aligned, the message sent by Skelgill before they left the Midlands:

"We think his name might be Billy Boothroyd."

And the response – left side again – within the last half hour:

"He reacted!!"

The nurse has added emojis that do not seem entirely appropriate. DS Jones is still woozy – her gaze lingers on the screen.

Then she remembers her dream.

They had gone to Duck Hall to find that Billy Boothroyd was an altogether different person – William was no longer there. And yet Skelgill had seemed unperturbed by the apparent substitution. And when nurse Ashanti had taken Skelgill by the hand to whisper confidingly into his ear, they had both looked at her as though she were the imposter – as if she were "Our O" and someone from whom the new 'Billy' must be shielded.

The dream was incomplete – its culmination abruptly truncated by the creak of Skelgill's handbrake.

She shakes her head.

'Oh, that's so good – I hope it brings about a small improvement.'

Skelgill seems momentarily diverted – as if he has detected her disquiet. But her compassion reminds him of his own underlying motive, when the piece of news has stolen precedence.

'Aye. I shouldn't like spending a year being called by the wrong name.'

DS Jones rubs her face with a washing action, as though to restore vitality. And now her response is more forensic.

'I don't suppose we should be surprised – I felt the McClays were convincing witnesses.'

Skelgill nods reflectively.

'Course – it don't prove owt, not yet. But at least it's the right answer. It's the next brick in the wall.'

That they each equivocate, to a degree, creates a hiatus in need of some catalyst. Skelgill releases his door catch.

'Howay, lass – make a run for it.'

He has ignored parking restrictions to get within twenty feet of the entrance – but it is still every person for themselves in the slanting rain beneath a stiff Cumbrian fell wind. Such conditions are well suited to flush out any last vestiges of lethargy.

They agree to rendezvous at the service counter, where DS Jones arrives to find Skelgill nattering with a girl she knows to be another that he claims as one of his many distant relations. In proof, he has been furnished with aptly mountainous portions of battered cod, chips and mushy peas.

He intercepts her reproachful gaze with the wave of a till receipt.

'I paid full price.'

'To feed the five thousand?'

The attendant seems to take the exchange as a compliment, and hands over a fistful of condiments.

Trays suitably laden, they weave their way to the most distant corner and settle at an isolated table.

The fish on his plate seems to prompt Skelgill. He taps the

crispy golden batter experimentally with the tines of his fork.

'Happen the arl fella didn't have bairns himself. Sounds like the father was busy with his job.'

DS Jones regards Skelgill intently. His tone is introspective, almost wistful. She understands better his preoccupation.

He catches her looking at him – there is a sheepishness in his reaction – he hands her a sachet of malt vinegar and bites open one of his own.

'Saves cooking, eh?'

DS Jones surveys her plate with a wry smile.

'Saves chopping salad.'

Skelgill indicates with his fork.

'Plenty of fibre in mushy peas. Taters – that's two of your five-a-day.'

She does not contest his claim. Unlike some, endowed with a less forgiving physiology, Skelgill does not outwardly resemble his diet.

A necessary silence ensues, before DS Jones's stream of consciousness leads her back to the subject of their mission.

'It seems unlikely that the McClays got it wrong about there being no wife.'

Munching, Skelgill nods. He appears unruffled by this contradiction that their trip to the Midlands has unearthed.

'Disinformation from the hospital. Duff gen, as Leyton would say.'

DS Jones regards him sharply.

'But someone must have told them that.'

Skelgill shrugs.

'Fits.'

She reflects on his earlier determination to reprise the scenario where the old man may have been abandoned at A&E.

But she reiterates the risk.

'We're relying a lot on hearsay. Something like that could send us in completely the wrong direction.'

Skelgill again seems happy to go along with her sentiment.

'Aye, I know. The arl fella mistook Cleopatra for a Border Collie.'

His lack of disputatiousness causes DS Jones to enjoin with his logic.

'Do you think that's like him mistaking you for his nephew? That it was the fishing that fired the connection.'

Skelgill shrugs.

'It did the trick. You can see why he'd expect his nephew's family dog.'

DS Jones nods.

'What do you make of that incident with the For Sale sign?'

Skelgill half closes one eye.

'Don't you want to tell me?'

She grins.

'Oh – I just thought you've been pretty free-thinking with this case.'

Her tone is teasing – and once more he obliges her.

'A deal fell through.'

He does not even intone a question mark.

DS Jones slowly draws away a strand of fair hair from her cheek and twists it absently.

'If Billy Boothroyd had already moved away – and his relatives were handling the sale –'

But she tails off, as though her reasoning has met a hitch.

'Go on, lass.'

'Well – the man who threw the sign – do you think that was the elusive Owen? That he is the nephew from across the road. Surely he is the most likely candidate?'

Where DS Jones has leant forward, Skelgill shifts back. It is plain that he is reluctant to entertain this notion. Could it be that, adopted by the old man as Owen by proxy, he is uneasy being cast in the role of knave?

She reaches into her shoulder bag and retrieves her notebook. Swiftly she scans her most recent entry.

'Evie McClay said Billy Boothroyd moved away two years and nine months ago. He was admitted to hospital in Kendal last September. Where on earth was he in between? That's over a year and a half.'

Skelgill seems alarmed by the bald calculation.

'Purley Way?'

That he glibly quotes Barry McClay's reference to the well-known South London thoroughfare highlights their present conundrum. Until they glean more information, they are no nearer the answer. And even if they do categorically determine that William is Billy Boothroyd, his name alone does not guarantee progress.

DS Jones's next point reveals something of her logic.

'Do you think there's any mileage in Barry McClay's remark about there being a fortune stuffed under the mattress?'

Skelgill tilts his head to one side.

'He might have been a successful gambler.'

'Isn't that an oxymoron?'

Skelgill ponders for a moment before he concedes.

'Right enough, Leyton's uncle – he was a bookie, and Leyton doesn't bet – so I suppose that tells you summat. Then again, I shouldn't want to be the one to tell Leyton's missus I've lost the housekeeping on a nag.'

DS Jones is about to reply, but they both see Skelgill's handset, on the table between them, light up with an incoming call.

'Talk of the devil.'

He allows a few bars of The Lambeth Walk to play out; it is jaunty, uplifting – he even mouths *any evening, any day* before tapping accept. They are well spaced from fellow diners and he switches on the speaker.

'I reckon we just met one of your distant relatives, Leyton.'

'What's that, Guv?'

'Never mind, Leyton – you sound like you're in a pub toilet.'

'I am, Guv – kind of –' The sergeant's disembodied voice momentarily falters, and there is a burst of interference on the line. 'I've been in benefits interviews all afternoon. I only just got your text about William's identity – that's flippin' great news.'

'We're not counting our chickens.'

DS Leyton seems keen to move on.

'Yeah – well – no – what it is – a colleague in the DWP wanted a word off the premises – on the q.t., like. About an idea we should follow up. Maybe we are barking up the wrong tree, looking for dead folks still receiving pension.'

'Fire away, then.'

'You see, it's not exactly the DWP's bag – more Social Services. Like you know, they organise the care home funding – but eventually that cost has to come out of the patient's assets. By law you're only allowed to keep something like your last twenty grand to pass on to the family. The relatives see this massive bill steaming down the tracks – and they conspire with the patient to squirrel away the cash. It's called Deprivation of Assets. By all accounts, this is quite common.'

DS Jones has an observation.

'But surely it's straightforward to identify any transactions?'

'That's exactly it, Emma – we'd soon rumble it. It's easy enough to find if a house has been sold or mortgaged, or premium bonds cashed in, or a savings account emptied –'

A sudden chorus of what sounds like raucous female laughter drowns out the end of DS Leyton's sentence.

'Leyton – are you sure you're in the right place?'

'Sorry, Guv – I'm in a unisex cubicle – it's that wine bar in the hotel on Warwick Road – seems these girls powder their noses mob-handed.'

Skelgill looks questioningly at his female colleague. The background cacophony persists, uncomfortable on the ear. He responds somewhat tersely.

'If it's easy to trace, what's the issue?'

Now DS Leyton seems to feel it necessary to whisper; they strain to hear his hoarse rejoinder.

'Easy to trace – but not if you don't know who the person is in the first place. Your William geezer – Billy Boothroyd – he could be being exploited by an unscrupulous relative and no one would know any better. If he dies, the trail goes cold.'

There comes another penetrating salvo of laughter and the two detectives simultaneously recoil.

In the absence of a response, DS Leyton continues hurriedly.

'I'd better scoot, Guv – I can only be away so long – I don't want to make it seem like the first thing I've done is report back.'

Skelgill looks relieved. His index finger hovers over the

handset.

'Aye – right you are, Leyton. Get back to your lady friend. Don't do anything I would do.'

'Wait on, Guv – what –?'

But Skelgill has terminated the call. He grins sardonically at DS Jones.

She is a little wide-eyed. But she opts to take the business line.

'That's – kind of – what we were just saying.'

Now Skelgill nods, but he leaves it to her to elaborate.

'It could explain why Billy Boothroyd was abandoned anonymously. And, if so, it has worked. All these government departments that are not joined up. They've just taken him at face value and looked after him as best they can.'

Skelgill gives a scornful growl.

'You're being too generous, Jones. When it comes to doing the hard bit – they just kick the can down the road.'

She regards him earnestly.

'Well – it's landed at our feet.'

Skelgill has a further lament.

'Aye – and only by fluke.'

She understands his meaning. It seems unlikely that their original strategy as part of Operation Community Chest would have led them to Billy Boothroyd's case.

Skelgill picks up his phone and gazes at the home screen.

'Are you thinking of trying to see him tonight?'

He starts, and hesitates to reply.

'I can drop you off – it's been a long couple of days.'

'I'd like to come.'

Her response is quickly volunteered.

When Skelgill does not immediately answer, DS Jones adds a caveat.

'But don't you think it's too late? He sleeps soon after dinner.'

Skelgill ponders for a moment and relaxes back into his seat.

'Leyton's keen – out on the town. He's normally changing a nappy if you ring him at this time of night. We could always crash his party. Rescue him from all those lasses.'

DS Jones eyes Skelgill suspiciously.

'What makes you think it was a female colleague?'

Skelgill shrugs and raises his tea.

'Call it male intuition.'

DS Jones simply grins, and spares him a second charge of oxymoron.

22. BILLY

Duck Hall – 10.15 a.m. Friday 6 October

'You didn't mention you had a girlfriend.'
'Who says I've got a girlfriend?'
Nurse Ashanti laughs, a little disingenuously, and reaches with both hands and clings to Skelgill's arm. He detects the musky tentacles of some invisible fragrance exploring the cool air between them.

'Thank you for coming back – and for everything you're doing.'
'I'm just doing ... doing my job. Just like you are.'
The girl gives him her broad white grin and there is a twinkle in her eye.

'Of course – of course we are.' Her gaze flicks past Skelgill and she lets go of him and takes half a step away. 'Here's your – colleague.'

Skelgill turns to see DS Jones approaching across the broad hallway. She looks a little startled – or perhaps it is that she has on some make-up that highlights the whites of her eyes and emphasises the natural prominence of her cheekbones. Her hair, unrestrained when it might normally be drawn back, seems momentarily to catch fire as she passes through a shaft of sunlight that penetrates the leaded light above the great oak door.

She nods politely to Nurse Ashanti and hands Skelgill his mobile phone. She raises the electronic tablet in her other hand.

'That's them all transferred.'

It takes Skelgill a second to collect his thoughts. Then he, too, displays his phone illustratively – now for the benefit of the nurse.

'We took photos. The ponds – and the village where they lived.' He frowns pensively. 'His old house is gone – replaced with a new building. The neighbours reckon he was never married – but there was a sister lived opposite. She had a son who might fit the bill – Owen's our best guess for his name.'

The nurse folds her palms over her breastbone; now it is she that is wide-eyed.

'You found out so much. Can you trace them?'

Skelgill inhales to speak, but DS Jones intervenes in a businesslike manner.

'We've got a team working on it. Now that we have the surname Boothroyd the DWP in Belfast ought to be able to identify him on their system. As for the relatives, they'll start with the historical electoral register and local property tax records. It's no guarantee of finding them – but the next step is to confirm their names.'

Skelgill points to DS Jones's tablet.

'We thought one of the shots might prompt him.'

But now the nurse's face falls.

'He's actually not too good this morning. I don't know what it is. There's a virus going round that makes you feel miserable – but if you can't tell anyone, what do you do?'

'Play it by ear.' It is Skelgill's response. 'We can always come back.'

The nurse nods her agreement and leads the way.

They pause at the entrance to the residents' lounge. The elderly man is over in his regular place, facing out by the bay window but still in his wheelchair. His head lolls forward as though he is asleep.

Nurse Ashanti lowers her voice.

'But you will see a difference – we're using the clothes you donated – and yesterday the chiropodist and hairdresser were in. We had a collection and paid for him. He looks so much better.'

Skelgill is frowning darkly.

'You shouldn't have to pay that, not on –' He checks himself, though it is probably apparent that his sentence would end on the words "your pay".

'It's okay – we want to do something – you've galvanised our energy.'

But Skelgill pulls his wallet from his back pocket and proffers all the notes. 'Here – let us know what you need – I'll keep a float topped up.'

But the girl backs away.

'It has to be set up formally – through Miss Bostick. It's to do with privacy and data protection.'

Skelgill returns his wallet to its place, but slips the notes into his breast pocket.

'I'll see her on the way out.'

They move forward a few paces, but now Nurse Ashanti holds up a halting palm. It is evident she does not want to surprise the elderly man.

She calls out, softly.

'Billy – Billy, you've got visitors.'

At the first word the man reacts – just slightly – but enough to suggest the name has registered when before William had produced no response.

The nurse turns to flash a gleeful smile – but her celebration is short-lived as they carefully move around in front of him – for his head remains bowed and his eyes closed.

The nurse indicates to Skelgill that he should go forward. He takes the tablet from DS Jones and squats in front of the wheelchair, just slightly to one side. The nurse takes the opposite position and gently she grasps Billy's hand. The touch prompts him to open his eyes, but he does not move his head or acknowledge those present.

Skelgill moves the screen into his line of sight.

'I went back, Billy – to Foster's Pond. Is this right? Is this it? Does it still look the same?'

The man's gaze is on the screen but there is no movement of his eyes, no scanning. Skelgill waits for a moment and then swipes to the next image, the Black Pit. But it receives the same reaction – or lack of – and so too do the remaining countryside photographs.

Skelgill flashes a forbearing glance at DS Jones – she is looking on anxiously.

He moves on through the photographs taken in Bull Furlong Lane and in the village centre – but while Billy's eyes remain on the screen, there is no discernible reaction.

Skelgill persists. He swipes back to the farm cottages, the shot taken from outside the front wall of what was Billy's bungalow.

'Billy –' Skelgill glances a little awkwardly at each of the women in turn; he is not comfortable with an audience. 'Billy – here's our house.'

Momentarily, Billy's eyes move to look at Skelgill.

Skelgill is plainly struggling for something to say. Only with difficulty has he inserted himself into the role. Then it strikes him simply to paraphrase his own mother.

'Me Ma would do her nut if she saw how they've let the garden go.'

Billy's features crease as if the knowledge is painful. Then he moves an attenuated hand to touch the screen. He inhales.

'Blue rose. Joy of joys.'

Skelgill's eyes widen in anticipation – but when there is no more forthcoming, and he makes to ask a question, he checks himself, for Billy's eyes close and he slumps to one side – so much so that the nurse moves to support him.

Skelgill stands up and joins DS Jones. He indicates to Nurse Ashanti that they will back off – that he recognises it has been enough for the old man – too much, even.

But just as the detectives step away the man speaks, unprompted and without opening his eyes. His voice is clear.

'Where's me shirt, our O? Lost me shirt on a gee!'

His tone sounds positively amused.

Skelgill makes a knowing face at DS Jones – but he leads the way out, for other patients, seeing them standing unattended, are beginning to vie for their attention.

Skelgill taps on the door of Miss Bostick's office and pokes his head in.

A regulation glower turns to mild toleration when she recognises him.

'Ah – Inspector – I gather you may have identified William – or should I say Billy?'

174

Skelgill steps aside to let DS Jones in before him. He notices the manager takes a moment to appraise his colleague's appearance; whatever the cause, she seems content with their presence.

Skelgill clears his throat.

'Madam, he may turn out still to be William – but I reckon he's accustomed to going by Billy.'

'Have you made any progress on that front?'

Skelgill indicates that DS Jones will answer.

'We've submitted enquiries to the DWP and the local authorities where he previously lived. We think there's a sister – if she's still alive – and a nephew – who is more likely to be. We should begin to hear back in one or two working days.'

She glances at Skelgill – it is plain from his subtle nod that he wishes her to elaborate.

'When we first looked at this case – it seemed the key issue was to reunite him with any funds or assets that belong to him. Although it is too early to say for sure, it appears he may have owned a house until comparatively recently.'

Miss Bostick is not slow to read between the lines.

'You are suggesting he has been financially exploited.' She makes the response as a statement. 'That would be very serious. Especially to take advantage of his dementia. I'm sure I don't have to tell you there is legislation surrounding Deprivation of Assets.'

Skelgill cannot suppress a scornful snort. The woman looks at him with alarm, as though he disparages her opinion. But he moves quickly to correct the impression.

'Aye – legally. But abandoning him – dumping him without a penny or a stick of clothing – no visits – not even a phone call – you wouldn't do that to a sick dog. That's the true crime – it's just not on the statute book. It's called Deprivation of Dignity.'

DS Jones is a little open-mouthed. It is rare for Skelgill to vent his feelings, let alone in what is – if not exactly a public forum – a meeting that does not guarantee the customary impermeability of the police's four walls.

But Miss Bostick's response once more belies her unyielding demeanour.

175

'It is indeed distasteful to think that he was regarded as too much trouble for someone to look after.'

There is a poignant silence.

It is Miss Bostick that resumes her narrative.

'I know we are just his temporary home – but the reality is that he has been left with us to die. The girls are finding it so distressing – that they get to go home to their families and friends at night and weekends – and he has no one.'

Skelgill shifts a little uneasily on his feet; it seems he carries some of the burden for the deficiency in guardianship. He reaches to take the wad of sterling notes from his pocket.

'Can I give you a sub? Take care of his basics.'

Miss Bostick's reaction is as anticipated.

'It is difficult with cash – especially given our holding position. There are all sorts of protocols – I am sure you will be familiar with this in your own line of work.'

Skelgill looks like he wants to dash the notes down on her desk. She interjects.

'You could apply to become his Appointee – it is a simple process.'

Skelgill glances at DS Jones – but it is plain she is none the wiser than he.

'How does that work?'

Miss Bostick picks up her pen and jots a note on her desk pad.

'I could organise with Adult Care to sponsor you. You say you are investigating with the DWP?'

Now DS Jones answers.

'That's right – it's the Belfast office that holds the national database.'

'You see – he must be eligible for state benefits. Pension credit, if not state pension.'

DS Jones is nodding.

'That's certainly something we're hoping to trace. It could lead us to a bank account – although we would need a court order to force full disclosure.'

Vigorously, Miss Bostick repeatedly clicks the end of her pen; by her standards, it is a display of excitement.

'Yes – but the beauty of becoming an Appointee is that you don't need to know anything about the person's bank account. Once you are approved as a fit proxy, any state benefits are diverted and paid directly into your account. You then deploy them on behalf of your charge.'

Skelgill's brow is creased; the office is unlit, and in the pale autumn light of the window his features take on the weathered highlights and shadows of Lakeland scree.

'Can anyone be made Appointee?'

'Within reason. It is purely an administrative function. Adult Care would liaise with the local DWP office and you would have an interview. They can sign it off on the day. Payments would begin almost immediately. The UK government is not entirely incompetent when it comes to those in need.'

'How much would he get?'

The woman presses the point of her biro into her pad.

'Well – here is the downside. The reason I am familiar with the procedure is because the bulk of a person's state benefits have to go towards care costs. He would be allowed to keep around twenty-five pounds per week for personal needs. But it is a lot better than nothing. Especially since William – Billy – is on only the most basic care package.'

Skelgill exhales; it is a sigh of reluctant cooperation, tinged with discontent. He spreads his open palms, though he knows the gesture to be rhetorical.

'He might be a wealthy man. If he's sold a house – where's all that gone? He can afford a lot more than a new toothbrush and a decent pair of slippers.'

Miss Bostick regards him pensively.

'Well, I quite agree. If that proves to be the case – he could afford transformative care. For instance, companionship visits – and more formal occupational therapy. It would be a travesty if he were being cheated out of support that could brighten his twilight years.'

Skelgill regards the woman intently.

'You reckon years, madam?'

She hesitates to answer.

'One never knows. He is certainly very old.'

Skelgill reluctantly returns his money to his shirt. He digs his hands into his pockets and exhales in frustration.

'All that said – it's his folks he's missing. That's what you'd want. Even if you didn't know. Who would choose to be abandoned?'

He stalks across to the window at one side of the office. He presses his forehead against the glass, as if to benefit from its cooling effect. The view is to the shady side; yellowing leaves nestle haphazardly upon a lawn that has missed its last cut; dense rhododendrons block any view. After a few moments, he speaks without turning.

'Aye. Start the ball rolling, will you?'

At the main doorway DS Jones is wrestling with the wrought-iron latch when footsteps patter towards them. It is Nurse Ashanti. She approaches close to Skelgill.

'He's fine, I think – he's sleeping. We moved him to his bed. It's the doctor's round today – we'll make sure she checks him thoroughly.'

Skelgill nods, but he backs away half a pace.

It is plain to DS Jones that he finds uncomfortable the role that is being thrust upon him – but also that he knows he has no other choice – until some next-of-kin can be identified. And then what? Such a person may be the bad actor.

The nurse reaches to touch his arm.

'I'll text you – if he perks up. So that you can try again with the photographs. Or call in – or – if you are fishing. We don't need any notice.'

DS Jones interjects; she addresses Skelgill. She gestures towards the nurse.

'Why don't we just send the photographs? Then if he has a lucid moment, they're ready at hand. I'll do it now, if you lend me your phone again.'

And she hauls open the door for Skelgill, inviting him to go ahead of her. She turns to smile in a somewhat perfunctory manner at Nurse Ashanti.

In Skelgill's car, they sit pensively for a moment, each preoccupied with their own thoughts.

DS Jones speaks.

'Do you think that was a reference to the bookmaker's – about losing his shirt?'

Skelgill nods reflectively.

'He sounded like it were a bit of a joke.'

'I thought that, too.'

Now another silence ensues; when DS Jones speaks again, this time she is less prescriptive.

'What are you thinking?'

'He reacted to his sister's cottage.'

DS Jones nods.

'What he said – it seemed descriptive, about the garden – but either Rose or Joy could be a sister's name.'

Skelgill looks sideways at his colleague.

'What about two sisters?'

'Oh.'

'If it were me Ma's family – of that generation – there'd be a good half-dozen.'

23. STRATEGISING

Carlisle – lunchtime, Monday 9 October

Since beating a reluctant retreat to the refuge of Portland Square Gardens, Morten Jenner has taken a liking to the leafy location. It may not be so conducive in winter, but on days like this when vestiges of summer cling to the backcloth of sun-dappled lawn and yellowing foliage, unmoving in the still air, it preserves a mystical energy; the flies that court in pockets of light dance a last tango before the season's curtain falls.

He eats his chocolate bar greedily, pushing too much at a time into his mouth, his wide rubbery lips contorting in the act of containment, not entirely successfully. The sugar begins to restore his depleted condition; two sides of a familiar sensation, each pleasant in their own way.

He crumples the foil wrapper. Methodically, he sets about his National Lottery scratchcards. He becomes consumed, scraping with his thumbnail, faster, more frantically. When the last is revealed to be a loser like all the rest he wants to fling them, to scatter them across the grass.

But he catches sight of the young woman with the pram, and reins in his flash of temper.

Instead he places them casually at his side.

She is dressed as if she is meeting someone. Or could it be to impress him? Slowly, she is working her way around the square in his direction. He pretends to look at his phone but he watches her. He can't help feeling a frisson, despite earlier, and he covets the finer form of this woman – indeed, everything about her – her designer clothes (is that a Chanel outfit and Louboutin shoes?) – the Georgian town house from where he suspects she emerged – even the ridiculously over-specified pushchair.

Surreptitiously, he casts an eye over his own attire. He, too, is well dressed – smart-casual, they call it – and he must look a good decade younger than his age – he could be taken for the director of a successful advertising agency, or a firm of architects, or perhaps a consultant surgeon on his day off.

He fantasises about chatting her up. He could compliment her style – or just pass the time of day, comment upon their mutual appreciation of the elegant green space.

And, if she's a regular here, then so can he be.

Last time – no, it was the time before that – she had been sitting on this very bench, reading her novel – some classic, undoubtedly, possibly a French translation – no chick-lit for a sophisticated woman like that. A pity that she doesn't have it to hand just now – that would be an excuse to make some informed observation.

Wait – his newspaper. He has The Times. By good fortune it was on a special deal with the chocolate, else he'd have bought The Sun.

But he has the damned scruffy carrier bag – and the rest.

He stuffs the bag with the chocolate wrapper and the wasted scratchcards and reaches to feed it, as unobtrusively as he can contrive, into the litter bin at his side.

He pulls out his pen and leans back and crosses an ankle over the opposing knee. He turns the journal so the masthead faces prominently outwards and begins to fill in the crossword on the back with random words – the first things that come to mind – he doesn't even register what he enters. It is the act that counts. He scribbles in short, decisive bursts, each one preceded by a moment's exaggerated concentration and – his eyes cast skywards – deliberation. It is as if the solutions are up there in the ether, and one by one – with his special powers of intellect – he plucks them down.

He must look clever.

The woman rounds the final corner of the quadrangle and begins to approach him.

Did he just catch her eye?

He bows his head to complete another clue, his pulse racing now. He has no sense of what he writes.

He has to time it just right.

Now.

He glances up expectantly, as if just alerted to her approach – only to see the woman in a single uninterrupted movement perform an abrupt U-turn, ten feet from him, and – striding more briskly – walk away and exit the gardens through the adjacent corner gate towards the town centre.

Morten wants to stab the pen into the newspaper.

But he diverts his fit of anger into finishing off the crossword – more random words and oaths, scrawled almost illegibly – before he crosses the whole lot out with a frenzied attack, tearing the thin substrate. Finally, he screws up the newspaper and thrusts it into the waste bin.

When he looks round, he finds an elderly woman in a heavy coat and carrying a bulging shopping bag has slowed to look at him. He stares her out. She opens her mouth as if to speak, but then thinks the better of it, clearly alarmed by his demeanour, and moves on.

Morten seems to freeze for a moment.

Then he smiles to himself.

She obviously remembered something – he must have reminded her – perhaps seeing him do the crossword made her think of an errand. She would have been impressed – perhaps it was something educational, to do with the child in the pram – perhaps to buy some of those alphabet building blocks or foam bath-letters.

Next time he'll be better prepared. He'll think in advance of something to interrupt her. Some way that he can help her – perhaps a fault with the buggy. He could palm a drawing pin and pretend to pull it from one of the rubber tyres. Flag her down as he spots it when she is passing.

It seems like she comes around lunchtime. That suits his schedule.

He gazes at the townhouses; gaps in the shrubs afford glimpses of pale perpendicular sandstone and white sash windows.

This is where he ought to own a second property. An apartment, at the very least, if not an entire main-door house.

And she is the sort of person he should rub shoulders with. A step up the social ladder – the status he deserves – busy man-about-town, a successful financier, with an attractive, sophisticated woman, hungry for his company whenever he can be free.

He compares it to his present arrangement, and his features work their way through a sequence of grimaces; resentment, discontent, resignation.

His little bird.

She pales by comparison to the society princess.

Though she's alright at what she does – she seems to enjoy it – and she's been more than useful – she's more than paid her way. He has to concede that.

But don't forget, she makes money out of all this.

Is that her game at the moment?

Casting doubt so that he keeps the funds flowing?

Is that why her enthusiasm for their little meetings hasn't dampened?

Keeping him on the hook.

Can he trust her to tell him everything she knows?

Can he really trust her at all?

After all, he's lying to her – what if she finds out more than is healthy?

Morten casts about the bench in case he has dropped a square of chocolate – he could do with another bar – and he rues that he left the last of the vodka – though he wouldn't have wanted the princess to see him on a park bench with a bottle, this time of day. Any time of day.

He gives an exasperated growl.

An absurd name – Community Chest.

But what she'd hinted at, he'd read about a few weeks ago.

The local paper had made a big splash of it.

He would have ignored it.

Another pile of piffle from pompous politicians who couldn't deliver a pizza, never mind a multi-million pound saving to the local purse.

But the words "pension" and "scam" in the headline had caught his eye.

Still, he had dismissed it.

183

But now his little bird has told him about it.

The suggestion of a clampdown.

And she can't know that Thomas has dried up. That's two weeks in a row the withdrawal has been declined. He's six hundred down. And how long will it continue?

What if it is part of a plan?

A malicious government ploy – that some kind of renewal is needed – an inspection – at a certain age. In Greece they say they pay dead people's pensions for decades. But that's Greece – and even there, didn't they put a stop to it as a condition of the German bail-out? Here there must be a system. He just doesn't know what it is.

And yet they don't seem to check. In a way it's amazing how little checking they do. If Billy, for instance, is still registered at his previous address – where he'd lived for donkey's years – why haven't they sent someone round before now to make sure he's still alive? Can they really be so useless? They deserve to be fleeced.

He hawks and spits – it is an act of disdain – but he realises that a man across on the far side with a dog is staring at him, transmitting his own vibes of disapproval.

Morten leans forward and rests his arms on his thighs and watches his hands in seeming entrancement as he wrings them.

A change of strategy is called for.

The change – it's the change he's had in mind – perhaps for a good while – but it has properly taken shape since he got the spare key cut for Harriet's front door.

Because if Thomas has dried up, what's to stop Richard drying up? And then Billy?

Thomas would be the eldest. If they're working their way down the years – stopping the oldest ones first – and if no pips squeak – then it's a simple saving for the government. If someone complains – *er, sorry, our mistake* – they just switch it back on.

Morten makes more facial contortions.

Hold on, though – is he overreacting?

Being hasty?

What if it's just some freak error, a gremlin in the works?

Friday's tentative inquiry, a phone call, with Rina posing as Mrs

Thomas Jones, had not borne any fruit. Listening in, he'd had to snap down hard to cut off the line when they started asking awkward questions about her identity that he knew she couldn't answer.

He snarls. They're so effing useless, the staff at these government offices.

But he can't be sure it's not some mess that Rina's made.

He curses.

Rina swears she has done nothing – but he doesn't trust her.

He suspects her of tampering with the mail.

She might even be looking at his stuff. Perhaps he should start using the padlock. Though he can't believe she could climb to his garret. She's never had a head for heights – she won't even set foot on a stepladder to prune her roses, she waits for him to do it. And he doubts that could be a ruse – she was like that even before he built his private study up in the attic. She might even struggle to fit the hatch – she's piled on the pounds in the last few years. She's not the best advert for her business these days. But then how much longer will she keep going?

Yes. How much longer will Rina keep going?

He gazes across the little park; the dog owner stands by while his pet urinates against the leg of a bench. Morten feels an urge to go across and strangle it. Drown it – that's what he'd like to do. Take it out to sea and strap it to the anchor and toss it overboard.

Then he realises the owner is glaring at him, more fiercely now, as if he reads his thoughts.

He lowers his gaze.

Rina. That's a question for another time.

It's on the far horizon, over the horizon. Barely a vague hint of dark storm clouds massing.

Thomas, by comparison, is upon them – a squall – too late to avoid – it must be sailed through.

And then it's what's in the offing that counts: lying low in the calmer waters beyond, sitting ducks, silhouettes against the sunset of their times.

First is the hulk of Harriet. She is one great whale of a cash cow.

Sort out Harriet, and there'll be no more sailing close to the wind.

Morten looks greedily at the Georgian roofs beyond the treetops – white smoke drifts symbolically from one of the tall chimney stacks, barely bent by the breeze.

The reality is, he made the decision as soon as he got sight of Harriet's documents. There's enough capital to pay cash for one of these town houses – with plenty to spare to entertain a princess who expects gifts of Chanel and Louboutin.

It hadn't been his plan – not so fast.

But there's the bloody idiot government and its ridiculous Monopoly scheme.

Rina or not, gremlin or not – he has to assume the worst.

It helps that he is disgusted by Harriet's presence, the great lump of Scotch lard, the lumbering old ox. And the chance has presented itself in a way he hadn't expected. Much more quickly.

He already has everything he needs.

With Rina's assistance they've applied for online banking. The passwords and access codes should come in a day or two. They've set up a mobile phone account in her name.

And he's got copies of all of her admin, including from the solicitors who have the title deeds of her house.

These days no one wants face-to-face meetings. Everything can be done anonymously, electronically and by Royal Mail. And if someone has to speak on the phone, Rina – she might be half-stupid – but where she's sure of her ground she's good on the phone – that gift of the gab, again – she's quick to improvise and win people over if she makes a mistake. She'll be an asset for being Harriet.

Besides, if he plays his cards right, there is serious income to be had. It might be trickier to sustain, but by the look of it, Harriet's got a gilt-edged index-linked government pension – from all her years in whatever deadly dull department she must have worked. And she's getting disability benefits – and there's probably more he could claim. Attendance allowance, for example. Harriet's income could easily replace the rest put together.

Why let Harriet drop anchor when he can cut her loose? Strip the assets and scuttle her. Davy Jones's locker ahoy.

He just needs to come up with a ruse to get her signature.

She won't even see it coming. She's as dim-witted as she's slow in moving around the house.

She's nearly incapable.

Look how she fell off the bed the other day!

Morten makes an involuntary scoffing sound.

What was Rina going on about? Getting suspicious. That Harriet must have made herself a cup of tea in their kitchen? Why would she go into their kitchen when she's got her own facilities? Rina said it would be an excuse to poke and pry. Nonsense. If the kettle were still warm – that must have been from his instant coffee before they went out.

Rina's getting paranoid in her old age.

She's getting paranoid about him.

He'll have to keep an eye on Rina.

He won't tell her about his plans for Harriet.

That can wait until after – just in case there ensue circumstances where she could let something slip. If it doesn't quite work out and they have to cover up.

Morten nods slowly to himself.

His thoughts begin to coalesce.

Now the nights are drawing in and it's getting chilly, he ought to offer to fetch the old-fashioned paraffin heater he saw at Harriet's house when he collected her charger. She might like it for a bit of background heat in the evenings – that sitting room of hers has a cold wall, facing north. She wouldn't know if the radiator had been choked off at the blanking valve.

He was surprised to see the old heater – they don't recommend them for domestic use these days. In an unventilated room, the carbon monoxide can be dangerous. Lethal, even.

Harriet. He wonders if she's accident prone.

She was lucky not to break anything when she fell off Rina's treatment table.

That could easily happen again.

If she fell and tangled the cables, she could even get an electric shock. Direct from the mains, a short-circuit would electrocute a person. All it would take is for one of those leads to be frayed.

It's about time he gave Rina's equipment a bit of a service.

He begins to nod once more.

Yes – and in the meantime he must inspect Harriet's mobility scooter. They can develop faults all the time. All it takes is a loose wire that can be impossible to detect. Without her scooter, Harriet would depend entirely on him.

Yes. The hulk of Harriet and Davy Jones's locker.

The image causes him to start – for there are two hulks – and he must deal with them both.

Because if they turn off Thomas, and then Richard, why wouldn't they turn off Billy?

Then, what would be the use of Billy?

In fact, what's the use of Billy, anyway?

They've had everything else they can get from him.

Why did they keep Billy so long?

Why didn't they just do the same as with Thomas and Richard?

"Because he's family, Morten."

Morten releases a snort of contempt.

Rina hasn't seen him since he went away.

She hasn't expressed a shred of interest in his welfare.

She couldn't give a tinker's cuss about Billy.

She was after the money, that's all – no different to him.

They took a risk with Billy.

There's still a risk.

The chances are small, but the consequences would be great.

The risk of remission.

That he'll be able to tell them who he is and where he came from, and where all his money went.

Billy, once a great asset, is now a great liability.

Morten stares once again across the square and beyond. There's a house there that would be perfect.

Billy is a threat to Morten and his ambitions. His princess.

Billy is a ghost ship that could sink them.

He needs to check on Billy – he needs a plan for Billy.

He needs to do it soon.

Belmont Manor. That's where he was. Morten realises he

hasn't heard from the cleaner in ages. She's probably had the sack. She was probably stealing. She was the crooked sort. He doubts she believed his sob story for why he couldn't visit – but she took the hundred quid to send a text every month: "Sorry, still no improvement".

Morten suddenly starts.

Billy could be dead.

Just because he's not dried up doesn't mean he's alive. They don't know who he is – so how could they stop his payments? That will only happen with this new scheme – if it is a scheme.

But, no – he mustn't get his hopes up.

He'll need to pay a visit.

He'll need a cover story.

He nods reflectively.

He takes out his wallet.

Yes – there it is, in the little zip compartment – the detective's calling card.

Morten had pulled it off then, okay – going back to the hospital after Billy was admitted – no one had even asked who he was – he could have been a terrorist, a poisoner, anything. He'd taken a risk – but he needed to double-check that Billy hadn't got on him the missing bus pass.

Then Morten had had a lucky break.

There beside Billy's bed was the card. The detective must have called in – paying lip service to finding out who Billy was.

In the days following, Morten had waited.

Rina had been on tenterhooks.

But a week went by – no one came, no one rang.

Two weeks – three – a month. More.

Morten grins at the card. Thank you, "Detective Inspector Alexander Useless".

Smart – *hah!* That's a joke.

Morten sits up straight. He presents the calling card as if he is displaying it to someone.

Find a junior member of staff – that's what you do. Someone who's used to obeying orders.

Morten affects an expression that is at once earnest and

insistent; he intones quietly.

'DI Alexander Smart, Cumbria CID. I'm making inquiries about one of your patients. I believe you know him as William. There has been a development in his case. It concerns his identification, and I should like to see him. There's no need to trouble the manager.'

That's it – get the lie of the land.

Visitors go in and out of these care homes all the time. The staff are paid a pittance and have their hands full. He'd get free rein to roam about, even if he weren't a detective.

Morten pushes back his shoulders.

He likes the idea of being a detective.

He would have made a good detective.

Except he's too clever to be a detective.

When you commit perfect crimes, you're a cut above a detective.

Morten laughs to himself, a sound that trails off into hysterical glee.

He rises, and straightens his jacket and bends to brush away flakes of scratchcard latex from his chinos.

No, he won't tell Rina about Harriet.

And he won't tell Rina about Billy

He strides away, buoyantly – all in all, the outlook is promising – Harriet, Billy, the princess – and even the little bird, who can keep him in the picture. He stretches his arms above his head; he is stiff from his exertions.

As Morten disappears through the gate in the direction of Aglionby Road, it would be to his chagrin, however, that from the entrance diagonally opposite emerges the attractive young woman, designer-clad, pushing the high-sided hi-tech perambulator.

She slows as she approaches the bench where Morten has been sitting – the bench where she previously read – but when she stops, she does not position the baby carriage in order that she may take a seat, but instead leaves it a little adrift.

Then she steps forward – and delves into the litter bin.

Quickly, she extracts the crumpled newspaper and carrier bag, and tosses them into the open-topped buggy.

She grasps the handles, turns, and strides away.

24. MIXED RESULTS

Police HQ – afternoon, Monday 9 October

'Wow.'

DS Jones remains literally open-mouthed after she utters the word, reading on the hoof and arriving at Skelgill's office to plonk herself down in front of the window with a single page of A4 paper held out in both hands.

'You look like you've just got your exam results, girl.'

She takes a moment longer before she responds to the seated DS Leyton, a nonplussed nod, as if she has not entirely taken in his meaning.

She transfers her gaze to Skelgill; it would be fair to say that his more subdued reaction is conditioned by the fact that her hot-foot arrival comes for once without a tray of refreshments.

'We've found him.' She brandishes the page. 'DC Watson has found him.'

She takes another look, her eyes now more thoroughly scanning the information of which she is evidently only just in receipt.

'Spill the beans, lass.'

Skelgill appears to have set aside his yen for tea.

DS Jones looks at him again, and now she nods urgently.

'It's not everything – nothing yet on the relatives – but about him – well, this is significant.' It is clear that she is still processing the content – but she understands she should convey the headlines. She stares at the page as she intones. 'The DWP in Belfast have him on their system. William Boothroyd, date of birth third of November 1933. And a national insurance number.' She looks up sharply, realising the potential contradiction. 'His name is officially William – but it's him alright – the address is Bull Furlong Lane, Middlemarch.'

She gives a little expiration of breath; there is more to come.

'They're paying him pension credit of £240 per week, and attendance allowance of £420 per four weeks. Last winter he received fuel and cold weather payments.'

DS Leyton does not immediately grasp the implications of what his colleague says.

'What do you mean, *they're paying him* – I thought the poor old geezer had no money?'

DS Jones regales him with a wide-eyed look.

'The funds are being paid into a National Westminster account at a branch in the nearby town – in his name, at his same old address. The FIU submitted a discovery request. The current balance is just over £400 and the account turnover in the past twelve months –' For a second the words seem to catch in her throat. 'Was – almost £17,000.'

It is perhaps just as well that Skelgill has no mug on his desk, for a small eruption now occurs.

He is on his feet and plainly incandescent, his expression conflating vindication and violence.

He would seem to be seeking a surface to punch – and it is fortunate, when he exits the open door, that no eavesdropper loiters in the corridor.

His colleagues regard one another anxiously as they hear his footsteps fade away.

DS Leyton requests clarification.

'Emma, what are we saying, here?'

She indicates to the incriminating page.

'Given that William Boothroyd – Billy – is incapacitated with dementia, and has not set foot outside a nursing home in over a year – and given that he isn't paying care costs and doesn't have two pennies to rub together – we're saying that someone has spent £17,000 from his bank account.'

'Struth. So there is a pension scam, an' all.'

'It looks that way.' Momentarily, she bites one side of her lower lip. 'But no capital sum. Your DWP colleague's suggestion – deprivation of assets – seems all the more likely.'

'We need a court order slapped on that account.'

They look up. A remarkably chilled Skelgill is framed in the doorway. He has three machine teas in a rigid holder and fourth plastic cup in his other hand. He seems to detect that they notice the asymmetry.

'You wouldn't climb a fell without a rock for the cairn.'

He places a cup for each of them within reach on his desk, and resumes his seat.

For a moment he casts about wanly, and even pulls out a drawer – and glances hopefully at the open door; but the afternoon tea trolley – today's special, ginger scones – is not due for an hour.

He finishes his first cup and makes a face of disapproval.

DS Jones picks up his direction.

'We have ample grounds to suspect fraud. I'll make the application myself. With authorisation from the Chief we can short circuit the FIU. I'll request the last five years' statements – that should expose the property transaction. If he sold his house, where has the money gone?'

They each reflect upon this, and it DS Jones who speaks again.

'Guv – Miss Bostick's proposal that you become Appointee. Now that we know Billy Boothroyd's receiving a regular income, you can intercept that and divert it for his benefit.'

But when Skelgill might admit at least a modicum of satisfaction in this potential outcome, it is apparent that he remains conflicted.

'Do we want to do that?'

DS Jones shoots him a sideways glance.

'I thought you did?'

But Skelgill only glowers and shakes his head.

'For a start – he only gets twenty-odd quid a week. I can fund that out of my own pocket – if they'll let me.' He makes a chopping motion in the air with his left hand. 'If we cut off the cash – that's a red flag to whoever's filching it.'

That he reveals he is one step ahead of his colleagues causes them each to take stock. DS Leyton is first to respond.

'And you reckon that's this Owen geezer – *Our O,* as he calls him?'

Skelgill does not answer. He picks up his reserve tea and rises, and moves slowly to the window to stand beside DS Jones, looking out.

Beyond, all is calm. The layered autumn sunlight discloses vast numbers of insects on the wing. It is the sort of day when Bass Lake lies like a millpond and its surface reveals every nuance of what goes on just below. Fins of fish testify to just how often they swim at the surface. He rues his absence – and there is Billy, watching from his wheelchair on the bank – a connection, a reason to be there. He could kill two birds with one stone; though he baulks at the phrase. But he has seen the forecast. If the Met Office is right this short-lived spell of Indian summer has almost run its course.

His answer, when it comes, is somewhat oblique.

'Nay, Leyton. This person's fly. If they're mobile – we might lose them. Why tip them off?'

DS Jones, as is the pattern of the case, reads the paradox that troubles Skelgill: that the old man holds ingenuous affection for the person who may be bleeding him. But she does not shy from playing devil's advocate, when ordinarily it would fall to her superior.

'One thing we must consider – now that we know that someone is spending Billy Boothroyd's money – is the extent that he might have granted permission.' When Skelgill turns sharply to look at her, she holds out an upturned hand pre-emptively. 'Guv, surely that's going to be the obvious defence?'

Skelgill snorts.

'Aye, reet. I'll live abandoned in dead folk's clothes – you live the life of Riley on my savings. Howay!'

He flaps at an imaginary adversary, as though a wasp has assailed him.

It is sufficient to win the argument.

DS Jones corrects herself.

'No – you wouldn't agree to that, would you?'

Skelgill remains discomfited, though he places a hand briefly on the shoulder of his colleague, as though to indicate that his contempt is not directed at her.

'You've just hit the nail on the head, lass. He *couldn't* agree to it – you've seen the state of him.'

DS Leyton, looking on, now has a point to add.

'Speaking with my DWP hat on – that pension credit – that has to go towards his care fees. He couldn't legally gift that to someone – even if he were compos mentis. And no one would be within their rights to take it – not even if they had Power of Attorney.'

There is concord, and Skelgill returns to his seat.

'It's not stopped them making hay, though, Leyton.'

DS Leyton leans forwards, resting his forearms on his ample thighs.

'Seeing as state pension's paid weekly – and there ain't a lot in that account – if they're making regular withdrawals from an ATM, we could catch 'em red-handed.'

Skelgill nods pensively; he is still troubled by the moral iniquity.

'They could be anywhere – abroad, for all we know.' He turns to DS Jones, before further speculation has them drifting into uncharted waters. 'You said there's nowt on the house – the sister, or the lad?'

DS Jones shakes her head and makes reference to the page of notes.

'All local authority records from that era are held manually. The register of ratepayers is somewhere in storage. And, of course, they've got staffing issues. As for the electoral register – we're waiting to hear from the National Archives.'

She flaps the paper a little impatiently, though her tone is not entirely downbeat.

'More promisingly, we've submitted requests to the Land Registry for the title deeds of both Billy Boothroyd's property and his sister's house opposite. Sod's law – there was a fee to pay and it sat in someone's in-tray for two days pending approval. It's away now – and we might just get the name of the sister and her spouse – depending upon how the ownership was registered – if they were tenants we'll need to wait for the local council ratepayers' report.'

Skelgill rests his elbows on his desk and blows through his long fingers, pressed together rather like inverted panpipes.

'What about you, Leyton?'

The question is entirely open-ended, unguided by reference or gesture; DS Leyton hems and haws for a moment as he finds some bearings of his own choosing.

'I'll need to tread carefully on this Billy Boothroyd case, Guv – especially if we don't want to rock the boat. Besides – if it comes to investigating deprivation of assets, then I'm in the wrong place – that's for social services and the council's finance department. You'd think their ears would prick up when they hear there's a hefty sum they can claw back.'

'You could take the credit for that, Leyton – we could get you transferred. Now there's probable cause, the Chief won't object to us changing horses.'

But DS Leyton seems unenthused by his superior's offer.

'I know what you mean, Guv – and it's me that's saying we started out on the wrong track, about dead folks' pensions – but, the thing is, I'm just getting me feet under the table. Getting the hang of it. I don't quite yet want to give up on our original idea. I've got a couple of little irons in the fire – I reckon I should see how they pan out.'

'Are you sure it's not the partying that's the attraction, Leyton – sounded to me like you've got a good little number going on there.'

Skelgill is grinning, and undoubtedly DS Leyton appears abashed; prevarication does not come naturally to him, and a little colour rises in his cheeks. He glances appealingly at DS Jones; she nods, encouraging him to elaborate.

'What I reckon – in social services, they're all do-gooders, ain't they? Now there ain't nothing wrong with that – it's their job to see the best in people – people in need. And like in Billy's case, it's not the old folks themselves what's doing the dirty deed – the fraud. It's the younger relatives – or, at least, them who've got their wits about them. But social services don't know them from Adam. But we know them – I mean 'we' at the local DWP office. Leastways, we know some of them – chances are, they're on our books.'

DS Jones has listened intently to her colleague's appeal; Skelgill it would appear to her less so, and that she suspects DS Leyton has an ulterior motive for hanging on to his formerly maligned assignment. She contributes on her colleague's behalf.

'You mean that it's possible that – well, let's say it could be

Owen – is already known to the DWP?'

DS Leyton shrugs and simultaneously nods hopefully

'We all know about repeating patterns of criminality. Robbing off your old uncle is going to come easily when it's been the habit of a lifetime.'

Skelgill's interest, despite his reservations, has been piqued. He casts an open palm towards DS Leyton.

'But how are you going to identify that person? Owen – the sister – whoever. We might never get a name.'

'I thought we could cross-reference suspected or convicted benefit fraudsters.'

'Aye – but cross-reference them with what?'

DS Leyton shifts a little uncomfortably in his seat.

'That's what I need to think out, Guv – like I say – I'm just getting me feet under the table.'

Skelgill inhales to present a further rejoinder, but DS Leyton interjects. He points an index finger vertically.

'I reckon maybe I can get a little bird to give the game away. It's just a feeling I've got. And what if it did bring me full circle to Billy Boothroyd?'

When hope might constitute a weak justification – intuition is a powerful tool when deployed against Skelgill – and he sits back and folds his arms. It is accurate to say that external information is what they need, and at this juncture they are at the mercy of others' whims. Counter to this, however, is the drumbeat of urgency that underlies his appreciation of the facts; Billy is living on borrowed time, and every day passing is another when he cannot enjoy what is rightfully his.

DS Jones appreciates her superior's dilemma.

'We are making good progress. It's quite possible that we'll have the names of Billy Boothroyd's relatives in the next couple of days. If there's a chance that more digging at the DWP will unearth a connection, surely it's worth giving it a bit longer? And – after all – we know that Billy's safe and in good hands with Nurse Ashanti.'

Skelgill glances at her from beneath lowered lids, his head tilted forwards; she makes a generous concession.

'Aye – I suppose it's not like someone's life's at risk.'

25. HARRIET ALOFT

Troughdale House, Whitehaven – 10.00 a.m. Wednesday 11 October

Harriet listens hard.

But rain has arrived and it's windy and tricky to hear.

The clang of the gates closing was muffled; she doubts she'd even detect the metallic sound that comes as a little early-warning before they reopen.

She gives it five minutes, remembering her rule for Jim, her late spouse.

She feels a little nauseous.

When she'd told Rina she didn't want her slimming session because she had a headache Rina had insisted she swallow two aspirin. They've never agreed with her stomach since she got an ulcer for taking too many when she had bad flu at university in Glasgow. It was before these modern drugs were commonplace in the supermarket. "Don't be surprised," one of her medical student friends had said, "It's salicylic acid – it attacks the lining of your intestines." Why do they ever sell it, then?

And Rina had looked like she didn't believe her. Which was awkward, because Rina was right to be suspicious, wasn't she? Over the course of a few days Rina has casually asked her some probing questions about last week – about how her fall could have happened – like whether she had been trying to get up to the toilet. Did she sleepwalk? Things like that.

Rina had looked strangely at Morten when she told him Harriet wasn't having her session.

Morten, however, had responded a little disdainfully – as if they'd been having a private argument, and he couldn't care less.

Harriet had said that at least they didn't need to worry about her – after last week's incident – and that Rina's appointment with the consultant was enough for her to have on her mind.

Morten had regarded her rather blankly. But if anything he has behaved more attentively in the past couple of days; asking her how she has been and whether she had suffered any ill effects from her ordeal with the slimming machine. One morning he'd knocked on her door and asked her to sign the draft tenancy agreement. He'd said it wasn't the final official document, but that it would cover her under Rina's landlord's insurance – just in case there were another accident – so that she, Harriet, could claim damages. Until, as they hoped, Harriet would go ahead with the purchase of the flat, and then she'd have her own insurance in place. He said her welfare was his number one concern.

Yesterday she had found him lying on the floor of her sitting room, working at the radiator with a spanner. He said he wasn't happy about the level of hot water reaching her flat – although it has seemed fine from the taps to her. And now he has said that while Rina's at the hospital he'll call in to her house to check everything's okay and pick up the paraffin heater he'd noticed last time. Then he'd get their shopping – and was there anything she especially wanted?

She had suggested that she would go to her house while they were away – that it made sense, rather than wait in on her own. But Rina had quickly said she shouldn't go out if she wasn't feeling well – what if it was something more serious coming on? And Morten had reminded her that there's a problem with her scooter – that he's noticed it doesn't seem to be charging properly. What if the battery went flat? To be stranded is bad enough, never mind in this weather. She should just stay and relax. He'd cooed, soothingly; those black eyes had reminded her of the snake in The Jungle Book cartoon film.

What they don't know – and this suggests they are unsuspecting – is that it has suited Harriet to be talked into remaining. This is the first opportunity since last Wednesday to do some more sleuthing. Now that she knows for sure there is sleuthing to be done.

Harriet glances down at her attire. In pink loungewear she doesn't look much like a sleuth – but then, if they came back, she wouldn't want to.

They've said they'll be at least an hour. Rina's got an outpatient's appointment at West Cumberland Hospital. It's only a five-minute drive – but they aways run late at these places – she thinks she has plenty of time.

She'll need some decent shoes if she's going to climb that ladder.

But it has to be done.

It is obviously where they – or Morten, at least – keep all of the materials, the mail and the admin and so on. Documents, certificates, statements. Evidence. Proof.

And she's going to need her phone to take pictures.

If she gets what she hopes for she could be out of here in a day or two. This whole charade could be over.

Her heart takes a little leap; though that is not the best thing.

If she gets what she hopes for she could leave directly – she could even take the originals and abscond before they get back. Head straight to the police. They'll have to believe her this time.

It depends what she finds.

She shudders.

There's the risk of being caught in the act.

Moreover, there's the problem of getting out of the 'compound' – as she has taken to calling the garden, with its seven-foot wall and electronic prison gates.

Though there is a ladder – she's seen Morten using it to prune Rina's roses.

Harriet thinks hard.

Maybe she should place the ladder ready?

Because what if she did decide to go this morning, and they return exactly as she is leaving? A sliding-doors moment that would not be good for her heart.

She should get over the wall at the rear of the house. Where they wouldn't see her.

If they came back in the car they'd enter through the front, or the kitchen door at the side.

That would give her time to escape – even though it won't be easy. Beyond the wall the hillside rises, a rough area of derelict orchard that must stretch to the main road to Workington.

She had better get moving; it will take her a few minutes.

She uses the wellingtons and an oilskin of Morten's by the kitchen door – it doesn't cover her adequately but it just about does the job. She finds the ladder where roses trail round the porch and she locates a likely spot, out of sight from the front, where one of the long curved coping stones is missing. The best means of egress will be through the French windows of Rina's treatment room.

She takes a long look at the ladder. It is aluminium; light enough. And surprisingly sturdy and rigid. She supposes if she could get on top of the wall, she could pull it up and then use it to descend on the other side.

She swallows – it reminds her of what is to come.

She returns via the kitchen door and replaces the wellies and the coat. Morten has already worn them this morning, so the fact of their being wet shouldn't be a giveaway.

She pads through to her flat and puts on trainers; not exactly her regular slippers – but she could say she had been trying out the little exercises that Rina has suggested to her.

She goes back to the kitchen and checks outside.

All is quiet in the driveway.

And once she is in the loft, she ought to be able to hear – these places generally have poor soundproofing.

She slips her phone into the hip pocket of her joggers.

Her heart is beating fast before she even sets foot on the stairs. She feels light-headed. She should have eaten some chocolate or biscuits for the sugar. And now her mouth feels dry and she realises she's hardly had a drink this morning, being too nervous to think about it. No breakfast. Just those confounded aspirins of Rina's.

But Harriet if she is anything is determined; you didn't get to be Chief Accountant at the council by being a shrinking violet. And she might be disoriented, but she forces her disoriented self to Morten's room and the foot of the ladder.

She sways a little as she grasps the nearest upright.

It is a challenge of an altogether higher order of magnitude.

Where the ladder at the back wall is a single piece, six foot – this one comprises three sections that fold away into the loft when they are shoved up with the hatch cover – and it must be eight or nine feet from the floor to the ceiling.

The contraption emits an ominous squeal as she steps upon it.

But she knows these things are designed to bear much more weight – big removal men who empty houses and heave heavy objects up into storage. She might be heavy, but she can't be that heavy.

Though it creaks and bends as she slowly ascends.

No wonder Morten leaves it open – he must think no one else would venture this way. And it probably suits him – she can see he's lazy, and the effort of folding it away, and then yanking it back down with the pole hook that's propped up by the bedroom door is probably something he can't be bothered with.

As her head and then shoulders rise up into the darkness of the loft, she stops.

There are two reasons for this, but she tells herself the priority is to get her bearings, to allow her eyes to become accustomed to the gloom.

Faint light emanates from the direction of what is the front of the house – it must be the roof-window where Morten has his study. Gradually she can make out what must be a partitioned-off section – not entirely right up to the roof itself – and a kind of walkway made of rough batons that leads over the exposed joists.

The loft gives the impression of being cavernous. In all other directions it disappears into blackness – but she can see enough to discern that the centre of the huge space is taken up by the brick chimney stacks that rise from the various rooms of the house and coalesce here into a single ten-foot-wide column of masonry. From the immediate surrounds she can see that the attic is not boarded; the gaps between the joists are filled with degenerated fibre insulation that is coated with thick dust and debris and cobwebs; balanced across the joists are piles of boxes and suitcases and dismantled furniture – bedheads, mattresses, blankets – nothing singular is large – but there wouldn't be anything like that – because the hatch opening is too wee.

And that is her real reason for stopping.

Is the hatch too wee?

As she takes another rung of the ladder she is met with the reality of this question.

Already she has been forced to turn sideways to fit her shoulders through.

Now there is pressure upon her torso; it tightens around her midriff like a hungry python.

Her progress is checked.

Panic strikes.

She begins to gasp.

The pulse in her temples becomes louder.

The pounding in her chest is becoming a pain.

She tries to descend.

But the python has her.

In a moment of clarity, she realises the chamfered decorative architrave has helped her squeeze through – but now the sharp angle of the rough-sawn inner frame is digging into her yielding flesh. It is like a lobster trap. And she must look puce like a cooked lobster.

The idea enrages her – the inner voice of determination cries out.

Heave-ho, Harriet!

Her body obeys – her legs pump, her elbows thrust – and she is free!

Inside.

She stands, panting, her feet still on the ladder, one arm around the closest timber strut.

She recovers her breath; gathers her wits.

No going back now.

Will she get back?

Don't think about it, Harriet.

No point thinking about it.

Do what there is to do, now you're here.

She clambers unsteadily onto the boardwalk, feeling for handholds above, bent for fear of protruding clout nails spiking her scalp.

She switches on the torch on her phone.

She can see more now – and the danger of a false step – she could fall through the ceiling – imagine if they came back to find her legs dangling through into Morten's or Rina's bedroom.

The boardwalk creaks and bends under her weight – but she makes it to what appears to be the door of a garden shed: vertical planks held by a zig-zag of boards, black T-hinges and a rim lock with a round handle. The key is in the keyhole. The door is unlocked.

She blinks as daylight floods over her.

The shed theme continues within. Rina had boasted of Morten's building of his "beautiful study". She has a mother's rose-tinted glasses. Morten is no carpenter, and a lazy craftsman to boot. The partitions are jerry-built, floorboards haphazardly nailed to vertical studs, themselves nailed askew to rafters, wherever he could find a point of anchor.

But it suffices, Harriet supposes. It sections-off a portion of the attic around the window, and it probably doesn't matter that the sides do not reach to the rafters, or have a myriad of gaps between the timbers – it does not have to be weatherproof and there is no sense of draughtiness. The floor is made of strips of chipboard, and partly covered by an old worn rug. The window is the Velux type, flush with the pitch of the roof. It is closed, though she can see it has a locking handle that can release a tilt mechanism. The glass is caked with grime, in keeping with the rustic condition of the booth.

The sound of the rain seems more intense. Perhaps it is because it streams down the window, obscuring any actual view; perhaps it has got heavier since she went outside.

Harriet stands for a moment and listens intently.

Would she hear them when they come back? The clang of the gates? The crunch of the tyres?

But she has to be out of here long before that.

Besides – she only needs a short while. If they are gone an hour, she's got a good thirty minutes in hand.

Beneath the window is a basic timber desk and on it an antiquated desktop computer.

She can see it is in standby mode. The keyboard is greasy. She

205

dabs at the space bar.

The screen lights up to reveal a pornographic website.

Harriet recoils.

But she can't switch it off – anything like that might give the game away. She'll have to wait until the screensaver comes on, or the computer goes back into sleep mode.

She averts her gaze. Beside the desk is a tall metal filing cabinet. There are four deep drawers with stickers on them, and initials in Morten's handwriting.

The very bottom one is "T.J."

Harriet pulls it open.

Inside hangs an array of suspension files separated by Crystal tabs, again labelled in Morten's distinctive spidery hand. The tabs are in alphabetic order, and the abbreviations include DWP, Lloyds, NS&I, Property, Stocks, and suchlike.

Harriet feels her pulse quickening once more – and it goes faster as she pulls out the first document, a letter from the Lloyds section dated only a few days ago.

Harriet begins taking photographs.

She works quickly, efficiently – she begins to get into a rhythm, a mechanical sequence of extracting and returning documents, photographing them in between, using the flash to make sure they are well illuminated and clearly legible. It reminds her of her days in the office, when she could process forms more quickly than anyone else. Her powers of concentration were always superior to those of her colleagues. She could shut out distractions – phones ringing, traffic noise, office chatter, doors opening.

Doors opening?

Harriet suddenly catches her breath.

Did she hear something?

Unnoticed by her, the rain has stopped.

She looks up – the vista is somewhat clearer – she can see the grey sky, occasional breaks in the scudding cloud that show a watery blue.

She leans close to the glass.

Below, there is a partial view – of the front wall, the gates, some of the rose beds and the lawn, and a section of the driveway.

And there is the back end of Morten's car.

Harriet turns in terror.

And then distant – from the darkness of the attic – from far below in the bowels of the house … a voice.

'Harriet? Harriet, dear – we're home!'

26. STORM BREWING

Bassenthwaite Lake – 5.50 p.m. Friday 13 October

Skelgill is not really fishing.

Just like he is not really getting anywhere with the case.

As he scowls discontentedly across the choppy waters of Bassenthwaite Lake he knows there are fish – thousands of fish – fishes, in fact. Dace, eel, minnow, perch, pike, roach, ruffe, trout, salmon, and the rare and elusive vendace – a few that spring to mind, to which he might turn his hand. But an answer to this conundrum he has been unable to discern.

The common strategy might be to go out with a rod, but the specific tactics vary as much as is revealed by comparison of the fishes themselves. Perch eat worms off the bottom; trout feed on flies hatching at the surface. Salmon don't feed at all; they bite only by instinct. It takes around one thousand minnows to make the weight of an average jill pike.

And with no clear objective in mind, progress is not possible. It is merely paying lip service to the task.

He has rigged up a spinning rod with four-pound line and a one-ounce silver toby. What logic there is guides him: it is too choppy for float fishing and the boat is shifting too much in the wind for ledgering on the bottom – it's Snag City down there, the rain has brought all manner of debris flooding down the Derwent in the past couple of days. He grimaces again. Even the toby is optimistic – the light is poor and fading fast – and fish might not have eyelids, but they cannot see in the dark.

But it gives him something to do.

For a man for whom *doing* is the modus operandi, *not* doing – waiting aimlessly – is anathema.

His colleagues see a paradox. He can concentrate for England when he knows what he is doing – or, rather, *why* he is doing it. A baited swim, clues gleaned from the elements and fine signs left by wildlife that reveal what species will be where, and when, and how they will behave. Waiting thus is purposeful. Waiting to strike. Waiting for the strands to intertwine, for the pieces of the jigsaw to click into place, for the emergent sun to transform a flat landscape into relief, shadow and highlight that reveal the weave of its fabric, the route to the summit, the path to progress.

And there is a second paradox nested within the first. 'Knowing' for him is not a standard that requires cognitive appreciation, a rationale that he could expound upon. It is grounded in intuition, gut feel that informs him he is moving in the right direction, just as surely as that same part of his anatomy tells him it is time for another bacon roll. But now, here, today, it is yet a level deeper – for, despite that it is something he knows in the usual way, equally it is something he does not want to acknowledge.

It is quite simple.

Billy.

A person might not visit a relative who suffers such a condition – unable to cope with the distress of seeing them like this – unable to process the metamorphosis. Unwilling to accept the reality. Rejecting the possibility of this being the lasting impression.

And there may be solace in that other members of the family can visit – who can cope.

While there is regret and guilt in being one who could not.

Skelgill blinks, several times.

He blinks away the shadow in the boat.

But he resolves – he must repaint the name on the prow.

The Doghouse.

It turns his mind to Billy. Not exactly the doghouse – that is a self-inflicted condition, merited by egoism or narcissism or selfishness, errant qualities of which Billy is plainly bereft, little though he can convey of his inner self. Billy is inherently kind and generous, if eccentric in the ways of the introvert.

Dead people's clothes.

It is strange that one small phrase – one aspect of which Billy

209

himself is totally unaware – is what most haunts Skelgill. It symbolises everything that has befallen Billy. The misdeeds of some (to be apprehended) and the failures of others, the police included (to be reprehended).

An all-consuming quest to restore dignity and see justice done.

This is why he is waiting; whatever the discomfort, it is a small cross to bear.

Skelgill sighs.

Even now, he is waiting for Nurse Ashanti.

Her text earlier had cheered him.

"Billy is good today. He has mentioned you. And the lake. Will you be fishing after dinner?"

By "mentioned you", Skelgill assumes *"Our O"*.

He wonders if she will come. Billy may have been good earlier – but he tires, naturally.

And the weather is hardly conducive. Blustery, with rain in the air, the charts show first a sequence of occluded fronts, predictable only in that they offer grey and damp – and a bigger storm to follow in a few days' time, the sting in the tail of a hurricane that has toured America's south, from Louisiana to Georgia, dropping in at Charleston, SC before taking off eastwards across the Atlantic.

He hears a text alert.

His first instinct is not to check the handset but to look up.

He half expects to see them, having emerged upon the ha-ha while he has been distracted.

The light is poor – sunset is around 6.20 p.m. – but the cloud cover advances dusk by a good hour.

In the gloom he spies a movement – but a mere shadow moving across a paler patch.

Is that Ashanti, checking that he is here? She, too, must doubt the rendezvous.

She could have stepped ahead to look for his boat – there is a tricky section passing through the rhododendrons where roots protrude and jam the wheels of the chair.

Nothing now.

Did he glimpse a human figure – or perhaps a roe deer, grazing the turf and now disturbed, slipping away?

He checks the text.

"Nearly there!"

And, sure enough, they appear.

Straightaway, Billy is waving. A curious urgency, in fact.

When Skelgill wades ashore, he sees the old man is more animated than usual. Though he does not now address Skelgill. Instead he glances about; there is something fearful in his manner.

Other than a greeting, Skelgill has not spoken – he looks expectantly at the nurse – but, though she smiles, her expression is resigned – that perhaps it is now too late in the day, that the best is past.

Skelgill tries some fishing chat, ruing his bad luck and blaming the weather – and bemoaning that Billy was not out there in the boat with him, to lend his knowledge. But to no avail.

'Thanks for coming, Dan.'

Ashanti turns from her charge to press a palm against Skelgill's flank.

'Aye, well – I said I would.'

The girl moves half a step closer.

'I thought you might have handed the case over.'

Skelgill jerks back his head.

'I'd come, any road – but what do you mean?'

His tone plainly surprises her; she withdraws her hand as if she suddenly feels a pang of guilt.

'Oh – there was a phone call – from another police officer.'

'DS Jones? Leyton?'

She looks anxious; the whites of her eyes gleam.

'He said his name was Detective Inspector Alexander Smart.'

'*Smart?*'

Now it is Skelgill who reaches out, to take hold of the other's arm.

'Yes – I think so.'

She is apprehensive, and he realises – and casually now he wheels away to stare out over the lake.

'It's probably no big deal. What did he want?'

His readjustment seems to calm her.

'He said it was just a routine call – that he was checking on the welfare of patients that had been dispersed from Belmont Manor – and asked about Billy.'

'What did he call him, as a matter of interest?'

'William Boothroyd.'

'And did he ask about anyone else?'

Nurse Ashanti looks momentarily perplexed, and shakes her head.

'No, he didn't. He just thanked me and rang off.'

Skelgill turns pensively.

'Would you recognise his voice?'

The girl sighs.

'Maybe. I'm not sure – it wasn't a very good line – it sounded like a mobile on hands-free, in a moving car, perhaps.'

'What about his accent?'

She remains doubtful.

'South of here.'

Skelgill grins wryly.

'There's most of England south of here.'

She extends her hands in a loose gesture.

'Well – it wasn't London. I would know that.'

Skelgill can at least find some consolation here, that DS Leyton is not up to some subterfuge – for he harbours vague suspicions in that department.

'Where's me shirt, our O – where's me shirt, for church?'

They each turn, having momentarily forgotten their charge.

Billy is grinning – but not looking their way – indeed, he has his eyes closed.

Rain is coming on.

Nurse Ashanti adjusts the rug over his knees.

'I should take him up.'

Skelgill nods.

'I'll give you a hand.'

'You needn't.'

But her tone is accepting.

'There's a tough bit through those bushes – you go first.'

At the main door there is a wheelchair ramp to one side of the steps. Skelgill halts and lays a palm on Billy's shoulder. He leans down to speak, though the man's head is lolled forwards and he appears to be sleeping.

'I'll see thee, Billy – soon as.'

'You're not going back out on the lake? It's almost dark – and this rain.'

Skelgill shrugs nonchalantly.

'It's my back yard. Plus my motor's on t' far bank.'

The nurse slides in front of him to take the handles.

'My shift ends shortly – my colleague Cara will see to Billy. Why don't we share an Uber – to your car?' She smiles engagingly, her face turned up to his. Her tight braids glisten as they catch the light of the porch. 'It's Friday night.'

Skelgill takes a half step backwards. Though it does not escape him that his car is parked conveniently outside The Partridge. And that he could easily drop her in Keswick. The row to Peel Wyke, into a gusting headwind, is not the most appealing option.

He contrives an expression of suitable reluctance.

'There's – there's summat I have to do.'

27. R FOR ROMEO

Police HQ – early evening – Friday 13 October

Skelgill has seen DI Alec Smart's latest flashy car in the parking area. Late on a Friday, when the cat is away, he doubts that he will find him in his office, diligently working at his computer.

He sticks his head around the door of the canteen. A group of uniformed constables break off from communal banter to look at him; at first surprised mid-laugh, their expressions collectively morph to that of respect – and then perhaps surprise again, when he retracts his head rather than strike a beeline for the counter.

Night has fallen, and along corridors he catches glimpses of himself reflected in black windows; a gaunt spectre in damp fishing gear, he probably looks like he has called in for some item he has forgotten.

Skelgill makes his way to the open-plan floor.

He sees DI Smart.

At once fawning and hubristic, he is perched, half-standing at DS Jones's desk, close beside its seated occupant, whose body language – to Skelgill's satisfaction, but also ire – is less accommodating of the exchange.

DI Smart's mustelid features reveal predatory intent – and, like the hunter, in turn always hunted, his small close-set eyes are quickly alert to Skelgill's presence. His minute reaction causes DS Jones to turn to see what distracts him. She plies Skelgill with a look of what might be relief, or exasperation – but it is certainly not an expression of complicity.

Skelgill, however, is focused upon DI Smart.

And his silent, relentless approach is sufficient to cause his opponent to stand upright, to take guard.

Nonetheless, he gets in the first thrust.

'Alright, cock? I didn't realise it was dress-down Friday. You're taking it a bit far, Skel. Are you being sponsored?'

His supercilious gaze appraises Skelgill's attire, while he absently preens the lapel of his designer jacket, and points the toe of a polished Chelsea boot. And he smirks confidingly at DS Jones, as if this is a private joke they share.

Skelgill does not attempt to parry the jibe, or even to issue a terse greeting.

'What's this about you phoning Duck Hall?'

DI Smart grins; he seems pleased with the question – as if he had feared far worse.

'I wouldn't know Duck Hall about it – *hah-hah-ha!*'

His cackle is self-congratulatory, and again he looks to enjoin DS Jones in his wisecrack.

Skelgill remains obdurate.

'You called them this morning, asking about the patient in the case we're investigating.'

Skelgill now senses that DS Jones reacts – looking at him and then at DI Smart. But he keeps his glare trained upon the latter.

'I reckon you need a quiet word with your supergrass, Skel. I've never heard of Duck Hall and if I had I wouldn't waste my time on your wild-goose chase.' He casts a bony hand to indicate loosely about their environs. 'Why would I want to be the laughing stock of the station? *Ha!* Duck Hall and wild geese – sounds about right for you!'

He stands smug and smirking, plainly believing that DS Jones can only be impressed by his incisive repartee.

For Skelgill there is the dual frustration of being thwarted and humiliated – and, make that treble, the rising realisation that he has started a fight he cannot win: that the sight of DI Smart at DS Jones's side inflamed better judgement, and has led to rash action and exposed flanks.

Words have dried up on his lips.

Now he would far rather punch his antagonist than interrogate him further.

But DI Smart's greatest instinct is for self-preservation. It is Mother Nature's most valuable gift; a maxim of Falstaff, champion of cowards: the better part of valour is discretion.

Theatrically, DI Smart makes a conciliatory bow.

'I don't know what you're up to, Skel – but you've got it wrong this time. Still, it's your funeral, cock. Let's see what the Chief's got to say on Monday.'

He leans towards DS Jones and extends a closed hand – it would appear to perform a parting fist-bump.

DS Jones does not move – and contrives to look like she does not understand what she is expected to do.

With a click of his heels, DI Smart spins around – as if he has not tried the act – and departs with an affected swagger, the hand now raised with its fingers split into a V-sign, as though it is a secret signal.

'Catch you later, Emma.'

Skelgill watches DI Smart's departure. It seems he has singled out a pair of female DCs in his own team, seated across the room. Skelgill's features are creased with distaste.

'Howay, lass – let's get out of here.'

DS Jones is eager to learn more – but she does not know what getting out entails. It could be anywhere between Skelgill's office and the pub – or even a riverbank. She quickly gathers up her laptop and some papers, and reaches for her jacket.

'Actually, Guv – is there a chance we can use the big screen upstairs? Just for a few minutes. There are some things that have come through that it would be useful to look at.'

Perhaps to her surprise, Skelgill does not demur.

'Aye – if they've not changed the code.'

They enter the lift, and when the door closes, DS Jones regards her superior inquiringly.

'Ashanti took a call from Smart – asking about patients sent from Belmont Manor – specifically a William Boothroyd. Then rang off.'

DS Jones hesitates for a moment, her large hazel eyes unblinking.

'Remember – social services told us they had received an email from DI Smart – a year or more ago.'

Skelgill nods, perhaps a little unconvincingly.

'Those details, Guv – he'd be able to get them from what we've posted on the internal system. He might just be covering his tracks. He let the case lapse and now he's worried it will come back to bite him.'

Skelgill grimaces, as though variously conflicted. He does not seem entirely happy with this theory.

But when he speaks it is in less cerebral terms.

'That's not all that'll bite him.'

DS Jones appears to see some attraction in the notion, but equal jeopardy.

'It would need to look like self-defence.'

A growl escapes Skelgill's throat.

'That's the trouble, lass – how could lamping Smart ever constitute self-defence?'

Timeously, the lift door slides open – and they become distracted by the task of cracking the coded lock of Room 101.

The most recent user has left the projector switched on, and DS Jones's laptop immediately displays its interrupted subject on the wall-mounted screen.

'Did you know you can go back in time with Google Maps?'

Skelgill, inevitably at the windows trying to discern anything in the rainy blackness, swings round, his interest piqued.

DS Jones indicates to the screen.

'This is Bull Furlong Lane, just over two years ago.'

The image is a brick-built bungalow, face on. It is not in great repair, and the garden is unkempt. Unappealing curtains are drawn at one window, half-drawn at the other. Paint peels from the front door at the centre, with junk mail sticking out of the letter flap. Frankly, it looks unoccupied.

Skelgill notes willowherb mostly gone to seed; it tells him this was probably late August.

'This is Billy Boothroyd's house – the one that was demolished.'

Skelgill nods.

'It's the same boundary wall – and that scraggy laburnum.'

DS Jones begins to manipulate the viewing position.

'But, look – if you approach from an angle. There's a For Sale sign.'

Skelgill steps closer.

She zooms in.

'See – it's a mobile number. Most likely the one that the McClays mentioned.'

Skelgill turns to her and inhales to speak – but she pre-empts him, raising her mobile handset.

'I called it – I withheld my number, naturally.'

Skelgill waits.

'It's active – it rang out – and no voicemail. I checked on the national register – it's a pay-as-you go supermarket provider – no contract. Possibly a burner phone.'

Skelgill weighs the likelihood. He nods pensively.

'If it were a bona fide estate agent – they'd have a proper number – public. And an answering service. Why miss a sale?'

'It certainly doesn't come up on any search. But I suppose it could have been that Billy had a phone.'

'But more likely the bloke that chucked the sign into the garden.'

DS Jones nods.

'We could get it tracked. It will take a few days to organise. It might lead us to the person we're looking for.'

Skelgill regards his colleague doubtfully. They both know that a cheap handset can only be geolocated by trigonometry, to an approximate position between three cell towers. Usually corroborating surveillance is needed – such as an unmarked police car following a suspect, or eyewitness testimony that they have entered a property and then moved to another.

But DS Jones makes a good point.

'At least it would tell us whereabouts in the country he is. That he's in Cumbria, or otherwise.'

'Aye.' Skelgill nods methodically. 'We should probably give it a go.'

He looks at his watch. It is not so difficult to read his thoughts, and DS Jones moves swiftly to leave the internet and open her mail app.

'Also – the Land Registry title search finally came through for the farm cottages. That was just before DI Smart came up to my desk. I only glanced at it. It looks pretty massive – loads of attachments. Not surprising, I suppose, given the age of the property – over two hundred years, according to the datestone at the gable end.'

Skelgill has remained standing thus far, and is shifting slowly from one foot to the other.

'Guv – should we have a quick look?'

He makes a face that tries for reproach but largely fails.

'Happen if we don't do it now you'll be clicking away at midnight.'

DS Jones wastes no time; her manicured nails get to work on the keys.

'Actually – look – the files are dated. That's helpful. The McClays said Billy's sister's family moved away in the Seventies. And –'

She clicks on an attachment that includes the numerals 1976.

It is a deed of conveyance exchanging title from a previous to a new owner.

'Oh, wow. This could be it.'

Her eyes devour the opening paragraphs – and her voice takes on a note of urgency.

'This deed conveys title to a Mr Stanley Bloxham. From 1966 to 1976 title was vested in Mr Bryan J. Romeo.'

'Romeo?'

Skelgill's rendition of the surname is sceptical.

'That must be the husband, Guv. Therefore the son's surname. Billy's nephew.'

A few seconds of silence ensue, before DS Jones speaks again.

'He ought to be easy to find – it can't be a common surname. And if he is Owen, that's not exactly a common a first name, either.'

Skelgill seems to harrumph.

'Sounds made up, to me.'

But DS Jones is busy on the search engine.

'Romeo – surname. Most frequent in Italy. Then the USA. Fewer than five hundred in Britain and Ireland.'

'That's still quite a few.'

219

She shoots him a sideways glance, and affects a frown.

'It could have been Jones.'

'Aye – we wouldn't want that.' Skelgill is forced to grin.

'I'll get DC Watson to run it through the databases we can access. I guess we'll have to wait until Monday, though – she's got all the necessary log-in approvals for this case. There can't be many in Cumbria.'

'We don't know they're in Cumbria.'

DS Jones taps the tips of her fingers together, and then resumes typing. Skelgill watches her progress on the big screen.

She enters "Owen Romeo Cumbria".

The result is not entirely promising – although the search engine finds a paragraph that contain this combination of words: a wooden sculpture in Grizedale Forest that at least causes Skelgill to narrow his eyes.

Seeing his interest, DS Jones makes a conversational aside.

'Where is Grizedale Forest? Isn't that near St Sunday Crag?'

'Nay, that's Grisedale with an S. There's no connection – apart from they both mean wild boar valley. Grizedale Forest's over by Hawkshead – Beatrix Potter country.'

DS Jones tries other combinations of words, but the presence of "Romeo" in the search box stubbornly brings up a series of Shakespearean actors with Owen for either a first or second name.

She sees that Skelgill is staring with a glazed expression – he might well be revisited by thoughts of DI Smart's jibe of a wild-goose chase.

But just as she is about to offer a consoling opinion, he blurts out a phrase.

'Try angling.'

'Guv?'

'Put the word "angling" into the search – with Romeo.'

She obliges, albeit seems a long shot.

'Looks like it's a popular name for a boat. Should we call it a day?'

'*Wait.*'

Now it is Skelgill's tone that is urgent.

'That last one – see – the proprietor's name.

DS Jones moves the cursor to rest upon the bottom line.

It reads: "Red Herring Deep Sea Angling. Nantucket, Mass. Prop: Eoin Romeo."

'That's USA, Guv.'

Skelgill seems undeterred.

'Aye – but what's that name?'

DS Jones frowns, now for real.

'You mean E-O-I-N? Isn't that another spelling of Ian?'

Skelgill does not immediately answer. Then he turns and casts an open palm at her keyboard.

She types.

'Oh, no – it's Gaelic – oh –'

Now they are both looking at the big screen, each slightly open-mouthed.

The entry she has found illuminates: *"Eoin. Same as Owen. Phonetically: O-in."*.

It would be fair to say that spines tingle.

DS Jones clicks back on the link, and reaches for her mobile phone.

Skelgill crowds her, leaning with two hands on the table, his head cocked to one side.

There is the unfamiliar American ringing tone, with its single burrs and long intervals.

They start simultaneously when the recipient picks up – but it has diverted to voicemail.

Unlike the burner phone however, there is a greeting, a male voice.

'Hey, you've reached Red Herring Deep Sea Angling, Number One in Nantucket. Sorry we can't take your call. We're all at sea at the moment –' (a self-deprecating laugh) ' – and out of cell phone range – but we'll be back in on the afternoon tide. Please leave a message after the tone. Thanks for your interest.'

The unfamiliar accent might be American – some eastern seaboard brogue – but, then again, it might not.

DS Jones reaches to end the call – it seems rational that they should gather their wits and make a plan. But Skelgill gently intercepts her at the wrist, and bends even closer. He intones calmly.

'Good afternoon. A message for Mr Romeo. If the name Foster's Pond means anything to you, would you please call me back as soon as possible. I am DI Skelgill from Cumbria Police in the UK.'

He relays a number – one that has DS Jones looking a little baffled – and now ends the call.

He turns and reaches for his jacket from the back of a chair.

'Howay, lass – time and tide wait for no man.'

28. RED HERRING

The Partridge – late evening – Friday 13 October

The Snug to themselves, Skelgill and DS Jones have prime position beside the fire. Skelgill is taking his time over a pint, and his companion, though not driving, has opted for now for tonic water. Skelgill occasionally prods at a log in the grate with the toe of his boot; there is an optimum state of affairs, but wood is not well seasoned at this time of year, and fine streams of steam protest as they escape the xylem; though it is a reassuring susurration when irregular gusts of wind rip at the surrounding trees and hurl sheets of rain against the old walls. The old walls – they have seen it all before; they have withstood a thousand gales and are good to withstand a thousand more. Their masons built them so diligently that four centuries later they even provide sanctuary from the mobile phone signal.

Ordinarily a feature Skelgill turns to his advantage, now the unfamiliar number he left in his message is explained to his colleague. It is that of The Partridge. And, alongside their drinks and empty packets of salted peanuts, on their table rests a handset belonging to the hostelry. Landlord Charlie is briefed to expect an international call.

Skelgill has determined that the flood tide at Nantucket Boat Basin makes highwater at just before 9 p.m. Greenwich Mean Time, minus five for Massachusetts.

Why wait in the office? Or some other location that puts them at the mercy of the unreliable mobile signal in these parts. And, if the call does not come, well – it is Friday night and they are in the pub.

A sigh breaks their silence.

Cleopatra, collected en route from her minder, always enjoys a sojourn to the old coaching inn. This evening the warming hearth makes a welcome addition to the regular snacks.

But perhaps she detects that there is tension in the air. It might be Friday night, and her human companions might be in the pub – but there is no disguising that they are a little on edge. If their search proves correct, the call when it comes could be a game changer. But there is a double jeopardy. Professional angler Eoin Romeo's connection to Billy Boothroyd may be blood relative – and also bloodsucker.

They shall have to caw canny.

As further proof of her sixth sense, Cleopatra lifts her head.

The handset rings.

Charlie has been briefed to put it through directly.

Skelgill stabs a finger at the button that activates the loudspeaker.

'DI Skelgill.'

There is a moment's delay as photons traverse the ocean bed, a six-thousand-mile round trip.

'Oh, how-do, officer. I just listened to your voicemail. This is Eoin Romeo from Red Herring Deep Sea Angling.'

It is the same voice as the recorded greeting – but surely now it sounds more British. Even the subtle hey/how-do shift. For his surname he stresses the middle syllable, as in *mayo*. Eoin, he most definitely pronounces as *Owen*.

Skelgill leans closer to the handset, his features strained. It is the look of a Skelgill that plays a fish on a barbless hook or an understrength line. There can be many a slip twixt cup and lip.

He dispenses with any formalities.

'Sir, do you have a relative by the name of William Boothroyd?'

'Uncle Billy? Oh, my – is he – is he okay?'

The response sounds grounded in authentic concern.

The detectives exchange wide-eyed glances. This is their man.

'Mr Romeo, I have a colleague with me – DS Jones – we've got you on speaker. We have a few questions.'

'Sure.'

Even in the single word there is the impression that the man is bracing himself for bad news.

DS Jones gets straight to the point.

'Mr Boothroyd is in a nursing home in our area. He is being well cared for. He is suffering from dementia. As part of a wider investigation he has come to our attention. We are trying to understand his circumstances.'

The man audibly releases a breath. 'Oh. Oh – I see.' Now his inflexion conveys puzzlement – but perhaps also a hint of remorse.

'Sir, when did you last see him or have contact with him?'

There is some hesitation.

'Well – I haven't really seen him properly for decades. The last time in the flesh was briefly at my mother's funeral. That would be eleven – no twelve – years ago. He couldn't stay long or attend the wake – he has a medical condition that embarrasses him.'

'What about other forms of contact? Mail or telephone? Online?'

'I don't know if he had a phone and I'd doubt he was ever internet literate.' Now there is another pause for thought. 'We produce a calendar – here at Red Herring – Catch of the Month. We mail it to our clients and friends instead of a Christmas card. I always send one to Uncle Billy. But you make me realise – I don't think we've had a card in return for a couple of years. I feel remiss in not making more effort to get in touch. I've kind of assumed that if he needed some help from me he'd holler, as they say over here.'

'To which address do you send the calendar?'

'To his home address – it's Bull Furlong Lane, Middlemarch.'

'Would I be correct in saying that is where you used to live?'

'Yes – right opposite. Until I was eighteen. I grew up there. In fact my Dad's job relocated to Croydon just before my final year at school. I didn't want to leave all my mates – so I actually moved in with Uncle Billy and my Nanna – Nanna Boothroyd.'

DS Jones glances at Skelgill. He nods, and leans in to speak.

'Sir, I mentioned Foster's Pond in the voicemail. That was a place Mr Boothroyd has spoken of – and we believe he refers to you.'

The man murmurs – there is an undertone of nostalgia and warmth.

'Uncle Billy – he was like a second father when I was a kid. My

Dad was away a lot with work. I was mad on fishing – and Uncle Billy used to take me – especially when I was younger and Mum worried about me being on my own near deep water. Just to the local spots we could walk to – nothing spectacular. Foster's Pond was one of them – actually it was private.' He laughs.

'What is it, sir?'

'Well – I don't know if you've worked it out. My mother's side of the family, the Boothroyds, they're from Liverpool. They moved down to the Midlands after the war, for work in the hosiery. It was one of Billy's jokes – that in Liverpool "Private Property – Keep Out" meant help yourself – you know, keep *owt?*'

Skelgill grins – he approves of the vernacular and the sentiment chimes with his own less-than-saintly boyhood exploits, such as where fruit orchards and keep out signs were concerned.

'As a matter of interest, sir – what does he call you?'

'Oh – it's always been *Our O.*'

'Aye – we've had a bit of a job getting from there to your actual name.'

Eoin Romeo gives an apologetic cough.

'There's Irish ancestry in my mother's family. I think she was determined to offset the Italian connection on my father's side. It made life interesting for me at school, I can tell you.'

Skelgill pauses, his features pensive. Thus far, the man has been unguarded in his responses. He looks at DS Jones, as if to canvass her opinion in this regard – but in the small hiatus the man speaks again.

'Is my Uncle Billy okay – I mean – is there anything I can do? Could I phone him or something – a video call?'

When Skelgill does not answer, DS Jones responds.

'That might certainly be welcomed, sir. He is confused, however. In the first instance, you can help most just by assisting us with some background information. You said that, other than briefly at your mother's funeral, you haven't seen your uncle for decades?'

'That's right. To cut a long story short. I got a place at St Andrews University in Scotland to study Marine Biology and met a girl from Nantucket. I'd never heard of the place – I'd never been out of Britain. But we took a trip to see Lizzie's folks after we graduated – they ran a guest house and we helped out. We married and here I still am. Lizzie took over the B&B and I set up the fishing business in the early Eighties. Now I'm close on retirement – if it weren't for the hit of Covid and the price of gas – I'd probably have my feet up with a fishing rod in more benign surroundings. It can get pretty hairy out there, off Cape Cod.'

Skelgill shifts in his seat – plainly he is tempted to digress, perhaps to suggest Foster's Pond, Massachusetts. He emits a growl of agreement – but the man continues.

'Sorry – I'm going round the houses. To answer your question fully – since my folks were in South London, close to Heathrow, we literally made flying visits to them. There never seemed to be time to get back up to the Midlands. Besides, my old schoolmates were dispersed about the country, some beyond.'

DS Jones moves quickly on.

'Sir, are you aware that your uncle's Bull Furlong Lane property was sold over a year ago?'

'Oh – no, I'm not. But – I suppose – as you say, he's moved into a care home. It's expensive, of course.'

DS Jones seems to know to wait. The silence is awkward – but perhaps Eoin Romeo also understands it is for his benefit.

'Naturally, officers, you've got me wondering what he's doing in Cumbria. And – well, frankly – the fact that the police are involved.'

DS Jones flashes a brief glance at Skelgill. She continues evenly.

'Do you know of any family connections in Cumbria?'

'I don't – no, none at all. I mean – obviously – he's originally from Liverpool – but that's still a good way off. As I said – the family line goes quite quickly back to Ireland. But – now I think about it –'

Evidently he does pause to think.

'Sir?'

'Well, to be honest, I would have expected the polar opposite – literally. Because I remember at my mother's funeral there was mention of him moving south to Cornwall.'

'Why Cornwall, sir?'

'My aunt lives there – my Auntie Rina. She's Uncle Billy's youngest sister – though I suppose she would be in her late seventies, now. I remember thinking it would have made sense, as he got older, to live near to her.'

'And is she still alive, sir?'

There is another moment's hesitation.

'To be honest, I've never really had much to do with her family. They lived in a village a few miles away. I know that Rina split up with her husband – he was Clyve Jenner – and she moved away somewhere. Though I don't think that was initially to Cornwall. I've got Leamington in the back of my mind. In fact, I think they moved round quite a bit. But they ended up in Cornwall, I'm pretty sure of that.'

DS Jones has listened carefully.

'She split up from her husband – but you say *they?*'

'Auntie Rina's son – my cousin, Morten Jenner – he lived with her, as far as I know. My mother told me Rina ran some sort of beautician's business from home – I think maybe he helped her with the financial side. I've also got a vague notion that he was ill – or was partially disabled, or something like that.'

'What age would this Morten Jenner be?'

'Well – younger than me – somewhere in his fifties, I guess.'

'Okay. We might like to trace them. Can I just check the spelling of their names – is Rina short for something?'

'No, it's just Rina – I've never heard any different. R-I-N-A. And M-O-R-T-E-N. Jenner with two Es and two Ns.'

DS Jones breaks out of shorthand for a moment.

'Do you have any idea of whereabouts in Cornwall they might be living?'

Eoin Romeo gives a tut of self-reproach.

'I'm afraid not, officer. You make me think I've not done a good job of keeping up family connections. I suppose I relied on my mother as the main conduit for news. And then I've got three female cousins on my Dad's side whose parents emigrated to Australia. We were bosom chums as small kids – but I've not set eyes on them since schooldays. One of them got in touch about the family tree a few years ago – we exchanged a few emails, but it kind of fizzled out. Your life fills up – Lizzie and I have raised five kids of our own. I guess that's my excuse.'

DS Jones waits for a moment before she continues.

'We received a report that Mr Boothroyd was initially admitted to hospital when his wife died.'

'What? *Wife?* No – that can't be right – he was a confirmed bachelor. I can't imagine he hooked up with someone in his eighties. The middle part of his life, he was a full-time carer for my Nanna.'

'Is it possible that he was living with your aunt and she was mistaken for his wife?'

It is evident from his delayed reply that Eoin Romeo is unconvinced by the suggestion.

'Well – that sounds more likely – I suppose a neighbour who didn't know any better could assume something of the sort. But –'

'Sir?'

'Well – I know I've just said I've had little contact with my extended family – but, if Rina had died, I think someone would have tracked me down to let me know.'

DS Jones presses on.

'Okay. Just for completeness, we have Bryan J Romeo for your father's name. What did the initial stand for, and was your mother called?'

'My Dad's middle name was James. He died a year before my Mum. She was Joy – just Joy.'

At this juncture the man might just choke a little. They hear him swallow.

DS Jones glances at Skelgill before she poses her next question.

'Did your mother grow roses? Your uncle has mentioned a blue rose.'

Again it seems he needs to manage his emotions.

'She did – that's right. I mean – she was no great horticulturalist – but she hailed from humble beginnings – a rented back-to-back in a tough part of Liverpool. Cheap wellies for shoes and an outside toilet and a postage stamp of a brick back yard. I think it was a dream come true when she married Dad and they eventually bought the cottage – and she had her own garden. There was a nursery in the village – the whole area was market gardens and smallholdings. She managed to buy a rare blue rose and had it in pride of place at the front. Sadly it died – and Uncle Billy always swore that some jealous neighbour must have poured weedkiller on it.'

Skelgill has been listening and taking occasional sips of his beer. He leans forwards at this juncture.

'When we spoke to your uncle's former neighbours, they mentioned he was interested in horse racing.'

The man's voice picks up.

'That's right – it was his lifelong passion. He'd spend hours studying form in a little room at the back of the bungalow. I used to creep round and tap on the window so as not to disturb Nanna. He always wore one of those green visors like telegraph operators in the old movies. He was striving for the perfect system to beat the bookies. He would tell me about it at great lengths – but I must admit – I was just a kid, and it mostly went over my head.'

'Did it ever put a strain on his finances? There's not many gamblers that do beat the bookies.'

'I reckon he operated within his means. And to be honest I think he was pretty good. He always gave great tips for the National. I don't recall he ever lost his shirt.'

'Your uncle doesn't say much – but he seems to have a catchphrase along such lines, *where's me shirt?*'

Now Eoin Romeo chuckles heartily.

'That's right – *where's me shirt, for church?* Actually it was a bit of a family joke – among the Scousers. They knew they all sounded different to the locals, and they'd exaggerate their accents at family gatherings. *Come 'ed, Our O – have a splash of whiskey in your Coke.*'

The man performs a convincing rendition of the Mersey brogue, imbuing the famous beverage's brand name with all manner of improbable lenition.

Skelgill develops the point.

'Your uncle – according to official records – is William Boothroyd. But we noticed he didn't seem to respond to the name William.'

'Well – I can explain that. He never was William. That was my grandfather – his Dad. So he was always called Billy.'

Skelgill is nodding. He is evidently growing increasingly relaxed as regards the suspicions they have properly harboured over the bona fides of their transatlantic interviewee.

'Aye – we were coming round to that way of thinking. But we've still not bottomed what he's doing in Cumbria. He was first admitted to hospital in Kendal. All they had was William, and no surname.'

He leaves the matter open to conjecture.

'Officer, I take it you wouldn't be asking me if you had some local point of contact. Is it conceivable that he sold up and moved – maybe into lodgings?'

Skelgill gives a nod to his colleague, indicating she should proceed.

'Sir, the reports of his medical condition – the advanced state of dementia – would militate against that possibility. We have reason to believe there could be another party involved.'

DS Jones stares unblinking at the handset. They have revealed something of their hand.

But Eoin Romeo is quick on the uptake.

'Do you suspect that some kind of malfeasance is at play?'

DS Jones is careful in her reply.

'We have to consider all possibilities. Especially an elderly person, vulnerable to financial exploitation.'

'That would be bloody awful.'

29. HARRIET HOPES

Troughdale House, Whitehaven – morning – Saturday 14 October

Harriet prays for rain. On the face of it, it is an unusual thing for a person to do in Cumbria, where it rains every other day; and she an expat Scot, at that. But she has not had a drink since yesterday evening.

When it rains she can collect run-off in the old kettle she has found. There is a rusted cast-iron pipe that passes briefly through the roof space and out via a hole in the soffit to join up with the main downspout on the outside rear wall of Troughdale House. It has a crack big enough in which to insert the spout of the kettle and divert some of the flow, albeit at a miserly trickle.

It also serves for disposal. Though there has not been a lot of need in that department.

As if on cue, Harriet suffers a bout of stomach cramps.

She is lacking her medication; her heart pills, her gastric capsules, the tablets for diabetes – although high blood sugar is not a problem right now.

She needs food – but she needs water first.

Next time it rains, she'll not rest until she has completely filled the cauldron that was among the crate of greasy pots and pans.

She sighs. How can it take so long to rain again?

Perhaps it rained last night. Was it night?

At least, while she had slept.

It had felt a long sleep – she was surprised at that, when she woke.

Perhaps it was the hunger, the thirst – they have made her weak.

Or the suffocating airlessness.

The only draught seems to follow the slam of a door downstairs, a pressure wave that must roll up through the hatch.

The hatch.

She has the hatch to contend with.

It might as well be a hundred feet up – or nailed down – as much use as it is.

She shifts position, slowly, so as to be silent.

The bed she has made, out of bedheads, an ironing board and some loose planks laid across the joists, with a mattress on top, is more comfortable than the bed in her flat. There is no shortage of blankets, for warmth, and to serve as pillows.

She realises now how convicts can make their cells habitable, and contrive improvised tools and dig improbable tunnels: when endless time is on your side, you can get a lot done slowly.

Now, she lies supine.

Thinking.

It is not quite pitch dark, and her eyes have become accustomed to the perpetual gloom.

At first, she'd had the torch on her phone.

She tries to swallow; her mouth is so dry; her throat feels like it is lined with sandpaper.

Almost immediately, Rina had rung her – luckily Harriet had kept her phone set to silent.

When she'd turned it off she'd realised it was on 1% – the battery was drained by all the flash photography. And when she'd tried to switch it back on later it was dead.

On tiptoes, she'd searched for a charger in Morten's cabin.

She'd found a plug bank with lots of wires – indeed, even a phone charger – but it did not fit her handset.

She ponders.

Her first reaction, upon hearing them return early from the hospital and her house, had been that she must get down and out onto the landing.

It might have seemed that she was in a peculiar part of the house – but she would have thought of something. She could have said she'd heard a noise – it sounded like an intruder – and that she went upstairs to investigate.

But she couldn't fit through the hatch.

She knew it. She'd known it all along.

In fact, she was lucky they didn't find her stuck there.

She has grazes all round her midriff, from her abortive attempt to get through – but even gravity was not enough – and she had been forced to return to the loft.

She was fortunate. When they began to search, their first thought had been that she had left the house.

Despite her panic and struggles, through the uninsulated roof she had heard Morten's voice calling Rina from the back garden. He had obviously scouted round outside and found the ladder.

And she still has that in her column.

Morten obviously does not think she could have got into the loft. Nor, had she somehow achieved the improbable feat, that she could possibly be hiding up here.

About an hour after they had returned, Morten had climbed up to the attic.

By then, she had found this spot, away in the darkness of the huge space, behind the great bulk of the chimney stacks. It is completely out of sight; even had he shone a torch – and not easy to get to – it had required careful picking of a route through the junk and bric-a-brac and heaps of boxes and trunks – treading so carefully on the joists.

The spot where she has since made her camp.

At first she had crouched, frozen, under a blanket between crates behind the chimney stack, on an upturned bagatelle board, praying it would hold her weight. She had felt like a down-and-out sheltering in a shop doorway.

He had not acted like he thought she was there.

He had gone straight into his cabin. And though he had begun by opening and closing drawers of the filing cabinet, it became clear that after a short while he took to watching pornography on his computer.

He has been up to do that a few more times, since.

Harriet has listened to the graphic audio track reluctantly, and to the sounds of Morten with distaste. She would prefer to plug her ears – but she has decided that she cannot risk not knowing what is going on.

She wonders if Rina knows what else Morten does in the attic.

He brings chocolate – but so far she has only found the wrappers; her stomach has protested as she has heard him feasting greedily, sucking and slobbering like some vampire that returns to his lair with his unconscious prey, draining them of their lifeblood.

She has worked out that her spot is above the empty bedroom stuffed with furniture – the one so full that it is unlikely anyone will enter. So the odd creak she might make if she turns in her sleep should go undetected.

Shortly after they had first arrived back Harriet had overheard a vitriolic row.

Morten had raged at Rina.

He told her she should have stayed. That he didn't need her at Harriet's house. He could have found everything he wanted. She should have waited to watch over Harriet, instead of circling like a vulture over her possessions.

They had sworn and cursed at each other. It had sounded like they almost came to blows.

But the long and short of it, is that they believe she has gone over the wall, defeated what they thought was the Harriet-proof compound. And even that she must have lowered herself down somehow on the other side, though she doesn't see how she could ever have performed such a feat without taking the ladder.

But Morten has been leaving open the hatch, and the door of his cabin unlocked.

After her 'escape' there had been an uncanny, almost silent hiatus.

There was the sense that they had hunkered down.

They had expected the worst.

But, after a couple of days, when no one had come, their movements and behaviour had returned to normal.

She had eavesdropped upon a further conversation they had in the hall below the landing.

Rina had suggested that Harriet might have forgotten to take her medication and that she had wandered off in a state of confusion. All of her pills were still in her bathroom cabinet. She said she'd checked Harriet's wardrobe, and as far she could tell, Harriet had gone in just a tracksuit. What if Harriet had fallen into a ditch or down an embankment? How long would a person survive without food and water?

Morten had answered cruelly – he said he didn't think food was the issue.

Harriet's heart had taken a great leap, right up into her throat, when Rina had said what if she went up into your loft, Morten? Before she left?

But from Morten's response, Harriet realised that this was Rina being sly, trying to quiz Morten about his private affairs. He'd replied what if she did go up – why would she want to? What difference would that make?

He had called Rina's bluff, and she had backed off the subject.

Morten had persisted, however. He said Harriet could never climb up there – that she'd break the ladder – that they'd find her wedged in the hatch.

How close they came.

Morten had sworn, and called her Humpty-expletive-Harriet.

Curiously, Rina had rallied to her defence. She'd said people can't help their natural weight, Morten.

Morten had scoffed, he'd said that it's called will power, Rina – that he didn't force feed himself with jam doughnuts.

Rina had pointed out that he likes chocolate – and that he metabolises it. Most people *store* surplus calories. It's natural – so when we were cavemen we could survive days on end in winter with no food.

Rina had suggested that Harriet must have walked back to her house – but Morten answered that they had driven home that way – they would have seen her.

Rina had countered that Harriet could have got an Uber – that her phone was gone, and it had rung out the first time, hadn't it?

Morten had pondered, and had decided he would drive round that night, to see if there were any lights on. But he doubted it. He told Rina that Harriet hadn't taken her keys, or her handbag.

Rina had been quiet for a few moments.

Harriet sighs.

Harriet had realised quite soon that she was compromised.

She could have phoned the police, while she had the chance –

while she had some battery power.

But she had been too panic-stricken to think clearly at first. She was terrified that she might be about to have a heart attack or a stroke or a seizure – and, anyway, what if it had gone wrong?

She had envisioned a scenario where the police came to the door – but perhaps only to the gates – and that Morten and Rina had fobbed them off – concocted a story that it was just Rina who had phoned – they'd had a family row and now they were fine – she could have pretended to be Harriet – Harriet knows she would have done that.

And then they would have come for her.

Morten would have come for her.

Harriet knows this for sure.

Because she knows what she has seen – what she has read and photographed.

And Morten would know.

Harriet ponders, staring up into the darkness where the clout nails protrude through the wooden decking like rows of vicious teeth, like she is inside the gullet of some great predator, the prongs all angled backwards to prevent her escape.

Harriet knows too much.

She decides – for the time being at least – that she should hide her phone.

She may not make it out, but one day the evidence might.

They've been keeping her as a de facto prisoner as it is.

Now they would never let her go free.

Prisoner is the best she could expect.

And she fears it would be much worse than that.

She inhales sharply, only partially managing to suppress a great shudder.

Her mouth is so dry.

She decides to think over her plan once again.

It is the best form of distraction.

Hope springs eternal.

She has to wait for them to go out.

She thinks she would hear Morten's car.

She could tiptoe to his cabin and peer through the glass when she hears the engine.

She is fairly sure she heard him go out yesterday. Was it yesterday? Was that Friday? She should have made score marks on one of the beams.

But it is not possible to discern who is in the car, even if she got to the window in time to see it leave.

For a while, when Morten went out, she thought Rina had gone with him, until she heard her voice. She was speaking to a client.

Harriet had thought about crying out for help. But what if the client didn't hear – or only heard vaguely? Again, Rina would brass it out. Then Harriet would be found. She would be done for.

In fact, Rina had had a client on a couple of occasions.

Harriet can't help a rueful smile.

Hah! "Rina's Reductions". Come and live in my attic without food and watch the pounds drop away!

Bizarrely, Harriet is banking on this.

Rina might be uneducated, but she knows things about diet. Harriet remembers her saying that if you don't eat you can lose three pounds a day – and every eight pounds is worth an inch off the waist. But why torture yourself when you can eat perfectly well and visit Rina's Reductions?

But if Rina is right, there really is the prospect that she'll lose enough weight to squeeze through the hatch.

She could probably already do it.

She wonders, if there were – say – a fire. Would she cast all caution to the wind? Force herself through – perhaps even risk going head first?

Head first – that's how you get a boy out of the railings, isn't it? The fire brigade tip him upside down and bring his head through face first.

Harriet might only have one chance.

Morten usually goes out alone on Mondays.

So she has to face the prospect of meeting Rina.

It's possible she could sneak past – Harriet has thought of the best time: Rina religiously watches the repeat of Ennerdale after Morten has left.

And if she met Rina face to face?

Surely she could overpower Rina?

She's much bigger than her.

But Rina's a street-fighter, that is plain. She wouldn't hesitate to pick up a brass candlestick or a poker or even a kitchen knife. And there would still be the problem of getting out of the garden. If Harriet couldn't find the remote that Rina has for the gates, it would mean using the ladder. And what if Morten has locked the ladder in the shed or chained it to something? She could find herself trapped in the compound until Morten came home.

She'd have to incapacitate Rina and hide by the gates and hope to slip out as Morten drove in. If he saw her, she doubts she'd get away.

Now she imagines him pursuing her – her breath coming in desperate gasps and her heart pounding in her head – the roar of the great engine running her down – the big car pinning her against a wall – Morten forcing her inside at the point of a weapon.

Morten snatching her phone.

She thinks again about hiding her phone.

She mustn't be caught with the phone.

She mustn't be caught.

She lies.

She listens.

Is that a bird pattering on the roof?

Harriet offers up a little prayer to the rain gods.

30. MISSING, INACTION

Police HQ – 10.15 a.m. Monday 16 October

'Where's that layabout Leyton got to?'

'He phoned in to say he's switched round his days at the DWP. Apparently there's something he wants to attend this morning.'

Skelgill scowls into his tea – unfairly so, as DS Jones has made a special detour to the canteen, rather than take the easy option of the machine at the end of the corridor.

'Some *thing?*'

'Guv?'

'Someone, more like. I'm getting worried about Leyton. He'll be applying for a transfer, at this rate.'

DS Jones looks like she is not convinced.

'Well, there does seem to be some attraction – but perhaps he'll surprise us with a breakthrough.'

'Don't hold your breath.'

She grins – and raises her notepad with an expression that humours her superior.

Skelgill finds her response obtuse, and he regards her more intently. The phrase 'calm before the storm' comes to his mind – it is a literal manifestation. She sits serenely before the unruly backdrop of scudding clouds and a late dawn that is darkening counterintuitively.

Yet she still has on the close-fitting sportswear from the class she has just taught – self-defence for females; now over-subscribed with a waiting list of male officers. She hardly has a hair out of place, and only the flush of her high cheekbones and a silky patina on her exposed shoulders as clues to her recently completed exertions. That she has checked her work station en route to change and come directly suggests she has some news.

She does, however, begin with a small caveat.

'It's still a case of two steps forwards, one step back.'

Skelgill's rejoinder is sympathetic, if somewhat cryptic.

'Traversing's often the fastest way up a fell. Too steep and you might end up on your rear.'

DS Jones guesses at the reason behind his amenability.

'I take it the meeting went okay?'

He frowns, however.

'Smart didn't turn up. He's another one swinging the lead.'

But Skelgill had been relieved. DI Smart's absence averted any targeted criticism over resources – that Skelgill has a pet project and one of his officers – DS Leyton – is patently wasting his time. Alec Smart would have been quick to point this out.

'We were well down the agenda.' He indicates to his colleague's notes, referring to Operation Community Chest. 'The Chief ran out of time. Top brass lunch meeting at some fancy hotel in Hexham. She wants a written report by the close of play.'

DS Jones tilts her head reflectively; but rather than opine, she opts to convey the facts to hand.

'Top line, we don't appear to have a Rina or Morten Jenner registered in Cumbria. There's nothing on the council tax register or the electoral roll. There's nothing in the phone book – and nothing coming up on an internet search or mainstream social media.'

Skelgill notes that she has used the word *registered* and not *residing*.

DS Jones continues.

'We've put in a request to Devon & Cornwall Police.'

Lifting his mug to his lips, Skelgill raises an eyebrow.

'You know they're on the naughty step?'

'Oh – no, I didn't.'

Skelgill, however, does not cast aspersions. Probably the least said about the trials and tribulations of another force the better. It is a tempting of providence. In these days of austerity one never knows what make-do-and-mend might be exposed by a visitation from the Police Inspectorate.

'Don't let it put you off.'

DS Jones nods.

'Border Force have been more forthcoming – I hope.' She wrinkles her brow as if a second thought crosses her mind; but she sets it aside. 'There is no record of Eoin Romeo entering the UK in the last ten years.'

Now Skelgill nods. The succession of negatives, in its own way, gradually adds up to a small positive sum.

'There's nowt from him?' He glances at his watch and corrects himself. 'Nay – it's too early.'

DS Jones looks like she concurs.

As a postscript to their telephone interview on Friday, Eoin Romeo had offered to look for photographs in suitcases shipped from his mother's home. But he had expressed the apology that he would have no time over the weekend, as the *Red Herring* (his forty-foot diesel sportsfisherman) was booked round the clock, and he must make the best of busy days and benevolent tides, heading into the off season. Clearly, he was having to toil to keep his business afloat.

He had independently volunteered a helpful idea: in the way that old photographs often have a scribble on the back – names, place, date – that perhaps he would come across a Cumbrian connection, a distant relation he did not know of – some cousin of his late mother's and Billy's generation.

They had also touched on the subject of Billy Boothroyd's will – if indeed he had made one. Eoin Romeo is of the view that his uncle would have made a will, but he doubts he would have employed a solicitor. As to its contents he could only speculate – but Billy being childless he would most likely have divided his estate evenly between his two sisters and their issue. He had openly admitted that, therefore, he would potentially be a beneficiary.

The detectives had skirted round their incomplete knowledge in this regard. Until they can sequester bank records, it is impossible to know the destination of the proceeds of the property sale. All they do know is that any such funds are not in his current account.

Skelgill drinks, and ponders.

DS Jones presses him.

'Have you had any further thoughts on Eoin Romeo?'

They had been starved of stimuli during their interview – just the disembodied voice, the mongrel accent that retained its distinctive Midland vowels among an American twang and occasional transatlantic phrases. There had been no body language to observe – when inadvertent shiftiness or affected enthusiasm can reveal inner sentiments and lies – but equally no distraction in this regard. In concentrating upon the voice – its tone and tenor – and hearing his subtle reactions to the news of his uncle, Eoin Romeo had sounded entirely natural. No alarm bells had rung for Skelgill.

He only shakes his head.

'You didn't ask him much about fishing.'

The statement is a question.

And now Skelgill perhaps does look a little discomfited.

He shrugs.

'I had a deek at his website. I reckon he knows his stuff.'

His reaction is restrained, his eyes lacking focus. DS Jones recognises that he is back on those troubled waters that have periodically consumed him during this case. His attention shifts to the rain-spattered glass at her back. His expression might reasonably be reserved for the worsening weather conditions. The foreknowledge of a storm imbues the skies with portents that would otherwise remain latent in the mind; the worst rarely happens; the perfect storm is a rare event.

'There's more to it?'

While Skelgill shakes his head, her question is perceptive. Though he is reluctant, almost embarrassed to answer.

'You wouldn't do that, would you?'

'What do you mean?'

'Like we've said. Rip off your old uncle. Dump him. Not when he's been so kind to you as a kid. Taken you fishing, time and again, when it's not even his bag. When he wants to study his horses. You'd have to be some sort of sociopath to be able to do that.'

DS Jones merely states the practical corollary.

'Then that's the type of people we're looking for, isn't it?'

31. UGLY MISTS

Troughdale House, Whitehaven – 10.40 a.m. Monday 16 October

Morten Jenner sniffs the air like a fox that has emerged from its lair – untrustworthy itself, always suspecting the worse of its surroundings.

His engine is running, and the driver's door open. He has got out to clear away a windblown branch from in front of the gates, ripped from a sycamore beyond the wall. Sycamores are not supposed to shed; they were gallows trees for that reason.

He tosses the branch angrily over the wall.

Then he stands for a moment, admiring the Mercedes and the imposing property beyond.

His features undergo convulsions; like the ebb and flow of the gale, one moment the malleable lips seem to smile, the next the teeth are bared in a grimace.

The car – the house – Morten fantasises about bigger things. Bigger and better. And beautiful.

But in the fickle nature of the storm he is reminded about the other things, those that are going wrong, that are thwarting his ambitions.

Harriet. Has Harriet thwarted them?

He is torn about Harriet.

They can still make Harriet work.

If Harriet has gone off and died – she might never be found – or never be identified, even if she is found.

Harriet requires a degree of patience that is hard to come by right now.

And it makes Billy more urgent.

He can't let another banker fall at the final hurdle.

He needs to act, decisively.

He stands, looking about the garden.

The memorial beds: Thomas and Richard. And the nameless one over by the wall.

The wall. Could Harriet really have scaled the wall? Pity she didn't fall right there.

'*Morty?*'

His thoughts are interrupted.

Rina must have overslept. She's in her dressing gown and slippers. Why is she coming out in this wind – with rain in the air and falling skies.

Rina looks around hopelessly, her precious roses at the mercy of the weather. The walled garden is sheltered as it goes, but the wind is gusting erratically, and malignant zephyrs swoop to strip petals from fragile late blooms.

'Morty – are you sure you should go? Why don't you leave it a week?'

He sniffs.

'She's been gone for five days.'

He leaves unspoken that this is sufficient time for what they need to have happened.

He adds a rider.

'If they were looking for her, or for us, they'd have been by now.'

But Rina persists.

'A couple more days, then?'

'I need to go. We're running short of cash – unless you want us to start paying for things by traceable means.'

'I'm sure we've got enough food in. There's all Harriet's.'

Morten is becoming irritated.

'I don't just go to a few cash machines and Asda, Rina.'

Rina pulls her gown together around her throat. She sticks out her jaw, her small, close-set eyes belligerent.

'Well – what *do* you do, Morty? What's so important it can't wait?'

Morten is momentarily taken off guard. He glances away.

'I have meetings, Rina – all this doesn't happen by magic.' He sweeps an arm about the garden and up at the house. 'There are people we have to keep satisfied – you don't know half of what I have to do – I don't trouble you with –'

He stops mid-sentence, his gaze trained high above the woman, as though he has espied storm damage to their roof.

'What is it, Morty?'

Morten's wide mouth is contorted now into neither its smile nor its grimace, but something altogether more sinister. His black eyes bore into their unseen object. His sallow skin is taut over the jutting bones of his face and his lank hair plastered unevenly over his anthropoidal skull.

Rina is transfixed – a little horrified – for Morten suddenly reminds her of Clyve Jenner, in those moments before he was taken away.

'Morty!'

Her cry is a mother's warning – that she sees danger about to envelop her child. She even stamps a slippered foot.

Morten responds – though not with a start. Only slowly does he come round, to look at her with vacant eyes.

'There's something I meant to do.'

He reaches into his Mercedes and turns off the ignition.

He slams the door and rounds to the boot.

He takes out some object.

Rina has been rooted to the spot.

'What is it? That's Harriet's heater.'

'Go inside, Rina. I'm coming back in for a minute.'

When he passes her in the hall he has the paraffin heater under one arm and the aluminium ladder from the garden under the other.

Rina loiters.

'What is it, then?'

Morten mounts the stairs. He answers over his shoulder.

'If you must know, I'm putting this heater on – so the attic's warm when I get back.'

'You've got an electric fire.'

Rina has blurted the words before she can help herself.

Now Morten turns and looks daggers.

Rina tries to brazen out her slip, that she knows this small detail.

'But that's a really good idea, Morty. It'll be cheaper to run, won't it? And Harriet's already paid for the paraffin, like.'

Morten is irked – but his mission is more pressing. He turns and continues upwards, his features grim.

Rina is emboldened by her minor success.

She calls after him.

'Why do you need the ladder? Are you shutting up the hatch, as well? I shan't be going up there, you know.'

'Never mind, Rina – go and watch your damned stupid programme.'

32. INTO THE ALLEY

Carlisle – 11.35 a.m. Monday 16 October

DS Leyton is feeling somewhat guilty.

His hopes – rather blind hopes at that – have not exactly come to fruition.

The senior departmental manager he had planned to see has been tied up in a meeting. His calls to the Adult Care section of the social work department have found him on hold for ages on end. And Deidre Wetherspoon has not come into work this morning, so he is limited without guidance on where to find admin and how to cheat the recalcitrant DWP computer system.

To add insult to injury, a brief call to Skelgill to touch base has received short shrift.

Alone at his borrowed desk he experimentally twiddles his thumbs.

He has always suspected there are occupations in which one becomes proficient in the art.

He is accustomed to putting his head down; to a whack-a-mole action list; to long full hours.

He thinks how Deidre is cavalier with her timekeeping; she takes long full lunch hours.

With a groan he rises and grabs his mackintosh from the coat stand.

He is about to leave when he remembers the hat – the fedora he wore on the walk from the car because of the rain. Also, perhaps just a very teeny-tiny fashion statement. Except there was no one here to greet his arrival.

Now he checks his reflection in the glass of the door. It is a hat ordinarily secreted in the boot of his car. Skelgill would have a field day. *"Hah!* Think you're Clouseau, or summat, Leyton, you donnat!"

But his good natured stoicism comes to the fore.

If there's nothing doing here, he may as well head back to the station after lunch. A peace offering springs to mind. Skelgill has been talking up Carlisle patties lately – but they are best served hot and might not travel well.

Then he is reminded of the banana dessert cake he almost took before.

The speciality of Deidre's little bolthole, the café tucked down the alleyway.

And now some intuition tells him it is the right move.

Or is it just the subspecies of presentiment that anticipates a sugary treat?

At the main door he has second thoughts. It is not so much the rain – it was heavier earlier – but the wind has further picked up. Pedestrians are uniformly bent like stick people in a Lowry, bound for the mill.

He glances up anxiously at the surrounding buildings, just as a seagull is blown off a ledge. Above, the sky is moving like a scene from a movie that uses time-lapse photography. He might be operating on various forms of gut feel, but vertigo is the sensation of the moment.

He ducks his head and presses down on the crown of the hat.

He is not a man easily buffeted.

Reaching the pedestrianised section of English Street, he extends his neck tortoise-like from his hunched shoulders to cast about. Now, where exactly was that alley? *Ginnel*, Leyton – he hears Skelgill's voice. He replays his last visit, when he came out ahead of Deidre Wetherspoon – that's right – it was diagonally opposite a large department store – and he espies the narrow thoroughfare.

The alley – or ginnel – offers respite from the gale. At its end he finds the windows of the café steamed up.

Inside it is surprisingly busy; a small port in a storm.

There is a comforting fug, warm and damp and imbued with the frying fat of breakfasts. For a moment his hunger pangs crave a savoury, salty satisfaction.

He had intended only to obtain a takeaway, and has joined a small queue at the counter; though now he is torn, and uses the time to weigh up his options.

But there are no tables obviously free, and hardly any seats he could comfortably squeeze into.

He reaches to take off his hat – and stops dead in the movement.

Slowly – unobtrusively – he tilts the brim, and reaches to turn up his collar.

Across the crowded interior, seated in the intimate alcove where Deidre had taken him, he recognises a man.

But it is not so much the man. The man alone would be small beer – but big beer is the man plus the woman seated opposite him.

The woman – side on to DS Leyton, in fact slightly turned away – is surely Deidre Wetherspoon.

And – back to the man – for the man is someone they have interviewed.

There can be no mistaking his distinctive features. Reptilian is the word that springs to mind. Skin that is taut and polished; something cold below the surface. Though right now it seems to DS Leyton that he flatters to deceive; his manner is once fawning and supercilious.

DS Leyton recalls the interview.

It was on his first day – when he had even less of a clue than he does now – and he knows that he'd seemed incompetent – much to this man's satisfaction.

Jones he was called. That's right, Jones. Naturally it stuck in his mind – because of his colleague.

He'd told them he was long-term disabled – and had an elderly mother with her own chronic ailments. His attitude was arrogant and entitled.

Yet Deidre had been munificent in her response.

That day the man was in a wheelchair.

DS Leyton steals a longer glance.

There is no trace of a wheelchair.

'What can I get for you, love?'

251

He is jolted from his covert observations.

When he stutters, forgetting his purpose, the woman behind the counter makes a suggestion.

'Like a bacon butty or summat – to take over to your friends?'

'Come again? Oh – no thanks, ma'am – nah – I'm just, er – just looking for a takeaway. Three slices of your banana cake and black coffee, to go – if you please.'

His rather disjointed answer does not seem entirely to dispel the woman's awareness of his interest in the couple huddled in the corner – but now he moves quickly to take a banknote from his wallet and proffer it in the direction of a large jar that sits on the counter, marked "Staff Christmas Box".

'Stick the change in there, girl.'

The note is generous relative to his order, and the woman is at once won over.

'Very kind of you, love – happen you're not from these parts?'

Such a question could take the conversation in various directions, when all DS Leyton wants to do is make a swift exit before the woman denounces him to his part-time DWP colleague and her sinister companion. As it is, he stands inelegantly hiding his features, as if he suffers from some arthritic condition of the upperparts.

To his relief – and before he can even answer – two elderly women enter the café and a gust must chase them along the alleyway, for the door swings open and bangs loudly before they can wrestle it under control. The distraction, and their attendance at the counter, forming a queue, causes the serving woman to grin and nod at DS Leyton and turn to the matter of his order.

During the minute or so that it takes, DS Leyton snatches surreptitious sideways glances. The busy café atmosphere is thick not just with aromas but the noise of chatter and crockery, hubbub and staccato that render deciphering any distant conversation impossible. All he can glean is that the couple are engaged in a confab that is undemonstrative but intense.

Each time the door opens the man Jones glances up, causing DS Leyton to flinch; but no inadvertent eye contact is made.

His order ready, DS Leyton is relieved to depart.

He takes gasps of fresh air; not just escaping the claustrophobic miasma, but realising he has been half-holding his breath.

He assesses the alleyway and determines it peters out; most likely they will emerge onto the market place. He crosses to the shelter of the department store's long veranda, where he sips tentatively at his coffee.

He is just thinking he could have a nibble of his portion of cake when Deidre Wetherspoon and the Jones man appear at the mouth of the passageway.

They each consult their phones – the suggestion that they are synchronising watches – like a married couple about to go their separate shopping ways and rendezvous later.

And indeed they split up.

A little to DS Leyton's surprise, it is the man who sets off back in the direction that will pass the DWP offices, and Deidre Wetherspoon who goes the other way.

A dilemma.

A split-second decision is required.

DS Leyton has the sense that it is an important decision.

What would Skelgill do?

He has a strong urge to follow Deidre Wetherspoon. The revelation that she is seemingly in cahoots with a client of the benefits office rings alarm bells for more reasons than one.

Then again, it may be an innocent relationship. And if she just goes home – that is not going to tell him a lot. And, should she spin on her heel and catch him unawares, she will almost certainly recognise him.

He follows the man.

He jettisons his coffee at the first litter bin – the brightly branded cup would mark him out as a tail at a second glance when his nondescript clothing might not.

The Jones man is smartly dressed. He wears polished boots and a long camel coat, and a Burberry tartan scarf tied in the fashionable manner, for ostentation rather than practical effect.

He is of average height and sinewy build. He is balding – more obviously from the rear, where straggly black Brylcreemed hair is less successful in concealing the condition.

Still the wind gusts, and rain streaks the air.

The pavements are slick, and plastered with fallen leaves and sodden windblown litter.

The man walks easily and briskly. There is no sign of an impediment that would require a wheelchair. Is he brazenly going to pass the Department for Work & Pensions?

He halts at a bookshop window.

Clearly, something has caught his eye. He enters and emerges a couple of minutes later with apparently a book in a carrier bag.

He continues. He takes a left, and then a right close to the DWP offices, and at the junction with The Crescent and Warwick Road another left along the latter.

In short order he stops at a cash machine. There is a youth ahead of him. But when another man joins the queue he quits waiting and moves on.

In two hundred yards he takes a right into Brunswick Street. The impression is suddenly residential instead of commercial. There is a notable absence of pedestrian traffic. DS Leyton hangs back. Ahead, on the left side, tall trees sway and detached autumn leaves swirl in the disturbed air.

DS Leyton is monitoring their progress on the maps application on his mobile phone. He sees that the trees represent a square, a small park.

The man diverts through the open gate at the first corner.

It is evident to DS Leyton that here is probably a popular cut-through for anyone wishing to exploit the diagonal.

He hurries – intending to take the long side rather than enter.

And just as well.

For the man is not walking on – he has settled at a bench about thirty yards inside.

DS Leyton glimpses a quadrangle of lawn edged by a narrow tarmac path. In turn shrubs and then trees border the path, and the entire public amenity is fenced in by cast-iron railings.

The keening of the wind in the leaves, and the constantly shifting foliage seem to DS Leyton to provide additional cover. He finds a point where he can peer through the railings and a gap in the bushes.

The man looks about – as if to satisfy himself that he is alone.

Briefly, he checks his mobile phone.

Then he brings out the book and stuffs the carrier bag into the litter bin beside his bench.

He settles one leg over the opposing knee and leans back to read.

DS Leyton squints to see better in the poor light.

It seems to be a classic novel. Certainly it is a weighty tome.

But now he witnesses curious behaviour. The man turns to roughly halfway through – seemingly randomly – and stares at the page. Periodically, he glances about. He does not turn the page.

Is this his rendezvous with Deidre Wetherspoon?

It would seem to DS Leyton to be an odd place – and these affectations – as if to convey some impression to an onlooker.

The thought strikes him that if Deidre is coming here – and should she advance along the same street as he – his prying is on full display.

No sooner he has had the premonition, than he feels a hand on his shoulder.

'Excuse me?'

He starts, and turns wide-eyed.

It is a woman. But not Deidre Wetherspoon.

She is younger – maybe early thirties – slimmer – and, strikingly so, considerably more attractive.

She is pushing a covered baby's pram, new-looking, an expensive model, he knows from experience.

Her appearance, make-up, attire – are commensurately immaculate.

She looks like the young wife of a well-to-do couple.

Startling blue eyes hold his gaze, and he has not yet found his tongue.

'Sergeant Leyton?'

Whoa. Yeah – I am, that's right.'

How can she know who he is?

The answer comes swiftly. She reaches into a pocket of her jacket and brings out a black leather card wallet – as she deftly flips it open he realises it is an official ID.

'I'm Sally Genever. I'm from the FEPS. The Fraud & Error Prevention Service. We're a national body – part of the DWP – but with independent powers of investigation. I'm working incognito for the anti-corruption unit.'

DS Leyton stares at her – she is far from what he would expect of an undercover agent.

But then – isn't that exactly what he *should* expect of an undercover agent?

His gaze falls on the pram.

She seems to understand, and reaches to draw back the rain hood. The pram is empty.

DS Leyton raises his eyebrows.

'Impressive.'

The woman smiles courteously.

'Sally – you said?'

'That's right.'

'You sound like you're from down south?'

She nods.

'I am on an assignment – out on a limb, you might say. A chance to prove myself.'

DS Leyton gives an ironic growl in his throat.

'Join the club.'

Now the blue eyes narrow conspiratorially.

'Well, I think our stars might have collided.'

'In what way?'

Her gaze shifts, through the railings, to the figure of the man on the bench.

'Sergeant – you're investigating Mr Jones, there?'

DS Leyton experiences a moment's hesitation – caught out performing amateur observation – and the peremptory introduction to a service and one of its representatives of which he has never heard – have him on the back foot.

'I might be – yeah. I mean – I'm not trying to be cagey. We've got this thing going – Operation –'

'Community Chest – yes – we know all about it.'

'You do?'

'Of course. We liaise with the police at a senior level. We've been hoping your activities might set a hare or two running.'

DS Leyton sighs.

'I'm still trying to get a peg in the ground. I've had me suspicions, like – and then –' He wonders whether he should come clean about his presence here – but it would seem churlish not to share his discovery. Besides, he has the growing sense that – never mind banana cake – here is the tangible progress he needs to take back as a trophy. He inclines his head in the direction of their mutual quarry. 'Last time I saw this geezer – he was in a wheelchair. Then – just now, seems he's right as rain – and he was with –'

'With Deidre Wetherspoon.'

'Yeah. That's right – Deidre.' Again, DS Leyton wavers. How much does this woman know? 'See – I've had me own reasons for suspicion – not about this Jones cove, in particular – but, now –'

The woman is regarding him intently.

'Now – I would say you are on the right track.'

DS Leyton nods gratefully. He peers again at the man, to make sure he is still there.

Then he seems to become conscious of their surroundings, the inclement conditions – the woman is sufficiently well clad – but not for prolonged surveillance, especially should the heavy rain that constantly threatens return.

'What do you want to do, girl?'

She seems to approve of his call to action, and his informal style of address.

She leans closer.; he can smell the subtle fragrance of her perfume.

'What I'd really like to do, is to see inside his house.'

DS Leyton furrows his brow.

'He's got an old mother, right – invalid?'

Now the woman looks like she knows more than she is ready to reveal.

'Our system – there is an AI algorithm that detects irregular patterns – it has blind access to external databases. It can identify –

well – for instance, a property associated with inappropriate or multiple claims. It assigns a statistical likelihood.'

DS Leyton reads between the convoluted lines. He cuts to the chase.

'You know where they live?'

She nods.

'Morten and Rina Jones, yes. Whitehaven. A large property called Troughdale House. Walled in, with security gates.'

'Jeez – it would be, wouldn't it? And he'd have no obligation to admit us.' DS Leyton clicks his tongue in frustration. 'Given a bit of time I could get a warrant. After what I've seen – one minute in a wheelchair, the next, he's fit as a fiddle – I reckon there's grounds to interview him.'

Sally Genever is listening inscrutably.

'Actually, I think if you kept out of sight – he would let me in. Let's say, while I've been watching him, he's been watching me, in a manner of speaking.'

She is unaffected in the way she is aware of her allure. But she adds a compliment for good measure.

'It would be reassuring to know I had a strong policeman standing by.'

DS Leyton shifts a little bashfully from one foot to the other.

'That's the old hitchhikers' trick, ain't it?'

Now she regards him more sternly.

'When someone's been defrauding their fellow citizens, I object to the word *trick.*'

DS Leyton grins.

'Sting?'

'I'll settle for sting.'

'Deal.'

33. SALLY FORTH

Troughdale House, Whitehaven – 2.15 p.m. Monday 16 October

'We must have beaten him here, don't you think?'

DS Leyton peers through the windscreen. His car is parked some fifty yards short of the frontage of Troughdale House. Their plan is that when the Jones man returns he will have to wait for the gates to open. Sally Genever will approach on foot, and ask to go inside and speak with him.

'Unless he knows some secret back-route. But I can't see it. That was more or less a dead straight line from Carlisle. And you saw the speed we came at.'

The young woman nods approvingly.

'I did.'

DS Leyton, however, is thinking that no doubt Skelgill would have found a way, despite the geographical truism, forty miles point to point, due south-west down the A595 with hardly a degree of deviation.

But he shifts to a more subjective matter, which has begun to trouble him as they have neared their destination.

'How are you feeling now – about going in alone?'

She smiles at him, detecting his conflicted emotions; chivalry, and a desire for action.

'I'm sure I'll be fine. It's not like we're dealing with a serial killer.'

A small silence ensues.

DS Leyton indicates to his phone in the cradle.

'You could call me before you go – so's I can listen in?'

She nods reflectively.

'Though I had planned to use my phone to record the conversation.'

DS Leyton clicks his tongue, reasonably thwarted.

'Given a bit of time, I could have got you a body-worn camera.'

Sally Genever turns to indicate into the back of his car. The seats are folded flat to make room for the pram.

'Actually, I've got one on the buggy – but it's specially concealed and I don't know how easy it would be to remove.'

DS Leyton frowns.

They have debated whether she should appear with the pram – in order to preserve the appearance to which Jones has become accustomed. But they have concluded it is too much of a risk – instead, if challenged, she will say that a local friend is taking care of the child.

Now she reassures him further.

'Look – I shan't need long – why don't we agree that you'll phone me after, say, ten minutes? That way, you'll know I'm fine – and if I need to, I can use it as an excuse to leave – I'll say it's an emergency call from my childminder – that she's got the baby in town and there's a problem – that I'll sort it out and come back.'

DS Leyton, however, remains looking worried.

'Are you planning to reveal your official identity? Or are you going to pretend you're the lady he's been watching, who's magically turned up on his doorstep? If you don't mind me saying, Sally – that seems a bit too good to be true, speaking as an ordinary geezer, like.'

She reads his awkwardness – but also she appreciates his concern.

'To be honest – I thought I would play it by ear. I would begin with, hello – may I come in and talk with you – and let silence do the trick. Once inside, I think – yes – show my credentials – but in such a way as to suggest this can't possibly be right – and perhaps he can clear up the confusion.'

DS Leyton, long experienced in such situations, knows a lot can go wrong, and often does.

He remains pensive.

'And you just want to see who else is living there?'

Sally Genever nods slowly, though she adds a rider.

'Or, rather, who isn't. Among other things. Like you said –

wheelchair – no wheelchair. Invalid mother – or perfectly fit mother? Et cetera.'

She does not elaborate on the et cetera.

DS Leyton ponders further. There is another aspect that has been preying on his mind.

'When you introduced yourself to me – you mentioned anti-corruption. When I hear that, I normally think of *Line of Duty* – insider trading, so to speak.'

'Correct.'

He swallows.

'So, what – Deidre Wetherspoon? Is she in your sights, an' all?'

But now Sally Genever equivocates. She tilts her head slowly from side to side.

'I think she has let her personal needs cloud her judgement – she has been manipulated. She is not the kingpin.'

DS Leyton allows a small sigh to escape – it sounds of relief, for Deidre's sake – although the basis for such a sentiment is less clear, even to him. Perhaps time will reveal exactly what his intuition has been trying to tell him.

Now he groans and shifts in his seat, and flexes his chest and yawns – as if to mask the hidden cerebral discomfort with that of his emasculated role in their plan.

'I could do with a stretch of the legs.'

Then he has an idea.

'I reckon I should just take a stroll up to those gates – see if they've got a doorbell camera, or CCTV – be handy to know that – whether you're being monitored when you approach. I'll just wander up to the end of the road and back – pass it both ways.'

She regards him sympathetically.

'Sure.'

He clambers out and hauls on his damp mackintosh. Still there is rain blowing in the air without it pouring. He reaches back in for his fedora.

'I don't normally wear this daft hat – it's just the weather and – well –'

She grins.

'Well?'

'I was going to say it helped me stay incognito – but a fat lot of good it did with you.'

'Ah – but I had the element of surprise on my side. Besides – it suits you – you look very suave – like –'

'Don't say Clouseau.'

'I was thinking more – *Columbo?*'

He makes a face, evaluating the suggestion.

'I'll settle for that.'

He pulls on the hat and turns up his collar.

'I'll leave the engine running – keep you warm – and so's the wipers keep the screen clear.'

She nods.

As he approaches the frontage of Troughdale House he appreciates the height of the wall. Its sandstone blocks and mortar joints are in poor repair, extravagantly sculpted, etched by loose debris and wind, like the patterns on rocks exposed by a low tide. But nonetheless it is a formidable barrier to both entry and view, a good seven feet in height. The gates are likewise in stature, though incongruous; rather ugly steel panels painted black, peeling. They are industrial, prison-like.

He passes slowly, casually glancing to his left.

He can see no camera of any description – not even the small doorbell type. In fact there does not seem to be a bell, and he wonders how they receive deliveries. He notes, though, that there is a large flap for mail.

He passes on, thinking this would be a good moment for drone surveillance.

*

Were a drone to hover at this very moment over the garden of Troughdale House – were it capable of flight in the torrid conditions – it would spy out a curious-looking personage only yards from where DS Leyton has just passed, on the inner side of the wall.

Rina Jenner – clad in Morten Jenner's oversized wellingtons and oilskin coat (the latter oversized in length but inadequate in girth to fasten by zip, and held only by a couple of poppers) – stands by a rose bed wielding a pair of secateurs.

But she is paying lip-service to pruning. It is cover – in case Morten should return and catch her loitering. She is loitering to intercept the post.

Her little charade is not entirely convincing, she knows. Morten would say, what the heck is she doing out in this weather? What good can she do while the storm is wreaking havoc? Better to wait and assess the damage another day. She'll say she thought she'd rescue a bunch for the vase in the hall – though as yet she has taken no such cuttings.

She listens; it is hard to discern much through the soughing of the gale.

If it were the postie's van it would have come right up and stopped outside the gates. Perhaps there is an engine running, a little way down the road. Perhaps it is the postie – having a quick break – a cigarette or a sandwich. They must have to stop somewhere. The call of nature in the bushes on the other side.

Certainly the mail is late today. But that could be the weather, too. It must take longer to do a round – Morten says the traffic is slower when it's stormy – that people drive over-cautiously.

She slips a hand into a pocket and feels the smooth plastic of the remote for the gates. She thinks of opening them to take a look – if it is the postie, then she could walk along and ask if there's mail for them.

But if Morten should come back at the exact moment, he'd see what she's up to.

But – then – he's the one who's up to something.

Ever since he's put a little padlock on the mailbox, she's been more suspicious than usual.

He'd said it was an extra precaution – in case Harriet somehow got to the mailbox before they did – or sneaked out when they were away.

But that doesn't matter now, does it? Harriet's gone.

He could take the lock off.

It must mean he suspects her, Rina.

She had waited until he'd left this morning, before going to look upstairs. He had closed the hatch to his attic. And there was no sign of the heater in his bedroom – he must have put that up there, like he'd said – and she could vaguely smell paraffin fumes and soot, as though it were lit.

But – and here's the thing – he'd also locked the hatch – with a little hasp and a padlock she's not noticed before.

Yes – close the hatch to keep the heat in – if that's what he wanted – but why lock it? You don't need to lock heat in.

That can only be to lock her out.

She makes a face, her features contorted.

That had made her all the more determined to intercept the afternoon post. Monday's always a big day for mail. She'll be able to see what there is – pop most of it back into the box for Morten to find when he gets home – and keep anything that looks interesting, to steam open later. Next time he's out. He won't know what's not been delivered.

She nods, satisfied.

She begins to snip at dead heads.

Yes, this is a good plan, Rina.

She begins to hum, *Please, please Mr Postman*.

*

Approaching his second pass of the gates, and feeling more confident now that he is not under surveillance himself, DS Leyton slows to a halt.

He glances at his car. He can't exactly see Sally Genever because of the reflection of the angled windscreen, but he gives her a little nod, all the same.

He tries to peer through the gap where the two gates join at the centre. But he is thwarted – there is a metal flange running down the inside of one of them, to create an overlap.

He wonders if the letter box affords a glimpse. Sometimes these things have just a wire basket on the other side. The flap is stiff, however; it needs oil and makes a loud squeal as he raises it.

'*Wait!* Don't post it!'

He steps back – and immediately the gates begin to swing

inwards.

'I'll take the mail, thank y–'

His first reaction is that he has been caught flat-footed for a second time today.

The gates clang back to reveal a small elderly woman, attired in an ill-fitting wet-weather outfit. He is vaguely aware that the arrangement of lawn and rose beds has the ambience of a memorial garden, and that the woman is holding a pair of trimmers.

Her expression – initially a smile of exaggerated sweetness – metamorphoses into one of bafflement infused with what seems to be panic.

But DS Leyton finds himself seizing the moment.

'Mrs Jones, is it?'

'What? Who are you? Where's the post? I thought you were delivering the post.'

DS Leyton realises he does not have a follow-up line.

He stammers.

'Whatever you're selling, we don't need it.'

Suddenly, as if by magic, he finds himself improvising.

'Madam – I've got a fare – she's waiting in the taxi because of the rain.' He raises an arm to indicate along the road. 'I've been trying to find the right house. She's here to see a Mr Jones?'

The woman takes a couple of steps forwards and peers cautiously around the gatepost.

'I can't see a taxi plate.'

'We just have them on the back these days – for safety reasons – same as motorbikes don't have front number plates..'

The woman turns a suspicious countenance up to DS Leyton.

'Who the hell is she – she's got no business here!'

DS Leyton raises his palms in a placatory manner.

'Dunno, madam – I'm just the messenger. Girlfriend, maybe? She's nice looking.'

The woman stamps a foot angrily, the too-big wellington flapping against her leg.

'I don't care if she's Raquel Welch – she's an imposter! And so are you! You've got no business here! Get away – before I call the police on you!'

The pitch of her voice is steadily rising, and the accompanying degree of vitriol.

She pulls out a mobile phone from a pocket of the coat and wields it, threatening to make good her promise.

DS Leyton is just thinking he will have to say that he *is* the police – and reproaching himself that he has completely blown Sally Genever's plan to gain a subtle entrance to the property – when there is an almighty crash.

The woman wheels round.

DS Leyton looks up, to the house beyond.

High above, it seems that an attic window, flush to the roof, has exploded.

The air is filled with a shower of glittering shards – and, as if in slow motion, a silvery box-shaped object roughly the size of a briefcase tumbles earthwards, leaking a spiral of fluid.

With a clang it lands in the rose bed below and instantly bursts into flames – a small inferno engulfing the bushes.

The woman howls in anguish and rage.

'No! My grandifloras! Why, you – you –'

But any further admonishment is pre-empted by a haunting cry that emanates from the shattered pane.

'Help!'

There is an unearthly moment of silence. Even the storm temporarily abates. The Jones woman is dumbfounded.

DS Leyton cranes to see the face of a woman – large and pale and doughy – and looking like she has confronted some great horror.

The shout from above is redoubled.

'Help – help – I'm a prisoner! Call 999! They're trying to kill me! You must help! They're murderers!'

DS Leyton, too, is speechless – but the Jones woman now finds her tongue.

She rounds upon DS Leyton, and begins to try to push him backwards over the threshold of the gateway.

'Go away! Take no notice! It's my sister – she's mentally ill – not right in the head – we have to keep her indoors – keep a watch on her – she's paranoid. Go away – and I'll deal with her!'

A tirade of cries continues to emanate from the attic.

'Help! Help! See – here's the proof! Take these to the police!'

A handful of papers is scattered into the wind.

The Jones woman grows rapidly more frantic, and begins to swear and curse at DS Leyton.

'Get away from here, I tell you – get off my property!'

DS Leyton has the advantage of bulk on his side, and is not easily put into reverse – but she begins to flail at him with the secateurs – and he has no alternative but to show his hand. Deflecting blows and beginning to puff and pant, he replies between gasps.

'Listen, madam – calm down, will you? You say you'll call the police – *I am the police!* Look, I'll show you my ID.'

The woman only becomes more ferocious in her onslaught – seething and spitting like a wildcat that has unleashed all its formidable array of weapons upon an unsuspecting domesticated Labrador.

DS Leyton manages to repel the surge, pushing her back, though sparing the force that could unceremoniously dump her on her backside – she staggers, but now merely stoops and claws up a handful of gravel and flings it at him with all her might.

He ducks, losing his hat in the process – and then has to duck and sway as she begins hurling one handful after another – and indeed she drives him to take cover on the street, behind the gatepost.

Suddenly he realises that the gates are closing.

He tries to step into the breach – but is met with another smarting volley of pebbles.

He shies away – and turns just in time to jump aside – for his car ploughs into the gateway – and the gates, designed with a built-in safety sensor, judder to a halt.

Sally Genever grins at him from behind the steering wheel.

34. LEYTON'S CALL

Police canteen – 3.30 p.m. Monday 16 October

'What the – ?'

Skelgill, about to drink, lowers his mug and bends over the handset of his mobile phone.

'What is it, Guv?'

It takes him a moment to muster a reply – though DS Jones cannot read the text message, she can see that it is hardly a dozen words – and what delays him must be its content rather than its form.

Moreover, now it comes to disseminating the latter, he seems reluctant to do so.

'It's – it's from the nurse – Ashanti.' He makes an indeterminate face, avoiding eye contact with his colleague. 'Smart's just turned up and asked to see Billy Boothroyd.'

'Oh. What – to interview him?'

Skelgill shakes his head very slightly – it is a "don't know" rather than an outright negation.

'But – surely he won't get very far?'

Now Skelgill looks at DS Jones, his brow creased.

'Happen that's what he wants to find out. Check that the arl fella's non compos mentis. That he's not going to drop him in it, by recognising him as the copper that couldn't bother his backside to help him. So he can't be accused of negligence.'

DS Jones looks doubtful.

'But surely DI Smart would have known that – if he visited Billy when he was admitted to hospital in the first place?'

Now Skelgill looks unconvinced.

'Confirm that he's not made a recovery?' He gazes pensively across the canteen; there is a group of DI Smart's junior officers in a corner where he can often be found holding court. 'Explains why he wasn't in this morning – he's out covering his tracks.'

Skelgill looks again at the handset – but as he does it springs into life – and he jabs at it instinctively – for it is DS Leyton calling, and the first few strident bars of The Lambeth Walk attract amused glances from a nearby table.

'Leyton.'

'Guv – wait till you hear this. I'm over at Whitehaven. A right flamin' palaver, I've had – literally flamin' – *hah!*'

DS Leyton is at once breathless and loquacious.

'Hold your horses, Leyton.'

Skelgill adjusts the volume and moves the handset to a point equidistant between himself and DS Jones. They both lean in a little.

'I'm with Jones – we've got you on speaker.'

'Righto, Guv. Alright, Emma.' He clears his throat, as if in a prelude to a more considered homily.

'Yeah – what it is – now, where do I start?'

The pair at the table exchange baffled glances. Skelgill offers a suggestion.

'Is there a headline?'

'There is, Guv – but bear with me a mo – else it won't make sense. See – I went into the DWP this morning – and it was like the flippin' Marie Celeste – nothing much doing, and I couldn't get hold of anyone that I wanted. So I thought – I'll get the crew some cake and head back to the station. Only I was feeling something ain't right – you see, I've had this suspicion – and blow me, if I don't get to the café and there it is.'

He has spoken without a pause, and now takes a breath.

Skelgill interjects.

'What is?'

'This geezer – a queer cove called Jones. Supposedly an invalid – in his fifties – we'd interviewed him about his and his old ma's benefits on me first day.'

'So, what – he's in a café?'

'He's in a café – but without his wheelchair – and not only that – he's tucked away in a cosy alcove with my colleague Deidre Wetherspoon – her who's been ladling out the benefits for him.

269

They were acting like they were in cahoots. So I followed him to this park – where he sits pretending to read a book. I'm watching him – then I realise *I've* been followed – there's a tap on the shoulder and it's an undercover investigator from the Fraud & Error Prevention Service. Seems she's been onto the same geezer – looking at a multi-layered scam with inside collusion.'

Again a pause to gather breath.

'I thought this Deidre was supposed to be your new drinking pal, Leyton?'

Now DS Leyton objects.

'Give us some credit, Guv – I never said that – I've been adopting your motto – and following me nose.'

Skelgill makes a face at DS Jones, that he has been duly admonished. He folds his arms, and sounds slightly bored.

'Carry on, then.'

DS Leyton, however, is undiscouraged.

'So, I agree to act as back-up for her to interview these Joneses –' He pauses to make an *ahem*. 'Sorry Emma, about them blackening your good name – they live at Whitehaven in this big house – walled in, with flippin' great security gates.'

He hesitates – but now perhaps for dramatic effect – and that he can tell his account is gaining traction.

'Pedal to the metal – and we get there before the Jones cove – and there's the old Jones lady, comes out in the street. Seems she was looking for the postman. I challenged her and she starts denying everything and chucking stuff at me and cursing like a trooper – then the next thing this window in the roof of the house is smashed open and there's another elderly woman up there – screaming blue murder – that's she's being held prisoner and accusing the Joneses of doing away with some other old folks.'

Both Skelgill and DS Jones now have their palms on the table, and in mirror image have each leaned closer to turn an ear to the disembodied voice that emanates from the handset.

'The Jones woman tries to make out it's her mad sister, who's got paranoid schizophrenia – but obviously I can't let it go. I pull rank and come clean about being a cop. I got pretty much instant back up from a couple of uniforms who were on patrol nearby –

we go inside – and find the other woman – name of Harriet Watt – she's locked in the attic. She'd had to smash her way into a little kind of den up there – where she reckons the Jones geezer had set a paraffin heater burning – with the aim of gassing her – you know, carbon monoxide? That's what she'd chucked through the window – and why I say it was literally flamin'. I've got paramedics here checking her out, and I'm just waiting for the local CID to turn up to get the full story.'

There is a small silence – it seems DS Leyton is anticipating some reaction from his superior. Skelgill duly obliges.

'Quite a little adventure you've had, Leyton – but where do we come in?'

DS Leyton now responds in a more considered fashion.

'Yeah – right – well I thought I should give you the background, Guv – then what I'm going to say maybe carries more weight. No surprise, the Jones woman is refusing to answer questions. Reckons she don't know anything about it – and that we need to speak to her son. Sally – that's the girl from the FEPS – she's had a word with the Harriet woman. She's particularly interested because there are benefit claims being made from this property in names of people she suspects don't live here. This Harriet is insisting that the Joneses have done away with her late friend's husband – himself called Jones – and that they've falsely taken his name. Seems she's moved into an internal granny flat – and she says it was previously occupied by the Jones woman's older brother.'

Skelgill makes a sound which can only reasonably be interpreted as an exasperated protest – that the story is not really making progress. But DS Leyton has a little ace up his sleeve.

'The brother supposedly passed away last September. Thing is, Guv – he's called Billy. What's more – this Jones woman – she speaks with a Liverpool accent.'

Skelgill and DS Jones now simultaneously sit back and stare at one another. When they do not speak, DS Leyton resumes.

'I thought – what if that's your Billy, Guv? That he ain't dead – and they're raking in his benefits – because that's what Sally's telling me is their game. They've been using the Jones name to make claims – and making double claims under their own real names.'

Skelgill does not take his gaze from DS Jones's large hazel eyes.

He speaks evenly, without the inflection that would naturally suggest curiosity.

'What are their real names?'

'According to Sally's information – the geezer – the son – he's Morten, and the mother's Rina. Surname, Jenner – the pair of them.'

There is another protracted silence, this one more profound than any yet. An observer might be wondering quite why Skelgill and DS Jones are engaged in such an intense staring match – and probably jumping to the wrong conclusion.

Not privy to the conversation that his colleagues have undertaken with Eoin Romeo, DS Leyton is unaware of the effect his revelation of the name Jenner has had upon them. He waits patiently at the end of the line for some feedback.

Skelgill is first to speak.

'You say the Jenner woman's there now?'

'That's right, Guv – she's been cautioned but not actually arrested.'

'And what about the son?'

'Seems he often goes into Carlisle. She reckons he should be back any minute – that he's normally home by two-thirty – but that's what – blimey, a good hour ago.'

After some consideration, Skelgill responds.

'You'd better hang onto him when he turns up. Happen we might want to talk to the pair of them.'

'Righto, Guv – I'd better go and get the patrol car moved – don't want to warn him off while he can still drive away.'

'Aye.' Skelgill's index finger hovers over the end-call button – but he manages to squeeze in a commendation. 'Nice job, Leyton.'

He does, however, end the call before his subordinate can offer a grateful response.

Skelgill remains staring at the handset.

DS Jones is bursting to speak – but she holds her peace. Skelgill's eyes are unblinking, and he has on the expression of concentration she has seen when he is fishing, trying to work out what is going on when there are insufficient clues – yet clearly there are clues. His upper lip pulled back reveals his front teeth. It is not the most endearing look, and injurious to such a craggy countenance – though he is unaware, while it signals significance to the knowing onlooker.

He points to the screen of his mobile phone. In terminating the call it has reverted to the open text message from nurse Ashanti. Without looking at her, he rotates the handset and slides it closer to DS Jones.

'You ever heard Smart refer to himself as Alexander?'

DS Jones blinks affectedly. She can discern that Skelgill has thought twice before posing the question; she understands that it implies a degree of intimacy that he struggles to acknowledge.

She reads:

"You said to let you know. Detective Inspector Alexander Smart is here to interview Billy. XX."

She shakes her head, as indifferently as she can contrive.

'Never, why?'

Skelgill does not answer.

Instead, he rises and pulls his jacket off the back of his chair.

'Nor have I.'

He fishes for his car keys.

'Howay, lass.'

DS Jones has to scramble to keep up with him – but she knows enough just to follow.

Almost breaking into a jog, Skelgill speaks over his shoulder.

'Phone Leyton back.'

'Now?'

'Aye – tell him to meet you at Duck Hall, double quick.'

'Meet *me* at Duck Hall? What about you?'

He turns, backing hard through the outer door to the car park.

'We pass Peel Wyke – you can drop me. In this wind, across Bass Lake's the quickest way.'

35. DARKNESS

Duck Hall Estate – 4.10 p.m. Monday 16 October

Morten Jenner narrows his eyes. Such heavy cloud cover has dusk descending early. He can barely discern the hills – the fells, the locals call them. There is an all-enveloping shroud, a sense of impending nightfall, a uniformity that blurs the surroundings and conceals his movements through the landscape.

The wind, too, tossing and turning the trees and the shrubs, like a sea of crashing waves, subsumes any sound. And, from ahead – down by the lake shore – there is an eerie keening where the gale rips at the crowns of the line of orange-boughed pines. It is plenty loud enough to conceal any cries of distress that might emanate from the little bay that is his destination.

His fleshy lips twist into a self-satisfied smile. His mission is going swimmingly. *Swimmingly!*

'You're not Our O.'

The first words uttered since his arrival.

He halts, and leans forwards to put his face close to the old man's ear.

'What's that you say, Billy?'

But no answer comes. The old man's eyes are closed.

He might have imagined it.

He pauses to stare ahead and survey the terrain. There is no path as such. They are crossing grassy parkland studded with ancient horse chestnuts.

But he had watched from the bushes on Friday, the route the nurse had taken, pushing the wheelchair to a point where a breach in the dark rhododendrons beneath the pines leads down to the shore.

She's too nice for her own good. And quite a looker. The

African beads in her braids and the big dark eyes and white teeth – and such a welcoming smile. He'd felt tempted when she'd touched his arm. It's a small shame he won't be coming back – she would have been a reason to visit Billy.

But then he thinks of the princess and his plan – now, they are in a different league altogether.

And this is part of his plan.

He pushes on, with more urgency – though the ground is soft and not well suited to the narrow wheels. He knows all about wheelchairs – he's an expert on wheelchairs!

Another of his incarnations.

One day Morten Jones, the long-suffering invalid – and now, another, the suave police officer, Detective Inspector Alexander Smart.

He grins. He wonders why he hasn't thought of it before. Now that he's experienced how 'being' a policeman opens doors. The fools just believe you. Ask no questions. Kowtow to your demands.

"Nurse – he's not very responsive. I'll take him for some fresh air. No – there's no need for you to accompany me. It's only a couple of very simple questions that I'm hoping to get answers to. It's better if we're alone. Easier to focus. Besides – Mr Boothroyd's answers could be confidential."

Hook, line and sinker.

Not that another guise wouldn't have worked.

Anyone could turn up and pretend to be an official or a relative – *hah* – there's the irony – he could have done this as a relative.

This place is a soft touch.

Perfect, really. A temporary care home with no decent security – no CCTV, reception desk, signing-in system – no nothing. Though why anyone would come to see an old codger who's practically gaga beats him. Unless there's money to be gained, of course.

Though in Billy's case, it's not about gain, but keeping what they've got. The capital sum. Because there's no knowing how long the benefits will keep flowing.

Morten pushes on, staring, unblinking, thinking.

The old man's head nods and bobs as they navigate bumps. Morten's concern is speed not comfort.

Billy has deteriorated since he last saw him.

He seemed to recognise him.

He seemed to shy away.

There was a time towards the end, when he lived at the flat, when Billy still used to call him Morty. But never "Our Morty" – then it changed – to "Our O".

Morten hawks and spits.

That had annoyed him.

It made it even easier.

Easier to be remorseless – and easier, knowing Billy's mind was gone.

Rina had taken a bit of persuading – though he reckons she was all crocodile tears. Like mother like son.

Except she couldn't countenance anything like what had happened to Thomas or Richard. No accidents, Morty.

But neither Thomas nor Richard had been gaga like Billy.

Billy's dementia had provided an alternative solution.

Even though it's come full circle – and now there has to be an accident.

Still, Rina will never need to know about it.

He doubts if it'll even make the news. What could they put in the paper? No obituary – there's nothing to know.

The council will pay for the cheapest possible funeral.

Another anonymous old person. An anonymous service with an anonymous priest and an anonymous undertaker.

William Doe, they would have called him in times gone by.

A shadow crosses Morten's mind.

It's strange that the nurse called him Billy.

In a lucid moment, could he have told them that? I'm not William – I'm Billy. I'm Billy from Liverpool. Whitehaven. Troughdale House. A flat. Sister – Rina. Morten.

No – he couldn't have told them anything like that.

Morten shrugs it off.

He can't have told them much – because they've obviously never traced him.

Hah – and why is that no surprise?

The incompetence in the public services. They can't be bothered. They'll do anything for a simple life. Look how easy it's been to get Deidre to pull a few strings – change a few names and addresses here and there.

Deidre – she has her uses.

Even if he doesn't quite trust her. For how can you trust anyone who does something for money?

And this latest thing – this inside information – for a moment, she'd unnerved him. But then he'd realised she thought she was doing him a favour. The police are sniffing around – and she's put them off the scent. Except she doesn't know about Billy – a different kind of iron in the fire. She's diverted them from one to another. She was only trying to help. Stupid cow.

That's all the more reason why he needs to be here.

Billy taken care of.

And – a little frisson – Harriet is back on, after all.

Once this is all sorted, he'll dump Deidre – and concentrate on his princess and his palace.

The princess.

She didn't come today.

Perhaps she didn't want to bring out the baby in this weather.

He must get there more often.

Perhaps the first thing should be a little *pied-à-terre*. In the square, or just around the corner.

Nice.

He notices that Billy is shivering.

It makes him think again of Harriet.

"I've got to keep the loft warm, Rina – it's getting colder by the day."

But what about after that?

It's not entirely a clear run in. There's disposal to think of.

He'd been lackadaisical about Harriet.

Why didn't he guess she was up there all the time?

Of course she wouldn't get over the wall.

But he'd underestimated her – even the basic physical fact, that she climbed into the loft.

He should have trusted Rina's instincts about Harriet. Rina's a sly old fox and she knows one when she smells one. He'll have to watch Rina – be careful what he tells her. She's useful for now – but that won't be forever.

And – right now – he reaches the gap in the rhododendrons.

The wind is funnelling through the gap. It's sweeping directly across the lake from west to east. He can hear the lapping of waves, actual breakers splashing like it's the sea.

Perfect.

He forces the wheelchair ahead of him.

It bumps and bounces over protruding roots, and Billy is jostled limply in his seat.

Through the bushes.

Nearly there.

The raised bank; the grassy knoll.

The steep slope down into deep water.

Black water that is seething and foaming.

Out there, some geese perhaps, riding the swell, flapping and flailing.

Morten positions the chair.

Suddenly Billy emits a choking gurgle.

'I never trusted you, Morten.'

Enraged, Morten gives the wheelchair a furious shove.

He watches for a couple of seconds, his lips curling venomously.

Then he turns, and strides away.

Time to make himself scarce.

He begins to trot.

But at the opening he turns – one last glance into the gloom, at the maelstrom, the thrashing, the voracious lake swallowing its prey.

Does he glimpse a head bob up?

Does he glimpse the raised wings of a goose – curious, coming to inspect?

Hah – there's no food thrown in there!

And Morten is gone.

Only a hysterical peal of laughter rises above the chaotic

crashing of the storm.

36. EVIDENCE

DI Skelgill's office – late afternoon Friday 20 October

CHARGING MEMORANDUM – HOMICIDE
for the Crown Prosecution Service
Prepared by DI Skelgill, DS Leyton, DS Jones – Cumbria
Constabulary
The Crown v Morten Jenner & Rina Jenner
SECTION 1:
Draft Witness Statements

Skelgill scowls at the legend on the front of his document.

'You volunteering to read it to us, then, Jones?'

'I thought you might want to take the Chief through it. It would be a chance to rehearse.'

Skelgill raps the papers with the back of his left hand.

'There's not a cat in hell's chance she'll believe I've written this. I can feel the weight – it's got way too many long words. You're our star scribe – I reckon you'll need to present it, lass.'

DS Jones glances at DS Leyton; he looks relieved that he is not up for consideration.

She smiles amenably.

'Shall I read it verbatim, and we'll save any discussion for at the end?'

She receives nods of agreement, and begins to narrate accordingly.

WITNESS STATEMENT OF DEIDRE WETHERSPOON

"I am an employee of the Department for Work & Pensions. My role is in the assessment and approval of state benefits claims made by members of the public. I have agreed to testify in full and without any form of plea bargaining. My age is 42. I am a single mother of two teenage children. In recent years a combination of price inflation and no pay rise has meant I have been unable to make ends meet from my wages alone.

I met one of the accused persons through work. He was a client of the benefits office, and I dealt with his application. At that time he gave me a false name, James Savile. It was only after I was interviewed by the police that I became aware of his real name, Morten Jenner.

I felt sympathy for him. He told me of his own incapacity, and that he was caring for an invalid mother, who also suffered from agoraphobia and was unable to attend the benefits office in person.

I found him most convincing. He was highly complimentary towards me, and began to lavish attention upon me, sending text messages, and on one occasion flowers. I must admit I found this flattering, and I had sympathy for his predicament.

During what he said was a period of remission he invited me out for dinner. Shortly after this we began a relationship.

He lived some distance away, at Whitehaven, and told me he was mainly required to look after his mother. Since evenings were therefore difficult, we began to meet at lunchtimes at my flat in Carlisle, when my children were at school.

After a while he asked if I would help him and his mother.

He told me that he had not wanted to bother me with his troubles, but that he and his mother were in a difficult financial situation through no fault of their own. He said his mother had been abandoned by her ex-partner, a man called Thomas Jones. They believed he was now living elsewhere with another woman. His mother had no assets or pension of her own and had been relying on Thomas Jones's contribution to the household budget. Additionally, his own bouts of illness made it impossible to hold down a job – and anyway he had to look after his mother.

He suggested that I could create an identity for his mother and himself in the name of Jones. His mother as the wife of Thomas Jones, and himself as their son. They would then be able to claim a range of state benefits.

He also offered to give me £200 per week out of the proceeds.

I am sorry to say that I accessed the DWP computer system and generated an emergency registration, in the names of Morten Jones and Rina Jones.

I convinced myself that the couple were entitled to receive benefits, and that I was only cutting red tape. However, I now accept that I was influenced by my own financial situation. An extra £200 per week was transformational to my circumstances. It meant I could clear some pressing debts and begin to feed and clothe my children properly.

I confess that I believed I was in a genuine relationship with the man I now know to be Morten Jenner, and that I was misguidedly in love with him.

I understand that his illness has been deemed a sham. On many occasions he was perfectly healthy, but he had explained that this was the intermittent nature of the condition.

He could be very charming and – I appreciate now – manipulative. And I was also just a little afraid – once I had done wrong I was entirely in his power. And he subtly made me aware of this – that the repercussions of exposure could be serious for myself and my children.

I fully realise this was entirely wrong and make no excuses, only an explanation.

I know I am liable to be prosecuted for these offences and that I will lose my job."

WITNESS STATEMENT OF SALLY GENEVER

"I am an employee of the Fraud & Error Prevention Service (FEPS), the division of the Department for Work & Pensions (DWP) responsible for investigating fraudulent and inappropriate benefits claims. I was assigned to the case of a mother-and-son couple, who were registered under false names with the DWP as Rina and Morten Jones. The pair, both residing at an address in Whitehaven, Cumbria, were in receipt of extensive benefits. It has now been established that they were also in receipt of benefits in their real names – Rina and Morten Jenner – claims that were first established at a domestic address in Cornwall over a decade ago.

These claims were largely maintained through online means, although the Jenners had mail forwarding in place to intercept DWP correspondence.

Sophisticated computer analysis indicated that other dubious benefits claims were connected to the Whitehaven address, and the couple in question. Further to the FEPS's own investigations and subsequent liaison with Cumbria Constabulary, ongoing false claims for state pension have been identified in the names of two deceased persons, Thomas Jones, and Richard Scawthwaite, both of whom formerly resided at the Jenners' Whitehaven address.

Furthermore, the Jenners have been siphoning off the state pension credit and associated benefits of Rina Jenner's elder brother, William Boothroyd, whom it appears they abandoned into care just over a year ago, having first gained control of his bank accounts. Such funds should, of course, have been diverted to pay towards Mr Boothroyd's nursing costs."

WITNESS STATEMENT OF HARRIET WATT

"Originally from Scotland, I am a retired employee of Allerdale Borough Council in West Cumbria, where I worked latterly as Chief Accountant in the Finance Department. My role included budgetary analysis of council expenditures and I have a good knowledge of local taxation and benefits systems. I mention this as it is relevant to my reasons for suspicion of the Jenners, as I now know them to be called.

However, my involvement with the Jenners has been for personal reasons.

A former work colleague and close friend of mine passed away suddenly about four years ago. Her name was Jaqueline Jones, and she left a widower husband, Thomas Jones, whom I did not know very well. Thomas was considerably older than Jaqueline, and she had expressed concern for how he would manage if he were ever left to fend for himself.

Due to my own disabilities I was unable to help in this regard, as I did not live nearby. However, sometime later, I did happen to notice in passing by bus that his house had been sold. This was a surprise to me, as it was specially adapted.

I made inquiries with neighbours, and I was told he had gone to live with a woman he had got to know through a connection of his wife, a lady who ran a slimming business from her home in Whitehaven, actually not all that far from where I lived.

I don't know why – maybe it is the stubborn Scot in me – but I decided to investigate. The story seemed unlikely: that someone would 'take on' Thomas Jones at a private address where there was a slimming business, when it would have seemed more probable that he would have needed to go into residential care.

I tracked down the business and began going for appointments. The woman – and her son – were using the name Jones. On no occasion did I see any sign of Thomas Jones – indeed, the only other occupant was a different elderly man, whom the woman I knew as Rina Jones referred to as her brother Billy. He kept to himself and appeared to be suffering from dementia.

A short time after, I was told that Billy had passed away. I continued with my appointments and I was offered the chance to rent and even buy the integral granny flat in which Billy had lived. The sales pitch was that I would have privacy but also company, and people to care for some of my needs. This had considerable appeal, given my physical condition, and isolation in my own home.

However, the main reason I accepted a trial period was to investigate the disappearance of Thomas Jones. It was the least I could do for my dear late friend, Jaqueline.

Through surreptitious means – though I believe reasonable under the circumstances – I soon discovered that, among other things, the Joneses were claiming Thomas Jones's state pension, despite that there was no sign of him – nor even that he was still alive.

I also found that they were claiming state pension credit and other benefits for the apparently deceased brother Billy. Moreover, I came across documentary evidence that they had received large capital sums from him, in return for purchase of the granny flat – but the transaction was never registered.

I realised that the Joneses – or, more accurately, the Jenners – were systematic fraudsters and that I was being lined up as their next victim. Morten Jenner had tricked me into providing a sample of my signature, and was beginning to make plans to sell my property without my knowledge.

I also became aware that I was being kept as a de facto prisoner. The garden was high-walled and the gates required a security key. My mobility scooter, after years of reliable service, suddenly developed a fault.

I felt I was in rapidly increasing danger, as was proved by subsequent events, which the police are best placed to describe."

WITNESS STATEMENT OF DETECTIVE SERGEANT LEYTON

"I was seconded to the Department for Work & Pensions (DWP) as part of the county-wide initiative known as Operation Community Chest.

Initially we had concluded that our resources would be best deployed in trying to identify cases of 'deceased pension fraud' – i.e. where relatives continue to make claims by not notifying the DWP of the death of a family member. There have been some high-profile instances reported in the media in recent years, amounts running into six figures.

However, I was advised by my temporary colleague Deidre Wetherspoon that 'deceased pension fraud' cases were rare, and that it would be more productive to identify 'deprivation of assets' cases – i.e. where relatives conspire with a family member to hide their assets prior to them going into local authority care. These assets should be used to pay care fees.

She said this was far more common. It also held the attraction that care fees are funded by local taxes – so from the perspective of Operation Community Chest it is a direct fraud against the Cumbrian taxpayer, and any savings would be recovered to the county purse.

However, I developed suspicions that I was being led off the scent. Deprivation of assets cases are a matter for the local social work department – which would have required a transfer of my position. Deidre Wetherspoon's enthusiasm in communicating this suggestion led me to wonder if she had a personal interest in pointing me away from the DWP.

However, I had no direct evidence.

At the time I was also unaware that the national body, the Fraud & Error Prevention Service (FEPS) was conducting its own undercover investigation, and had identified Deidre Wetherspoon as a possible insider in an ongoing benefits fraud.

However, I put two and two together when I observed Deidre Wetherspoon in a clandestine meeting with a client of the benefits office, the man we now know to be called Morten Jenner. I had interviewed Mr Jenner – then masquerading as Morten Jones – with Ms Wetherspoon a few weeks previously. He was awarded significant extra benefits, in relation to himself and his invalid mother, 'Rina Jones' – whom we know to be properly called Rina Jenner.

Events took a dramatic turn when I agreed to accompany Sally Genever to interview Morten Jenner and his mother at their home in Whitehaven. Mr Jenner was absent, while his mother – far from being invalided – was violently obstructive.

I refer the reader to the separate incident report for details. The result was that we discovered the elderly and somewhat infirm Harriet Watt not only imprisoned but apparently in mortal danger. She had been locked in an unventilated attic, where Morten Jenner had set a paraffin heater burning. Expert opinion has concluded that she would have been overcome by fumes, and death from carbon monoxide poisoning would have ensued had she not managed to partially break free.

I understand Sally Genever has provided details of the multi-layered benefits fraud perpetrated by Morten and Rina Jenner. I also understand that there will be a range of criminal charges in this respect, and that these will be prosecuted by the FEPS legal department.

Therefore, I now come to crimes against the person.

The police will seek a charge against Morten Jenner of the attempted murder of Harriet Watt, and accessory to the same in the case of Rina Jenner.

However, there are more serious matters still.

A comprehensive forensic operation is currently in progress.

Human remains – of two elderly adult males – have been found buried beneath the rose beds at the Jenners' property, Troughdale House, Whitehaven.

Identification has not yet been confirmed by DNA analysis; however comparison against dental records indicates a match for a Mr Thomas Jones and a Mr Richard Scawthwaite, both former local residents and men whose names are connected to the Jenners' ongoing benefits fraud.

Pathological tests are currently in progress to establish the cause of death in each case.

Preliminary indications point to murder charges against Morten Jenner and Rina Jenner."

WITNESS STATEMENT OF DETECTIVE INSPECTOR SKELGILL

"Through a chance personal contact I became acquainted with the predicament of William Boothroyd, a resident of a temporary nursing facility at Duck Hall, close to Bassenthwaite Lake.

It became apparent that Mr Boothroyd had been abandoned in suspicious circumstances by a person or persons unknown. His dire financial position also indicated that he may have been financially exploited, along the lines raised by my colleague, DS Leyton.

Mr Boothroyd's case, therefore, was wrapped into Operation Community Chest and was further investigated by myself and DS Jones. However, a combination of Mr Boothroyd's condition – his inability to communicate about himself – and the covert manner in which he had been abandoned made it very difficult to establish who was responsible.

From limited local authority sources we learned that he had been dropped off at A&E at Westmorland Infirmary in Kendal. This was just over a year ago. There was a message that his wife had died – as if to explain why he was now being left alone. Understandably, his treatment was given priority, but there was a failure to gather vital contact information.

Initially, we had only the first name William, and no surname. This made it virtually impossible to verify his back-story. We now know that he was always called Billy (and thus was not responsive to "William"), and that he was never married. Moreover, as a further smokescreen, he was driven over sixty miles to Westmorland Infirmary, when West Cumberland Hospital was fewer than two miles from where he had been living.

He was left with no apparent access to savings or pensions, and was unfortunately placed on the minimum council-funded care package. This could be described as 'no-frills', and left him to be supplied with replacement clothes from deceased residents. He received no visits during the entire period he was in care.

To quote the care home manager on one occasion, *"He is here to die"*.

Careful interviews with Mr Boothroyd provided some limited clues to his background. He had a Liverpool accent but referred to a person we believed to be a younger relative, with whom he had fished in the Midlands. We identified the locality and, in turn, former neighbours of Mr Boothroyd. It was at this point we established his full name, and that he was in receipt of state benefits – or, at least, they were being paid into his bank account, and being withdrawn by an unknown third party.

The neighbours knew of a sister and nephew of Mr Boothroyd, though not their names nor where they lived, nor even whether they were still alive. These we regarded as persons of considerable potential interest.

The nephew we traced to Nantucket, USA, where he has spent most of his adult life. His mother was deceased. However, he told us that, at her funeral some twelve years ago, he had heard mention of the suggestion that Mr Boothroyd would move to Cornwall to live with a second sister – of whom we had hitherto been unaware – a Rina Jenner, and her son, Morten Jenner.

We put into motion a request to trace the Jenners through police channels in Cornwall, should they still be living there. More immediately, we could find no evidence of them residing in Cumbria. We now know this is because they were falsely registered locally as Rina and Morten Jones.

At this juncture there was no indication of an imminent threat to the safety of Mr Boothroyd.

However, some misgivings did arise when we learned that the nursing home received a telephone inquiry about Mr Boothroyd, apparently from a police officer unconnected with the case. This took place on Friday 13th October.

On the following Monday, as a result of the incident at Troughdale House reported by DS Leyton, my colleague DS Jones and I learned of the presence of the Jenners in Cumbria.

Accordingly, we were apprised of their role in a complex benefits fraud, and their alleged imprisonment and attempted murder of Harriet Watt.

This elevated to *critical* the level of seriousness of the investigation.

Rina Jenner was apprehended by DS Leyton.

Morten Jenner's whereabouts were unknown.

We then received a real-time message from an alert member of staff at Duck Hall – that the abovementioned police officer had arrived, unannounced, to interview Mr Boothroyd.

We suspected that the 'police officer' was probably being impersonated.

The impersonator was Morten Jenner.

And Mr Boothroyd's life was in jeopardy."

WITNESS STATEMENT OF DETECTIVE SERGEANT JONES

"Following the events described I drove with all haste to Duck Hall. I had made an urgent call to rendezvous there with my colleague DS Leyton.

En route, I dropped DI Skelgill at a small harbour beside Bassenthwaite Lake, from where he used his private fishing craft to cross the water to Duck Hall. This was a much shorter distance than the long perimeter road, which on the eastern shore requires navigation of a network of narrow, winding lanes. There was the attendant risk of a road being blocked by a fallen tree or bough.

Our aim was to apprehend the man we believed was Morten

Jenner, and to do so before any harm came to Mr Boothroyd. Given what we had learned from DS Leyton about the circumstances at Troughdale House in Workington, we feared that it must be Morten Jenner's aim to 'silence' Mr Boothroyd.

On arrival I was met by the nurse who had admitted the person claiming to be a police officer. The description she provided did not fit that of the named officer.

The nurse told me the 'officer' had insisted that he take Mr Boothroyd, in his wheelchair, for "a little fresh air" – using the excuse that it might make him more wakeful, and able to answer questions.

I was further alarmed by this news. The weather conditions were hostile, and far from suitable for wheeling out an elderly person.

I first searched a courtyard at the side of the mansion house, and an area of abandoned stables and workshops. I then began to widen the search – in the light of my torch I found what looked like wheelchair tracks in the wet grass, heading down towards the lake. There was a single line of tracks.

Out of the gloom I noticed a man approaching me.

From the description we had obtained of Morten Jenner, I realised it was him.

He was alone – there was no sign of Mr Boothroyd or the wheelchair.

As we closed the man began to smile, and made as if to greet me in a friendly manner.

Without warning, he attacked me.

I do not recall exactly what happened for the next few moments, or for exactly how long – but I realised that DS Leyton had arrived on the scene.

We successfully subdued Morten Jenner.

I was uninjured, but DS Leyton sustained some small injury to his knuckles.

I left DS Leyton in charge of the handcuffed suspect, and ran on down to the lake.

As I broke through the bushes at the shoreline, I encountered DI Skelgill wading from the lake, cradling in his arms a limp human figure.

He cried out to me to phone for the air ambulance."

END OF SECTION 1

DS Jones takes a breath, and looks to Skelgill, for his reaction.

He seems a little choked, as if he is reliving some of the events – perhaps even reproaching himself for what he might have done differently.

He starts, and grins at her, though unconvincingly so.

'See – there's upwards of a dozen words in there I don't even know the meanings of.'

DS Jones chuckles.

'Sorry – but I think the CPS will understand these are drafts, paraphrasing the recorded interviews. No doubt their lawyers will want the full tapes and transcripts in due course. I've tried to avoid overlap and unnecessary duplication – just to communicate the main gist of the story from the perspective of the witnesses. Evidentially, I think it will seem more convincing.'

DS Leyton slaps a thigh in a congratulatory manner.

'It's a great job, Emma. And a neat bit of sleuthing you did – finding those wheel tracks in the grass. I don't reckon I'd have thought of that. The geezer might have given me the slip.'

DS Jones smiles gratefully.

'Well – a neat bit of rallying, you must have done – to get there in that time.'

DS Leyton shrugs modestly.

'You know me – any excuse to drive at the speed limit.'

Skelgill makes an appropriately disparaging noise.

'Just as well you pair took him into custody. I might have had to take him back down to the shore.' He grimaces, as if he suffers a sudden stabbing pain in his temple. 'Then again, I wouldn't want Bass Lake polluted with that kind of scum.'

His colleagues regard him pensively.

DS Leyton voices a connected observation.

'I notice we're not chucking DI Smart under the bus.'

He sees that his colleagues exchange a quick glance; evidently they have discussed this aspect.

Skelgill glowers.

'No point sinking to his level, Leyton.'

DS Leyton nods slowly. Then he brightens.

'Talk about chucking folk under the bus – sounds like the Jenners can't incriminate one another fast enough. Singing like canaries, according to DC Watson – and that's just when you take 'em a cup of tea!'

And now DS Jones has a query to raise.

'I hear Sally Genever has produced what amounts to a signed confession from Morten Jenner?'

DS Leyton grins.

'The Times crossword?'

'Yes.'

'She fished it out of the litter bin because the FEPS wanted a sample of his handwriting – to compare against forged applications. She didn't bank on his deranged scrawl – *KILL BILLY, KILL HARRIET – KILL RINA*. The secret thoughts of a flippin' madman.'

Skelgill is shaking his head, his expression one of grim disbelief.

DS Leyton now muses contemplatively.

'She's a smart cookie, that Sally. Ambitious, dedicated – not afraid to go out on a limb. The DWP could do with a few more like her.'

Skelgill raises an eyebrow, and his tone becomes lighter, teasing.

'You seemed to hit it off with the ladies in this case, Leyton. Rendezvous in the park – nights out on the town. I'm only surprised you want to come back to us.'

DS Leyton looks to DS Jones for moral support.

'Give over, Guv – you don't think I would actually fall for all that flannel, do you? Cor blimey – Deidre Wetherspoon made more passes in the first half-hour than England did in the whole game against Bulgaria last week. I've had half a lifetime to work out the meaning of flattering to deceive.'

DS Jones weighs in.

'I do believe Deidre Wetherspoon regrets everything she did – not least trying to mislead you. Morten Jenner had her under his spell. She's a single mum, financially distressed. A lonely lady wanting some company and attention. She fell for his sob story and his charm. Then the spell became an iron grip. In my book she's a victim of the Jenners, just like all the others.'

DS Leyton is nodding.

'Yeah – well, let's hope the CPS go easy on her. They could do well to learn from her – it takes an insider to know the loopholes. As I see it, this whole case has exposed failings in just about every local and national government agency.'

DS Leyton's analysis implicitly includes their own organisation's role. Indeed, Skelgill is moved to comment in this regard.

'At least we got there.'

There is sufficient emphasis on the *we* to generate collective accord – *they* did get there – against the odds – through solid police work, the serendipity that such brings, and – not least – Skelgill's sheer bloody-mindedness.

DS Jones offers credit where it is due.

'Your instinct about Billy, Guv –'

But Skelgill shakes his head, his features creased in denial of the suggestion. And perhaps that to claim any victory would be pyrrhic.

'It weren't about instinct –'

His colleagues wait for him to pronounce, but he seems unable to produce words to match his sentiment. Indeed, for a second time, he seems uncharacteristically choked.

And then the moment of awkwardness is interrupted by a knock on the door.

DC Watson appears stoically; she brings a sheet of paper.

She grins self-effacingly – and silently looks around and chooses to hand it to DS Jones – perhaps as her direct report – and she bows out, closing the door behind her.

'She's a lass of few words.' It is Skelgill's observation.

DS Leyton has an alternative set of facts.

'You should hear her on the rugby pitch, Guv. I passed the ladies training the other night. Turned the air blue, they did – very creative use of the English language.'

DS Leyton sounds like he was most impressed.

Meanwhile, DS Jones has been digesting the missive; her colleagues now notice her silence.

They turn to her – and her face lights up.

She brandishes the page.

'A telephone message from Eoin Romeo. He's booked flights and is asking if "DI Skelgill and team" can be present when he collects Billy from hospital to take him to the States.'

There ensues a hiatus, for this information to be absorbed, and its implications processed. And, perhaps, a tear shed.

DS Jones is watching Skelgill closely – there can be no doubt he is conflicted.

Allowing a moment more, she poses the question.

'What are you thinking, Guv?'

He rouses himself.

'Two things.' He looks first at DS Jones, and then DS Leyton. And then back to DS Jones. 'You said there was a Foster's Pond in Massachusetts, aye?'

She nods, inviting his further rejoinder.

But he merely nods himself, introspectively – but perhaps now with a glint of satisfaction in his eye.

After a moment longer, DS Leyton offers a prompt.

'What was the other thing, Guv?'

Now Skelgill blinks a couple of times, and seems to revert to his regular bluff demeanour. He points to a carrier bag that DS Leyton on arrival placed on top of the filing cabinet next to his chair.

'What's in there?'

DS Leyton grins widely.

'Ah – the Missus reminded me. That banana dessert cake I bought – when I spotted Deidre Wetherspoon and Morten Jenner in that café? I took it home and she froze it.' He reaches up and pulls down the bag. 'Should be good to go, by now.'

Skelgill is rising and heading for the door.

'Let's hope the canteen's got a fresh mash on.'

***

> *Oh, dirty Maggie Mae*
> *They have taken her away*
> *And she'll never walk down Lime Street any more*
> *Oh, the judge, he guilty found her*
> *For robbin' the homeward bounder*
> *That dirty, no good, robbin' Maggie Mae*

Liverpool folk song; recorded by The Beatles in 1970.

NEXT IN THE SERIES

WHAT GOES AROUND ...

Lakeland's most famous 24-hour fell running feat was accomplished by local man Bob Graham, who in June 1932 scaled 42 peaks over a distance of 66 miles, with an attendant height gain just a little shy of Mount Everest – arriving back at Keswick Moot Hall with 21 minutes to spare. 'The Bob Graham Round', as this route came to be known, is etched into Cumbrian folklore, not least because the 42-year-old Keswick B&B owner ran in tennis shoes, long shorts and a pyjama jacket. His record stood for 28 years.

Fell running gear has evolved beyond recognition in the near-century since, but the *Bob Graham's* arduous nature, the fickle mountain weather, and man's (and woman's) competitive spirit mean that this challenge is fraught with risk. And, when something goes wrong in the fells, help is not always at hand.

It sounds like the perfect setting for a Skelgill mystery.

'Murder in the Round' by Bruce Beckham will be released in July 2024.

FREE BOOKS, NEW RELEASES, THE BEAUTIFUL LAKES ... AND MOUNTAINS OF CAKES

Sign up for Bruce Beckham's author newsletter

Thank you for getting this far!

If you have enjoyed your encounter with DI Skelgill there's a growing series of whodunits set in England's rugged and beautiful Lake District to get your teeth into.

My newsletter often features one of the back catalogue to download for free, along with details of new releases and special offers.

No Skelgill mystery would be complete without a café stop or two, and each month there's a traditional Cumbrian recipe – tried and tested by yours truly (aka *Bruce Bake 'em*).

To sign up, this is the link:

https://mailchi.mp/acd032704a3f/newsletter-sign-up

Your email address will be safely stored in the USA by Mailchimp, and will be used for no other purpose. You can unsubscribe at any time simply by clicking the link at the foot of the newsletter.

Thank you, again – best wishes and happy reading!

Bruce Beckham

Printed in Great Britain
by Amazon